NEW STORIES
FROM THE SOUTH

The Year's Best, 2008

NEW STORIES
FROM THE SOUTH

The Year's Best, 2008

Selected from U.S. magazines by

ZZ PACKER with KATHY PORIES

with an introduction by ZZ Packer

Algonquin Books of Chapel Hill

Published by
ALGONQUIN BOOKS OF CHAPEL HILL
Post Office Box 2225
Chapel Hill, North Carolina 27515-2225

a division of
WORKMAN PUBLISHING
225 Varick Street
New York, New York 10014

CONTENTS

INTRODUCTION
The Double Indemnity of the South

Though I'm not a "Southerner," I am a "southerner." I don't pride myself particularly upon being any more hospitable than those hailing north of the Mason-Dixon, nor do I defend foodways one step away from roadkill masquerading as Southern delicacies (headcheese, chitlins, hog maws, and squirrel brains—if truly Southern—put my intestinal tract somewhere north of Rhode Island). I don't believe that one should stay in the same county as one's grandfather *just because,* nor can I get on board with pronouncing "library" as "lie-berry" or "ask" as "ax"—though I am adamant about the pronunciation of my Kentucky hometown, Louisville—which is never "Lewis-ville" or "Looey-ville" but always and forever "Lou-a-vull" (rhymes with "You a bull").

White Southerners, we are told, ooze with hospitality and charm—that is, when they're not tying up unsuspecting passersby, *Deliverance*-style, demanding their quarry squeal like a pig to the tune of "Dueling Banjos." Born in a land of contrasts, the men are either Cavaliers, brought up on a diet of buttermilk biscuits, bourbon, and cigars, or the redneck yeomen whose enormous wads of snuff are rivaled only by the more impressive enormity of their goiters. They are always going about, these Southerners, quoting either Faulkner or Thomas Wolfe or Aeschylus or Jeff Foxworthy. The females of the species are hardly better—belles and well-bred spinsters alike concerned largely with lunching and pastel foofaraw. Keeping their husbands aswim in seersucker in June, they spend their weekdays mixing juleps—often sipping on them beneath their insane, cantilevered Kentucky Derby hats. And if they're poor, the toothless, bra-less wonders whoomp it up at NASCAR rallies passing around Wonder Bread and Miracle Whip sandwiches.

Black Southerners, if we're to believe Faulkner's Quentin Compson, "laugh at things that aren't funny and cry at things that aren't sad." They are sage subliterates who, if not Mammys or Uncle Toms or Amoses or Andys, are most certainly minstrels of another stripe: the lazy—albeit colorful—buffoon, the saucy Negress, the barbarized insurrectionist; add water and the parade of Kara Walker silhouettes blooms to life. When they accompany whites (see above paragraph), however, they are Magic Negroes, imminently risible, ready to help or aid someone else's story from slipping into irrelevance without good old-fashioned grounding in common sense. They are not intelligent so much as wise, they are not studious so much as talented, they are not hard-working so much as naturals, they are not eloquent so much as articulate. They have no agency, these black Southerners. Except, of course, when they commit crimes.

These Southerners, in full possession of that capital "S," stroll through life with an unassailable sense of right and wrong—right: chicken-fried steak, Jesus, zero taxation; wrong: vegetarianism, psychiatry, Birkenstocks. The "southerner," lowercase, does not stroll so much as simper. Whereas the Southerner is always assured of knowing where the "absolute best barbecue in the world" is to be had, the lowly southerner knows that the best barbecue joint has only a smidgen to do with quality and everything to do with which one gives you free brisket every odd visit.

If being a southerner and not a Southerner means one is not quite so self-assured, it also guarantees some reflection, some twisted-arm compromise, a kind of double indemnity of the soul peculiar to thinking folk. One can not inhale the gothic miasma of

Flannery O'Connor's *Wise Blood* without being forced to reckon with one's own sense of mortality and failings, as one cannot read *The Sound and the Fury* without witnessing those cardboard cutouts *nostalgia* and *sentimentality* handily slain by bitter, awful truths.

The same voice that has given rise to nearly every original form of American music—jazz, the blues, zydeco, country, rock and roll—finds its way welling up through the pages of prose, each word vibrating with its own music, rhythm, and beat, sentences weaving their own harmonies, so that when one has finished a collection of stories by Savannah native James Alan McPherson, or a novel by Kentuckian Gayl Jones, one is buoyed by the symphonic strains of human music, sounds that reverberate like those church organs whose deepest notes can only be felt in one's nerve endings and capillaries.

It is telling that a culture alternately cheered and derided for its unapologetic obsession with the past should find its most perfect expression in literature, a medium destined to record our secret past in greater detail than any of our histories. Both Southerners and southerners do not tell so much as retell, they do not create so much as cajole, and they do not offer resolutions so much as revelations. Their very disinclination to adapt is borne out of being forced to do it, time and time again, as no era of Southern history has dovetailed peaceably into the next, leaving its citizens relaxed and refreshed, ready to inaugurate new relations with a smile. It has always been bloody and embattled: colonization, slave revolts, the Civil War, Reconstruction, Jim Crow, the fight for civil rights, integration, the heady commercialism of the "New South." It has been a zigzag course, a jolting ride with nary a denouement before the next uptick sends one hurtling in a new direction, hungry and ill-equipped, late before one has even started.

If Southern history is indeed noted for its lack of neat and meaningful resolution, then this very state of imprecision allows demagogues, rogues, and caudillos of every stripe to attempt to comfort and unify through dogma, through romantic overtures to moribund traditions—witness Orval Faubus, George Wallace, and Strom Thurmond. But such lack of resolution also serves as a sort of carte blanche for the Southern artist to fulfill her destiny, composing those final, as-of-yet-unwritten chapters, providing testament to how we ended up, after all.

In selecting the stories for this collection, I wasn't surprised that I found myself drawn to the stories by southerners over Southerners. The Southerner has pride in the past glories of the South while the southerner stakes his pride in the small daily miracles of the South—the progress that is made each day of our lives, often absent any viable examples. There was no question my sensibilities ran toward the latter. But I was surprised that I found myself attracted to stories that managed to straddle the southern-Southern divide, stories that paradoxically evoked the mythic South as well as the somewhat bastard South. I often felt as though I was not editing *New Stories from the South* so much as *Stories from the New South,* stories that seem to ask "How do I get out of here?" or "How can I ever piece my life back together?" These were stories of struggle, tales of those who wrestled with demons and often came out losing, but the authors, the characters, refused to whitewash said demons into angels, or to prettify (or for that matter, uglify) their trailer parks, greasy spoons, halfway houses, or meth labs in order to make us readers feel some sense of familiarity with the South we're apt to find simulcasted to us from the twinkling electrostatic of our TVs.

These are stories of people who have gone afar afield—not just from the South, but from their moral centers. These are the stories of those who sometimes returned, grateful for the frigid air of the Winn-Dixie and the maze of the Piggly Wiggly; the absurd two-thousand-calorie Goo Goo Clusters from the Loveless Café; the Cracker Barrel restaurants and their stupid triangle golf-tee peg puzzles; and prepackaged Moon Pies—twelve to a box. They've returned, wiser for the journey, wiser for the homesickness, more inclined to choose sentiment over sentimentality.

Living in New Orleans post-Katrina, I saw the wreckage of a very real Ninth Ward displacing the cried-over ruins of an Old South that never was. Similarly, a month-long stay in Wilmington, North Carolina, put me squarely in the same town that decimated its black population in 1898, then proceeded as genteelly and graciously as if nothing of consequence had happened. I chose stories that refused to gloss over such inequities or pretend such travesties never occurred. I wanted—needed—stories that would remind me that stories are all about problems—that literature is the halfway house for conflict, and that there wasn't a fiction invented that did not question myth or meaning. Whatever our Southernness amounts to, these stories seemed to say, it doesn't amount to much if our talent for dressing a bird, loving our neighbors, or serving life with a spoonful of sugar can't square with our utter superiority at telling tales of woe and our penchant for wrong choices.

Yes. I love the South. There's the sweet iced tea, and the bourbon, and mint juleps, but there's also the low-brow Rally's and Checkers and White Castles. There are New Orleans Saints games and the Pegasus Parade; there are the daily reminders that you are indeed alive in the form of a thousand mosquito stings, the awful, wonderful heat of the sun that burns like no other. There are the everlasting pine woods and the dusty roads of Mississippi and the surf of Wrightsville Beach. But there are also family trees stunted by lynchings, mob violence, Emmett Till–style "justice." There are Guatemalan and Mexican immigrants living ten to a house picking tobacco in Kentucky, or the Hmong harvesting rice in the Carolinas. No, we can't anethesize ourselves so long as the ghosts of the murdered are still living; we can't pretend our land is filled with magnolias and dogwood and honeysuckle without remembering the Strange Fruit that used to hang alongside the spanish moss and catalpa. We cannot forget Selma, the Edmund Pettus Bridge, the Greensboro Four, the Montgomery Bus Boycott, Rosewood, or those four murdered girls in the church basement in Birmingham, Alabama.

And yet we also can't forget that the solution to the problem—the sit-ins, the marches, the hope of better days—began in the South as well. Every other region can jam its fingers in its ears and and shake its head and tunelessly chant "Not in My Backyard," but not so the South. The South *is* the backyard. And as backward as we've been portrayed—or as backward as we've sometimes portrayed ourselves, slipping behind a curtain of innocent and naive agrarianism, rural somnolence, and sleepy everlasting vowels—the truth is that every awful and beautiful thing that has happened in America happened in the South first.

So turn the page and get to reading.

NEW STORIES
FROM THE SOUTH

The Year's Best, 2008

Holly Goddard Jones

THEORY OF REALTY

(from *The Gettysburg Review*)

I.

When Ellen was a girl, she spent her summers down the street at the Hoffmans', paddling around three or four hours a day in their in-ground swimming pool and frying her skin with baby oil. The Hoffmans were, it seemed to Ellen then, grown up but not old—maybe her mother's age—and they had a big, fancy house and sad eyes. All the neighborhood kids who swam at the Hoffmans' place, and that was most of them, knew the story about Caleb Hoffman, Mr. and Mrs. Hoffman's little boy. A while back, some teenagers had used scrap wood and aluminum to piece together a couple of bike ramps on either side of Town Creek. If you got a good, fast start up on Poppy Street and aimed your wheels right, the rumor went, you could fly over that creek *Dukes of Hazzard* style, though you risked screwing your bike up in the process. All of the boys tried it, however, and Caleb was practicing by himself one evening in late summer when the first ramp collapsed, sending him headfirst into the ditch. The creek was barely a trickle in August, but the fall knocked him unconscious, and he drowned in about four inches of water. He was eleven years old. Ellen had been six when it happened, and from then until the time when she was more interested in talking on the phone than roaming the neighborhood on foot or bike, the name *Caleb* was her mother's near-daily refrain: "You stay away from that creek, now. Remember what happened to Caleb," or "I don't want to lose you the way poor Greta lost Caleb."

Ellen didn't remember much about him, but it seemed to her that he was a constant, invisible companion whenever she, her brother, Andy, and the other kids played at the Hoffmans'. There were pictures of him in the house: on the kitchen counter where Mrs. Hoffman served them sweet tea and lemon cookies, on a shelf in the bathroom where Ellen went to pee or to change out of her wet bathing suit. He'd looked like every other boy in the neighborhood, like Ellen's own older brother: brown haired and skinny with crooked teeth and freckles. When Mr. and Mrs. Hoffman were together, smiling but faraway looking, it seemed to Ellen that the space between them was always about as wide as Caleb would have been.

Later, Ellen would consider the irony of that pool ritual. Caleb Hoffman died in four inches of water, and Town Creek became a death place, but that rectangle of blue water, the sound of children cannonballing and belly flopping, was somehow holy and necessary, even to the other parents. "Go to the Hoffmans'," they'd say if the late-afternoon doldrums set in. "They'll appreciate the company." And they did. Even as a girl Ellen knew the look of loneliness, and her heart then was of the tender sort; she was the kind of kid who felt guilty when she saw a man eating by himself at Dairy Queen, and the sight of her own mother laughing too hard—eyes squinting behind cheap plastic-framed glasses, cigarette stains prominent on her two front teeth—made Ellen's stomach knot with pity and shame. Mrs. Hoffman was a tiny woman, thinner and prettier than Ellen's mother, and she was always offering to braid Ellen's hair or paint her fingernails. One time, she invited Ellen into her dressing room—such a big, lovely place, with pink-tinted lightbulbs and a makeup table cluttered with delicate, pastel glass bottles—and showed her how to put on eyeliner.

"Just a smidge on the lower lid," she said over Ellen's shoulder with her soft voice, demonstrating. "Right here in the corner. Not too much, or you'll look cheap. Now here." She guided Ellen's hand. "Just past the edge. It widens the eye. Oh, that's lovely. Now look at me.

Ellen did.

Mrs. Hoffman riffled through a makeup bag and pulled out a tube of mascara. She held up the wand. "Big eyes," she said, showing Ellen, making her own eyes pop out. Left eye, then the right: a few strokes on each side. "Okay, take a look," Mrs. Hoffman said.

Ellen turned and faced the mirror, then caught her breath. Her eyes looked bluer and brighter, almost glittery. She blinked, pleased with the new heaviness of her eyelashes. She felt like her old baby doll, the one she'd named Kissy Kay, whose eyes fluttered shut if you laid her on her back. The doll that she still allowed herself once every couple of weeks or so, when she felt sad or bored or overwhelmed by school, and when she was sure no one—not her mother, especially not her brother—was around to see her play with it. Looking at herself in the mirror, Ellen had an insight that was almost grown-up: *This is the person I'm giving up the dolls for.*

"You're such a darling girl," Mrs. Hoffman said. "I always wanted one."

And then there was Mr. Hoffman. Ellen saw less of him, which usually suited her fine; he was a nice enough man, but she'd grown up watching TV movies with her mother, the kind with titles like *Sleeping with Danger* or *No Means No,* and she knew that some middle-aged men—not a lot or even most, but some—were rapists or girl touchers or the kind who slapped their wives if the casserole didn't come out right. For all she knew, Ellen's own father could be any of these things; he'd left her mother when Ellen was three and now lived down in Miami, Florida, with his new wife and their eight-year-old twin daughters. Once a month he sent a child support check, which Ellen's mother split evenly between her checking account and Ellen and Andy's savings accounts, and he always mailed fifty dollars for birthdays, one hundred for Christmas. Ellen sometimes thought this was a better bargain than an actual dad. Two years earlier, when Ellen was eleven, he'd invited her and Andy down to Florida to hang out for two weeks and meet their half sisters, and the whole thing was a disappointment. He lived in an apartment—not even a real house—that was so far away from the beach that you had to take a cab to get there, and the twins just wanted to stay inside and play Nintendo all day. They didn't even have tans. Also, Janet, her stepmom, cooked everything in weird ways: spaghetti with butter and green flecks but no tomato sauce, hamburgers with onion soup mix and red peppers mixed into them, stuff like that. She also served buttered toast with every meal, which was a good thing, because that was all Ellen could bring herself to eat the whole time she was down there. "Bread and water," her father kept saying at mealtime. "I'm not running a prison here. What'll your mama think if I send you back to Kentucky ten pounds lighter?"

Fathers, she decided, were probably overrated.

She had to admit, though, that Mr. Hoffman was a lot of things that her dad wasn't. Handsome, for starters. He was tall and sandy haired—her own father's hair was mostly gone—and he wore the kind of clothes Ellen usually only saw on TV: suits when he was coming home from work, khaki shorts and white button-down shirts with the sleeves rolled up for sitting around the pool or in the kitchen. The sight of that white cloth on his tanned forearms fascinated Ellen. He was an engineer at Logan Aluminum, Ellen's mother had told her, and everybody knew that Logan was the best factory in town. He had a nice voice, too: proper, like a TV anchorman's, and not punctuated with the *ain't*s and *fixin' to*s that her teachers had deemed ungrammatical and just plain ignorant sounding. The way her mother talked, for starters. She asked him why one day, and he laughed. "Greta and me, we're not from here originally," he said.

"Where are you from?"

"Ohio," he told her. "Columbus, Ohio."

They were sitting by the pool during this conversation, and Ellen felt okay about talking to him because Mrs. Hoffman was a few feet away spreading a towel out on a lounge chair and Andy was in the water with his best friend, Kev Brewster, doing clumsy flips off of the diving board. Also, Mr. Hoffman had his shirt on. When Mr. Hoffman stripped down to his trunks for a swim, Ellen was usually so embarrassed that she made up an excuse to dry off and go to the bathroom. Or home. She knew that the sight of Mr. Hoffman in his trunks was nothing to feel anxious about, but she did all the same. She thought about all the times she'd walked in by accident on her mother changing, or how they sometimes collided in the hallway between the bathroom and their bedrooms, towels wrapped around their middles. She tried to picture her dad in swimming trunks — or in just a towel — and shuddered. Grown-ups didn't seem to worry that much about what they exposed you to: private, ugly, or otherwise. She didn't want to know about her mother's stretch marks. She didn't want to know about the strip of wiry hairs between Mr. Hoffman's bellybutton and shorts.

"Is that a big city?" she said.

"I didn't think so when I was there." He laughed again. "But moving to Kentucky has a way of putting things in perspective for you, no offense."

Ellen liked the fact that he said that: *no offense.* Casual and not sarcastic at all, like they were equals.

"That doesn't bother me," she said. "I hate it here. I bet Columbus is a whole lot better."

Mr. Hoffman shrugged. "Ah, it's not so bad here. The weather's better. And you can have a whole lot more house for the money. This place cost me eighty thousand. Two-story house with a pool and an acre, and I'm a five-minute drive to work. I've been here almost ten years and I still can't believe it. Now when you live in a city, houses get a lot more complicated. It's all about location. Have you heard that saying before? Location, location, location?"

Ellen wasn't really sure what he was talking about. She shrugged and nodded at the same time, so that she could seem knowledgeable without actually being deceptive.

Mr. Hoffman adjusted his lounge chair so that he could lie flat. "I'm probably boring you silly. How old are you? Ten? Eleven?"

"Thirteen," she said.

He lifted his sunglasses and looked at her. "Huh. How about that. Well anyway, here's the best advice I know to give a little girl like you. When you go to college, get as far away from here as you can. Go somewhere totally different from Kentucky, like New Mexico or Oregon or, hell, Europe. It's only four years of your life, and you can always come back." He took a sip of something: a short glass with ice cubes and amber-colored liquid.

"What's that you're drinking?" Ellen said, sensing that the question was inappropriate but unable to help herself.

"That's a straightforward question." Mr. Hoffman said. "So I'm going to give you a straightforward answer. This is an alcoholic beverage called bourbon. The brand name is Maker's Mark. Come to think of it, this is another reason why Kentucky isn't necessarily so bad. Did you know that all of the world's bourbon comes out of Kentucky? There's a fact for you to take some pride in."

"Adam," Mrs. Hoffman said sharply. "For God's sake."

He winked at Ellen. "Don't mind her."

"Can I try it?" Ellen said.

Mr. Hoffman looked like he was thinking it over. "I guess not," he said finally. "The thing about bourbon is that you can't mistake the scent, and you can't really cover it up either. Lean in."

Ellen did, and he exhaled into her face: a burnt, tangy smell that made her eyes water. His lips were only a few inches away from hers. "Uck," she said.

"You see what I mean, then," he said. "That's basically how it tastes, anyway. Did you know that 90 percent of taste is smell? That's why food doesn't seem as good when you have a cold."

"I don't think I'd like it," Ellen said.

"That's probably for the best," Mr. Hoffman told her. He pulled his sunglasses back down and reclined again. In another couple of minutes he was snoring.

"You shouldn't mention the bourbon to your mother," Mrs. Hoffman said after a moment. She looked at Mr. Hoffman's sleeping figure and sighed—the sound Ellen's mother made when she was frustrated with Andy, when she said things like, "I'm at the absolute end of my rope here." It was odd, seeing that kind of frustration directed at an adult; odd that she was allowed to share in it. "Come over here, dear," Mrs. Hoffman said finally. "You need some sunblock on your nose.

Ellen let her apply it, enjoying the coolness of Mrs. Hoffman's fingertips. Everything about her was more delicate than Ellen's mother. Her touch, her voice, her smell: sweet but not overpowering, not like the apple-scented body spray Ellen's mother used when she didn't feel like showering. Ellen loved her mother—too much, it seemed some days when the love felt like something that could wrap itself around her heart and crush it—but she was certain then that she'd do whatever Mrs. Hoffman told her to, that the Hoffman's pool was a place with its own secrets and rules, a place that had to be protected. A haunted place. If she looked out at where Andy and Kev were in the water, now playing volleyball—if she half closed her eyelids and let her vision blur—she could almost make out a third figure, a Caleb-shaped figure. Turning toward her. Smiling.

Two weeks after the bourbon conversation, Ellen ended up at the Hoffman's pool alone. Andy had gotten an air pellet rifle for his fifteenth birthday—their mother's compromise, because his heart had been set on a real rifle, a .22—and all he felt like doing anymore was setting up Shasta cans in the backyard and practicing his aim. He wouldn't even let Ellen try it.

"Mama'd be pissed if you shot a window out," he said.

"I wouldn't aim at a window, dummy. Anyway, those stupid pellets probably couldn't shoot through a slice of bread. It's just a baby gun, anyhow."

He shrugged and took aim, not bothering to look at her. "Then what's your problem?" He missed the can. "Shit. Anyway, you're one to talk about baby stuff. I saw you playing with that doll the other day."

Ellen felt her face go hot. "You're a liar. I don't play with dolls anymore."

Now he looked at her, and he was grinning. She wanted to smack him. "Sure you do. I saw you through the window when I was weed eating." He let his voice go soft and girly: "You was brushing her pretty blonde hair wis your itty-bitty brush —"

"I hate you," she said, kicking a clump of dirt his way. He just laughed.

"Go swim or something," he said. "I've got to practice. Kev's dad said he'd let me use his rifle the next time they go deer hunting."

"I hope you shoot yourself in the foot," she told him, running to the back door. She slammed it behind her, and her mother yelled from the living room—that bellow Ellen couldn't stand — "Don't slam the goddamn door!" She couldn't win.

She went to the bathroom, where her bathing suit was hanging—now dry—and stripped down, tugging the spandex over her hips and shoulders with angry jerks. She pulled on a pair of cut-offs, then grabbed a towel and the baby oil. She looked at her reflection in the mirror, trying out different faces and angles, searching for the combination that would age her, that would show Andy just how invincible she was. But the grown-up she'd spied in Mrs. Hoffman's dressing room was gone. She was round faced and red blotched, with tears trembling on her eyeliner-less lids. She was a child.

She usually approached the Hoffman's backyard slowly, at an angle; if no other kids were there, she'd slip back toward home before anyone could see her. She couldn't explain why she did this, but it had something to do with that space between her and adults who weren't her mother. The sense of formality she felt around them, and also unease. Kids could be bad, of course. If Kev Brewster were at the pool and feeling bored, he'd sometimes grab Ellen and force her underwater, not letting her surface until she was

thrashing with panic, or until one of the Hoffmans came outside.
A couple of weeks ago, he'd shoved her down with Andy's help—
Andy, who was usually just a laughing bystander—and straddled
her shoulders, tightening his thighs around her ears until Ellen's
world was nothing but a distant sense of wetness (she'd remember
later on, more than anything else, the grotesque push of his groin
on the back of her neck) and a high-pitched, alarmlike tone. She
couldn't hear anything else. When he finally let her out of the vice-
like trap of his thighs, she'd come up gasping for air, so tired that
she'd barely been able to keep her head aloft before throwing up
in the water. Kev had teased her and made her use the bug net to
clean it up herself, but he never played that trick on her again. At
least, he hadn't yet.

Kids could be bad, but their cruelty was familiar to Ellen, something she understood and even initiated. (Wasn't she the first to
tell Darryl, the retarded black kid who rode her school bus, to "kiss
the window"? Hadn't she laughed—cackled—when he did it, leaving big, smeary lip prints on the already dirty glass?) The cruelty of
grown-ups was harder to pin down: mystifying, really. Ellen had a
girlfriend, Ray, whose mother was single just like hers. But Ray's
mom, Gloria, was different. She was small and flat chested, and she
dressed a lot like Ellen and Ray; she wore short-shorts and T-shirts
with sayings like *Flirt* or *Call Me* written across the front in sparkly
cursive, and on Saturday nights when she didn't have a date or a
party, she'd take Ellen and Ray cruising through Russellville and
buy them all Diet Cokes and tater tots at Sonic. She'd play songs by
Roxette ("It Must Have Been Love") and Michael Bolton ("How
Am I Supposed to Live without You?") loud out of her car's sound
system and explain why the lyrics were special to her. Usually her
stories were about old boyfriends from high school, like Toby
Taylor, who had "long hair and a hot Trans Am." On other nights,
she'd leave Ray and Ellen home alone while she drove to the Ex-
ecutive Inn in Bowling Green with some girlfriends. Sometimes
she returned laughing and in high spirits; she'd wake Ray and
Ellen and show them the cherry stem the bartender had tied with

his tongue, or she'd tell them about the "nice man" she'd met and how he promised to take her to dinner at 440 Main as soon as he got paid the next week. Sometimes she came home with her eye makeup smeared, mouth tense and almost old looking, and on those nights she wouldn't talk to Ray and Ellen at all; instead she stormed through the house and ran water in the bathroom for long, uninterrupted spans, smoking and having intense conversations on the cordless phone. Ellen never knew which version of Ray's mother to expect, but she feared them both.

The adults of the world gave permission and took it away, stocked the refrigerator, punished you, drove you to soccer practice. But you still couldn't trust them.

So happening upon the Hoffmans' that afternoon the way she did was an accident. She was almost to the pool—head down, every stomp of her foot a release of the anger she felt at Andy—when she realized that no other kids were around, and no Mrs. Hoffman either. Just Mr. Hoffman, kicked back in a lounge chair with a book folded open over his face, and he didn't even have his shirt on. His nipples looked like wads of bubble gum. She stopped all at once and thought about backing away slowly—she'd seen this in a movie, when a guy who was camping didn't realize that a bear was a few feet away until he'd unzipped his pants to take a whiz—but Mr. Hoffman must have heard her. He took the book off of his face and sat up, squinting. "Ellie?" he said.

"Ellen, " she said. "My name's Ellen."

"I was close, though." He waved her over. "Don't mind me. I was just snoozing."

"I was looking to see if my brother's here," Ellen said, the lie coming to her lips so quickly that it stunned her. "I guess I better go find him."

"Aw, hell," Mr. Hoffman said. "You have your suit on. Go on and swim. I won't bother you. Probably don't want to get stuck in another conversation about real estate, huh?"

Ellen shrugged.

"Go on and swim," he said.

She went to the edge of the pool and sat, sketching the surface with her toe. The water was sun warm and pleasant, and Mr. Hoffman had already reclined again, book back on his face, so she wriggled out of her cut-offs and slid into the pool, quiet as possible. As always, she made herself open her eyes underwater, grimacing through the sting of chlorine, and touch bottom. It was her lucky charm, one of many; if you could force yourself to do something scary or hard, Ellen believed, then good things would happen. She had a few other habits along those lines—at school recess, as a little kid, she'd always make herself jump out of the swing at the height of its arc, for instance—and she often made up charms on the spot. One time, she'd wrapped thread around her pointy finger until the tip turned blue and cold, promising herself that if she could keep it that way sixty seconds, she'd make an A on her fractions quiz. Another time, she decided that Robby Barrow would like her back if she could run around the house twenty times without stopping.

When she resurfaced, Mr. Hoffman was sitting up again, watching her. She felt a flush break out on her face, spreading to her neck and chest like a rash. Wasn't this just like those made-for-TV movies? In another minute, he'd say, "You're growing up so fast, Ellen" and invite her to sit beside him in the lounge chair. The thought was sickening, but also kind of exciting. How would she escape? Was Mrs. Hoffman inside? If Ellen yelled, would she come running?

"So what do you think?" Mr. Hoffman said. "Want to try some alcohol?"

"I probably shouldn't," Ellen told him.

"Well, that's true," he said. "Greta would have your ass and mine, too."

Ellen swam to the ladder, sorry that she hadn't left her towel close enough to grab without getting out of the water. She thought about Andy teasing her and wondered if he'd ever had anything to drink. He probably had, over at Kev's house. Maybe Kev's dad had even offered it to him: Andy was always bragging about how cool

Mr. Brewster was. And she knew that her friend Ray had snuck tastes from her mother's drinks, that Gloria had even given alcohol to Ray once when her girlfriends were over and everybody was cutting up and laughing really loud. The next day, Ray had bragged about how good Kahlua mixed with rum tasted, and she'd said that sipping it had made her feel "fucking great," and that her mother's friends had bragged about what a "trip" she was. Then she had acted cool and sophisticated for a week or so, hinting to Ellen that she'd have to catch up or bug out—that she was hanging with a much better crowd these days. A week later, after her mom had refused to let Ray go cruising with her, Ray gave Ellen a carefully folded note that read "Still BFF?" in purple ink. "Circle Yes or No." Ellen circled "Yes," but she also circled the "No" and then scribbled it out. just to let Ray know that she was on thin ice.

Ray would be impressed if she drank a wine cooler, Ellen thought now.

"Maybe I'll try it," she told Mr. Hoffman. She was still in the water, the bottom rung of the ladder hard and bumpy beneath her right foot. She realized how quiet the afternoon was: a distant car, some birds, the occasional hiss of the pool filters—lazy sounds, the kind that just made the silence louder. Mr. Hoffman stood, and Ellen saw that he'd gotten badly sunburned before hiding beneath the shade of his book: bright strips of red across his forehead, nose, and cheeks, the skin on his collarbone almost purple looking. It occurred to her how early in the day it was—an hour after lunch, maybe—and she wondered why Mr. Hoffman would be home already.

"Now you're talking," he said. "Wait here. I have just the thing."

As soon as he went inside, Ellen climbed out of the pool—heavy with the water, moving slowly—and grabbed her big towel. The air outside was freezing. She was fumbling into her jean shorts, legs sticky with the damp, when Mr. Hoffman returned. He had four bottles in his left hand; he was holding one between each finger, by their necks, and when he lifted his hand to show her he almost lost his grasp on them. "Shit," he said, quickly unloading them onto an end table. He had a glass of the brown stuff—the bourbon, Ellen guessed—in his right hand, and he took a big sip from it as he got in his lounge chair. He looked sweaty and a little sick, like he'd eaten something that wasn't sitting well. He grinned.

"Wine coolers," he said. "They're Greta's. Girls love them."

Ellen examined the bottles. They were small with foil wrappers, wet with condensation. She chose one called "Tropical Sensation" because orange was her favorite color, opened it, and took a sip. It was sweeter than she expected, good tasting—not as bad as she'd feared, at least—but strange, too. The alcohol hit her tongue right before she swallowed, alien and familiar all at once. A barely concealed bitterness.

"What do you think?" Mr. Hoffman said.

Ellen nodded. "I like it."

"I figured. I told Greta—I told Mrs. Hoffman, what I meant to say—that I was going to give you your first drink. Told her that I bet somebody on this block knows how to have a good time. She was real raw about it, but she never told me 'no' outright." He squinted, like he was thinking. "Mrs. Hoffman doesn't *say* 'no,' you gotta understand. She thinks it and expects you to read her mind."

"Where is she?"

He wiped his forehead with the corner of the towel he was lying on. The skin that hadn't reddened was pale, almost white. He took another sip of his bourbon.

"At her mother's place up in Cincinnati. Visiting." He shrugged. "'Just visiting.' Like it says on Monopoly."

"Cincinnati's pretty far away, huh?" Ellen said. She drank some more of the wine cooler, sugary citrus taste coating her tongue, alcohol already starting to hum a little in the bottom of her stomach. The goosebumps were gone, and she was starting to feel the sun again.

"Honey," Mr. Hoffman said, "she may as well be on Mars. You know what I'm saying?"

Ellen took another sip.

"It's all about location," he said. "It's distance. The distance between points A and B. I could write an equation out for you, Ellie. You know that? I could write a proof explaining the distance between Russellville and Cincinnati, and the answer would be infinity. We couldn't get there in our lifetimes."

"I don't get it," Ellen told him.

Mr. Hoffman laughed. "You know what I'm going to call it? The Theory of Realty. Hoffman's Theory of Realty. I haven't worked out the particulars yet. But I'm onto something."

"I think I better go," she said.

Mr. Hoffinan grabbed one of the wine coolers and held it to his forehead. His eyes were squeezed shut. "You haven't even finished your drink yet," he said. "Christ alive, am I that hard to be around? Do I smell bad?"

"No," Ellen said. She sat down across from Mr. Hoffman, her face and neck hot—from the alcohol or from nervousness, she wasn't sure. He looked sick, and he looked sad: the kind of sad Ellen remembered from the days—the years, even—after her father left, when her mother would start crying out of nowhere, for no apparent reason. Her mother cried at the grocery once, in front of a stock boy and everybody else, clutching a package of Oreos until the cookies inside started to break. She was wearing lipstick that day, Ellen recalled: a bright color, garish and greasy, that Ellen didn't recognize from before and hadn't seen since.

"You're a good kid," Mr. Hoffman said. He looked at her again, peering as if she were on the other side of a keyhole. "Are you old enough to remember Caleb?"

"I remember a little about him. But maybe I think I remember because I see the pictures of him in your house."

Mr. Hoffman drank the rest of his bourbon in a single gulp. His eyes were red and wet. "Good lord. Do I know that feeling. And I was his father, saw him every day of his life for eleven years. We were a close family. Greta and Caleb would come with me on business trips, even." He took an ice cube out of his glass and pitched it at the pool, skipping it like a stone. "But every now and then I forget what he looked like until I take a picture out and examine it. Then I have to focus on a detail, like his ear, and remember in my hand what his earlobe felt like." He rubbed his thumb and forefinger together, looking at Ellen like she ought to be able to see the piece of flesh between them. "Sometimes it clicks for me and sometimes it doesn't. Sometimes I see a picture of us down at Gulf Shores and I know what's in my memory is the real thing and not made up. Because I can remember how Caleb screamed when a wave went over his head, and I know how the shrimp down there tasted—these big shrimps, hon, like little mini lobsters—and I even remember what Greta looked like in her red bathing suit. She was a knockout. You couldn't tell she'd had a kid." He stared into his empty glass like he might be trying to conjure up more bourbon. "But there's this one photo that worries the shit out of me. Caleb was maybe four when Greta took it, and he's bopping me in the head with a Nerf bat, and we're both laughing like crazy. I can hear his little giggle in my head, but the only thing I can see when I try to go back there is the photo, so I'm seeing him and me, too, and you know that's not how a person's head works. Right? If I really remembered I'd be seeing him out of my own eyes."

"Maybe it doesn't matter," Ellen said.

"Maybe not," Mr. Hoffman said. "But maybe it's the only thing that matters."

Something had happened. Mr. Hoffman had entrusted Ellen with his grief, and though she wanted to withdraw from it—though she sensed that this confession was as inappropriate as his offer of alcohol had been—she also felt his heartbreak, his despera-tion. She didn't want to run away like a kid, to pretend that she didn't comprehend his pain. So she did what the women in those TV movies did when they finally found a decent man to confide in: she put her hand on Mr. Hoffman's forearm.

"Mr. Hoffman," she said. "I wish I could help you."

They stayed that way just for a second—long enough for Ellen to register the tremble in Mr. Hoffman's arm muscle, the texture of his thick arm hairs under her fingertips. And then he was shaking her off, roughly, and she stood up so quickly that something in the middle of her forehead throbbed, as though the blue vein that she usually hid with bangs had ruptured.

"I think there's been a miscommunication here," Mr. Hoffman said loudly, slurring a little on *miscommunication*. He looked sick still, but also something else: scared, disgusted. Caught? Whatever it was—or the combination—made Ellen so nervous that she grabbed her tennis shoes and backed away.

"I'm going," she said. The taste of the citrus wine cooler was still in her mouth, cloying and almost bitter, and she felt like she'd be sick if she didn't lie down soon.

"That's right," he said. "You take off. And you might watch yourself a little better from now on, Ellie. You're at that age. I wouldn't want to have to call your mother."

She ran the whole way home, stomach sloshing, eyes hot and sore with her sudden tears. She crossed two gravel drives barefoot, the pain almost satisfying, and she didn't make it inside before the little bit she drank came up on her: first in her mouth, thick and hot and almost chemical, and then in the bushes next to the back door of her house. She pressed her forehead against the glass of the storm door. Her mother had opened the window on the door a bit, so air could circulate, and she could hear home through the screen: *Guiding Light* playing loud on the cabinet TV; water running in the kitchen, where Ellen's mother was probably getting ready to mop floors, her Friday afternoon ritual. Ellen would have an excuse, at least, to creep to her bedroom through the den and into the hallway, skipping the kitchen and her mother; she was always catching hell for tromping across wet linoleum.

She yelled, "Home, Mom" from the living room, wiping her face with her beach towel.

"You better rinse that water off quick," her mother called back, as she almost always did. "That chlorine'll turn your hair green."

A shower didn't seem like a bad idea: she felt scummy, felt like she wanted to scrub with hot water and brush her teeth two or three times and never drink anything orange flavored again. She crossed the hall, treading lightly in her bare feet past Andy's bedroom—his Sega was blasting that infernal Sonic the Hedgehog theme song, the one that got stuck in Ellen's head some days until it made her half-crazy—and went to her own room, planning to grab a clean pair of shorts and one of her tank tops. She was already pulling a bathing suit strap over her shoulder when she realized that Kev was there, standing in front of her dresser. Her underwear drawer was open.

"Oh." That was all she could say.

His back was to her, and he stiffened, his neck all at once red and blotchy. But when he turned, his face was casual, teasing: the face he wore right before dunking her in the Hoffmans' pool. He pushed the drawer shut with his bottom. "Later," he said. He walked out with his hands plunged deep in his pockets, and Ellen shut the door behind him. She wished that she had a lock, but her mother wouldn't allow it, even when Ellen had explained that Andy came in sometimes and stole her babysitting money. She went to the drawer, opened it, and looked at the tangle of cloth and straps, wondering what Kev had touched and why. Everything was thin and cotton, some patterned with flowers, most with popped elastic in the leg holes or waistband. Some of her underwear had faint stains in the crotch, and at least one pair was smeared with a ghostly red-brown: the imprint of washed-away blood. Seeing this, and knowing that Kev had seen it, made her want to cry again. There wasn't anything private. There wasn't a corner of this world — of her own room, even—that she could stake claim to, that belonged to her and her alone.

II.

The morning after what happened with Mr. Hoffman, Ray called and asked Ellen to come over for the night. "Mom might stay home this time," she said. "If you come, she said she might. I've almost talked her into taking us cruising with her."

"Yeah?" Ellen knew that she should be excited—Ray sure

sounded it—but Gloria seemed like the last person she needed to be around right now. She thought about what Mr. Hoffman had said at the pool, the look on his face as he said it: *You might watch yourself a little better from now on, Ellie. You're at that age.* Hadn't he been right? What did Kev's presence in her room mean, if not that she was doing or saying something—putting out a signal— that she shouldn't be?

"Yeah," Ray said. "The FOP is doing the summer carnival thing again out behind Pizza Hut, and she mentioned wanting to go out there. Say you'll come, okay? I always wanted to go, and she'd never do it. She said it was silly. But she's into it for some reason this year. What do you think?"

"Mom might not want me to," Ellen said.

"Oh, bull. Please, just come. If you don't go, she'll probably take off somewhere. And there's nothing to do around here."

"Okay," Ellen said. She knew what Ray really meant: *She'll take off somewhere, and I'll be alone.* "I can talk Mom into it."

"Wear something cute," Ray told her, and hung up.

Ray and her mother lived in a duplex on Second Street, close to the sewing factory where Ellen's mother worked. When Ellen went there for sleepovers, her mother always made her write the phone number for the factory in pen on her arm—up above the wrist, where she wouldn't wash it off—and promise to call if anything seemed wrong or even unusual. "You call," she'd tell Ellen just before dropping her off, which was pretty often that summer. "Don't worry about bothering me. If you hear anything funny outside, or if Gloria brings a man home—that last, especially. Do what I say, now. You promise?"

Ellen would promise.

"All right then," her mother would say, ruffling Ellen's hair, eyeing the house—Ray's half of the house—with suspicion. She'd have her work clothes on: the gray shirt and slacks, the big denim apron. "Make sure you give Ray some money for the pizza. I'm going to drive by when my shift ends and make sure things look quiet over here."

And her mother always did. At midnight, when Gloria was still who knows where doing God knows what, Ellen would peek through the mini blinds and see her mother's slow drive by. It was a comfort, especially those times when Ellen and Ray *did* hear strange sounds in the surrounding neighborhood—barking dogs, loud teenage laughter, and once something they were both sure had to be a gun shot — and the doors seemed like paper, like nothing that could come between them and a person who meant them harm. A house—a half of a house — was nothing.

But Ray wanted her over there, and Ellen wanted, at least a lot of the time, to be there. They had fun together. Gloria would leave them money for pizza, and there were usually movies to watch, because Gloria managed Get Reel and got all of the new releases the weekend before they officially went on the shelves. Ray had a real grown-up's room, too. Her mattress and box spring were on the floor—"so we can just crash," was how she put it—and her walls were covered with posters of bands that Ellen had never heard of, all of the members long haired and greasy looking with black boots and layers of rings on both hands. She hadn't witnessed Ray listening to their music, ever, but the posters themselves were dark and dangerous and impressive. Best of all, Gloria didn't make Ray pick up after herself — and she sure didn't pick up after Ray, the way Ellen's mother would do some days out of pure frustration—so the carpet was covered in clothes and fashion magazines, a kind of happy mess that made Ray's world seem fuller than Ellen's, that hid treasures: the scatter of jewelry on top of Ray's little black-and-white TV; the Caboodles case, stuffed full of Gloria's old, powdery compacts and glittery eye shadow and tubes of lipstick, on the floor next to Ray's pillow. She had a line of empty beer bottles on her windowsill, too—her mother's—the labels colorful and all different, like tiny flags: Corona, Budweiser, Miller High Life.

By six that evening, Ellen was wearing the cutest thing she could find in her closet—a denim skirt and a blue silk shirt that she'd splurged for with her birthday money, not great, but the best she could do—and sitting on her front step, overnight bag between her feet. Her mother had already left for her shift, grumbling about working on a Saturday but clearly glad for the overtime nonetheless. She'd been feeling Andy out recently about finding a part-time job—just a few hours a week, something to help her cover his equipment costs for baseball in spring and basketball in the winter, plus the eating out and stuff he liked to do—but he got to grumbling about it in typical Andy fashion, and the conversation appeared to be dead, at least for the time being. Ellen wanted to love her brother, and there were times when he was almost all right, like the afternoon a few weeks earlier when he walked with her down to the Bethel Dipper for milkshakes, but most of the time he was nothing but a loud laugh and a bad smell coming from the room across the hall, and she just about hated him. It was no wonder she liked staying at Ray's place, strange sounds and Gloria drama and all. Maybe her mother even understood that.

Gloria's red Firebird pulled into the driveway, and the horn sounded. The windows were tinted dark enough that Ellen couldn't see inside from this disance, but she knew that Ray was probably squeezed up next to the gear shift so that they could share shotgun. She felt a little thrill despite herself. Whatever else you could say about Ray's mom, she was fun: she spent money easily, not checking tags and agonizing over a two-dollar pair of earrings the way Ellen's mother did, and she talked to Ellen and Ray like they were her own age, like friends. As if she'd read Ellen's mind, the dark window on the driver's side rolled down part way, and Gloria stuck her head out. "You going to stand there and show off your outfit some more, or are you going to get in? We've got places to go, sugarbunch." She was grinning.

"Coming," Ellen said, waving too hard, like a dork, in her giddiness. She tossed her bag into the backseat and squeezed in front next to Ray, who smelled like Aqua Net and watermelon-flavored Bubblicious. Like her room, Ray was scattered and occasionally overwhelming, but full of good if you looked hard enough. Even Ellen's mother had to admit to that.

"You look great," Ray said.

"You sure do," Gloria chimed in, backing into the road fast enough that her tires squealed a little before she braked and shifted. She had to sit on a couch cushion to see around her own headrest. "Cute as a button."

The windows were down. Warm evening air funneled into the car, blowing Ellen's hair across her mouth, and she put her hand out slightly, letting it ride a current of wind, jumping driveways and mailboxes with her fingertips. She saw a couple of teenage guys skateboarding by the old bank and smiled, feeling powerful and gorgeous, like a movie star. She didn't know if they'd seen her, but she turned to Ray and hugged her suddenly, knowing somewhere deep within her that a night like this was fleeting and too soon forgotten, a fragile thing, a treasure.

"I'm glad I'm here," she said, and Ray hugged her back.

"Me, too."

As soon as they drove out of the thick of buildings around town square, the carnival was visible: a huddle of multicolored lights where there was usually only a dark parking lot, the arc of a Ferris wheel. One of the things Ellen liked about summer was the way things cropped up out of nothing: carnivals, sure, but also tent revivals—she'd never been to one, but the idea of them appealed to her in ways that regular church didn't—sno-cone stands, the old guy who parked off Stevenson Mill Road every June and July and sold produce out of the bed of his truck. When you drove past him, he always sounded the same call in a tongue that seemed ancient and a little exotic: "Canna-loop, wadda-meyon."

They parked behind Pizza Hut, not far from a row of pickups and low riders—most of them souped-up with chrome wheels and metallic detail work, all of them playing music, a mix of rap and country that hurt Ellen's ears and made her heart feel hijacked, forced into a rhythm that wasn't its own. Young men leaned out of windows, watching as Gloria climbed out of the car and made a big show—even Ellen could see it—of bending over to adjust the ankle strap on one of her high-heeled sandals. "Girls," she said loudly, looking their way but not seeming to see them. "Let's get a move on." There was a whistle, and Gloria didn't acknowledge it, only smirked a little and picked up her pace. "Damn rednecks," she said.

Then the parking lot music gave way to carnival music—the waltz of the merry-go-round, last year's New Kids on the Block playing out of speakers above the funnel-cake stand, the electronic hisses and beeps of the Bullet and Gravitron—and Ellen felt better. This was familiar; these were the sounds of a lifetime of carnivals, the kind of music meant to blend together and fade out, a backdrop to the lights and the smells and the fun. She couldn't listen to music the way the older kids, the way those guys in the parking lot, did: so loud that it wiped out thought. Some teenagers, she'd noticed, gathered around a boom box like it was a fireplace, like it was something that could warm them. Even Andy. He'd lie in his bed and play Nirvana's *Nevermind* album over and over some nights, and he'd get pissed if Ellen came in to ask him a question or tell him that dinner was ready, as if he didn't already know the words to every song.

Gloria stopped them at the ticket stand. "Here's some money," she said, handing Ray a ten. "That should keep you guys busy for a little while, at least."

"Aren't you going to hang out with us?" Ray said.

Gloria craned her neck, searching the crowd. "I'll be around," she said. "You girls have fun and don't run off. If I haven't seen you by ten, I'll meet up with you in this same spot. Okay?"

"But, Mama," Ray said. She tried grabbing Gloria's hand, but she pulled away.

"You're so serious all the time. Why are you so serious?" She smiled nervously and smoothed her curly brown hair. "We'll hang out. We'll get a pizza when we're done here and go home and stay up late. How does that sound? I'll do my tarot cards on you."

Ray crossed her arms and turned away, so Ellen spoke up: "That'll be fun."

"You're a good girl," Gloria said to Ellen. She walked away before Ray had a chance to turn around again.

"Fucking bitch," Ray said.

Ellen nudged a piece of gravel with her toe.

"I know what she's doing. I know why she brought us here. I'm so stupid."

"Why?" Ellen said quietly.

Ray walked to the ticket stand and traded the ten-dollar bill for a strip of tickets. "This won't even last us an hour," she said miserably.

Ellen linked her arm through Ray's. "I have some money. Let's just have fun, okay?"

Ray looked in the direction her mother had walked off, eyes dry. She nodded.

They rode the Ferris wheel first, and when they stopped at the top, waiting as the next bucket was loaded, Ray closed her eyes. "This is where you're supposed to kiss if you're with a guy. Mama told me that. She said that her first kiss was at the top of a Ferris wheel."

Ellen hadn't had her first kiss. She thought about Mr. Hoffman again and wondered if she should tell Ray what had happened. She could be casual, totally blasé about it: "So yeah, I had a wine cooler yesterday." Ray would like that. She'd want details, and for a few moments, Ellen would be the powerful one in their friendship, the one with knowledge and experience, the one with a story worth telling. But she didn't feel blasé about that drink and what Mr. Hoffman had said to her, the way his trust had turned so quickly to disgust. And if power came from this kind of knowledge, she wasn't sure that she wanted it. Could she explain that to Ray? Because if she revealed the part about the wine cooler, she'd have to spill the rest of it; and she knew that her explanation wouldn't justify the way she felt, the guilt and the emptiness. Ray would say, "It was just one drink," and she'd write Mr. Hoffman off as "an old perv" or even a "dumb fucker," and that would be that. "Nothing happened," she'd say. "What are you so bent out of shape for?" Ray was Ellen's best friend—her BFF, the person she liked most and had liked longest, since they were assigned to be study buddies in fifth-grade social studies. Ray was a good person, she knew, but maybe being around her was costing Ellen something.

You might watch yourself a little better from now on, Mr. Hoffman had told her. *You're at that age.*

Ray's eyes were open again. She leaned over the edge of the basket, looking down below them. "Mom's doing a cop," she said. "That's why she's here."

"That doesn't seem so bad," Ellen said. "I mean, at least it's a cop."

The Ferris wheel started moving again, fast this time and not stopping. The rush of warm air was pleasant, and the sun was just setting to Ellen's right. The basket they were in creaked with each descent, as though a screw somewhere were working its way free.

"It's Robo Cop," Ray said. "Do you know who I'm talking about?"

She sure did. He had white blond hair and blue, almost clear eyes, and he was investigated a year or two ago for using his nightstick on a fourteen-year-old boy. A lot of people were pissed when he wasn't fired, including Ellen's mom, who told her and Andy that there was a lesson in what happened: "Cops can get away with anything. Not a thing you can do about it."

He also had a wife and some kids, Ellen was pretty sure.

"Wow," she said.

"Yeah. Wow is right." The ride stopped, and they wandered over to the line for the Scrambler. "He's a jerk. He comes over real late on weeknights, and he leaves before I get up in the morning. He parks his cruiser right out front like he doesn't give a care. My mom is such a slut."

As if summoned, Gloria appeared, grabbing them each by an arm. "I need to borrow you guys a few minutes," she said. "I was looking all over for you."

"What's up?" Ray said, brightening.

"Let's go to the Gravitron," Gloria said. "Everyone's saying how fun it is. You two ought to ride it."

They went to the line, which was pretty long—at least twenty or twenty-five people—and watched as the Gravitron slowed its spin. It was white and cylindrical, like a soup can, and you couldn't see inside it. Just watching its motion made Ellen uneasy, as did Gloria: she looked high-strung and determined, like she was up to something; she kept standing on tiptoe so she could look over the heads of the others in line. "Be damned," she said suddenly. "I see her."

"Who?" Ray said.

Gloria adjusted her blouse, fluffed her curls.

"Who do you see?"

The doors to the Gravitron opened, and people started streaming out, some laughing, some sick looking. Ellen could guess which category she was going to fall into. The line moved, and Gloria grabbed Ray by the elbow, almost pushing her into the man ahead of them. "Go on," she said in a loud, hard whisper, and for a moment Ellen felt the sudden and irrational fear that Gloria was going to force them in the Gravitron, then abandon them. She looked down at her arm, where the phone number to the factory was usually written, and realized that she'd forgotten it this time. Her mother, in a hurry to get out the door, hadn't reminded her. She could look it up, of course, or she could call Andy and get it, but its absence seemed like a bad omen. Ellen was as conscious of bad omens as she was of lucky charms.

She saw Robo Cop just before they reached the entrance. He was sitting at a folding table, collecting tickets, and a woman was seated next to him—his wife, had to be. She was chubby but attractive, and Ellen guessed that she hadn't always looked like somebody's mother. The woman was smiling and bobbing her head as she collected a ticket, and then she was tearing the ticket in half, and then they were in front of her, handing their own tickets over. Robo Cop was giving Gloria a look—angry, maybe, or desperate— but his wife didn't notice it.

"I'll wait out here," Gloria said. "You girls go on, you're holding up the line."

"I don't want to ride," Ray said loudly.

Robo Cop looked at her and stood, nudging his wife with an elbow. "I need a smoke," he said in a low voice—a cold and emotionless voice that seemed closer to the nickname than anything physical about him—and he walked off. Gloria laughed, a high-pitched sound, almost hysterical.

"A smoke," she called after him, and now his wife *was* noticing her, and the look on her face was confused but also sort of resigned, too—like she knew enough about trouble to recognize it, but she hadn't figured out the brand yet. "What?" Gloria said, putting her hands on her hips and leaning over, so that her face was just a few inches from the woman's. "Who do you think you're looking at?"

The woman shrugged. "I don't know you," she said, keeping her voice low. "And I don't want to know you."

"Your husband knows me," Gloria said, and that's when Ray broke line and ran, sending a swirl of gravel dust up behind her. Ellen started to follow, but Gloria caught the tail of her silk shirt as she turned, yanking her back. The ride hadn't started up yet. Everybody was watching.

"You tell her—" Gloria stopped, face drawing up into something ugly and despairing. She put her hand to her eyes and pressed, like she was smoothing, and it seemed to work—when she pulled her hand away, she looked like herself again. "You tell her to get her ass in the car and not move until I get there." She opened her purse and felt around, then pulled out a ring of keys. "Take these and stay put."

Ellen found Ray in the parking lot, sitting on a curb and scratching her initials onto fresh blacktop with a piece of limestone: RAW, a light gray against a darker gray. Ellen sat beside her.

"Ray Anne Whitaker," Ellen said, rubbing her fingers over the letters. "I hadn't noticed that spelled a word out before."

"Yeah, well, it's stupid," Ray said. "Because my mom's stupid. Didn't even know that Rayanne is one word."

"I like your name."

Ray shrugged against her shoulder, then leaned into it, resting her forehead on Ellen's neck. Ellen could feel her cheek, cool and dry, and she took Ray's hand in hers. They sat that way for a while, watching the carnival, listening to Mr. Big blasting out of somebody's lowrider: "I'm the one who wants to be with you . . ." Gloria loved that song. She turned it up when it came on the radio, which was a lot these days, and sang along without embarrassment, like the lyrics touched her somewhere deep, and she wasn't going to hide it.

She came out maybe an hour later, face bright and triumphant, pulling the neck of her shirt out and fanning with her free hand. "Sorry about that. The carnival sucked, right? But the night is young."

"I want to go home," Ray said flatly.

"No pizza?"

Ray shook her head, then glanced at Ellen, checking. Ellen nodded.

"Just home."

They both rode in the backseat this time, and when they got to Ray's place, Gloria went straight to her room and her telephone. Before long the house started to smell like perfume and hairspray and that low burn of a curling iron against hair, and Gloria's high-pitched laugh carried across the house every now and then, bold as an exclamation point. Ellen and Ray watched a video. When the doorbell rang at eleven, Ray didn't budge. "It's for her," she said. "She can get it."

"Is she going out?" Ellen whispered.

"Probably."

Gloria came to the door and paused, hand on the doorknob. "Ray," she said. "I know you're upset. Just don't mess this up for me, okay?" She was wearing a different outfit now: cropped pants and a tank top, no bra. Her brown curls trembled at her shoulders.

Ray stuck out her middle finger, eyes still on the TV screen. Ellen couldn't believe it.

"Let me tell you something," Gloria said. "My life ain't easy. Things didn't turn out how I planned. Maybe someday you'll get a taste of what that's like. It's real easy to be a princess when you're thirteen and somebody else is making the payments. You hear what I'm saying?"

The doorbell rang again, followed by three hard raps. Gloria opened it, and Robo Cop came in, still wearing his uniform. "Hey," she said, standing on tiptoe to kiss his cheek. He didn't say anything back, just stared at Ray and Ellen like he was trying to figure out who they were, how they'd gotten into Gloria's living room. Gloria took him by the hand and pulled. "We'll be in my room," she said. "Watching TV." They walked to the back of the house, and in another few minutes the stereo was blaring. When the first song ended, the sound of bed springs echoed for a couple of seconds, and Ellen focused on the streetlamp outside, aware that her face and neck were reddening. Ray turned up the volume on the television.

"At least she's here," Ray said, sounding like she might cry. "Right? That's something, isn't it?"

"I guess."

Ray jumped to a stand, grinning. "Hey! We can have drinks!" She went to the kitchen, stopping in the doorway when Ellen didn't follow. "Come on, Mom won't care."

"I don't want any," Ellen said.

"Bullshit." Ray disappeared, and Ellen could hear the refrigerator door open and close, then the roar of the freezer. "I'm making you one," she yelled over the bass line of a new song. "This is my own invention. It's just like cherry Sprite."

Ellen looked at Ray's living room: the big-screen TV with the image that warped on one side; the coffee table littered with ashtrays and an old HBO guide and a half-dozen glasses, different sizes, all crusted with the remains of milk or juice or beer. This wasn't a home; it was a hotel room. And Gloria was no mother. Ellen had loved Ray enough all these years not to see what was right in front of her, but she was too old now to play stupid, to let Ray and Gloria turn her into something she didn't have to be.

Ray came back with two large tumblers. She handed one to Ellen, took a big swig from the other, grimaced, then smiled. Ellen looked down at her glass and sniffed. The liquid was bubbly with a reddish tint, and the smell was nauseating, like nail polish re-mover.

"Check this out," Ray said. She took Ellen's hand and flipped it over, pulling her fingers open so that the palm was exposed. "This is your life line," she said, tracing around Ellen's thumb with a sparkly painted fingernail. "This is your career line. And here on the side—" She showed Ellen a few faint lines marking off the edge of her palm, just below the pinkie. "These are marriage lines. Mama knows all about this stuff. You know what's funny?"

"What?"

"She put our hands side by side one time," Ray said. "And the lines were almost the same. She said that means we're soul mates." She let go of Ellen's hand. "What do you think?"

"I think it's all a load of crap," Ellen said, and it seemed true, even though there were days enough when she felt like her own life hinged on the tiniest thing: how many twists to remove an apple stem, how many laps she could run in P.E., dozens of oth-ers. Forgetting to write the number for the factory on her arm had felt like a bad sign, and perhaps it was, given the events of the night, but she knew that her mother would be driving by at a few minutes after twelve, and that kind of certainty had nothing to do with charms or superstition or luck. She looked at the digital clock on the end table: 11:45.

Ray frowned and gulped down more of her drink. "You're just jealous," she said. "I mean, your mom's nice but it's not like she's pretty or fun or anything."

This hit Ellen square in the middle, stealing her breath for a moment. She tried to think of a retort, of evidence to prove Ray wrong. But Ray was right. Her mother was chubby, with dull graying hair and old acne scars on her face. She wore sweatpants and T-shirts around the house, and her idea of a good time was watching *The Golden Girls* with a tin of Charles Chips in her lap. When she tried to be spontaneous—like the day last year when she took Ellen and Andy to Bowling Green to watch a movie—she always made some kind of miscalculation. That last time, the movie had been lame, the popcorn was cold, and they'd argued the whole way to the theater and back. Her mother had said, "Lordy mercy, prices sure have gone up" to the teenager working the ticket booth, and Ellen had wished that a piano would drop from the sky and land on top of her, putting her out of her misery. Her mother's efforts inevitably led to such cataclysmic failures.

She loved her mother, though—scars and bad teeth and everything else—and she felt that she owed it to her to say why now, to put Ray in her place once and for all. But "I'm going outside" was all she could manage.

"Wait," Ray said. "What do you mean, outside? Why would you do that?"

Ellen rose. "To wait for Mom to get here."

Ray ran to the front door, stumbling a little, and stretched her arms out in front of it. "Don't go, okay? I'm sorry. I'm being a bitch because I'm mad. But we can still have a good time." Now she was crying, the first time Ellen had ever seen her do it. Ray held up a hand—*just hold your horses a sec*—and went to the phone. "You're hungry, right? Let's get a pizza. Anything you want."

Ellen put her hand on the doorknob and shook her head.

"Please, Ellen," Ray said. Pleaded, really. She lowered her voice. "I'll pour the rest of the drinks out. We can go straight to bed if you want. Just don't leave me here alone with them. If you're my friend, you won't."

Ellen felt the brass of the knob getting hot and wet under her palm. She could stay this night with Ray, she knew, and everything would be fine. Robo Cop would leave. Gloria would be in high spirits the next day; she'd get up late and make chocolate chip pancakes, and then they'd go to the mall. Tonight wouldn't seem so bad in the morning, because Ray wouldn't let Ellen remember the way things had gone down. At her mother's side, she'd be too happy, too satisfied, to do anything but pretend and forget.

"I've got to go," Ellen said finally.

"Okay, sure, I understand. But take me, too." Ray came over and grabbed her free hand, then hugged her, not seeming to notice or care that Ellen didn't return the embrace. "I'll go home with you and your mom. Your mom is great. Okay?" She squeezed Ellen tighter, and Ellen felt the hot press of Ray's face against her neck. "Ellen, *please*."

Ellen pushed her away. She knew she was being selfish, but she was also being practical: Ray couldn't stay with her forever. This was, she'd think later—and with more sorrow than she could ever have anticipated—her first real adult decision.

"I'll see you at school," she said, and stepped outside. The door slammed shut behind her, so hard that the living room window rattled in its frame.

"Bitch!" she heard Ray scream, the closed door and the loud stereo making her voice seem puny and distant.

There was a swing on the neighbor's side, but using it seemed rude, so Ellen sat on the front steps, legs pulled up to her chest. The night was warm and strangely bright—there was a not-quite-full moon out, riding high in the sky—and she waited, sitting up straight when she saw headlights, relaxing when she realized that not enough time had passed, that it was too soon yet.

Her mother came just after midnight. Ellen didn't know the time, but she knew her mother well enough to be sure of it.

She looked surprised when Ellen came to the car, but she didn't say anything about Gloria as Ellen had worried she would, only stared at the house—the police cruiser, dark and silent in the drive—and touched Ellen's shoulder. "Is Ray all right in there?"

Ellen nodded, feeling like a liar. She wondered what Ray would do now: watch TV, go to bed? Finish what was left of her drink and Ellen's too?

"Are you okay?"

"Yeah," she said. And that much seemed true. Her mother put the car in drive, and Ray's house—her half of a house—disappeared around a dark corner.

Ellen marked the changes outside her window. As you drove closer to the square, the duplexes gave way to older houses, and then the houses east of town, in Dellview, were the nicest, where the doctors and lawyers all lived. Gloria called it Pill Hill, and this one time, when they'd gone cruising, they'd driven through Dellview with their windows rolled down—Ray and Ellen squeezed into the front, like always—screaming the lyrics to "Blueberry Hill," saying, "I've had my thrills on Pill Hill" instead. On West Ninth you passed Arthur Baldwin's house, which was the biggest and fanciest in town as far as Ellen was concerned, but just a few streets later you got to the Shell station and the cemetery and Kip's Garage, which always had tires piled in the back so high that you could see them over the roof of the building, and then you got to Ellen's subdivision, which wasn't the worst in town but sure wasn't that great either. In the dark you could see what a difference a mile—what a street, even—made. Ray was back behind her, and Mr. Hoffman's place was just ahead, on the right, the windows all dark. She thought about Mr. Hoffman's Theory of Realty, feeling the first dawn of understanding. Ray still lived right across town, and Ellen would inevitably cross her path at school. But they would never be close again.

"Mr. Hoffman's wife left him," she told her mother.

Her mother signaled, and they turned off of Sycamore and onto Forsythia, where the split levels like Mr. Hoffman's gave way to small ranch homes, shabbier as you got further away from Ninth. "How did you hear about that?" her mother said.

"I don't know," Ellen told her. "It's just going around."

They pulled into their driveway. "Well, folks aren't happy unless they've got bad news to spread, I guess." Her mother sighed. "Don't I know it."

"She's in Cincinnati."

Her mother nodded as if this made sense, as if Cincinnati were the destination for women who left their husbands. "Things hadn't been the same for them since Caleb died. We all knew that. But Greta—I shouldn't say this, but here I go—she could be a real handful."

Ellen remembered Mr. Hoffman, sunburned and angry, and the taste of that wine cooler, the one that had once been Mrs. Hoffman's. "I thought she was nice. She helped me with my makeup one day."

"A girl your age has no business wearing makeup, anyhow," her mother said. "If I'd known about that I would've thought twice about letting you go over there."

"Whatever," Ellen said.

"*Whatever.* I hate that word. That's your answer to everything." The car's headlights hit the door to their garage and reflected back faintly, making her mother look old, jawline set but soft, wrinkles around her eyes more prominent than Ellen remembered them being. "Walt's a nice man. Women like her don't know a good thing when they've got it. They're always looking out for better."

"You think Mr. Hoffman's a good thing?"

"I think a girl could do a lot worse." Ellen saw the faraway look in her mother's eyes, could read the dream in them that her mother would never acknowledge and certainly never act on; she and Mr. Hoffman and a house with a pool, a life that had nothing to do with late nights spent sewing pockets into cheap blue jeans. And what else? Sex, sure. Something Ellen didn't know much about outside the science of it—the things she'd learned in seventh grade, when Ms. Burchett split up the girls and the boys and taught one half while the other got an extra thirty minutes in activities period—but it had to do with the way a shirt folded up onto a tanned forearm, the tangle of panties and bras in her dresser drawer, the noises Gloria and Robo Cop were making in that back room, audible in the pauses between song tracks. Because sex, she figured, was just another way of saying *secret:* the secret lives of grown-ups. She looked at her mother and realized that she knew something about Mr. Hoffman that her mother did not, and she understood that the power between them was shifting—slowly and maybe imperceptibly now, but shifting nonetheless. And she didn't want it to. She craned her neck so that she could see through the window, trying to find a star to wish upon, a charm to bring her luck. But her view was blocked by a nearby streetlamp: the only point of light in a sky the size of infinity.

Holly Goddard Jones was a 2007 recipient of the Rona Jaffe Writers' Award. Her fiction has appeared in *The Kenyon Review, The Southern Review, The Gettysburg Review, The Hudson Review,* and *Epoch* and has been reprinted in *Best American Mystery Stories* and a previous volume of *New Stories from the South.* A graduate of the MFA program in creative writing at Ohio State University, she now teaches at Murray State University, in her home state of Kentucky.

BRANDON JONES

*T*heory of Realty" was my attempt at a coming-of-age story, but I actually had a pretty specific set of goals in mind for it. I was bent on writing about a girl who embodied some of the strange superstitions and fears that I had when I was Ellen's age, most notably the sense of being constantly at risk, corruptible. The first half of the narrative is one of those girl-in-jeopardy stories come to life, though the threat turns out to be much different than the kind Ellen had anticipated and even halfway hoped for. I see the second half of the story as a kind of response, or answer, to the first: Ellen trading the child's disillusionment for the adult's. The form is a little unconventional, but I stood doggedly by it; I like the idea that a story can sometimes work like a novel in miniature, with multiple arcs and pauses for reflection.

Pinckney Benedict

BRIDGE OF SIGHS

(from *Zoetrope*)

From the darkness of the barn, my father lumbered out into the yard, blinking like a baby in the sunlight. He shaded his eyes with a flat hand until he saw the farmer, a fellow by the name of Woodrow Scurry, standing in the stiff mud, still as a scarecrow. That was what he looked like, Scurry, a scarecrow, with his too-big overalls and beat-to-shit steel-toe boots, his hair sticking out like straw from under his ball cap.

He was leaning far forward, like whatever was holding him up was about to give. He'd been standing that way since my father went into the barn. He'd been standing just like that for a full five minutes. I was keeping an eye on him. Sometimes they went a little batty.

"I count thirteen head in there, Mister Scurry," my father said. He looked at the clipboard in his hands. "So we're four short." It was always a mystery, how many animals these fellows were hiding. It might be a couple steers, like Scurry, or it might be a dozen. It was always some, though. They couldn't help it, trying to keep something back. They didn't know how serious it was, or they pretended not to know. They were shifty and ignorant, and they were a danger to us all.

"Is that right?"

"There is nothing covered that shall not be revealed," I said. It was the first thing I had said since we got there, a thing my father always told me after he'd finished work at a place like this. "Neither anything hid that shall not be known."

"What's that?" Scurry asked. He turned to look at me — I don't think he'd even noticed I was there until that moment — and his cheeks were hollow, his eye sockets filled with shadow beneath the bill of his cap.

I was sitting on the hood of my father's big black Chrysler Imperial, long as a limousine. Most cars you couldn't sit on the hood without dimpling the metal, but that Chrysler might as well have been armored. We had ridden up here to Scurry's place from the county seat, my father and me, listening to Cowboy Copas loud on the radio and singing along with "Tragic Romance" until we lost the signal among the rocky hilltops. I was tall enough that year that the heels of my Dingos touched the chrome of the bumper. The hood ornament, the Imperial eagle that my father had ordered specially, sat calm and solid beneath my hand.

The massive motor poured out waves of warmth, even though it wasn't running. My butt and the backs of my legs tingled from the heat and ran with sweat. The bright light of the sun made my head ache, but it couldn't fill the darkness where Mister Scurry's eyes ought to have been. The metal of the engine block ticked as it cooled. Under that I could hear something else, a soft whispering like many voices. The sound of water running over rocks. I was suddenly thirsty.

The epizootic was running mad in those days, sweeping through the highlands like wildfire, threatening to clean out our valley as well. It was like a charnel house up on those high farms. And we were lucky, where we lived. In other places it had arrived earlier and traveled faster, and there was nothing left. We heard about it on the radio. Places where there were no cattle anymore at all, no pigs, no sheep. Places where poultry barns—long white buildings holding, some of them, as many as a hundred thousand birds—had simply been set alight and burned flat.

Places where it had wiped out the dogs. I tried to imagine that, a world without dogs, but my imagination just wouldn't frame it. I thought about all our dogs, swarming the Chrysler as they would when we pulled into the yard that evening, barking into their own reflections in the bumpers, the chrome wheel wells, the hubcaps. Standing on their hind legs, grinning in through the windows at us with their tongues out, their spit flecking the glass. My father would shout at them to get out of the way, promise to run them down if they didn't shift, and they'd ignore him. A world without dogs. It was impossible.

And in some of those other places, we were now hearing, the epizootic had made the leap over into human beings.

"Thirteen," Scurry said, turning back to my father. The corners of his mouth came up in a tight, lopsided smile. There was nothing here for him to smile at. He looked embarrassed. Sometimes they were belligerent, the stockmen, sometimes they were confused, sometimes they were just humiliated and wanted to get it over with. The belligerent ones were easiest, my father said. You didn't mind doing what you had to do when a fellow argued with you. "Do you have to kill them all?" Scurry asked.

My father looked at him, then at me, peering at us again from under the visor of his hand. He had sensitive eyes and was all the time squinting against the light. "I need them all," my father said. He waved the clipboard in Scurry's direction.

"That's all I got is right in there," Scurry said. "You can look around the place if you want. All the good it'll do you." He gestured around him, at the barnyard, the barn, the house that stood crookedly, as crookedly as Scurry himself; at the pastures and the woods that stretched everywhere.

The sound of running water seemed louder to me now, and I swallowed in a dry throat. There was a creek nearby. I had spent a good part of the summer looking for a mud puppy, one of the fat brown mountain salamanders, big as your hand, and I wondered if there might not be one in some shallow cool-water pool along Scurry's creek, lurking among the stones and the ferns.

"This doesn't give me any pleasure, Mister Scurry," my father said. "I don't do this for the enjoyment of it." He was talking to me, not to Scurry.

Some of the extermination men liked their job, and some of them that didn't care for it at first got to like doing it after a while. Not my father, though. He came from a farming family himself, and killing livestock cut pretty close to the bone.

"You know what it is, don't you?" he asked me on the way up to Scurry's farm. "This epizootic, these germs they talk about. It's the Gadarene Swine. We've been told this story. If we don't stop it in the animals, it'll kill everything. This fellow"—he glanced at the clipboard that sat beside him on the wide bench of the Imperial— "this Scurry, he'll say, 'Please don't do this, mister.' He'll beg me. But will I listen to him?"

"You won't," I told him.

"No, I won't," he said.

I hopped down off the hood of the car and went around to the trunk. My old man had opted for the Flight Sweep trunk lid, the one with the shape of a spare tire stamped into it. It was supposed to be fancy, but it looked like a toilet seat to me. He cared for it, though. He got everything extra there was to get on that car. He said he felt like he deserved it, with the work he was doing. He could afford to, I guess, with the bounties from the epizootic. We never had anything like that Imperial before. I popped the lid.

The Exterminator sat in the trunk, goggling up at me with its cloudy glass eyes. It gave me a thrill to look into them, like looking at death and seeing myself reflected there. Twice, once in each lens. The Exterminator had a long, flexible snout, like an elephant's. Skin like an elephant's, too, thick and gray and wrinkled. No mouth. Massive sausage-fingered hands.

My father didn't do the killing. The Exterminator did the killing. It kept the demons off of him, and it did the killing for him, and it kept him clean and safe inside it, no matter what went on outside. He was like Jesus, in a way.

My father was talking to Scurry in low tones. Explaining to him what was about to happen. Showing him the paperwork on the clipboard. Explaining how it was good agricultural hygiene, and it was the only acceptable way, and it was the law. Scurry just kept wagging his head. I laid hold of one of the Exterminator's legs and dragged it out of the trunk. The rubber was heavy and cool and slick. I put one foot on the ground behind the car. The leg stood up by itself, folding over at the knee. I got the other leg, stood it beside the first. Then I went after the body, the coverall and the apron. Assembling the Exterminator: that was another one of my jobs.

I wouldn't touch the head. That was the one part I wouldn't do. The head just lay there in the well of the trunk, right next to the star wrench and the rear evaporator and the bolted-down spare tire with its brand-new tread. The head peered up at me as I worked. It seemed like it wanted to tell me something, but with no mouth there was no way for it to speak. What kind of voice would it have, if it could speak? A voice like the crunch of dead leaves under a boot, I thought, soft and mean and brittle.

The Exterminator made my father look like something other than my father, made him look like a giant insect. But really he was a good and happy guy, always whistling and humming around the house. My mother loved him, and she would never love anyone bad.

"You just sit up there on your porch," my father told Scurry. Scurry stood with the paperwork clutched in his hand. The hot sunlight was getting to him too; he was a thin, dried-out-looking guy, but he had big sweat stains down his back and under his arms, darkening the fabric of his shirt. It was hard to believe he had that much water in him to lose. The papers he held were wrinkled and damp. I was still thirsty.

"It's hot as blazes out here in the sun. Be cool," my father advised him. "Be comfortable."

They always hid the animals, but they never hid them well. It wasn't in their nature. My father always found them. Usually they just put them in an unused shed or barn. Sometimes we'd find a calf or two bawling and half-crazed, standing knee-deep in the water of a cistern. I think the farmers knew my father would find them, or somebody, the sheriff if we had to call him, so they didn't go to a whole lot of trouble.

One guy hid a bunch of Angus in an abandoned saltpeter mine at the back of his farm, and it took my father the better part of a day to figure out where they were, trudging across the fields, peering into empty outbuildings and tilting silos. They were miserable, those half-dozen bulky steers huddled together in that wet, shallow cave. Their moaning sounded like they were trapped in a tin can.

The humane killer stayed in its box next to the jack. I didn't touch the killer either. It was off-limits. The head of the Exterminator wasn't off-limits; I could have touched it if I wanted to. But it gave me the shivers, the way it looked at me. Its missing mouth, its snorkel nose. The flat black circles of its eyes.

The killer looked like a long, skinny hammer. Stamped into the handle were the words W. W. GREENER LONDON & BIRMINGHAM. The Greener company made the killer, and they made shotguns too. Expensive shotguns. Fancy, like the Imperial. My father had started talking about one day buying himself a Greener 12-gauge side-by-side, for bird hunting. A Greener with a tight choke on it had a long reach, he told me. Pick up those whitewings far down the field, the ones that were always getting away from him.

Below the maker's stamp it said GREENER'S .455 HUMANE CATTLE KILLER. When I was younger I thought it said "Human Cattle Killer," and that was an idea that gave me nightmares. For a while I saw a lot of people like that. The Fuller Brush man when he came to the door to sell trinkets and to sharpen knives, he was a sad-eyed Jersey. The man behind us in line at the post office, looking at my mother, his nostrils flared, his head tossed: a Brahma bull. The men in the barbershop sighed and grunted like the gentle Herefords just up the road at Seldomridge's. But then I asked my father, and he explained to me that "humane" just meant kindly. Gentle. After that I didn't see the human cattle so much anymore. When you're a kid you'll believe anything is possible.

None of the other extermination men used a killer like my father's. Some of them used what they called captive-bolt pistols, and most of the rest just used a rifle behind the ear. One great tall man used nothing but an eight-pound Master Mechanic's sledge. But my father used the Greener, which seemed like a privilege, since it had come so far and from such a prestigious manufacturer.

A fellow named John Keeper gave it to him. My father had worked with him at the big state abattoir up at Denmar. The slaughter line was the job my father had before he took this one. They recruited almost all the extermination men from their jobs at the state slaughterhouse, but they never got John Keeper. He just walked off one day: handed the Greener to my father and got in his truck and went. And then the Greener was my father's.

My father struggled into the Exterminator's hip boots and lifted the rubber apron out of the trunk. He nodded at me and I retrieved the disinfectant sprayer, sloshed it back and forth, the gurgle in the canister telling me that we had plenty. That was another one of my duties: spray him down after he had done the job, pump the disinfectant—the sprayer looked just like a big bug sprayer in the cartoons—all over the Exterminator until it was shiny and wet and gave off a smell like ammonia and licorice.

That disinfectant smell, which could beat the odor of the demons, the stench of blood and brains, of shit and fear—that smell had come to mean the end of the day's work to me. It meant getting in the car and driving back home, back into the valley. Cranking up the air conditioning and turning on the radio and singing along at the top of our lungs as we rolled along the narrow blacktop, back toward our house and our yard and our dogs. Maybe Pee Wee King would be on the air when we got back in range of the station. I loved good old Pee Wee King.

After we got home, my father would do the job a second time, pin the Exterminator up over the clothesline and scrub it down with a long-handled, stiff-bristled brush. The dogs would loop around his legs. I could almost like the Exterminator then. It looked harmless, pinned to that line with its gangling arms outstretched, its mouthless face tilted toward the ground as my father went after it with the brush, sweating and grunting with the effort. It was really getting the treatment then, and I could feel sorry for it.

But right after the job—right then, as I pumped away at the sprayer as hard as I could, working the piston until my arms were sore—then I often pretended that the choking cloud I was soaking it with was acid, that it would melt the Exterminator down, melt it like a lead soldier on the stove and leave just him, leave just my father standing there in the puddle of it.

"Keep him company, you hear?" my father told me. He meant Scurry. I lowered the disinfectant sprayer, which I had been holding like I was ready to use it. But the job wasn't done yet, the job hadn't even begun. To Scurry he called out, "My boy here has some stories he can tell you. He doesn't look like much, but he can spin a tale." Thirteen steers was going to take him a while, after which we would have to find the hidden ones. He touched the side of his nose with one of the Exterminator's gross gray fingers, and I knew that meant I should find out where the remaining steers were.

He pulled on the head of the Exterminator, fumbling a little because the gloves made his hands clumsy. He twisted the head from side to side until it sat comfortably and he could see out through the goggles. He gave the top of its skull a funny little pat to show me that he was still in there, shifted his shoulders to loosen them, and then set off with the Exterminator's sloshing gait toward Scurry's barn.

We were sitting around watching TV one evening, about the time my father left the state abattoir, my mother and father and my little brother and me. A cartoon was on, and it was a surprise and a pleasure to be able to watch a cartoon in the evening, because mostly it was just news programs about the war and other things I didn't much care about. The epizootic was just beginning to get a grip around that time. Most people didn't even believe in it yet, I don't think.

The cartoon was funny at first, and I enjoyed it, two men that hated each other fighting in various ingenious ways, ways you'd never think of, with magnets and rockets and matches and rubber bands, hurting but never killing each other. I had the idea it was a very old cartoon of a sort they didn't make much anymore. We were all enjoying it, even my mother, who hated anything violent or cruel, and my little brother, who was scared of most things. It was the difference my father marked between us, because we were only a year apart in age. Similar in size and appearance, and people often mistook us for twins: I was the one who didn't get scared, and my brother was the one who did.

But then the cartoon changed. It seemed like the two men had run out of inventions and ideas for ways to hurt each other, and they just began hitting each other over the head. *Wham, wham, wham,* with these hammers, great wooden mallets. I knew about the man from the abattoir who killed with the eight-pound sledge. This was how that man spent his days, I thought. On and on. He had grown a hump, a big ridge of muscle between his shoulders, from swinging that sledge.

My mother and my brother were fixated. I could see them out of the corners of my eyes. My father was sitting in the big chair directly behind me. It seemed like the two men hitting each other was going on too long. I'd been sitting cross-legged in front of the television for hours, watching this one thing over and over. My face ached from smiling at the cartoon, and my lungs hurt from laughing. My mother and brother were laughing too. Tears were shining in their eyes. The music was strange and full of foreign, shouting voices and sounded like it was made out of metal; "The Anvil Chorus," I have since learned it's called, an Italian song. I tried to blink, but my eyes stayed open.

I wondered if my father was trapped the same way we were.

Was he watching? I couldn't hear him laughing. If I could get him to understand what was happening—that the cartoon wouldn't end—then he'd figure some way to free us. He'd switch off the TV. Above the metal music that was whamming away, I could hear the wind rising. It was howling around the eaves of the house. The ground started chattering under me, as though it were trembling from the cold. I felt sick, and I was still laughing and grinning.

I cranked my head around. I've never done any harder work than that: the air was as thick as oil; I thought at any second the bones of my neck would crack and splinter. And I saw, sitting in my father's chair, the Exterminator, its glass eyes reflecting the television screen: the bright colors, the hammers rising and falling. My own body in the center of each eye, flat like a cardboard cutout. I stopped grinning. I stopped laughing. I screamed.

My mother leaped up. My father gaped at me—it was him and not the Exterminator at all. My little brother ran from the room. They had not been laughing. I turned back to the TV, and it was easy to move my head this time. There was no cartoon on the screen. It was the news. On the news, a man with a flamethrower strapped to his back was burning out a bunker while other soldiers watched. They were smoking cigarettes.

"That's a terrible story," Scurry told me.

Bang. And Scurry jumped. It had started and it wouldn't stop. Twelve more times, and I knew Scurry would jump every time. They never got used to it. We sat on his porch. I wanted to ask him for something to drink, because I was thirsty beyond belief, but I knew it wouldn't be right to ask him for a favor while the Exterminator was killing his cattle.

"You ought not to tell stories like that," Scurry said.

"I made a mistake," I said. "I thought it was a cartoon on, but it was the war. I thought everyone was laughing and enjoying theirselves, but they weren't."

"Do you make a lot of mistakes like that?" Scurry wanted to know.

"I used to," I said, "when I was little. But I've learned to tell the difference a lot better these days. Between what's happening and what I think is happening. My father helps me with that."

I was pretty sure that this conversation was actually taking place between us. Scurry's words matched up pretty well with the movement of his lips. I could hear voices too, little quiet voices in the distance—no idea what they might have been saying—but they didn't worry me, because they sounded like the voices that come from a radio that's on with nobody paying attention to it, way in the back of a house somewhere. Maybe it was the water I had heard earlier, the creek. I licked my burning lips.

Bang. Scurry jumped again. "What happens next?" he asked.

I didn't know exactly what he meant. Did he mean what happened next in my story? Next my old man picked me up and shook me and my mother cried and my little brother cowered in his room like the scared pissant he was. Next my old man told me, *Don't you ever scream like that again. You're frightening your mother. You're frightening your brother.* That's what happened next: exactly what you might expect.

I didn't say anything about the cartoon, but my father seemed to know. He knew that the world had stopped matching up to itself for a while, and now that I had screamed it was matching up again, rolling along just like it was supposed to. He knew that sometimes it stopped matching up. You didn't need to scream when that happened. You didn't need to look around. You just waited for it to start matching up again.

These were all things my father told me later, when we took to riding in the Imperial together. About the world jumping its tracks, and how you just held on until it came back onto them again. Not to scare the women and the little kids—that was half the job, when you were a man and the world got trapped in itself, turning over and over and seeming like it would never stop.

Was that what Scurry meant when he asked, "What happens next?" Or did he mean what would happen next on his farm?

Bang. Jump. That's what.

•••

I asked my father what happened to John Keeper after he handed over the killer and walked out.

"He crossed the Bridge of Sighs both ways," my father said.

The Bridge of Sighs was the ramp of steel grillwork that led up onto the slaughter line. It was where the animals came to be slaughtered, shouldering one another out of the way to get to the other side like they were getting on Noah's Ark or something, the stock handlers sticking them with poles and electric jolts. The metal incline clanged and echoed from the blows of hooves, and the bellowing and wailing rang off its surfaces. It was the way the workers came in as well, the men who stood on the slaughter line. They wore rubber hip boots, and their feet made no sound on the bridge at all.

You never crossed the Bridge of Sighs both ways. That was what they said. The animals, because when they went in, they died. And the men, because when they went in, they never left. Maybe their bodies did, but not their minds. They stayed in the state abattoir forever. All except John Keeper, who handed the Greener Humane Killer to my father and strode into the outside and was never seen again.

"But you left," I said to my father.

"No," he said. "I'm still there."

"It's not him that's doing the killing," I told Scurry. "It's the Exterminator." When he looked at me like he didn't understand, I added, "The suit. The rubber suit."

Scurry shook his head. "No," he said. "It's him. He's doing the killing all right. The suit just keeps the blood and the gore off him."

I decided not to argue.

It was then he asked if I wanted to go down to the creek. He said he had something he wanted to show me. I hoped he meant a mud puppy even as I knew he didn't. How could he have known what I spent my summer looking for? He just wanted to get away from what was happening in his barn. Still, I asked him, "Do you have mud puppies along in there?"

Bang. But this time he didn't jump. I liked him for that. He was getting used to it.

"Mud puppy?" he said. "You mean those big lizards?"

"Salamanders," I said.

"Yeah," he said. "We call them water dogs up this way. But we've got them. Keep your eyes open and you might see one."

We followed a little gully that opened beside his house, followed it as it deepened, became a steep, rock-sided ravine. An easy climb down but a tough climb back up. I wondered how Scurry would handle it.

The voices in the creek sounded pleased to be talking. They never seemed to repeat themselves. I wanted to kneel down and get a big drink. The water was clear, the rocks of the streambed smooth and clean beneath its moving surface; it looked cool. The sunlight wasn't so bright here in the shadow of the trees that grew along the banks of the creek, broken up as it was by the branches, with their hefty loads of leaves. I wanted to lean down and cup handful after handful of the cold water into my mouth.

My father jumped out at my little brother and me from behind the front door of our house. We'd just come home from school. He was wearing the Exterminator, the first time he'd put it on, and he thought it would make a good costume to surprise and scare us. My little brother disappeared for a couple of hours, didn't even make a sound, just vanished back through the door. I stood like I was rooted as this thing, this bug, lurched toward me, its arms outstretched.

When it reached me, it swept me up in a great big embrace. It lifted me up high, and my head brushed the ceiling, exactly the way it did when my father picked me up. Even through my clothes, the touch of the Exterminator was clammy and dank, like something freshly dead. It smelled like a public swimming pool as it nuzzled its face against my cheek. I was stiff. It was trying to kiss me, or eat me, one or the other. It bashed me in the eye with its short, swaying trunk of a nose.

My eyes were near to its eyes. Up close like that, the eyes didn't reflect. I could see through them. I could see inside the head of the Exterminator, into its skull, into its brain. And what I saw, behind its blank eyes, were the fond, familiar eyes of my father. I suddenly thought, *This is what it's like to be a grown-up man.*

My mother drifted through then, scolding my father, slapping at him, her hands making wet noises against the flabby skin. "Put the boy down, for the Lord's sake," she said. "Can't you see he's frightened to death?" I wanted to laugh, but my tongue was still caught against the roof of my mouth. I couldn't say anything. "What gets inside you?" she continued. "I swear I don't know."

Then she noticed that my brother was gone, and the search for him began. We didn't find him until well after dark, hiding among the foliage of one of the great silver maples in the back, twenty feet off the ground. It took my father another hour and an extension ladder borrowed from the people across the road to finally get him down.

Scurry didn't seem interested in that story either. It always made my father laugh to think of my brother way up in that tree. He was not much of a tree climber, my little brother, either before or after that first encounter with the Exterminator. But Scurry didn't smile or anything.

"There's not really any mud puppies down here, are there?" I asked him. He shook his head sorrowfully, like he regretted having told me an untruth.

"There used to be, when I was a kid," he said. "I don't know what happened to them since then."

Bang. Very muted and far away. I had lost count, but it had to be pretty near the end now. My father would come back out of the barn and he'd be looking for me to have the disinfectant canister out, ready to spray him down and help him get out of the sweaty, foul-smelling Exterminator. He would want me to put it back into the trunk of the Imperial, where it belonged.

We came to a point where the creek shallowed and broadened, parting around a small, sandy island in the middle of the current. On the island stood the missing cattle, bunched together and gazing at the sheet of water that passed near their hooves. I should have guessed they were what Scurry wanted me to see. Sometimes that happened: the farmers just gave in and took us to their hidden animals. I was glad I hadn't drunk from the creek, downstream from the beasts as we had been. Cholera, diphtheria: it would all be in the water from their waste.

The little group of cattle broke apart when they saw Scurry. They thought he was bringing fodder with him. They were well fed and sleek, and I knew how much effort it was, bringing feed down to them in this rocky place, so far from his house. How hard he was working to keep them alive and safe on their little island.

And I saw that there was something else on the island with them. Something small and terrible in the shifting green shadows beneath the trees. Something that had been hidden behind their bulk. One of the mutants that I had heard the epizootic could bring about. Misshapen: six legs, maybe seven. Grotesquely twisted body. Two heads. My breath stopped in my throat, and I felt the world begin to unhinge. A monster. Time would stop, down here by the island. Who knew how long I would spend in this ravine, with Scurry and his horrible calf. Maybe an eternity.

"You see?" Scurry said to me. "They're not sick. These ones aren't. You can see that, can't you?"

The water was talking. Or maybe it was my father, calling out from the barnyard. He had probably wrestled the Exterminator's head from his own, the job done, and he was wondering where I had got to. Me and Scurry. Maybe he was even a little afraid, alone like that. One of the monster calf's heads wailed, and the other answered it. Their bawling bounced crazily off the rock walls around us and drowned out the voices of the water.

Then I looked again and saw that it was no monster. It was just two spring calves, two little bulls standing folded together, twins and small for their age. One of them trotted down to the edge of the island and sank its muzzle into the water and started to drink. My dry throat tightened.

Scurry's voice was loud in my ear. "Nothing," he said. My father would soon find us, the way he had found my little brother, way up in that tree. "There's nothing at all wrong with them, is there?" he said to me. He wouldn't be satisfied until I said it. My saying it would do nothing, it wouldn't change what had to happen, but he wanted me to witness, to tell him what he already knew. Nothing was wrong. Nothing wrong at all.

Pinckney Benedict has published two collections of short fiction and a novel. His stories have appeared in, among other magazines and anthologies, *Esquire, Zoetrope: All-Story, StoryQuarterly, Ontario Review,* the O. Henry Award series, the Pushcart Prize series, and *The Oxford Book of American Short Stories.* He is coeditor, with his wife, the novelist Laura Benedict, of the 2007 anthology *Surreal South,* and he is a professor in the English department at Southern Illinois University in Carbondale, Illinois. This is his third appearance in *New Stories from the South.*

*B*ridge of Sighs" *combines my paranoia about the coming pandemic with my love of the music of the great Cowboy Copas (who died in the plane crash that killed Patsy Cline) and my lust for a fully restored classic Chrysler Imperial. Plus my fear of germ-warfare suits. My only regret about the story is that I didn't manage to get in the name of Hawkshaw Hawkins, who is, like me, a native West Virginian, and who also died in that awful accident.*

Amina Gautier

THE EASE OF LIVING

(from *Colorado Review*)

It was barely the summer—just the end of June—and already two teenaged boys had been killed. Jason was turning sixteen in another month and his mother worried he might not make it. A week after the double funeral, she cashed in all of the Series EE bonds she'd been saving since his birth and bought him a plane ticket to spend the summer with his grandfather. Distance, she believed, would keep him safe.

She waited until the day of his flight and told him over breakfast. "It's not forever," she said, polishing off her coffee. "Besides, it's a done deal." The ticket was paid for and they both knew she couldn't afford it. He had no choice. She was working only a half day in order to ride with him to the airport. She set the mug down and hurried out the door. She had neither finished her breakfast nor cleared the table. On the table she left a small plate holding the crusts from her toast, crumbs and dollops of jelly clinging to chipped china.

She had ruined his morning.

Usually, he couldn't wait for his mother to leave so he could go outside and chill. His boys would appear a half hour after she'd gone, and they would have the day all to themselves. This was the time of day Jason loved. The short yellow bus had already come

51

and taken the retarded people who lived in the middle of the block out for a day trip. The adults with jobs were at work; the others were in their homes watching talk shows and soaps. A few girls were scattered on the stoops up and down the block, braiding hair and giggling at nothing. All the boys dumb enough or lucky enough to get summer jobs were out somewhere, supervising kids running through sprays of water, price checking the produce and bagging the eggs separately, or flipping burgers and asking if you wanted fries with that. But not Jason. Not him and his boys. They had the whole summer to themselves. They could ride down to Coney Island if they wanted. They could go downtown to the movies and sit in the Metropolitan or the Duffield all day to make up for the lack of air conditioning in their own homes. They could each buy one ticket, then sneak into as many different shows as they could manage until the evening brought cooler breezes and they could go home once more. Or they could go to the park and watch the girls run around the track in those tiny blue shorts with the white trim. Or they could go to the pool and jump in the deep end with their shorts and sneakers on, dunking all the girls who had slighted them and messing up their hair. They could do any-thing they wanted. They could even just sit out there on the stoop all day long smoking blunts and saying whatever came to mind. He liked that best of all, but now he had to leave it. He would miss it, the times that couldn't be pinpointed to a specific action, the times that were as numerous as the days of summer vacation, when he didn't have to think about school or listen to the things his mother said or accept that the deaths of his two friends meant nothing would ever be the same again.

"Hey, yo!" a voice called up to his window.

He pulled out his duffel bag and threw it on the bed. Then he went to the window. He stuck his head out and called, "Be down in a minute!"

He didn't know anything about the South or its weather, so he didn't know what to take and what to leave. His Timberlands, of course, would go. He didn't need to pack them; they were already on his feet. His favorite baseball cap with the brim broken in half to shade his eyes. His basketball jerseys: Jordan, Ewing, and Starks. His Walkman. His favorite mixtapes. His clippers so he could stay smooth. His wave cap and brush. His underwear, socks, and toiletries. The overalls he had gotten his name spray-painted on at the Albee Square Mall. A stack of T-shirts, another stack of jean shorts. A tiny vial of scented oil he'd bought off a Muslim in the street. Everything he needed fit into one bag.

They were crowded in on his stoop. Four boys with blunts and a forty. A dark stain of liquid made an uneven circle on the bottom step of the stoop, where they had already tipped the forty to Kiki and Stephen's memory. Three weeks ago, they had all attended the double funeral. They passed the forty, quickly demolishing it before Jason came down. Then they lit up.

"Took you long enough," Howie said, rising slightly to give him a pound. Half of Howie's hair was braided into cornrows that followed the contour of his head and then ended in tails at the back of his neck, the other half of his head was wild where he had picked the braids loose.

"I'm here now, right?" Jason said.

"What, you was sleeping or something?" Smalls asked.

"Nah," Jason said.

"You wasn't—I mean—you know," Dawud said, making obscene hand gestures.

"No," Jason said, "I got your girl Tanya for that." Then he told them he was leaving for Tallahassee in a few hours to spend the summer with his grandfather.

"Damn," they all said at once, shrinking away from him as if he had a disease.

"Florida," said Howie. "And not even Miami where all the honeys are. That's the South for real."

The package of Easy Riders came out for those that didn't have blunts.

Smalls and Justice were seated on the same step. Justice laughed. "Man, you still rolling them little things?"

"Shut the fuck up, nigga. This shit is better than nothing, like my man over here." Smalls pointed at Jason.

Howie said, "That's all right. I got him. It's his last day and shit. He know I got him. Right, son?" Howie passed Jason the blunt. Jason took it and lost himself in it, focusing only on getting high one last time before he left.

Smalls said, "Damn! Come up for air. This nigga act like he on death row or some shit."

"Damn near," Jason replied, coughing.

"Leave him alone. This might be his last blunt for a while. Who know what the fuck they smoke down there? Trees and shit. Corn husks," Dawud said.

"Nigga, you a fool," Smalls and Justice told him.

Howie pushed Jason. "Damn, nigga, pass that fucking el. I know it's your last day and all, but you can't take all that shit!"

They all laughed at him sitting there, puffing like his life depended on getting high. Then Howie asked, "Why you ain't never tell us you had you no rich grandfather?"

"He ain't rich," Jason said. Then he shrugged to show that he wasn't being defensive. That he couldn't care less.

"Got enough money to just up and send for you," Smalls said. "He something."

"Just old," Jason said. "Bored, I guess. Lonely." His mother had paid for the ticket. He was being *sent,* not *sent for,* which made all the difference. Being sent for was a privilege, a vacation, a luxury that meant he could do what he wanted and enjoy himself. Being sent was a punishment and a threat. His mother was sending him to get him away from his boys. Away from Howie, Dawud, Smalls, and Justice. She was scared he would be next to die. It was not a luxury, not a vacation. Pure and simple, it was surveillance. A more motherly version of prison. But his boys didn't need to know that.

"You'd be lonely too if you was living in Hicksville, two towns over from the middle of nowhere!" Dawud said and laughed. A girl with braids roller-skated by and ignored them when they called to her.

"You gonna be down in one of those backwards towns like where all that Freddy Krueger stuff be going down. Little ass towns where people don't be locking they front doors and be knowing each other's name and be all up in your business," Howie said. "Better you than me."

"I'll be back before you know it," Jason said.

"Don't come back up here talking all that *y'all come back now ya hear,* know what I'm saying?" Justice said.

Smalls said, "This nigga gonna be square-dancing. Talking about yee-ha!"

"Gonna be listening to some Dolly Parton. He come back and be like, *Biggie who? Tupac what?*" Dawud joked.

Smalls said, "Least they got honeys down there. You know, them big-legged, cornbread-eating girls."

"Church girls," Justice said.

"Yeah." They all said it.

"Good girls. Go to church on Sunday, turn you out on Monday," Howie said.

"Put a hurting on you," Smalls teased.

"Yeah, clear up all them bumps on your face. Skin be mad clear from all the play you'll be gettin'," Justice said.

Dawud said, "Won't know what to do with yourself. Put some in your pocket and save it for later."

"Maybe I'll just airmail some back to you niggas. Be all you ever get," Jason finally said. He had let them go on at his expense because he had the feeling he would miss them, because he knew the jokes hid the envy.

Better you than me. They had all been thinking it when Howie said it. But even if they'd wanted to, none of them could have switched places with him. His mother wasn't a crackhead. They were poor because she was raising him by herself, not because she was smoking her money up or giving it to some fool who was constantly going upside her head. Jason knew who his father was—every once in a while he even came by whenever his mother asked him to "talk some sense into" Jason. Many of his friends had Southern relatives, but none of them would ever be sent Down South. He and they were different. He didn't relish the difference, but he recognized it. He didn't think it made him better; it just set him apart. And Howie and Dawud and Smalls and Justice all knew it, too.

Which is why they left him out of some things. They never asked him to walk to the store with them because they didn't want him to see them using food stamps and their sisters' WIC checks. He didn't have any children either, but some of the boys his age already had two or three. He was almost sixteen and he was still a punk. Whenever he and his boys caught the train and jumped the turnstiles, he always went second or third to let someone else get caught. Inside he turned to jelly each time while he waited to see if a police officer would come out from behind the door to the fake janitor's closet. He only sold weed to people he knew. He only broke into the public pool at night, when it was all full and no one would be able to pinpoint him specifically if the cops came and broke it up. He didn't go anywhere with his boys on the first of the month if he could help it. He wasn't into robbing old ladies and their home attendants for SSI checks. He was a punk in thug's clothing and he knew it and they knew it, but they were kind enough not to say it out loud. He was with them because there was nowhere else for him to be. He wasn't smart; he wasn't athletic or artistic or talented in any way. He played basketball and tried to freestyle because everyone else did, but he wasn't even good enough to be mediocre at either. He had no plans and no prospects. He was a black boy—without exceptional height or skill—who could not ball and who could not rap, and as such, no one cared what he did or where he went or what he became, least of all himself.

He didn't talk to his mother as they sat on opposite sides of his duffel bag and let the taxi take them to the airport. She cast worried glances at his profile; he pretended not to notice.

"I'm sorry I had to do it like this," his mother said, "but you know how you are."

When he didn't answer her, she pressed her hands into the cracked leather of the seat. She was still dressed for work and began to play with the cuffs at her wrists. "It's just for the summer," she said. "Just a change of scenery. I just want you to get away from all this—this *madness* for a little while." *Madness,* she said, as if it were temporary and had only just come. As if it would not still be there waiting when he returned. As if he could come back and find out that a joke had been played and Kiki and Stephen were still alive.

She continued as if she couldn't stop. "Spend some time with your grandfather." She turned to look at him. He could feel her eyes on his face. He continued to watch Queens's fast approach as they neared the airport. "He hasn't seen you in a while and he's getting on in his years. He can't move around like he used to."

To Jason, her words sounded lilke the plot for a made-for-TV movie. Or like those programs that cities and states were coming up with where they thought that sticking a city kid out in the country for a month would solve all of the kid's problems. He felt like an experiment.

When the cab pulled up to the curb, Jason's mother didn't get out. She kissed him and pushed a wad of rumpled bills into his hand. She laid her moist palm against his cheek and whispered hopefully, "Maybe tonight, you'll be able to get some sleep."

His grandfather's home attendant met him at the airport. She was holding up a cardboard sign with JASON printed carefully on it. Though unnecessary in the small regional airport, the sign made him feel important.

She introduced herself as Miss Charlotte. When she spoke, her voice made him think of family gatherings and holiday dinners. "I know Cal wanted to be here to pick you up himself, Jason," she said, "but he can't do all the things he wants anymore."

Two years ago, his grandfather had fallen in the shower and had a stroke. Jason's mother had flown down to Tallahassee to look after her father, leaving him with the apartment to himself for two whole weeks. He'd used that time to convince Chanelle to come over and stop playing hard to get. He had not thought of the paralysis that took over the left side of his grandfather's body. He had thought of that time as a vacation.

This was not the house his mother had grown up in. His grandfather had moved from a two-level, three-bedroom house to a one-level, two-bedroom home after the stroke made it difficult for him to climb the stairs. Miss Charlotte gave Jason a tour, taking him all over and through the house, showing him what she clearly thought of as the main attractions. She took him into the bathroom and pulled the shower curtain back to show him how the bathtub had been altered to fit his grandfather's special needs. "Now he won't have any more nasty falls in here," she boasted.

Jason pointed to a large silver-looking handle shaped like an upside-down U reinforced in the middle of the side of the tub. "What's that?"

"That's so he's got something solid to hold onto when he climbs in and out of the tub," Miss Charlotte said.

A small rubber mat with upraised bumps lined the bottom of the shower so his grandfather wouldn't slip. A wide white plastic chair sat on top of the mat. It looked like more than one person could sit there. Jason lifted it up easily and set it on the small square of tiled floor in the cramped bathroom. The plastic was hard; it didn't bend or give. It was bone dry. It would have looked like something he could take to the beach if it hadn't had so many perforations in it to allow the water to run freely. Miss Charlotte explained that his grandfather had to sit to take his showers because one of his legs wasn't strong enough for him to stand long enough to shower on his own.

"That's his shower chair. I set it in the hallway to dry each time Cal is finished with it so it won't get mildewed," she said. "You can go ahead and put that back the way you found it now."

She was about to take him to the kitchen and show him the bottle opener she used to keep all of the bottles in the house untightened but closed when Jason heard his grandfather's raspy voice.

"Is that you, Charlotte?"

"Coming, Cal!"

"Hurry up. I want to see him!"

"We're coming, you old goat! Keep your pants on!"

"Why don't you take them off for me, woman?"

Jason hadn't known a woman her age could still blush. Miss Charlotte led him down the hallway to the bedrooms and apologized. "You've got to excuse his language, Jason honey."

The voice shouted, "Don't make excuses for me! I don't need them."

"Don't pay him no mind, Jason. He's pleased as punch to have you here. He's been talking about your coming the last three weeks. Cal, look at what I brought you," she said, pushing Jason forward as if he were a gift.

The overpowering smell of Bengay made Jason's eyes water. The two windows in the room were both closed and the smell of the liniment mixed with the musty, stale air. The room was sparsely furnished and everything seemed to be in precise order. One lone bottle of cologne sat on the dresser next to a short hairbrush and a nail clipper. A wheelchair was positioned to the left side of the bed and the man who was his grandfather half sat and half reclined in the bed with his back against the headboard. He wore a white sleep shirt with faded blue stripes. A heavy gray blanket, the kind Jason had seen in Army Navy stores, was spread over the bed.

"So you're here," the old man said, staring. Jason stared back. Surprised to see that his grandfather's face was his own. He looked nothing like his own mother and father, and although he had seen pictures of his grandfather, he'd never noticed any resemblance. But it was here in the uncompromising features of the old man staring back at him; the same seal brown skin, the same aggressive nostrils, the same bushy eyebrows that almost connected above the bridge of the nose, the same full lips and pugnacious chin.

Jason didn't like the way he talked to him. He didn't like the way the old man sat there, looking legless, as if he ended at his torso. "Yeah, I'm here," Jason said. "Where are your legs? You lose them in a war?"

His grandfather rolled his eyes. "I still have them, youngblood, but I can only count on one. The sroke affected the left side of my body. My left leg is basically useless."

"Oh."

"I guess that's not cool enough for you."

Jason shrugged, not caring one way or the other. "Nah, it's okay."

"If it makes you feel any better, for as long as you're here, why don't you just pretend that one of my running buddies, my home-boys as you'd call it, didn't like the colors I was wearing one day or didn't like the way I rolled my joint and decided to smoke me but missed and only caught me in the leg. Is that any better?"

"Whatever," Jason said.

The old man asked, "Is it true that they shot those two boys down and killed them?"

"Calvin!" Miss Charlotte's exclamation broke the silence. "What a way to begin—"

The old man cut her off. "Well, boy?" he demanded. "Is it true?"

He knew his grandfather knew the answer to that question. Surely his mother had told him. Surely, the old man had been forewarned. His grandfather's blatant disregard angered him. His mother carefully stepped around the issue. They had never actu-ally discussed the death of his friends since the funeral, except for a few cryptic sentences in passing. But this old man who surely must know better had no sense but to bring the subject up right away. Jason didn't know what to think, except that he would have liked nothing more than to wheel the old man out into traffic. Since the funeral, he'd felt only numb indifference; now he claimed a pleasurable anger. His palms itched to hurt the old man. His grandfather smiled as if he could read his mind, as if he welcomed the challenge. Somehow, with his sunken body, the old man man-aged to give the impression that he could spring at any moment and kick ass.

"Anyway. Can I use the phone? I told my mom I'd call."

• • •

Miss Charlotte called them to dinner. The chair was removed from the head of the table to accommodate his grandfather's wheelchair. The sight of his grandfather sitting there, the back of his wheelchair making him seem like a king seated on a throne, brought back the anger.

"What's for dinner? I don't know if my mom told you or not, but I don't eat squirrel or possum," Jason said. "I'm allergic."

"Boy, this is Tallahassee, not Davy Crockett's wild frontier."

"Don't y'all eat that stuff? Rabbits and deer and all?"

"Rabbits and squirrels are just as much rodents as rats. You'll never see me putting any of that anywhere near my mouth. Come here, youngblood."

Jason rose and approached him. His grandfather began to pat his chest and pockets. Jason jumped back. "Man, what you think you doing?"

His grandfather said, "Checking for weapons."

"You're crazy. I ain't carrying nothing."

"You gonna get in my car and go do some drive-bys? Or maybe sell me some drugs? Or are you gonna wait 'til I'm good and asleep and then steal my basketball sneakers to sell on the corner?" his grandfather asked.

"What are you talking about?"

"You want to indulge in stereotypes, I can oblige you. Now sit down."

Jason sat. He shook his head. "You need to stop watching rap videos. It's not all like that up there."

He had begun to eat when his grandfather's hand shot out and grabbed his wrist, applying pressure. "We give thanks for our food before we eat it," his grandfather said quietly.

"I don't do church."

"Then just be still while I say something over the food."

The boy thought about it. He could refuse. This man was not his father; he didn't have to obey him. But the pressure of his grandfather's good arm told the story of strength. Veins, thick and prominent straining from knuckle to wrist, reminded Jason that this was the same man who could split a watermelon as easily as a head, the same man who had snapped the necks of chickens, blown the heads off rattlesnakes, and torn the hide off his mother's behind when she misbehaved. Jason released his fork.

His grandfather and Miss Charlotte bowed their heads.

"Lord, I don't have much, but I thank you for what I have been given. Please bless this meal and all who come under this roof. Bless us all with a nourishing meal and a good night's sleep."

Jason refused to look up when his grandfather mentioned sleep. He waited until his grandfather began to eat, then he followed suit. After some time, his grandfather spoke again.

"You play any sports, boy?"

"Nah, not really."

"Watch any?"

"Just basketball," he said.

"Who do you like? Bird? Johnson? Thomas?"

Jason thought of Michael Jordan's Gatorade commercial with everyone singing, *I wanna be like Mike*. What he wouldn't give to be like Michael Jordan, have Michael Jordan's money, his skill, his arrogance and confidence, his nobody-can-touch-me bravado. What he wouldn't give to hang in the air like he was free from all restraints, switch hands up in the air and keep everyone guessing, constantly watching, waiting for his next move, hanging on him, all eyes reflecting his image so that he saw himself wherever he went. What else was there for him if he didn't want to be like Mike? All of his friends wanted to ball or rap. No one believed in school anymore. It was just a free version of day care. Just a place to contain society's knuckleheads and keep them off the streets for a few hours. In school, he was expected only to pass the tests that would move him into the next grade. He was supposed to memorize, regurgitate, and repeat. He was not supposed to think. All of the students who could think had been weeded out and parceled into magnet schools, gotten scholarships or vouchers to private and boarding schools, or tested into Brooklyn Tech, Bronx Science, or Stuyvesant. He and his friends were leftovers.

He said only, "I like Jordan. He's nice on the court."

"I always wanted to be Satchel Paige myself. Or Jackie Robinson."

The boy looked confused.

"Baseball," his grandfather said. "Don't look at me all cross-eyed like that. Don't stay up too late. We get up early around here. No exceptions."

"What are we gonna do? Milk the cows? Go fishing or something?"

"Boy, you've been watching too much TV."

He dreamed the first night. He was back in Brooklyn, back on his stoop. Howie, Smalls, Dawud, and Justice weren't there, but Kiki and Stephen were. They were sitting at the top of the stoop, and Stephen was holding a forty. Stephen and Kiki rose and gave him a pound when they saw him. Kiki took the bottle from Stephen and twisted the cap off. He tipped the bottle and poured the first few drops onto the concrete stoop. Kiki said, "This is for you, son," and Jason woke up covered in sweat.

By night, Jason dreamed, unless he could manage to stay awake. By day, he avoided his grandfather, spending the bulk of his time holed up in his room, listening to music and trying hard not to ever fall asleep. Sometimes he wandered outside, looking for something to do. He wore his headphones throughout the house, listening to his music. When his batteries ran down and he had to recharge them, he watched television. Music videos and stand-up comedy if he had the living room to himself. Watching TV wasn't the same when there was no reason to turn the volume all the way up—his grandfather's street was quiet; there were no noises to drown out or ignore. He pretended that he lived alone, maneuvering around Miss Charlotte and his grandfather as if they were furniture. There was nothing to do in his grandfather's house. Nowhere to go and nothing to see. There was just himself and his grandfather, a man he didn't know at all.

So it went.

His grandfather gave him chores the first week he was there, saying, "It's time you started doing some chores to earn your keep. This here is not one of Koch's welfare hotels."

"Ain't this what you got Miss Charlotte for?" Jason asked, balking at being used for manual labor, especially when a home attendant was present.

She's a home attendant, not a housekeeper. She just helps me do the things I need to do for my daily survival. She helps me bathe, prepares my meals, and does the food shopping. Everything else is extra. If I want the mirrors polished, the tables dusted, I have to do that myself. She's not my personal slave, you know?" his grandfather said. "Huh. I wish she was a harem girl. Then maybe me and her could have us some fun."

Jason was to polish the old man's shoes every day, even though his grandfather only went out every other day to the doctor's. His grandfather wore his good shoes all day long in the house, even though Miss Charlotte kept a pair of brand new slippers by the side of his bed.

Jason had to scrub the bathtub if he was the last one to use it. And he had to sweep the long hallway and sweep the living room. He had to bring in the newspaper and wash the dishes after Miss Charlotte cooked. There was no fried food anywhere in the house. Everything was steamed, boiled, baked, or broiled. And he was responsible for dinner. Miss Charlotte cooked their breakfast and lunch and left instructions for dinner. There were certain things his grandfather could eat and certain things he couldn't. A diagram with cartoon drawings of mustard, salt, red meat, soda, ketchup, and many other foods crossed out with big black Xs was fastened to the refrigerator with a magnet. The diagram had been drawn to be cutesy. The forbidden foods all wore diabolical grins and raised eyebrows.

He also had to make both his and his grandfather's bed every day and tidy his grandfather's bedroom, which included dusting down a dresser which was never dusty. He came to hate that chore.

Standing in front of that dresser, he was forced to see himself in the big wide mirror, forced to lift each item and wipe the wood beneath it to make it gleam. First the Bible, then the heavy brush with no handle, then the bottle of cologne. He always sniffed it although he meant not to. His grandfather would wheel in and check on him to make sure that he had really cleaned the dresser and Jason had to stand there with the reflection of his grandfather's head and torso next to him in the mirror, reminding him each time of who he looked like and who he was.

The dreams were vivid but not nightmarish. He saw no blood-stained bodies. His boys had not turned into effigies or zombies. They appeared in his dreams as they had appeared in life. Kiki, full of bravado and clad in the newest fashions, Stephen slightly shy and hanging back. They always met him on the stoop in front of his house. He'd never been alone with just the two of them in real life. Howie and Dawud or someone else from their crew had always been there. In his dreams, Kiki held out a forty to him and Jason tipped it back and drank without thinking. Kiki and Stephen watched him and when he wiped his mouth and handed it back, Stephen said, "You're next," and pushed him. As Jason stumbled backwards off the steps, Kiki always said, "Better you than me," and Jason would wake up with his body leaning halfway out of the bed and one palm flat on the floor.

The boy and the man lived near each other, but not together. His grandfather demanded his presence at meals; other than that they kept apart. Jason pretended not to notice the physical therapy sessions when it took all of his grandfather's strength to squeeze a small red ball, when the therapist laid his grandfather's hand palm up and exercised each finger. All the therapist did was massage and rub each finger separately, then try to bend it at the joints, but his grandfather made faces as if the woman were cutting his hand off at the wrists. When it was time for the therapy, Miss Charlotte stood at his grandfather's side with her hands on his shoulders. Jason tried not to walk by the kitchen when the therapist was there. His grandfather had caught his eyes once and held him there until he felt something like guilt pouring through him. In that arrested moment in the kitchen, Jason could guess at the things his grandfather must have had to go through in his life to get him to that point in the kitchen when he could sit and quietly endure the pain that was clearly excruciating, the ability to endure pain with a quiet acceptance that this pain, too, like everything else, would pass. Jason was no great student and had gotten much of the history he learned in school mixed up. He wasn't sure how old his grandfather was; he didn't know if he had lived long enough to have fought in any of the major wars, but he guessed that just the plain simple living of getting from one day to the next might have been something like war for the old man.

He didn't like to think of the old man, but he did anyway. He wondered what his grandfather had done before he arrived, if he was intruding, if his grandfather liked being alone. He had never really thought about what it meant to be by one's self. He knew that in coming here, he had left his mother alone for the first time and he wondered if she was missing him, if she was lonely without him. He tried not to think about his boys at all, and he barely spared Chanelle more than a passing thought. By the time he got back, she would be with somebody else and she'd cut him with her eyes and act like she didn't even know him.

But he did think of Kiki and Stephen.

Stephen's body had worn a black suit with a tie. He'd looked as if he were dressed for graduation or picture day at school. He had looked alive. Jason hadn't wanted to get close, but his mother dug her nails into his arm and made him. "Take a good look," she'd said. "Any day now, that's you."

Her prediction terrified him. She had not said, "This could be you" or "See what can happen to you?" She had spoken without subjunctives and conditionals, without mercy. Her unrelenting words made him see that when it came down to it, really came down to it, there was no difference between himself and the boys in his crew even though he had tried to cultivate one. It *was* him in the casket. Any day now, it was him. He'd looked at the corpse then. No longer Stephen Townsend, his boy, his friend, his acc. Now, a black body, a black boy, a statistic, a number, as in "one less on the street." A corpse, a cadaver, an absence.

They had taken the bodies to Merritt Green. There had been no trees near the twin plots, just the hot June sun shining straight down on everyone. The heat left damp circles in the armpits of his suit. He and his friends served as the pallbearers. They'd slipped on the white gloves and lifted the coffins. As they'd marched, Jason remembered things Stephen had told him about his family. He remembered Miss Townsend's own mother had passed two years earlier and now, without Stephen, she was all alone. At the funeral, she'd looked gaunt and brittle, as if a strong wind could knock her over. She'd sat there so still, hands folded and head bent, that Jason wondered if she was really there or if she had just left the shell of herself. Seated in the pew behind the immediate family, Jason remarked to his mother that Miss Townsend didn't cry, and his mother said, "Maybe she's done with crying. Maybe she cried for him all the while he was living and doesn't have any tears left now that he's dead."

When it was her turn to view the body, Miss Townsend fell out on the casket, crying without sound. She cried and her eyes were terrible and her mouth opened and closed around words as if she were talking, but not a single sound came out. It had felt like a trick, like watching a favorite TV show with the sound turned all the way down. Try as he might, Jason couldn't forget that.

The day his mother told him she was sending him to see his grandfather, he'd asked how she could afford it and she told him about the savings bonds she'd been holding for him since he was a baby. "I was saving them for you to go to college," she'd said.

"But if I don't get you out of here and away from them, you might never live to see the day."

The dream was different this time.

Kiki looked at him as he approached the stoop and asked, "Yo, where did you get those kicks, son?"

"I got them downtown at Dr. Jay's."

"For real? I ain't even seen those the last time I was in there." They're brand new."

"How come I ain't seen them then?"

"You were dead by the time they came out," Jason said.

Kiki and Stephen backed away as if Jason were holding a gun on them. Stephen said, "I gotta get back to my grandmother." Then he was gone, but Jason didn't see him leave.

Kiki wound his arms around the stoop's railing and pulled himself up to sit on the top rail. He motioned for Jason to join him. "At least I ain't go out like no punk. At least I went out like a man." But he hardly looked like a man at that moment with his feet hooked around the bottom railing to keep him steady.

"But you're a boy," Jason said. Then Kiki leaned backwards over the railing, falling and pulling Jason with him.

Jason struggled against the arms around him that kept tightening like bands, squeezing him so he couldn't breathe. It was like someone was pushing him into a coffin and trying to force the lid down. He couldn't see anything, only darkness. There was only a thick blinding shroud of darkness and the suffocating feel of arms.

He was being shaken. He was covered in sweat. His body felt as if it had been dipped in water. He kept hearing a voice saying, "You all right. You all right." A calm thread of sanity and assurance thrown out to him like a lifeline. He could follow the steady sound of the phrase and the voice and let them pull him back to shore, realizing that the arms were an anchor, not a snag.

He could breathe again. He felt as if he had been submerged underwater and now had to learn to breathe in the open air again.

He opened his eyes and found himself half-sitting up in bed, the covers pooled at his waist, his chest sweaty, his gandfather holding his shoulders and shaking him slightly. "You all right, you all right, boy," the old man continued to say, long after Jason had opened his eyes and left the dream behind.

"Do you ever stay over, Miss Charlotte?" Jason asked the next day when he found her in the kitchen and she showed no signs of leaving. She had set up the ironing board and was pressing creases into a pair of slacks.

"Sometimes when it's needed," she said. "Off the books, you know. But you're here now."

"I ain't no home attendant."

"No, but you're a body in the house," she said. "Cal's been through so much, seen so much. Now it's like he just wants to pull into himself, pull away from everybody else. Only he can't because his body won't let him. That's hard, wanting not to need anybody, but needing them anyway, even if just for the little things. I don't like leaving him alone to fend for himself. It's not that he can't do most of these things for himself, because he can. It's the loneliness. People do things when they're alone that they wouldn't think of doing with people around."

He thought about that. There were plenty of things he couldn't do while he lived with his mother, and he couldn't wait to get out and have some privacy. But Miss Charlotte made it sound like a bad thing.

"I know what you mean. Man, when I turn eighteen, I'm getting out of my mom's crib and that's my word," he said.

"What're you going to do?"

"Get up when I want. Play whatever music I want. Loud as I want. Do my thing. Don't answer to nobody. That's all I got to say. A man's got to be a man, you feel me? That's the only way I'll ever be able to get her to stop hounding me."

His grandfather's front wheel turned into the kitchen. "So she's hounding you, huh? Let me ask you something, youngblood. Do you think it's her job to love you and take care of you?"

"We take care of each other. I help out too, you know." His mother paid the bills and provided him with a roof over his head, but he felt they were mutually dependent upon each other. He was, after all, the only man around the house. Neither his father nor grandfather were there to help out. He was the one who had to fix things without thanks, to change the lightbulbs, to throw rock salt on the snow-covered stoop when the city workers didn't come fast enough to suit her. He was the one who had to beat mice senseless with the broom, carry the groceries, and fix the storm windows and realign them back into their grooves. So, yes, it was her job to love him. He had earned it, paid for it. He had not deserved to be sent away.

"Helping out is a small price to pay when somebody works to feed and dress you and keep the lights on and the cold out. It's a small price to pay for those sneakers on your feet, those jeans hanging halfway off your ass, and that little gold ball in your ear. It's a real small price to pay to have somebody watching out for you and waiting up for you when you don't even have to say thanks. No, all you have to do is tell her your whereabouts and show your face every once in a while." His grandfather looked down at his hands, running the thumbnail under the other nails to clean them. He continued to survey his nails as he talked, making Jason feel small. "Yeah, you got it real bad. Got somebody to love you and here you are complaining about the thing that's keeping you alive, keeping you from being laid out there like your little dead friends."

The old man snatched a small orange pill bottle off the counter and wheeled himself out of the kitchen.

Jason turned to Miss Charlotte. "Damn, what I do? He's been coming down on me since the moment I got here and I ain't do shit to him. The day I walked in the door he started in on me and he's always talking about my boys!"

For some reason the old man had it in for him. All he ever did was bring up the murders. Jason thought a man his grandfather's age should know better. After all, wasn't that why he had been sent here? To get away from it? To forget?

Later that day, after Miss Charlotte had gone home for the evening, Jason went to his grandfather's room. The door was wide open. The old man was seated in his wheelchair, polishing his black shoes, a chore which Jason had forgotten to complete.

"Don't lurk in the doorway, youngblood."

"I just wanted you to know that I'm gonna call my mom and ask her to change the ticket so I can be up out of here. I don't know why you so mad at me when I ain't do nothing to you."

"I'm not mad at you."

"Then what's your problem?"

"What's yours?"

"I don't have one," Jason said. "I just wanna go home."

"You think everything down here is small and beneath you, but I can't see how what you have back at home is so much better. At least I can say I have what I want. Nobody gave it to me and that means nobody can take it from me."

"Look, I ain't come in here for a lecture. I just wanted to let you know how I felt—"

His grandfather stopped him. "You ever stop to think that maybe one of those boys could have been you?"

"What?"

"That you should be grateful it wasn't you? No, you just want to jump right back in, doing what you were doing, going nowhere fast. Your mother wanted you to come down here so you could get away from all of that mess, and I guess I felt sorry for you when I heard that your little friends died. Your mother thinks you got smarts. She thinks you can turn yourself around before you end up like your little friends."

"Stop saying that! You don't have the right to be talking about them all the time—"

"I have the right," his grandfather said. "Last night was not the first night I heard you."

"Huh?"

"I'm up every night you are. I hear you every time you have one of those dreams."

"No you don't!"

"Those boys, the ones in your dreams or the ones out on the street, can only take what you give."

"Shut up! What do you know about them? You don't know nothing about them! Don't say nothing about them! Don't say—" He was tired of hearing about it, tired of being vigilant night and day. Each time his grandfather talked about it, it did something to him. Made it so he could barely breathe. Made it so he felt as though he were the boy in the coffin, in the suit, with no smile. As though he were the one dead, dying and already buried. Buried alive.

He started to cry. A boy his age. Sixteen years old and crying, but he couldn't help it. He told his grandfather that they weren't even really aiming for Kiki and Stephen. That the boys who shot them didn't even know them. That it had nothing to do with them. Revenge he could understand. Revenge was cold. Calculated. Methodical. Logical. Everybody got even. But the bullets that had killed them weren't even meant for Kiki and Stephen. This thing that happened was accidental, careless. Murder. He thought his friends deserved better. Someone should have at least known who they were.

It had only gotten worse after they died. They had been used as examples. All of the young boys older than six but younger than fourteen, dressed in borrowed brown, black, and navy suits, had been led up to the caskets by relatives and been forced to look at the boys. Kiki and Stephen had become an example of what could happen to them and all other black boys that didn't stay out of the streets. The accidental part of the shooting only made the adults feel that much more justified. The adults whispered that bullets didn't have anyone's names written on them, the phrase he'd heard on nights after a shooting when his whole block turned off their lights and pulled their shades and closed their windows to

repel the stray bullets. Because it was a funeral and the dead boys'
mothers were present, the adults kept the other words under their
tongues. *Serves them right,* they wanted to say. Jason knew they
all believed it was just deserts just because of the people Kiki and
Stephen knew and hung out with. *Sooner or later something like
this was bound to happen,* they wanted to say. He knew the adults
felt the same way about him. They kept their distance when he
walked down the block. No one ever gave him a five-dollar bill
and asked him to help carry a shopping cart up the fourteen steps
of the stoop to their front door. To them he was the same as Kiki
and Stephen, and Kiki and Stephen were the same as the boys who
had shot them. So they didn't speak to him. Instead, they watched
him and waited for him to die.

He told his grandfather about the shooting. Jason had never
seen a boy die before. When it happened, it wasn't at all like in the
movies he and his boys sneaked into all summer long. The gun
going off hadn't had the loud clap sound it has in the movies. At
first Jason had mistaken the sound of the gunshots for firecrackers
going off. Then the popping sounds started folks on the other end
of the block to running. When the girls and the children scattered
and hid he saw that Kiki and Stephen had fallen. Then the popping
had stopped. Then he had run himself.

"Get yourself together," his grandfather said when he was
done.

Sympathy would have shamed him, but the command released
the tightness in Jason's chest, made it so he could breathe. He
stopped crying, but he didn't wipe his eyes. He stood and waited
to see what the old man would do.

"You can sleep in here tonight if you want," he said. "Get in."

Jason kicked his boots off and got into his grandfather's bed,
just as he was, dressed in his baggy jeans and basketball jersey.

"You ought to take better care of your shoes."

The light went off. Jason heard the roll of the wheelchair, heard
it settle on the other side of the bed, then heard the shuffle of a
dead foot and the creak and heave of a body settling into bed. He

rolled onto his back and tried to focus on the ceiling fan to keep awake, but the absence of all the night sounds he was used to and the comforting silence that remained instead was slowly claiming him. His eyelids were starting to meet when he stifled a yawn and asked, "What's it feel like, having a stroke?"

The silence was thick with his grandfather's breathing. He thought he would not answer, that maybe he had asked too much.

His grandfather finally said, "You don't need to know. Settle down and go to sleep."

His grandfather's caustic answer only made Jason desire the answer more. "Tell me," he said. "Please. I can't sleep unless I know." As soon as he said it, he knew it was true. He believed he would never have a night free of wakefulness unless his grandfather told him what he wanted to know.

His grandfather said, "It feels like one half of you is gone. Like half a body is all you got left. But you still know the other half is there, you know? You can see it, this other side of your body that you're just dragging along with you, hoping that one day it's going to wake up and get started again, knowing that it won't. So you have to pretend that something can be done with it since you can't just cut it all off. It feels like having somebody you don't like coming to eat supper with you every night and then that person has to make a big deal of the fact that he's there so a man can't enjoy some peace and quiet with his meal—no, this person has just got to keep reminding everybody he's there."

"You talking about me?"

"No, son. That's what it feels like when you can't use a part of your body. Anybody that tells you it don't feel like nothing or they don't notice it anymore is lying. It never goes away."

"So then what?" Jason asked. He thought there must be some secret and that the old man must have it, something that told him how to do it, how to live, how to survive, how to make it through another day when half of him was dead and dragging by his side. "I mean, what do you *do*?"

"Nothing to do. Nothing but live with it."

"I guess that's not so bad," he said. "I mean, it doesn't sound so hard."

"Who told you that?" The boy felt his grandfather shift in the bed, felt him looking at him through the darkness. "Living ain't easy. It's about the hardest thing a body can do."

Over forty of Amina Gautier's stories have been published, appearing in *Callaloo, Chattahoochee Review, Kenyon Review, North American Review, Notre Dame Review, Shenandoah, Southwest Review,* and *StoryQuarterly,* among other places. Her work has been anthologized in *The Sincerest Form of Flattery: Contemporary Women Writers on Forerunners in Fiction;* honored with scholarships and fellowships from Breadloaf Writer's Conference, Ucross Residency, and Sewanee Writer's Conference; and awarded the William Richey Award, the Jack Dyer Prize, and a grant from the Pennsylvania Council on the Arts.

*A*s a child, I always thought of summer as the most crucial of seasons. *Perhaps it was because school was out and we were free to do as we wished. Grown-ups pushed us kids out the door as soon as we woke up— sometimes even without breakfast—and sent us on our way with warnings not to come back until it was dark. Without school to divide the time between night and day, weekday and weekend, summer was an immeasurable, seemingly limitless season. Summertime was supposed to be a season of easy living, according to the popular song, but I had never known it to be so. Anything could happen in Brooklyn on a hot summer's day free of adults, anything at all. And that thing that happened, whatever it happened to be, would become the memorable event to mark the summer. That was the summer that So-and-So got married. Or had a baby. Or went Down South and never came back. Or got shot and killed. Even when the thing was not a terrible*

thing, it would characterize that particular summer, making it unlike any other summer that had ever come or ever was to come again.

I wanted to write about a summer marked by a double funeral. The two dead boys in this story appeared as two live ones in "Yearn," another story I published many years before, the prequel to "The Ease of Living." When I wrote the first story, which takes place several years before this one, I already knew what the two boys' fates would eventually be. In this story, I wanted to explore the effects of their deaths on their community. Mostly, though, what I really wanted was to know how it might touch the life of one boy and change this one boy's definition of summer. I don't think I need to say where I got the idea for the title, do I?

Kevin Moffett

FIRST MARRIAGE

(from *Land-Grant College Review*)

They noticed the odor outside Tucson the day after they got married. They were driving on a bleak stretch of highway and Tad thought they might be near a rendering plant or a dead coyote, but twenty miles later the odor hadn't dissipated. It was putrid and dense and seemed to be getting denser. Amy drove with her hand over her nose while Tad rolled down the windows and breathed.

"Don't worry," he said. "We're not far."

They were headed to Bisbee in a car, a Volvo, that belonged to a man named Gar Floyd who expected them in Jacksonville, Florida, in eight days. This was their destination or, more accurately, their halfway point. The car was part of a program called Drive Way. In Florida they'd be given somebody else's car, which they would drive back to California.

"It's thickening on my tongue," Amy said. "It's like we're being punished."

The odor swelled. It ate at the air. It was as if some giant blood-rancid bird had dragged itself into the backseat and spread its wings and roosted there.

In Bisbee the station attendant sat in the driver's seat and closed his eyes. A few seconds later he stepped out of the car, coughed, wiped his hands on a blue towel, coughed again, and said, "It's animal."

Tad and Amy looked at each other. Amy handed over the keys and she and Tad walked their luggage to their motel: a cluster of Airstream trailers decorated with atomic-print throw pillows and chintz curtains. Theirs was the Royal Manor. Tad rifled through the cabinets while Amy showered. He found an old Saltines tin filled with condoms, a drawer of taped radio shows from the fifties. He found a book with GUEST MEMORIES on the front. He looked through it, the road still humming under him. CACTUS WRENS IN THE OLD CEMETERY. THE SHRINE AT DAWN, ONI MADE HER SPECIAL BEANS!

He found a pen. TODAY'S THE SECOND DAY OF OUR FIRST MARRIAGE, he wrote. WE HAVE NO SPECIAL BEANS, BUT WE'VE TASTED VICTORY AND DEFEAT AND BOTH WERE WONDERFUL.

The last part was something he'd read in a book about the Civil War. It used to be his slogan, when he had a slogan. Now he had no slogan. He listened to Amy mashing shampoo into her hair. He felt consigned and content and resigned. He fished one of the condoms out of the tin, undressed, and got under the covers. He felt like a costume waiting to be worn, an odd feeling but not at all disagreeable, not at all.

They climbed a rounded bluff to see the shrine, built by a father to his son. There were plastic carnations and school pictures of a smiling black-haired boy. On the east-facing side of the shrine the pictures had faded to beige in the sun. The shrine seemed cheap, disused. Noticing a shelf for offerings, Tad searched his wallet and found a punch card from the Sub Hut, which he parted with. "Enshrined," he said. He lifted the collar of his shirt and smelled it. It smelled like shirt.

He looked at the town: laundry lines and kiddy pools and satellite dishes mounted to roofs and trained to the same remote object. Farther on, the copper pit, cactus and scrub, barrenness.

He sat down, closed his eyes, and listened to the click-and-advance of Amy's disposable camera. She'd been taking pictures since they left, gathering evidence of their good time. She was sentimental, discreetly. She saved birthday cards. She couldn't pass a missing-pet sign without noting how tragic the child's handwriting was. Sometimes when Tad looked at her he saw someone stronger, more permanent and at ease with herself than he would ever be. And other times he saw something less certain, a question unanswered, a teetering pile of wishes. . . .

When he opened his eyes she was scrutinizing the camera. "Won't zoom," she said. The abrubt way she spoke made it sound German. "Hey, maybe they'll take our picture."

A middle-aged couple in khaki shorts and fanny packs approached, their voices seeming to speed up as they neared. The man said, "The clerk at the hotel keeps saying. 'I'd eat the streets, I'd eat the streets.' He's trying to say the streets are clean."

The woman accepted the camera from Amy. She held it to her face and counted, her top lip quivering like a dreaming dog's, three, two, one.

"We got married this morning," Tad said after she returned the camera. "This is our honeymoon."

"How wonderful," the woman said. She surveyed her husband until his truculent expression softened.

"I just realized I left the bouquet in the car," Amy said. She put her hand to her face tentatively. "It's probably ruined."

"We can pick another one," Tad said.

"No. Are you serious?"

He supposed he was. Unthinking, but serious, he supposed. "Of course I'm not serious."

Amy watched him with puzzled amusement. She watched him like a child waiting for a top to spin itself out.

"We're so in love," Tad said to the couple, "we could fall off this bluff and it wouldn't be tragic. It'd be romantic."

"Poetry," the woman said.

"Horseshit," the man mumbled.

There seemed nothing else to say. Tad noticed the couple was dressed identically except for their fanny packs, which were as un-alike as could be. This heartened him, the fact that they'd been unable to coordinate the fanny packs.

"Speaking of which," the man said. "I believe one of us stepped in some." They lifted their feet to check. Tad smelled his shirt again, a mixture of fabric and fabric softener. "Don't let Frank ruin your moment," the woman said.

Back in the trailer, Amy lay down and Tad put in a radio show called "No One Left." A man wakes to find that everyone has disappeared. At first the man, who lives alone and despises his neighbors, is thrilled. He goes to the beach, takes what he wants from stores. But soon he's lonely. Six months later he's raving in the streets. "I can't do it anymore!" he says. "I need to be seen!" He goes into a pharmacy and swallows a handful of sleeping pills. Just as he does, a pay phone rings, rings again, again.

"What a cruel turn," Amy said.

"It was probably just a telemarketer."

She sighed, exasperated. "You're always saying things like that. Clever, insignificant things."

This seemed excessively bitter, but he let it pass. Besides, she was right. She was almost always right. Recognizing this and conced-ing to it allowed him a little dignity, he hoped.

She sat up and rubbed lotion onto her shins. She'd packed a bat-tery of lotions to fight the desert air, a lotion for each body part. Tad began kissing her stomach, arms, legs, neck, stopping to smell the different lotions. It was like a theme park, where you could visit eight countries in a single day.

"Are we really married?" she asked.

He held out his hand to show her the thin band of turquoise they'd bought at a souvenir shop near the courthouse.

"I mean, I'm still figuring out how to feel about it. I used to think it'd be like getting my ears pierced. Only, I don't know. More."

"Don't try so hard," he said. "Let's enjoy our honeymoon. We can always get divorced on the way home."

"That's what I mean! You keep doing that, diminishing it. Acting like it's nothing special."

"Finding each other was special, but we've been together three years. Getting married's just confetti after the party."

"We should at least pretend."

Tad felt like he was being led through a series of increasingly smaller doors. "Okay, let's pretend. Let's talk about all the things we'll do."

"Sometimes it's like you're talking underwater." With her thumbnail she scraped at the skin on her knee, then studied the results unfondly. "I mean, I know you're doing your best."

"I always do my best," he said quickly. Then, "What do you mean?"

"I don't know. I'm beat. I'm married."

"Confetti," he said. "Come here."

She acquiesced. Her body was warm, moist, and unsurprising. Tad closed his eyes and pretended they were trapped on a Ferris wheel. It was their first date and they were nervous and then the Ferris wheel stopped. They held hands and soon began kissing and taking off each other's clothes. Tad imagined the Ferris wheel starting up again and spinning faster. Their trailer seemed to buck and sway, in tune with the scenario. Their inhibitions were brittle, they flaked off like skin.

They'd gotten married the day before in Lake Havasu City. Lake Havasu City was HOME OF THE LONDON BRIDGE, the billboards said, but they must have driven past it or across it without realizing it. They parked in front of the courthouse, went inside, and took a number.

Tad, wearing eel-skin boots and a bolo tie, looked like the brother of somebody famous. The judge asked him if he was in the military; it seemed like he was in a hurry, the judge said. The bailiff took pictures with Amy's disposable camera. Afterward he handed her a bag of sample-size dish soaps and detergents, FOR A FRESH HOUSEHOLD, the label said.

She drove while Tad read the owner's manual and reprogrammed the radio stations every hour or so. It felt good to be logging miles, to command something so imperative. They discussed Gar Floyd's likes and dislikes. Gar Floyd liked raggedy women, they decided. Gar Floyd did not like the idea of milking a goat. The rear armrest folded down to reveal an oval opening to the trunk and Tad and Amy tried to guess its purpose before Tad looked it up in the owner's manual. "Snow skis," he told her.

They'd guessed it was where Gar Floyd stowed open beers when the police pulled him over. An air hole in case Gar Floyd was trapped in the trunk.

"Our first marriage," Tad kept saying as they drove south toward Phoenix. They passed cinder-red rocks. Saguaro cactuses shaped like people being robbed. The wildflowers he picked for her bouquet were drying on the dashboard. "What are you thinking about?" he asked her.

"You," she said. "Me. You and me." She was wearing the white linen sundress she'd bought for the ceremony. She looked drugged, lovely. "I'm trying to decide what sort of life we're going to have."

"Uh oh," he said. He reached over to her with an imaginary microphone. "What kind of life are you deciding to have?"

"I can't say really. It's more like a hue, a general mood."

"What kind of mood?"

She peeked down at Tad's hand next to her chin. "Unfamiliar," she said.

Parked between two snoring semis at a highway rest stop, they had sex in the backseat of the Volvo. They planned to do this in every state they crossed. Sex in Gar Floyd's car was a wonderful novelty, like life itself. Back on the highway they passed a Tercel with blinking hazard lights and JUST MARRIED soaped on its back window. Amy honked the horn, Tad waved. Behind the wheel was a bearded man in a tuxedo, and next to him, a woman in a peach-colored dress.

Tad thought, Right here, this moment, no before, no after. He couldn't recall where he'd heard it. It was either from a philosophy book or an aerobics video. He felt a fierce contentment. He wished there was a way to ration it out to make it last longer. But there was no way. It ignited, it burned up, it was gone.

The man in the tuxedo lifted a can of Schlitz and toasted them as they drove past.

The Volvo sat in the garage, a fan perched atop a toolbox blowing into the open door. Tad approached the car and, leaning in, sniffed. The odor reached out like a slap, sharp and undiminished. It smelled to Tad like membrane or groats, not the things but the words.

"At first we thought it was on the engine block," the mechanic said. "It happens, with kitties especially. They crawl up there to get warm. When you start the car, the fan belt just annihilates them. You would've noticed that." He seemed pleased with his story so far. The odor still reached Tad from where he stood, or else it'd stayed in his nose.

"It was a snake, from the looks of it," he continued. "Probably went in through your wheel well and couldn't get out. Starved. We pulled the backseat and there it was. Little old coral snake."

The mechanic paused while the office door creaked open and a black dog trotted out, followed by an elderly man in spotless coveralls. The spotlessness of his uniform seemed proof that he was in charge. The dog lay down the instant he stopped walking. "It's a shame," the man said. "It was a nice car."

"Was?" Tad said, adding, "It's not our car." He looked at his watch. The minute hand pointed to one number, the hour hand to another. "We need to be in Florida in eight days."

The old man laughed noiselessly. "You're just about through with Arizona. All that's left is New Mexico, Texas, a few others. What takes you to Florida?"

"I don't know, what takes you to Florida?"

"I'm asking you. People often have reasons for going to Florida."

"Oh," Tad said. "The way you said it, I thought it was a joke."

The old man laughed again. Just his shoulders shook. "It's no joke, son. It's a goddamn predicament!" The dog perked up when the man raised his voice, and the man patted him softly. "We'll keep air on it, but it takes time. Right now it's a scream. Might be down to a yelp tomorrow. Didn't you say you're on your honeymoon?"

Tad nodded. He was looking into the car at the bouquet, still drying on the dashboard, remembering something before he retrieved it.

"Why are we talking about snakes then? If I were you I'd be celebrating. Hell, I'd be back at your motel having fun. What do you say, Jeff?"

Tad waited for the other mechanic to say something but it turned out that Jeff was the dog. Jeff didn't say anything. "This is ridiculous," Tad said. "Can't you do anything else? This car belongs to a very impatient man."

The old man scratched his shoulder. Where his neck met his clavicle Tad noticed one of those flesh-colored nicotine patches that always made him a little sick to his stomach. "Sure we can," the mechanic said. And then to the other man: "Go in my office and grab that other fan."

Looking at the bouquet once more before he left, Tad left.

He bought a six-pack of beer and walked back to the trailer as the sun set. The horizon was violently radiant and the wind sung with borrowed nostalgia. It was growing colder. He passed the immense copper pit, a fenced-off canyon of wrecked earth at least a half-mile across, staircased and very still. Tad peered through the fence. The damage looked cataclysmic up close, but seen from space it was nothing. Seen from space it didn't amount to a pinprick. This struck him as a nice, comprehensive thing to realize. He wanted to realize more things like it, but it was getting too cold to concentrate. On the road again, he decided that if anybody asked what he was doing he'd say, very casually, "Just passing through." But no one did.

In grade school he used to pretend to chew gum in class. When the teacher asked him to spit it out, he would pretend to swallow it. This was what he remembered while he looked at the bouquet. The old man reminded him of the teacher, something about how he lazily regulated the conversation.

In the trailer, Amy sat on the edge of the bed, her head pitched forward slightly on her long neck, as it did when she was unsure of something. He came closer and she said, "Tad." The word released a smell like sweet dough. "We aren't moving, are we? It feels like we're being pulled behind a truck."

He told her about the snake and waited while his disappointment became their disappointment. "That's so awful," she said. Tad's impulse was to make her feel better, and why not? There were a hundred ways to make her feel better, a hundred possibilities. But as he stared at the white underside of the comforter, scorched with an iron mark, he was dim with hesitation.

She said, "I was remembering when I was little, how I'd lie naked in bed after a shower. I'd feel this amazing thing happening inside me. This event. Like my body was just the thinnest husk to hide what was going on inside. I'd try to imagine what my husband would be like, what he was doing at that very moment."

"Probably thinking about girls like you, naked in their beds."

"I hope not. I was nine."

"Maybe I was riding my bike. Was it summer?"

"I imagined him traveling a great distance, suffering setbacks."

"A hero, earning his way to you."

She closed her eyes and smiled. Her face looked slightly misshapen. Was something happening inside her? He waited for her face to show signs of relief. He was distracted by the sound of a coyote. Ah-oooooo. So faint and wavering, it sounded like a coyote practicing to be a coyote.

If there was only one way to make Amy feel better, instead of a hundred, he would not have hesitated.

In a few minutes she was asleep, gripping the pillow like a flotation device, a castaway at rest at sea. The sight of her sleeping always made him a little envious, the way conversations in other languages did. He was ignored, left behind. It seemed unfair that she could close her eyes and make him, sitting right next to her, invisible. As he left the trailer, he made a lot of noise, trying unsuccessfully to wake her.

He carried the beer into the cemetery that neighbored the trailer park. The hundred-year-old tombstones were crooked like tombstones in a Halloween play. KILLED BY INDIANS, some of them said. The ground was loamy and uneven and he suspected he was stepping on unmarked graves so he found a bench and, sipping the beer, watched a distant quiver of spotlights spread out and revolve and reconverge in precise increments, brusquely sweeping the sky.

When he was a child his mother took him to an Indian mound. He was excited for days beforehand but it was just a big green lump scattered with railroad ties. The sort of place you visited without leaving your car. In protest Tad began running up the mound and down, up and down. A man in a blue uniform stopped him and said, "You're running on the bones of my people."

The man's lips held a toothpick. He clenched his jaw, a sheriff ready to pull his gun. He smiled. "Just kidding," he said. "About my people, I mean, not the bones."

Tad thought of a few things he would've said to the man now. His thoughts were a junkyard. He hounded the edges, distracted by any oddity or shiny trinket.

The spotlights danced in the sky as he finished the beer and began constructing a list of demands for himself and Amy. It went: We must take care of each other. We must be the best versions of ourselves. We must inoculate each other from unhappiness.

Contented, feeling as if something serious had been achieved with very little effort, he walked back to the trailer. A pair of tombstones were pitched against each other in an interesting way and Tad scrutinized them like something he might sketch. He felt expansive, blameless, a bit drunk. "Just passing through," he said to the tombstones. He said it how Gar Floyd would. He made it sound dusty.

All night a harsh wind shook the trailer on its moorings and he brought the sound into sleep with him, dreaming that they were being pulled down the highway. Into the unknown, into the unknown. In the morning he was awoken by the ticking of the trailer's metal ceiling in the sun.

They ate breakfast in a diner with framed articles on the wall about paranormal phenomena. They took a tour of the copper mine which was cold and long and garishly informative. Amy sat with the disposable camera in her lap waiting for something photogenic to occur. Their guide, who'd worked in the mine before it closed, said everyone on the train had to ask one question before the tour ended. "Any advice for me and my new wife?" Tad asked him.

He thought about it for a second then said, "Never don't say goodnight."

Afterward they went into antique stores and picked things up and set them down. Amy bought a petrified rock that said OF-FICIAL ARIZONA SOUVENIR and a dream catcher for Gar Floyd's rearview mirror. This cheered them for a while. A trifle distresses, a trifle consoles, wasn't that how it went? They looked around for consoling trifles. They returned to the trailer and listened to the radio shows.

A man keeps seeing someone who looks exactly like him. A woman begins speaking another language, one that no one, including her, understands. The shows were really about aloneness, Tad decided. He helped Amy pull off her shirt and then licked a line straight down her back. He licked dots along each side of the line like a surgical scar. He studied her back and tried to decide what else to do.

What else was there to do?

•••

The Volvo had been moved to the front of the service station, one fan blowing into the driver's-side door, another into the rear-passenger door. Beneath the wiper blade was a piece of paper which Tad freed. THE HAPPY HAWKER, it said. WE PAY TOP DOLLARS FOR IMPORTS. There was a drawing of a car with dollar signs for headlights.

He leaned in. The odor, though not as harsh, was still there. Still insistent. The remains of the remains outlived the remains, Tad thought. And the wildflower bouquet remained on the dashboard. It looked happy there.

Inside the station, the old mechanic sat eating a sandwich half-wrapped in wax paper. He listened to a portable radio and chewed in rhythm, as if eating the song.

"Still stinks," Tad said. "Any more fans?"

He swallowed thoughtfully before speaking. "People used to put dead fish inside hubcaps, as a joke. Maybe someone's playing a joke on you."

"I told you, it's not my car. It's Gar Floyd's."

"Maybe someone's playing a joke on Gar Floyd."

"Maybe. And maybe we're all clowns in a giant circus."

"Maybe."

The other mechanic came in from the garage and whispered something to the old man, who said, "Christ," and stood up with his sandwich. They walked outside. Tad followed them behind the station where, in a packed-dirt clearing, Jeff was stooped over the picked carcass of what looked like a turkey. When he saw the three men, his front shoulders went rigid and he took the carcass's spine in his mouth, waiting, it appeared, for a reason to run away with it.

"He acts like we don't feed him," the younger mechanic said.

The old man breathed through his nose. "He's not acting like anything, Lon. It's instinct. He's made to think every meal's his last. It's how he survives."

"I bet he'd bite me if I tried to snatch it from him."

"What would you do if someone tried to take away your last meal?"

Tad had the feeling that this exchange had occurred before, perhaps hundreds of times. After a while, Jeff relaxed and began gnawing at the carcass, crunching the bones ostentatiously.

"Stranded in Bisbee," the old man said after a while, continuing to admire his dog and eat his sandwich. "That could be a hit song. It'd be sad, but not too sad."

"Something's wrong with this place," Tad said. It was one of those things that he didn't know he was going to say until he said it. "We were happy till we got here."

"What rhymes with Bisbee?" the old man said.

"Frisbee," the other mechanic said.

Tad waited for something else to happen. The old man bit so close to the wax paper that Tad was sure he was going to take a hunk out of it, but the old man knew, apparently he knew, what he was doing.

He and Amy had dinner in town. He ordered a buffalo burger because he thought it might make things more exciting but it didn't. The way the waitress handed him the plate and said, "Here's your buffalo," and then later, "How's your buffalo?" and then "How was your buffalo?" depressed him. He felt like a baby with a toy. A man at a nearby table said to the young boy across from him, "Pretty soon, you'll get to sleep in a bulldozer. How's that sound?"

The boy seemed suspicious but interested.

Amy smiled from time to time to let Tad know their mutual silence was okay. The smile was a token that stood for something to say. It reminded him of the edge of a curtain being lifted and let go.

A group of waiters came out of the kitchen singing "Happy Birthday." One of them presented a single-candled cupcake to the boy, set a coffee filter atop his head, and told him to make a wish.

The boy kept his eyes shut a very long time, then, all of a sudden, his face came alive again and he blew out the candle.

Tad said, "I keep thinking of that stupid commercial that goes, 'If this hammerhead stops moving, he dies.'" He tossed a napkin over his half-eaten burger. "It's probably not even true."

Amy looked at him solemnly and said, "There is so much we don't know about the hammerhead."

They laughed and then it was quiet again.

"For my birthday one year," she said, "my dad gave me *The Odyssey,* the children's version. There's a part where Odysseus returns home disguised as a shepherd to claim his wife. His dog is old and blind, but he sniffs him and immediately recognizes him. I loved that part. That's what I always thought my husband would be like."

"Like Odysseus," Tad said.

"No," Amy said. "Like his dog."

They waited for the check. Tad took Amy's hand and kissed it, inhaling the brackish sea-smell of zinc oxide. She brushed crumbs off his shirt. He had a premonition of her doing the same thing fifty years from now, so familiar to each other they'd be strangers. He thought: there is so much and so little we don't know about each other.

Back in the trailer he was restless. More sex? They'd already had sex twice. Doing it again would be strictly remedial; it would diagnose their dissatisfaction. Instead he complained about the trailer, which was starting to seem like a decoration left out too long. The carpet was filthy. The trash can was filled with condom wrappers and used condoms. Tad threw away an uneaten orange to make the trash can look more domestic.

Then he had an idea. In his wallet was a Drive Way business card with the phone number of Gar Floyd's motel in Jacksonville. He found the card and dialed the number. After the clerk connected him to Gar Floyd's room, it rang five times before someone on the other end picked up, fumbled the receiver, and said hello.

Amy studied his expression. "Who is it," she whispered.

"Gar Floyd?" Tad asked. Gar Floyd said yes tentatively, as if expecting bad news. He sounded nothing like Gar Floyd.

"You don't know me," Tad said, "but I'm driving your car to Florida. I wanted to tell you that I, that we've, been wondering about you. You spend time in a person's car and you begin to wonder about him."

"Abort," Amy said, waving her hands. "Abort."

Tad had forgotten why he originally wanted to call. Gar Floyd was clearing his throat, breathing roughly. What had he expected Gar Floyd to say? "Oh," he said. "I thought you were calling from the hospital. My wife's getting treatment. She's sick."

"I'm sorry to hear that," Tad said.

"They prescribed these sleeping pills and, ever since, I keep dreaming I'm back in the Air Force. I'm doing something wrong but no one will tell me what. That's just what it was like." He paused to catch his breath. "Listen, my wife's not doing so well. What time is it?"

Tad looked at his watch and told him.

"Well," Gar Floyd said after a while, "how's the car?"

"It's great," Tad said. "It's a great car."

"The transmission's been rebuilt. The tires are brand new."

"The tires," Tad said, "are unbelievable." He felt his stomach tighten. "We shouldn't have bothered you."

"Who's there with you?"

"Amy, my wife. We're just married." Telling him this, Tad remembered that this was what he'd called to tell him. He thought it would be funny to tell Gar Floyd about getting married. "We're in Arizona."

Amy stared straight ahead, implacable, like a rigidly disciplined athlete.

"What a great time," Gar Floyd was saying. "Careless."

"Sure," Tad said. "We're seeing all there is to see. Your car's in good hands, that's what I called to tell you. We're checking all the fluids, using high octane. You'll have it in a few days."

"I've got a rental now," Gar Floyd said. "An Escort. It's a lousy car. The wind blows it all over the road. What kind of car do you drive?"

Tad drove an Escort. He didn't say anything. He watched Amy flop down on the bed and thought about his lousy beef-brown Escort and waited for Gar Floyd to ask another question.

"You woke me up," Gar Floyd said. "The least you can do is talk to me."

Silence on both ends of the line, Tad in Arizona and Gar Floyd in Florida. Tad apologized again. He wished Gar Floyd and his wife well. He stressed the imminence of their arrival. Goodbye, he said. All right, Gar Floyd said.

He sat next to Amy on the bed and patted her arm while she studied the ceiling. "Just married," she said. "Just married. Say it one way and it sounds like one thing. Say it another way and it sounds like something else."

"I thought it'd be funny. It wasn't. What do you want me to say?"

"Nothing, everything. I want you to know when to be serious. Act like this means something."

"I'm excited we're married, I'm ecstatic."

"I'm not just talking about being married."

"What then?"

"This. This moment we're in. Life, Jesus, look at me, you never look at me."

Indeed Tad was staring at the percolator on the counter, at its clear nipple, using it as a focal point. He looked at Amy, at her wide wary face. Whenever she exerted herself her cheeks flushed with ghost acne, like fingerprints on a steamed-up mirror.

She put her hand under his chin and held it strangely. She didn't blink for a long time. "What are you doing?" he asked her.

She let go and said, "Wishing."

After Tad turned off the lamp, passing headlights lurched and danced inside the trailer. He watched them for a few minutes and resolved to leave town in the morning, whether the odor was gone or not. El Paso, Houston, Baton Rouge. He wanted to be looking at Bisbee through a telescope of better days.

"Goodnight," he said.

"Goodnight," she said.

In the morning they walked their luggage to the service station. The Volvo was no longer in front, nor was it inside the garage. Looking around, Tad was surprised by the relief he felt, the sense of absolution.

"Where'd it go?" Amy asked.

Mexico, he hoped, where it'd be stripped, sold, scattered.

"They probably just moved it," he said.

Inside the office, the two mechanics sat next to each other, reading sections of the same newspaper. The younger mechanic looked up and grinned at Tad while the old man kept reading. Jeff was sleeping on a folded towel in the corner, beneath a sign for Bar's Leaks.

"My partner thinks he had an epiphany," the old man said.

"It came to me in a dream," the other man said.

Tad looked at Amy, who had her arms folded over her chest. She knew he was looking at her, he could tell by how her expression went vacant. The four walked behind the station, Jeff trailing behind. The Volvo sat in the clearing with its doors open.

The younger attendant ran to the car, gawkily animated. He arched forward and leaned in for a big cartoon sniff. "Delightful," he said.

"Potpourri," the old man said, shaking his head. "Lime scented."

"Country summer lime," the other mechanic said. "Get in! It smells so damn clean in here!"

Tad and Amy sat in the backseat, their feet crunching down on something as they got in. Tad saw that the floorboards were filled with dark green wood shavings and dried buds. Inhaling the sweet sour smell, he was reminded of those scented soaps he was always tempted to take a bite out of. The dead snake odor was no longer perceptible.

"It isn't bad," Tad said. "It's better than it was."

"My girlfriend buys it in bulk. This is what my bathroom smells like."

The old man sat down in the passenger's seat. Tad hadn't noticed how big he was until he got into the car. He had to slouch forward so his head didn't touch the ceiling. Jeff jumped onto his lap and laid his snout on the headrest, panting.

"No charge," the other mechanic said. "That's the best part."

Tad reached down and grabbed a handful of the rough, ridged wood and then let it go. "No charge," he said to Amy.

"On the road again," she said, holding her hand out for Jeff to sniff, which he did, and then looked around warily. "Will you hand me that?" she said, pointing to the bouquet on the dashboard. The old man groaned as he reached forward and then handed it back to her. It looked brittle, careworn. She held it in her lap.

"No charge!" the young mechanic said. He started the car and pulled out of the clearing, kicking up loose dirt.

Out front, Tad loaded the car. He hung the dream catcher on the rearview mirror while Amy drove off, waving to the mechanics who responded with succinct nods. As they headed east into New Mexico, the landscape started to make sense again and Tad felt an agreeable recession. Time, he knew, was vast—seen from a distance, each moment was nothing, a ripple, barely perceptible, nothing. Soon they would stop at a rest area and make love while other travelers gamboled in their designated areas. They'd stay in a motel shaped like a teepee. By the time they arrived in Florida with Gar Floyd's car, Bisbee would be no more than a mere layover, a place where—look, here's a picture, Amy and Tad smiling at the shrine—they were as happy as they'd ever be.

Kevin Moffett was born and raised in Daytona Beach, Florida. He is the author of the short-story collection *Permanent Visitors*. His stories and essays have appeared in *Tin House, McSweeney's, A Public Space,* the *Believer,* the *Chicago Tribune,* and *The Best American Short Stories.* He is the recipient of the Nelson Algren Award, a Pushcart Prize, and a fellowship from the National Endowment for the Arts. He teaches writing at Cal State University San Bernardino.

CORINNA VALLIANATOS

I remember a comment a former writing teacher once scribbled at the end of one of my stories: "This reads like barely rescued autobiography." It was written in blue marker. I stared at it for a long time, trying to figure out if it was a compliment or a complaint. Based on the word "barely" I decided it was a complaint. I hate that I think about this comment when I'm writing anything that skirts up close to true life, but I do. "First Marriage" started with an autobiographical fact, a three-day-long stay in Loxley, Alabama. No smell, no snake, but a burned-out clutch and a mechanic who showed me the grease stains on his palms and said, "My hands haven't been clean in fourteen years." This line was the original germ for the story, but I forgot to include it.

Robert Drummond

THE UNNECESSARY MAN

(from *Arts & Letters*)

Three-and-a-half hours—that was all Michael got with Charlie Johnson. Three-and-a-half hours beginning at eighteen minutes past six on a Tuesday night, when Michael Bailey came running into the house certain his mother would be angry that he was late to supper. Instead, she wore a ridiculous smile on her face and sat across the kitchen table from a tall man with a long neck and dark eyes.

"Michael," his mother said, turning, "this is Mr. Charlie Johnson."

Michael knew the name. And though it was true that after that day he wouldn't be able to think of the name without also thinking of what he would witness later that night—the confused violence, the way a man's body could crumple to the sidewalk—at that moment Michael knew only what he'd been told. He knew the name and how to spell it, knew that Charlie was sometimes Charles and other times Chuck, knew the name Kenneth came between Charles and Johnson. Knew all this though Michael had never seen the man once in his eleven years. And so he looked at the man and waited for him to confirm or deny his identity.

Charlie Johnson chewed a toothpick and looked with appraising eyes down at Michael. Michael watched the toothpick travel from one side of his mouth to the other. "Sure enough," Charlie Johnson said at last, and winked.

Charlie Johnson stayed for dinner. Doris had prepared sloppy joes, the soupy meat simmering since morning in the crock pot on the counter, and Charlie Johnson ate with vigor, smacking the meat off the roof of his mouth and swallowing audibly. Before he was done Charlie Johnson ate four sloppy joes. He would finish one sandwich and lick a finger and already Doris was up and making another without the man having to ask.

Michael followed every single word of the conversation, though the remembered stories and names meant nothing to the boy. But, because near everything Charlie Johnson said was hilarious to Michael's mother, Michael did his best to laugh along with her. "And if that wasn't enough," Charlie Johnson said to Doris between bites, "your dumb son-of-a-bitch cousin walks out of the bar with the basket, like he'd had it the whole time." And Doris laughed again, laughed in a manner Michael neither recognized nor appreciated. She did not normally toss her head back and look at the ceiling, gripping the table to stay upright, and then wipe the tears with the back of her hand and look at the man making her laugh as if he had hung the moon all by himself.

When she finally stopped laughing, Doris looked with shining eyes at Charlie Johnson and asked him where he was staying, and would he be in town awhile?

Charlie Johnson said he was leaving first thing, but that he hadn't as yet settled on a place to stay the night.

"Is that so," Michael's mother said, and for the first and only time in his life Michael heard the pull of sexuality in her voice— though at that moment he understood only that her voice rose in pitch, that her words slowed in a new and mysterious way, twisting the end of the sentence with a delicate drop of tone that almost, but not quite, faded to a whisper. Is that *so*.

• • •

When Charlie Johnson had eaten his fill, Doris put on a pot of coffee and excused herself to step to the restroom. Michael and Charlie Johnson sat in silence and listened to Doris's footsteps retreating down the short hallway, the closing of the bathroom door, the overwhelming and sudden silence of the small house. From the corner of his eye Michael watched the toothpick find its way back into the mouth, where it seemed to rest or float as if in extension of the tongue. When the silence filled with the splashing stream of his mother's business in the bathroom, Michael felt heat rise to his face. He was mortified. He looked up to find the man looking back at him.

Charlie Johnson raised his eyebrows and smiled. "Now, why don't you tell me," he said, "where your mother hides the beer?"

In the bathroom the toilet flushed. As if to cover its sound, Michael said quickly, "We don't have any. She doesn't like it." His first words of the evening.

Charlie Johnson sucked his teeth and nodded grimly. "Don't I know it," he said. The toothpick retreated behind his lips, then reemerged a second later when Charlie Johnson smiled and winked at Michael, as if it was their secret, Michael's and this man's, that he had asked for beer in the first place.

It was decided that Charlie Johnson would sleep on the living room couch, and a big show was made of arranging it. The man helped Doris drape the sheets, and he said no, he wouldn't need such a big blanket, and Doris sent Michael to fetch an extra pillow from his own bed. In short order the couch was made up and three people stood in the crowded living room looking at it.

The clock on the wall ticked thunderously. Michael stared at the carpet around his feet and waited. Suddenly his mother laughed. "You know what?" she said. "I just thought, I don't have a *thing* for breakfast—milk included." She laughed as if this was the funniest thing in the whole world, and then she put her hand on Charlie Johnson's long arm, her bare fingers touching the skin of his bicep, just below the sleeve of his tee shirt, and said, "Would you be a dear?"

Charlie Johnson said he couldn't be anything *but*.

"I'm sure you'd like us all to think so," Doris said, rolling her eyes. "Good then. That'll give me a chance to get this boy to bed." She looked at Michael and for an instant was once again his mother.

"Could do," Charlie Johnson said. Then he shrugged. "Or maybe the boy could come with me."

Michael felt, rather than saw, his mother go rigid. "It's already past his bedtime, Chuck." None of the wispy, mysterious tone of voice now—pure house manager.

"Aw hell, Doris. Let him take a ride with his daddy."

Michael would have put the odds at one in a hundred that his mother would let such a thing happen, but this man was a magician, and when he spoke that foolish smile came back to Doris's face. She laughed, looking down at Michael, and said, "Do you want to go with him?"

Michael felt a thrilling pulse in his stomach; he hardly managed a nod. His mother laughed again, laughed though it was past eight o'clock and Michael had done no homework nor cleaned his room nor bathed, and Michael wondered what other powers Charlie Johnson had.

Charlie Johnson said to Doris, "Maybe I'll take your car," and he raised his eyebrows and grinned as if he went to the store for her five nights a week.

Doris raised her eyebrows in return. "Maybe you'll gas it up for us," she said.

Charlie Johnson chuckled. "Maybe so," he said, and when his back was to Doris he winked at Michael for the third and final time.

Before that night, it had been three years since Michael or his mother mentioned the name Charlie Johnson. It happened as they sat in front of an episode of *Family Feud* and Michael asked why Charlie Johnson had never appeared.

Doris was sewing a patch over a hole in Michael's jeans. She gave no sign of surprise or distress at his question. "Because we don't need him to," she told her son without bothering to look up from her work.

Michael said that every one of his classmates at school had a father.

"Maybe everybody else needs a father," Doris said. "You don't."

Michael was just old enough to understand that her tone and manner indicated the topic was settled. Michael did not need a father; this, apparently, was the fact of the matter.

But now this unnecessary man was here, now Michael sat an arm's length away from him in his mother's Oldsmobile as they drove to the Kroger's. Michael recognized this as his chance to find some things out, to question this man sitting across from him. But the pulsing thrill that began in his stomach at the prospect of going out with Charlie Johnson had worked its way into a shaking, confused energy in Michael's arms and hands, and the things he thought to ask were too strange to say out loud. He wanted to ask the man if he ever felt something inside him that was just a little off from others, if he ever felt entirely separate from every other living person in a room. He wanted to ask how this man knew where the grocery store was without asking, if he was born here, if he grew up here, if he went to Michael's school. If he had already lived Michael's life for him, if maybe he could tell Michael how it would all turn out.

But Michael couldn't form the words, and neither of them said a thing to each other until they were inside the grocery store, and Charlie Johnson had filled his basket with eggs and bacon and coffee as Michael trailed after him. In the dairy section Charlie Johnson grabbed a half-gallon of whole milk from the bin, though Michael and his mother drank 2 percent, and said to Michael, "Carry that for me, champ?"

At check-out Michael saw that Charlie Johnson's wallet was connected to a chain, which was in turn secured to a belt loop on his pants. This seemed to Michael an extraordinary precaution. He looked at the drooping silver chain and wondered where this man had been, what he had done, that such safeguards were necessary.

When they were back in the car and pulling quickly out of the lot, Michael was determined to start a conversation, but he stopped short when they turned the wrong way, heading in the opposite direction of the house.

"You play ball, then?" Charlie Johnson asked. He looked straight ahead when he asked the question.

"Oh," Michael said, nodding quickly. "Yeah."

"Which?"

"Baseball and basketball. I'm better at basketball."

"No football?"

"Nah," Michael said.

Charlie Johnson was quiet.

"But, you know," Michael said, "I'll probably play football this coming year. Most likely."

"That so?" Charlie Johnson nodded once. "You ought to. Toughen you up."

Michael wanted to ask if he needed toughening up, if something about him made this immediately apparent to Charlie Johnson, but he said nothing. They crossed Omaha Street, taking them further from Michael's house. At Main Street Charlie Johnson went straight instead of left, driving past Tilly's, the restaurant Michael got to eat at twice a year on his and his mother's birthdays, past the bowling alley, past the car wash and the Discount Drug, and Michael tried not to wonder what was happening, not only where they were going but what rights this man had to Michael and to his mother.

"Give your mom much trouble, do you?" Charlie Johnson asked.

Michael wasn't sure of the correct answer here. Would it seem un-tough to say he did not, that his mother was not a woman to abide foolishness of any sort, as she herself had reminded Michael many times? But if he lied, if he said he did as he pleased, the man might later verify his answer with Michael's mother. "Not really," Michael said.

"That's good, kid. That's the way to do it." Charlie Johnson nodded again.

Michael flushed with a kind of pride. The compliment, if that's what it was, emboldened him. "I was just wondering," Michael asked, "where you live usually?" The boy looked out the window as he spoke. He didn't know the street they were on.

"Usually?" Charlie Johnson asked, then fell silent for several seconds. "I haven't really settled down, not yet. Curse of Cain, they call it. Been in California, though. Don't you know that about me?" He didn't wait for an answer, but nodded, as if this made sense. "Well, that's where I've been lately."

As he spoke Charlie Johnson was slowing the car and looking at the buildings lining the road. He eased to a stop, then, and expertly parked the Oldsmobile parallel to the curb. Just ahead and to the right was the only commercial building on the block, a windowless place with MURPHY's lettered in green neon above the door.

"Well," Charlie Johnson said, putting the car in park and killing the engine. "You just sit tight a minute or two, little man. I need to make a quick stop."

The Oldsmobile door creaked heavily as Charlie Johnson opened it. He stood, looking up at the sign and down each side of the street, and then he sauntered up the sidewalk and inside the door, looking tall and swift and purposeful. To the boy watching from the car, the man moved like a giant of the earth, legs striding, arms swinging.

The door to the bar clapped shut and the night fell still around Michael. He waited and watched, his seatbelt cutting across his neck. He inspected the faint green flicker of the sign's neon tubes. He counted the bricks above the wood siding, and saw the remains of daytime construction work at the building's near corner, where the sidewalk was torn away and yellow tape circled an area at the wall's base; a piece of the wall was missing, revealing pipes and framing, a pair of shovels and a jackhammer.

Twenty minutes passed, then thirty. Michael's mother would be worried and Michael himself might get in trouble. She would think something happened. Michael tried to will Charlie Johnson to emerge from the bar and take them home.

As if on cue, the door to the bar whipped open and a mass of men burst from the entrance as if riding on a great rush of water. Michael counted six, no seven, as they scattered across the side-walk, and Charlie Johnson was among them. Michael focused so intently on him that it took the boy a few seconds to understand that the commotion involved two other men.

"The hell you did," said one of them, short and stocky, wearing a red baseball cap and leather jacket. The night was still and the road without traffic; Michael could hear him plainly even with the car windows up.

He was talking to a taller, bald man whose back was to Michael. "Oh, I did," that man said. His voice echoed quickly off the bricks of the bar. The surrounding men formed a loose semicircle around the two, with Charlie Johnson nearest the building. "You god-damn right I did," the bald man said, and he took one step forward and spat. The smooth skin of his scalp looked a sallow green under the neon light.

The shorter man looked for the briefest of seconds at his shoes, and then he was lunging forward, moving at and into the bald man, arms windmilling. The bald man took a step back and to the side, attempting to corral his adversary around the head, but all he managed to do was knock off his hat. When the two came together again it was with a ferocious swiftness, the collision accompanied by tangled arms and groping hands, the two bodies alternately clinging and separating for space enough to swing a fist.

And these fists, when they struck, made no sounds Michael could hear, no TV-like smacks as they collided with a shoulder, or the side of a head, a neck. The whole of it was chaotic and uncoor-dinated, lacking grace and choreography. No clean, decisive blows, just mauling and clutching, an occasional swing of a white-green hand. When at one point the smaller man found himself backed up against the wall of the bar, he ducked and burrowed his head into his opponent's midsection, reaching his arms around the back of the man's legs in an attempt to lift and pivot him to the ground. The bald man did not go down. Instead he rained blows on the exposed back of the shorter man.

Michael felt his heart pounding in his neck. He looked to Charlie Johnson, trying to understand his involvement or risk. But Charlie Johnson only watched, nodding. Now the bald man had a hold of his opponent's jacket, and he used it to pull and push and fling him toward the wall of the bar. The shorter man tried to keep his footing as he flew across the pavement, but his velocity overcame him and he toppled, rolling awkwardly to the cement. The bald man was on him before he could stand up, coming in a run and kicking with full force into his ribs. The downed man dropped flat, the air forced from his lungs in a wheezing grunt. When he lifted his head from the sidewalk in an effort to rise, the bald man reared back and delivered a second kick that struck him under the chin. The head flopped up and back down as if its neck contained no bone or muscle or ligament.

Quick as that it was over. The semicircle tightened, the men murmuring and emitting low whistles. The shorter man, incredibly, remained semi-conscious, his head raised but otherwise motionless, strands of blood and saliva bridging his mouth to the sidewalk. The bald man stood over him still, speaking down on him in a low voice. The group began to break up, then, all of them going back inside except for the combatants and two other men: Charlie Johnson, who turned and walked toward the car, and another man, one from the crowd, who went around the building to the right and returned a moment later with a shovel. The bald man, unaware, was still speaking to his fallen adversary when this third man approached him from behind and brought the shovel down on his head.

This time Michael did hear something—a peculiar, concussive

thud as tempered steel met skull. Charlie Johnson, who was almost to the car, turned to look, and the sound reached Michael's ears a second after impact, so that by the time he heard it the bald man was already commencing his slow fall. The image seared on Michael's brain after that night was not so much the fight itself or the two savage kicks or even the glinting swing of the shovel, but this—the way the bald man dropped. There was something horrible and unnatural about the slow leaning, the body going stiff and soft at once, falling with knees locked, head slumped, hands limp at his sides. The hands fell more slowly than the rest of the body, in fact, trailing behind the torso so that the knuckles were the last things to reach the asphalt, all that straining time between the sound and the body coming to rest.

In the car Charlie Johnson seemed exhilarated, charged through with an energy that expressed itself in wild hand gestures, with fast driving and fast talking. "Now," he said to Michael, "you saw how the little fellow came right at him? No fear?"

Michael nodded, worried his voice would tremble if he spoke. His heart still pounded so fiercely that he felt each beat behind his jaw.

"Well, that's how you've got to be. Size doesn't matter one bit. You remember that." Charlie Johnson shook his head. "Look—there's always going to be bullies. You have to deal with them, I'll tell you that right now. And the only way to deal with them is what you saw right there tonight." He locked his eyes on Michael. "You hear what I'm saying to you?"

In Michael's mind the bald man kept repeating his slow fall. "Do you think he died?" Michael asked.

Charlie Johnson looked straight ahead for a moment. Then he said, "Look here, now. Don't you worry about all that. You listen to what I'm saying, because it's as important as anything your mom'll ever tell you. A moment will come, every single time, where you can either run or fight. Period. And when it does, you better let him know you'll go until you can't go no more. No back-down in you. That's what this little fellow did here tonight. You hear me?"

And then, perhaps because he saw something in the boy's eyes, Charlie Johnson said, "Okay, then," and he laughed. He laughed, but he did not wink, and behind the laugh Michael saw again the tipping man, the way his body stuck motionless when it hit the concrete, face down, palms up and open.

The drive home after that was silent and short. Charlie Johnson pulled the car into the driveway outside the one-level house. But before he shut off the engine he turned to Michael and said, "I guess that extra little side trip, you know, I guess that'll be our secret. Yours and mine."

Michael turned from Charlie Johnson and looked out his window and down the street where he'd been growing up. He said, "What've they got out in California?"

"Well," Charlie Johnson said. "They've got the Pacific. And as much soft, warm sand as you want. Other than that, it's not much different than anywhere else."

"California," Michael said. He felt the word in his mouth.

"Yes, sir," said Charlie Johnson, and then he turned the key and the engine fell silent, and with nothing left to be said they got out of the car and walked together toward the light glowing in the kitchen window.

And even then, the night not yet over, walking step for step with Charlie Johnson, the boy's mind was already misremembering the events of the evening, slowing them down and rearranging them, so that when he recalled them it was as if the activity outside the bar had occurred under water, not in the frenzy of its reality but painfully slowed, every movement clear, the chaotic surging of fists and feet untangled and made orderly and deliberate, the green neon catching and holding the shovel's steel for its long arc through the air. And though it didn't happen all at once that night, it did happen that slowly, gradually, Michael's memory placed Charlie Johnson beneath the swing of that shovel, so that when the dull thud reached the boy's ears the sagging face of the man beginning his slow descent was not the bald fighter but his father's—Charlie Johnson's locked knees, Charlie Johnson's trailing arms, Charlie Johnson's dark hair parting for the shovel's impact.

Michael remembered it that way not because he wished Charlie Johnson any particular harm, but because such an outcome presented a tidier finality to the night than the one offered by reality. Because Charlie Johnson beneath that shovel better explained the next morning, when Michael arose early and anxious and hurried from his bed to the living room to find the couch empty, the blankets folded and put away, the strange car gone from the driveway, and his mother at the stove, dressed for work and stirring the eggs and listening to the radio as if that morning was no different than any other, as if the entirety of the previous night was a singular experience lifted whole and struck clear from the record of their lives.

Robert Drummond's fiction has been nominated for a Pushcart Prize and named as a finalist in the *Glimmer Train* Short Story Award for New Writers and the *Nimrod*/Hardman Short Story Award. His short stories have appeared in the *Sycamore Review, Phoebe,* and *Arts & Letters.* He has lived in various U.S. locales, from Ann Arbor to Los Angeles to New Orleans. He currently teaches expository and creative writing at American University and lives in Arlington, Virginia, where he is finishing his first novel.

KATHRYN DRUMMOND

*W*hen my grandmother was a young girl she saw her father struck and killed by a man with a shovel. The two men had been shoveling snow and began to fight for one reason or another. She watched from the window of her home and was the only witness—later she testified at the man's trial. When I learned about this as a boy I was both horrified and intrigued.

I tried to imagine what it must have been like for her to see such a thing, how terrible and shocking. When I was older I made several attempts to turn her memory into a story, but I could never carry it off in a way I found worthy or workable. After several false starts I gave up entirely.

The idea reemerged in disguise a few years later, however, as I was working on background notes for a character in the novel I'm writing. I intended only to write a flashback to the protagonist's boyhood and his brief interaction with a long-absent father. The pair ended up witnessing a fight, and when one of those fighting men appeared with a shovel in hand, I was as surprised as the bald man in the story. I realized the source of that idea about the same time I understood that I was dealing with a stand-alone story.

Stephanie Soileau

SO THIS IS PERMANENCE

(from *Tin House*)

For the first time since she'd given birth, Sarah was left alone with her new baby. Her mother and sister—run ragged for two weeks seeing to duties that Sarah avoided by, say, hanging out in sitz baths for hours with a vampire novel—had escaped at last, back to work, back to high school. Ever since the later months of her pregnancy, after she had packed up the contents of her locker, turned in her textbooks, and left high school, apparently for good, Sarah had taken to her room, giving herself over completely to sleepless hours alone with the growing boulder of a belly and the strangely comforting idea that if only she were a spider, she might cast this thing off on a windowsill in a bundle of silk and let it hatch on its own. Her attitude after the birth was no better. But Sarah had promised herself and her mother that she would rally, and to her credit, she had successfully fed and changed the baby twice the afternoon before.

On Monday morning she heard none of her mother and sister's bustle to tend the baby and get themselves ready for work and school, nor did she wake when her sister, on the way out, quietly opened the bedroom door and wheeled in the crib. Of course, they both fully expected Sarah to loaf in bed until the crying reached decibels impossible to ignore. But she did not. Her alarm clock went off only moments after her mother backed the car out of the driveway, for last night, in a sleepless agitation, Sarah had been inspired.

From her closet, she extracted four wire hangers, and she took a roll of twine from a shelf in the laundry room. After some digging, she found pliers in her father's neglected tool chest, which had once been so impeccably organized but now, not even a year after his death, wouldn't close because of the odd angles at which the women tossed in the hammer, level, screwdrivers, and wrenches. Having laid the hangers, twine, and pliers on the kitchen table, Sarah took a peek at the crib. The baby was starting to stir. This was fine. She was expecting this. She knew exactly what to do.

In the hospital, the nurses had tried to teach her how to slip an arm under the baby's bottom and up toward his head, how to grip the head gently but firmly, like an egg. At the time, she simply refused to learn, and this caused a stir among the nurses, who would wheel the baby in on a cart every three hours and fuss loudly enough for the *good* mothers up and down the hall to hear: *Whose baby is this, young lady? Whose?*

Now she scooped the baby up more or less as she had been taught, and clutched him awkwardly to her chest. Tightness spread through her breasts, this gravitational pull of milk to baby, baby to milk. She felt a fleeting impulse—like the one that compelled her sometimes at the grocery store to pocket a blossom-pink lipstick or a sequined headband—to lift her shirt over her breast and press her nipple to the baby's mouth. It was mortifying and exhilarating, this feeling, and she would rather forget it than try to explain it to herself.

Sarah clutched the baby tighter and poked a bottle of formula at his mouth. She whispered his name, which her mother had given because Sarah had not bothered to think of one, and leaned close to his head, smelling powder and a lingering stink from the diaper, and underneath all that, something almost nice, like her own hair when she had not washed it, or the foreign-familiar scent of another person that hid under perfume.

When he was done after only two ounces, she propped him up

in his carrier, stationed him too on the kitchen table, and left the rest of the formula on the counter for later.

If Sarah had once been curious, it was so long ago that she hardly remembered what it felt like, or what she might have been curious about. The anoles in the camellia bushes? Penguins? She still loved music—that was a constant—but only in the way most teenage girls loved music, that is to say, enough to mold an identity from it, but not enough to pick up a guitar and search for chords or scratch lyrics on napkins at cafés. Certainly not enough—or in the right way—to beg her mother for lessons and her own instrument. Even if her parents would have paid for lessons. Which they wouldn't have.

But where had everything else gone? To the top shelves and buried corners of closets, then to garage sales. Now recovered and laid out on the kitchen table, the remaining artifacts of Sarah's dead interests were these: a shark's jaw from a field trip to Galveston Island, a five-inch plastic penguin, a shoe box of rubber Smurfs. As a supplement to these things, Sarah brought out a stack of raggedy *National Geographic*s.

The baby, she realized, could be her coconspirator. In the empty house, she could finally show herself, not only to herself but to this other creature.

She held the penguin close to the baby's eyes and wiggled it. "Emperor penguins are the largest of all the penguins," she said. "And what's cool is the lady penguins lay the eggs and then go off to sea and forget about them, but the daddy penguins stay and carry the eggs on top of their feet. You'd be in a heap of trouble if I was a penguin. Ha ha."

She knotted a little noose of twine and slipped it around the penguin's neck.

"And sharks!" she said, picking up the gaping skeletal jaw. "One day you'll love sharks. One day, when you get a little older, we'll watch *Jaws*."

With no one to see and conclude that whatever she was feeling was not the right thing, or worse, that it *was* the right thing and she would be a good little mother after all, Sarah—she couldn't help herself—kissed her baby on his smooth, round forehead and let him curl his hand around her finger. They held on to each other like that for a little while, and she thought that at last they had reached an understanding, come to some agreement.

By noon, the mobile was well under way. Sarah had manipulated the wire hangers until, all joined together, they formed an asterisk that could be hung from the mobile's center. She dangled the penguin from one arm of the asterisk, the shark jaw from the next. These she counterbalanced with a constellation of Smurfs carefully arranged on the opposite arms.

Still, there were gaps to be filled. She turned to the old *National Geographic*s. Most of the best pictures had already been plundered for school projects, but Sarah found that her aesthetics had changed. Whereas she once might have cut out the prettiest—seals, tigers—or else the most revolting—insects, innards—she now lingered on humans, masked dancers, totems, and statues, on faces reconstructed from prehistoric skulls and given intelligent, watchful eyes under their apish brows. She cut out the skulls and the faces, and the in-between stages of their restoration, and pasted them to pieces of the shoe box. As they dried, she attached these too to the arms of the mobile.

The baby had fallen asleep, and all around his carrier on the kitchen table and scattered across the floor were bits of paper and twine, small puddles of glue, and sharp little bits of metal that had snapped off the hangers. The mobile itself lay in a tangle in the middle of the mess. Sarah felt a little too focused, and a little gnawed; she was both the pencil and the teeth that chewed it. It would be good to have a cigarette, but there were none in the house, and she was just deciding that the baby would probably sleep through a ten-minute trip to the convenience store on the corner when she heard her mother's car outside.

As soon as Sarah's mother opened the door, her expectant

smile—the one that usually preceded *Where's that baby? There's that precious baby!*—turned to horror. "What on earth?" she said.

Sarah wiped at the spilled glue with a ball of torn magazine pages. The baby opened his eyes and wiggled.

"Sarah, you left this out?" Her mother snatched the bottle of formula from the counter, de-nippled it, and dumped the contents into the sink. "Sometimes I think you've got no sense. Did you remember to boil the water first?" She sniffed the empty bottle. "And this mess, you're going to clean this up before you do anything else." With her giant sack of a purse still on her shoulder, Sarah's mother shook out a new trash bag and indiscriminately swiped scraps into it. "For goodness' sake, Sarah. I can't do it all."

"Stop! Wait, I was doing something," Sarah said.

But there was no stopping her mother. Sarah's projects—and there had been few—had always upset the equilibrium of their house, had always been a dreadful, galling inconvenience. Since Sarah's father had died, her mother had been forced to get a job—her first and only job, ever—in the records department of the hospital, and her will to power over the household had only grown as a result, her home and daughters becoming more and more like unruly colonies in an overextended empire.

"Come on," Sarah said to the baby. He was huffing and tossing his arms around, gearing up for a cry. Sarah gathered up the mobile and the baby carrier, and left her mother holding the trash bag.

In her bedroom, she hung the mobile from a blade of the ceiling fan and tried to distract the baby with it. The baby's eyes opened and rolled, dizzy in his floppy head. He could not focus on anything for more than an instant of stupid amazement. Sarah realized with frustration that this was probably for the best. If she were one week old and had to look at that hideous spidery contraption hanging over her head at night, she'd—well, she'd scream, or puke, or pee her sheets. Maybe all three. Now, what kind of mother would inflict such a thing on her child?

• • •

Beneath Sarah's bedroom window was a row of thick camellia bushes that she'd never believed she could jump into or over without hurting herself. They were a great deterrent, these bushes, and Sarah, in most things, was easily deterred. But on Friday night she decided she would do it. For the first time in her life, she would catapult herself over the camellia bushes—courage, courage—not for long, only to walk down to the convenience store for smokes: ten, fifteen minutes tops, because for Christ's sake she just needed some air.

She had improvised maternity wear out of her death metal T-shirts, ripping them up the front and stringing chains of safety pins across the gap, then adding more pins as the months passed. It wasn't a bad look, she thought. She took away some of the pins and put on one of these shirts, along with a gauzy black skirt and boots; her cozy old ripped-up jeans still wouldn't close around her belly. After her sister had gone out and her mother to bed, Sarah brought the baby with her into the bathroom and spent an hour drawing cat's-eye points of eyeliner nearly to her temples, blackening her lips, and teasing her indigo hair into a masterpiece of abstract impressionism, a blown-forward asymmetrical arch that plunged down into a jagged fringe over her right eye. She inspected herself in the mirror and found she looked like hell, in the best possible way.

What would her poor old father have thought? In the old days, he would have shaken his head, lit up another cigarette, and gone back to watching the TV. He might have said, as he had when she first experimented with eyeliner and lipstick, *Has your mother seen that stuff on your face?* And if it came down to it, if her mother made too much fuss, he might have done his fatherly duty and succumbed to the idea of a spanking, threatening Sarah without much conviction, as he had done once or twice over smaller transgressions. But she didn't dress like that then. In the weeks before he died, when Sarah first turned up at the hospital looking like an imploded star, her father only winked at her as though they were sharing some joke and groaned for more Dilaudid. While her father was sick, sneaking out was never necessary; dressed any which way she wanted, she would simply exit by the front door, her mother too exhausted, too sad and distracted to do anything about it.

Back in her bedroom, Sarah put on some quiet music and painted her fingernails until the baby finally fell asleep. Just in case he should start to cry, she built a soft nest of blankets and pillows on the floor of the closet and nestled him into it.

Only ten or fifteen minutes, definitely no more than twenty.

She turned out the closet light and quietly closed the door.

She perched on the windowsill for a while, gauging the distance to the ground. Finally, Sarah gathered her skirt, launched herself over the tops of the bushes, and tumbled to the grass, bones atingle from the impact, as suddenly and bewilderingly free as a cat fallen from a balcony.

She heard the kids in the parking lot before she saw them, their loud country music and a girl yelling, "Hey, heeeyyy. Get off me!" A group of about a dozen were clustered on the bed, the roof, and the hood of someone's ratty old pickup truck, like crows on a dead rhinoceros. Sarah scanned the group for her sister, and when she was sure her sister was not among them, she revealed herself in the buzzing orange light of the parking lot.

Normally, she would have ducked under her hair and slid quickly past these kids. She knew them from school. She didn't hate them, they didn't hate her, but they didn't know quite what to do with each other. After all, what could Sarah find to say to girls who went to church on Wednesday nights and then again on Sundays, who gathered every few months in front of the Wal-Mart to testify and wash cars for Jesus? Mostly, though, she resented the way that, when pressed to be cordial, the perkier ones always tried dutifully yet warily to draw her out.

But tonight she was high on her daring. She felt a reckless urge to wander a frontier, hop a whaling ship. Short of that, she'd settle for climbing to the top of that beat-up old truck and having a cigarette or two before she went home. So after she bought herself a pack of smokes, she lit up and squinted at the group of kids to find one she could casually flag down. There was among them one boy, Brent Stelly, who was sort of a floater. He was as likely to tuck in his shirt for a Wednesday night church service with the Baptists—his family was French-Catholic, like Sarah's—as to deck himself out all in black, plunge a safety pin through his earlobe, and spend the night wandering back roads with Sarah's strange tribe.

"Sarah girl!" He leapt off the hood of the truck and jogged up to her, holding out his fist, wide silver rings on every finger. "*Comment ça va,* my cher-ree?" Seventeen years old and small, bouncy, Brent Stelly aimed to be everyone's favorite uncle from the boondocks. He was the youngest son of a huge family of Cajun fishermen turned riggers, and he played it up, the wild Cajun, the swamp rat. His tongue rode its backwoods inflections like a bucking bull.

"*Ça va ça va,*" Sarah said, blowing a stream of smoke. She smacked his fist with her own.

"Shoo," he said and reached for the uppermost spikes of her hair. "Can I touch?"

"Yeah, sure."

"You out for the night, Sarah girl?"

"I guess I'm out for a little while."

Two of the girls slipped off the truck and strolled over to meet them. "Hey," said one, in the languid, sad, reluctant way teenage girls had around there.

The friend went in for a hug that Sarah accepted stiffly and broke quickly. "How's that new baby, sweetie?"

Sweetie.

"Um, okay, I think. I don't know. Fine? He doesn't really confide in me these days." Sarah felt the examining eyes of the girls prodding at her stomach, felt them lifting and dropping each tight, over-large breast. Or maybe, after all, they were only checking out her badass safety pin chain mail.

"Are you coming back to school?"

"I don't know."

"What are you gonna do if you don't come back?"

"I really don't know."

"So, what's the bee-bee's name?"

"I don't know."

"Quit pulling my leg, you."

"I'm not pulling any legs."

"Come on, Sarah, what did you name him?"

"I didn't name him."

"Well, he's got a name, doesn't he? What is it?"

The quieter one said, "I like your shirt."

Stelly linked his arm through Sarah's, pulling her toward the truck; some kids squeezed together to make room for the two of them on the hood. They smoked and watched cars pass on the strip, then pass again, and sooner or later turn into the convenience store and pull up alongside, honk, hoot, then return to the strip for a few more laps. When Stelly slid a flask of whiskey her way, without thinking overmuch about it, Sarah drank.

Fifteen or twenty minutes turned into almost an hour, and though a distant anxiety crackled in Sarah's bones, she stayed, free from her mother's say-so and the tyranny of infant. She listened to the kids bitch and laugh about the desolate crappiness of this place, none of them, not even Sarah, realizing of course that no matter what, no matter where, adolescent years were spent cruising a strip of one kind or another; that this nervous, dreamy pacing in the dark corridors of town, this poking around for surprises in dusty corners and sounding of walls for secret passages would come to nothing much, and ultimately a good many of them would relish the onset of complacency, would become dentists and dental assistants, or flunk out of dental school and become offshore roustabouts, real estate assessors, and school board clerks, would buy a large house on the lakefront or a small house in a neighborhood of elderly people, marry, go to church, have babies, baptize their babies, and many other common, decent things that now, in their restiveness, most of them, especially Sarah, would call giving in.

Sarah and Stelly reclined next to each other against the windshield. They smoked steadily and drank when the whiskey came around. One of the boys reached inside the truck and turned the radio up for an old country song they'd all heard since kindergarten, a slow and faraway good-bye song. The kids passed the flask and sang and swayed arm in arm to the lovely, aching promise of nostalgia.

It was all very bizarre, and seemed more bizarre by the minute, that Sarah should find herself in the parking lot among these kids, especially when she ought to be home—and how very, very strange that she ought to be home doing the things she ought to be home doing. Her head drooped between her knees and she remembered the startled eyes of the creature that had been extracted from her numbed lower half barely two weeks ago. It made her giggle, the thought of herself in labor, the absurd lump of her belly, the rock-star paroxysms of her face, and the blessed disembodiment as painkiller after painkiller was pumped into her. It was a joy, sure, a relief to be at last free of the weight and movement inside her. Then that creature—and here she giggled harder—that strange, groping alien they laid on her chest and insisted was hers!

When Stelly leaned into her ear now and said, "How come you ain't dancing, Sarah girl?" she could hardly stand it. She quaked with laughter in spite of herself, whiskey-warm and wild, until the talking around her, the boys' teasing and the girls' shouts, stopped altogether, and she felt Stelly's arm snake around her shoulders and squeeze, then the welcome suffocation against his hard little chest, smelling first of cologne and then of human sweetness and heat.

One of the girls said, "Is she okay?"

A boy said, "I think she's laughing."

"Is she laughing?"

A hand touched Sarah's back. "Are you okay, sweetie?"

"She's okay," Stelly said. Then he whispered to Sarah, "Let me take you home, chere. It's time you went home."

Sarah said to her knees, "Good God, I don't want to go home. Take me somewhere else."

•••

They drove south. Each time they paused at a crossroads, Stelly asked, "Which way?" and Sarah answered, "Straight, straight, just drive." After about half an hour, the flat, grassy pastures turned to marshes and canals, and they crossed one drawbridge after another until they finally reached a ferry that took them over the intracoastal ship channel connecting the waterways of their town, twenty miles inland, to the Gulf of Mexico.

The dilapidated beach resort at this time of year was nearly empty and, except for a few small and widely spaced streetlights and lighted windows, entirely dark. Sarah and Stelly left their car on the road and their shoes under the porch of a deserted camp. The water was still warm after the long summer and remarkably serene, the waves low, reticent; shouting and laughing, the two bared their legs and plunged in. They made more noise than the sea itself, and this seemed to Sarah a magnificent thing.

After a while, drenched to the hips, Stelly turned back toward shore. Sarah's skirt was hiked up to her waist, waves splashed against her thighs. She tested each step with her toes and went on. A rig flickered in the far distance, so small, so isolated, that it might have been sparked by a fisherman's Zippo. It would be easy, really, to keep wading toward that light.

"Don't go too far," Stelly shouted. "Hey!"

Miles from this beach, somewhere in the middle of that moving darkness, were a thousand men and women who lived their lives like Sarah's father had, intermittently, two weeks on, two weeks off, napping on the couch or puttering in the house, yard, town for fourteen-day stretches, and just when the harder questions of living begged for answers, they were off again to the rigs, questions forgotten, decisions unmade. They were whisked away in helicopters to a place for which Sarah had no reference in her imagination. Not a trace there of family life, of children, no pictures or toys, no sentimental accumulations, the Gulf a mile deep beneath and miles around, reflecting only the rig, the night sky, and nothing of home.

"Sarah!"

"All right!" Any moment she could plunge into deeper water. "I'm coming back."

Sarah and Stelly lay down in the sand, shoulder to shoulder, wrist to wrist, foot to foot, and shared their last cigarette, brushing fingers when they passed the butt back and forth, and lingering upon casual touches just past the point of necessity. This was the sign. It could be taken or left.

For the longest time, they just lay there and breathed.

At last Stelly said, "I seen Daniel the other day at that diner off the highway."

"Yeah, he's always there."

"How come you don't tell him—you know?"

Sarah put out the cigarette, stood and brushed the sand from her skirt and hair, which had wilted in the moist air and was clinging, sticky and limp, to her forehead and neck. "Hey," she said, "want to hear my death rattle? I've been practicing, listen." She let her head sag to her chest, and a ghastly, dry croak escaped her throat.

"If the baby was mine," Stelly said, "I'd want to know."

She made the croaking sound again.

"Sarah."

"I'm sure he can figure it out."

"If it was mine, I'd want to do something about it." Stelly reached for her foot and traced the tendons down to her toes and to her toenails, with their half-moons of chipped black polish. From his knees he tugged at her skirt, drew her down to him, and she was on her knees too then. She heard a rush in her ears, felt a pounding of waves on her chest when their noses touched. Stelly slipped a hand under her shirt, but Sarah grabbed that hand and held it; not so long ago, her breasts had answered even the slightest touch with a humiliating trickle of warm colostrum. She buried her face in the soft nook behind his ear. She said, "Yeah? What would you do about it?"

"I'd—" He dug his fingers into her flaccid stomach. They crept under the waistband of her skirt as he kissed her neck, her ear, her mouth, as his other hand found its way again into her shirt, groped, caressed, and stopped. "Wait," he said. He sat back on his heels. "Hold on. No."

"God," she breathed. She needed to do something sudden, violent, so she seized a handful of sand and threw it hard into the wind. She threw another handful, then another, and the fallout blew back into their faces.

"Quit it," Stelly said.

Sarah did not quit it. Stelly turned away, shielding his eyes with his arm. "Stop!"

Sarah did not stop.

"I'm taking you home."

"Fine! Take me home." She launched the next handful at his back.

He stood and dusted himself off. "Well, get dressed. Come on, get up."

She straightened her clothes, but didn't move. A gull dipped and circled just above them, trilled quietly, and then glided out over the water, where the first few fishing boats were leaving the channel and chugging toward the horizon.

"Get up, Sarah."

"No!"

"Come on, girl."

"Wait!" She clutched at his damp, sand-caked jeans. "Let's stay here. Let's live here!" Stelly shook his leg free and took her hand to pull her up, but she went limp like she would as a little girl when her mother tried to carry her to the bathtub or to church. The dead weight of her body dangled from her up-stretched arm, which Stelly held firmly by the wrist. He dragged her a little way through the sand before finally giving up and letting go. Sarah let her head and arm fall at deliberately bizarre angles. "Ghhhhaaaah," she groaned.

"Come on, what are you doing?" Stelly poked her once with the toe of his boot. "Girl, get up. We have to go."

Of all the possible moods Sarah imagined she would walk into at home—resigned annoyance in the best case, wild fury in the worst—none approached the silence with which her sister met her at the door and shadowed her through the kitchen and into the living room, where the baby, rescued from the closet, now squirmed on the floor amid the debris of her sister's all-night vigil. He seemed carelessly discarded there, along with the empty soda cans and bag of potato chips, the fashion magazines and catalogs, like he might easily be swept up and tossed away. His hands flew up and wriggled in the air; according to the maternity ward nurses, this ancient and adorable reflex meant the baby thought he was falling from the tree. *So fall,* Sarah thought and felt remorse, almost immediately.

Their mother slept on the couch with a Bible tented on her chest. In moments of distress, their mother would take up the Bible as though it were a magic eight ball; asking silent questions, worrying silent worries, she would let it fall open in her lap and start reading at the first word her eyes latched on to, and always she found the kind of contorted and ambiguous relevance—or so it appeared to Sarah—that her sister found in, say, the horoscopes of *Vogue* and *Cosmo.*

Exhausted, her shoes and clothes and hair prickly with sand, Sarah went immediately, casually, to her bedroom. She rooted through disorganized, overstuffed drawers for her pajamas while her sister stood in the doorway, watching her. Finally, when Sarah flopped heavily into her bed and heaved a most defiant sigh, her sister said, very quietly, and with more wonder than reproach, "You didn't even pick him up. You didn't even bother."

In the weeks that followed, the less effort Sarah put into the care of her baby, the less her mother and sister assisted her. He might cry or be hungry or sit in his own filth much longer, but neither of them would lift a finger. Some conspiracy was afoot between them. While before her father's death there had been predictable and equal alignments in their domestic loyalties—sometimes Sarah and her sister against their mother and father; sometimes Sarah and her father against her sister and her mother—Sarah now found herself without an ally, her privacy infiltrated by this sensitive little infant spy who would blow the whistle, loudly, on any negligence or indiscretion.

Except to roll the stroller up and down the block or to run to the grocery store, with baby in tow, for formula and diapers, Sarah never left the house. She was bored. She was lonely. Not long ago, dropping out of school had seemed like the one good thing to come of all this, but now she sometimes talked about going back, and when she did, it was as though she had made some insipid comment about a character on TV, and she might get an inattentive answer but more likely she would be ignored altogether.

One Saturday around noon, the baby started crying and, like an angry god, would not be appeased. Sarah cycled through every possible desire; she offered feeding, diaper-changing, entertainment, then feeding again. She sang to him from her repertoire of disturbing dirges by the Cure, Joy Division, and Bauhaus, and was even getting sort of into it, inventing a two-part harmony—as nearly as one voice can—for "Love Will Tear Us Apart," when her sister said, "Do you know how off-key you are? If you don't cut it out, *I'm* going to cry." Her mother suggested walking around with him, keeping him moving, so Sarah propped the baby on her shoulder and wandered through the house, jiggling him and humming *uhhuhhuhhuhhum* in breathy bursts, a completely unmusical but comforting sound her mother used to make when she or her sister was inconsolable.

Still he cried. He cried through the afternoon and into the evening. He screamed until he was hoarse, until his whole body hiccupped, choking itself on some mysterious distress. He clawed at blankets, at Sarah, at himself until he drew blood on his own neck and she had to mitten his hands in tiny socks: a tiny straitjacket for a tiny madman.

This was not part of their agreement. This bawling thing—this was the very creature that had moved unbearably in her body for months, yet he did not know Sarah from anyone else, and in fact, he did not seem to know person from thing. When he scratched himself, he did not know the cause of the pain or how to stop it—he could not even tell himself from himself. How could she love a creature like this? How did people find it in themselves to love such a thing?

Sarah knew that this was the point when some mothers lost it completely, when one way or another Dumpsters and rivers started to look like viable options. And Sarah did not know herself well enough to be certain where she actually meant to go when she snatched her mother's keys off the kitchen counter and announced that she was taking the baby for a ride to see if maybe, by the grace of God, that would shut him up.

Nearly a year ago, just after Christmas, Sarah had gone to the hospital and found her father—who had been articulating the most precise and vivid hallucinations only the day before—entirely receded, the skin of his hand and cheek a dry spongy bark, his wasted body too dense, too heavy to be budged by the tiny kernel of life lodged and buzzing in his throat. Her mother and sister would wait with him until the end, but Sarah called her friends to pick her up, and until he was laid out in a casket four days later, she did not see her father again.

She spent those four days mostly with Daniel, in self-imposed exile in a freestanding backyard kitchen that Daniel Sr. had built when Mrs. Daniel banned the cooking of meats in her house. He practiced guitar there, the younger Daniel, because that had been not banned but annoyingly encouraged in the main house, and often, if he'd gotten into some trouble that his parents might detect on his person, he slept there, camped out under a card table in a sleeping bag, absorbing into his clothes and long hair a pleasing aroma of garlic and gristle that he would carry around all the next day. It made Sarah hungry, being near him.

For those four days, he let her live there with him, and every night she watched him assault the guitar before she cuddled up next to his light, fluttery body and let his hands dance over her.

They were careless, it's true, but there was comfort in their carelessness. And it had not seemed possible that a boy who looked so much like a girl that new acquaintances sometimes called him—accidentally, impulsively—Danielle could ever father anyone, could ever be complicit in her body's mean betrayal of her wishes.

It baffled her even now, as she watched him through the window of the diner. He was sitting in the booth at the rear, fooling around with a pennywhistle and ignoring a conversation that came to a halt entirely when Sarah, with her wailing baby, flung open the door and approached. It was unclear to Sarah exactly what Daniel knew, or whether he had indeed drawn the obvious conclusion from the evidence presented to him. Regardless, confirmation of a host of rumors was now about to join him at the table, kicking its legs and screaming bloody animal murder. To discuss the situation would be, Sarah thought, redundant.

"Hello," she said and shoved the baby carrier into the seat between herself and a boy she knew vaguely from last spring's geometry class. Daniel dropped a curtain of hair over his face and would not be coaxed out by greeting or question. Across the table next to Daniel was a boy Sarah didn't recognize. She appropriated his ashtray and shook a pack of cigarettes that was lying on the table. For a moment the new boy made eye contact with her. "Can I bum a smoke?" she said.

He said something she couldn't hear over the crying. "What?"

"I said it's my last one."

"Do you have one, Dan?"

"Nope. Quit."

"You didn't quit," she said.

"This is just crazy," said the boy from geometry class. "I mean, I can't even believe it, right? Can you believe this came out of Sarah?"

Daniel said, "You're so fucking stoned," and started a different tune on the pennywhistle, something twittering and ticklish that for a moment diverted the baby's attention from his own misery.

"Wow. That's the first time he's stopped crying in hours," Sarah said. "Are you all really telling me there are no cigarettes at this table?"

She got up to bum one from an old man at the counter and when she sat down again there was whispering between Daniel and the stranger. The stranger quivered with stifled laughter and Daniel grinned under his hair, his lips pulled back, teeth gripping the pennywhistle. A snicker sputtered down the pipe and seemed to flick out like a tongue.

"Where did you find that thing anyway?" she said.

"It's mine," said the stranger.

"Oh. And who are you?"

"He's our guy," said the boy from geometry.

"You're their guy?"

"Yeah."

"What the fuck does that mean?"

More whispering commenced on the other side of the table. Tucking the pennywhistle and a cigarette lighter into a back pocket, Daniel shooed their guy out of the booth and together they skulked off toward the men's room. The restroom door slapped closed behind the two boys, and that was all there was to it.

The problem was that she understood how he felt, she really did, and she could not hold it against him. If she'd been in his position, she would have treated her the same way, no question. In fact, she would have gone further. She would have used every trick of math and misremembered chronology, all the hostile confidence of forensics and gossip, to prove what could not be proven, to make true what was so unmistakably false. And the names she would have called herself! The things she would have insinuated! And she—the she she actually was—the sixteen-year-old mother of a baby confronting the seventeen-year-old father of a baby, would at least have been granted the dignity of outrage, instead of this slow, creeping embarrassment, this paltry and invisible disintegration.

She would not have sat there and said nothing at all, she would not have sneaked into the men's room like a worm to get high on whatever they were getting high on.

Or else she would have. In fact, she would have, so she was back to this after all: she could not blame him.

The boy from geometry swooped down on her baby with a crazy face, going, "I'm gonna eat you! I'm gonna eat you!" The baby was twisting up his mouth and jerking his feet, sucking in air that would soon be expelled again in a deafening screech.

"Hey," Sarah said, can you watch him for a minute? I need to get something out of my car."

She truly had not planned it, but it couldn't have been easier. Not the old man sipping coffee at the counter, or the two young roustabouts eating fried cheese, or the woman playing video poker, or the waiter who moved aside to let Sarah pass—not one of them protested or even raised their heads as she walked out the door started the car, and simply drove away, leaving her child there in the booth, like leftovers or a purse.

This interstate, if one took certain exits and cloverleaf turn-arounds, led exactly nowhere, and while Sarah was looping around the city at seventy miles per hour, past the petrochemical plants along the lakeshore, past the mega-stores and chains on the out-skirts of town, the seafood markets and shotgun houses of the older neighborhoods, over the bridge and back around to the pet-rochemical plants again, she was debating whether she, like certain of her rougher cousins, had what it took to actually drive away from this place and toward another one, effectively stealing her mother's car, sleeping on strangers' couches or in strangers' beds, working a more depressing job than she had ever feared until she was inevitably apprehended and condemned to a juvenile detention center for the rest of her adolescence. She just might.

It was so hard to do anything about anything. It was so hard to love anything, and she could not find a way to love anything more, or to hoist herself out of this pit. She saw the shadows of others moving around up there; sometimes a face peeked down. Where was the rope?

When she had first discovered she was pregnant, she searched the yellow pages for abortion clinics, of which there were, of course none. So she called a hospital and asked evasive questions in all the wrong ways, got no answer, and fretted in her room until several months had passed and her pants no longer fit and she had to tell her mother. By then, it was too late to do anything about it, and even if it weren't, her mother would never have allowed it, would have rejected the idea out of hand and been appalled that it had occurred to her daughter in the first place. If Sarah were a different kind of person, she might have begged a ride into another town, worked connections, asked bold questions.

Instead, she was left with this impossible choice, and no way of knowing how to make it.

She imagined the boys—and this made her laugh out loud— re-abandoning the baby on the front steps in an elaborately stealthy maneuver, a trio of gutter-punk anarchists depositing a home- cooked bomb. She could also imagine Daniel hunching over his newborn son in the backseat of a crummy and rattling old hooptie, abashed as she had been by the growing resemblance between that tiny, near-formless face and his own.

One day the child would speak to her, would ask her questions and develop preferences for, say, drums over trumpets, for cucum- bers over tomatoes, would—in other words—become remarkable in the small ways that people inevitably become remarkable to those who must observe them every day. But now, what was he? He was one more thing that failed to interest her.

For a moment, when he was first handed to her in the hospi- tal — there was something. He had been so much like a feather- less, fledgling bird, but not in the way her mother or the nurses thought. *Look at those little bird lips, look at my hungry little bird.* No.

More like the sad, naked beasts she'd seen as a little girl in the bleachers of dolphin shows and football games, fallen like ripe figs from their nests in the rafters, and crushed, or soon to be, jerking their heads on stemlike necks, jerking their not-yet wings.

She had longed to squash them under her shoe, and to cradle them in her hands. She had wanted to touch their rubbery skin, to pry open their blind, bruise-blue eyes, to hide them in a shoe box and to bake them in a pie. And whenever she reached for one, whenever her exasperated mother grabbed her collar, yanked her up onto the bleachers, and knocked the filthy, dying creature from her hands, her father's complacent drawl had spread over her like an umbrella. *Let her be, she's fine. Just let the child do.*

<hr>

Stephanie Soileau's short stories have appeared in *Gulf Coast, StoryQuarterly, New Stories from the South 2005, Best of the South: From the Second Decade of New Stories from the South,* and *Tin House.* They have received awards from the Illinois Arts Council and the Vermont Studio Center, as well as a Pushcart Prize nomination. She is a graduate of the Iowa Writers' Workshop and is currently a Wallace Stegner Fellow at Stanford University, where she is working on a collection of stories and a novel about fishermen in coastal Louisiana.

I wrote the first draft of this several years ago, but it just wasn't working. When I finally picked the story up again, I had just spent over a month in my hometown of Lake Charles, Louisiana—the longest I'd been there since I left at sixteen, and long enough to remember, viscerally, what it was like to come of age there. Almost every day during this visit, I'd stop for coffee at a little diner on the main drag, where all the strangest, most out-of-place teenagers would gather and horse around and complain, waiting for the moment when they could finally get out *(as out-of-place teenagers do, no matter where they are). I wondered what would happen to the ones who didn't leave, or couldn't, and I thought again about the wayward mother in my story. She had been shadowy before, not fully realized, but here she was now, sitting in a booth in front of me, making lethargic jokes and squinting under her shaggy hair at the pick-up trucks cruising the strip outside.*

THE GREAT SPECKLED BIRD

(from *The Southern Review*)

Preston Clearwater, prematurely gray, squatted near a black 1950 Chrysler four-door sedan and, using a broken quart jar, dug a shallow hole where he buried part of the automobile's glove compartment contents and a billfold. Clearwater wore glasses with octagonal lenses and no frames. He packed fresh dirt with his hand, smoothed over the small mound with his fingertips, and then scattered leaves and pine straw. The sky above was just dark enough to show the first stars of evening, and far across a nearby field of broomstraw stood a long line of black pines, above which lay a strip of yellow sky.

"There's no tool like the fingers," said the tall, pointy-headed boy leaning his butt against the front fender of the Chrysler. His wrists and hands hung from a sports coat that was too small.

Clearwater had picked him up two weeks before. The boy had been standing in front of a grocery store in Smyrna dressed in a black suit, white shirt and tie, with a suitcase and valise by his side, and holding out a long red thumb. What Clearwater saw in the boy as he stood by the road was something he'd evaluated as drive—something smart and businesslike.

"Go bring the other car," said Clearwater. "Here's the keys."

He hadn't noticed the boy's eyebrows coming together until he had hopped into the front seat that day, looked across, and said,

"Hit's mighty fine to be picked up right when you're praying it'll happen. It makes you know the good Lord is taking care of you." But then when the boy said he was selling Bibles, especially given his red-rimmed eyes and a kind of chalky paleness, Clearwater whiffed deceit—and figured the boy might be of some use.

For the first few days he felt a kind of kinship to the boy, but now he wasn't so sure about him. He talked too much, for one thing. And Clearwater didn't like the way he let the leftover end of his belt hang down without putting it back through the first loop. And the eyebrows. He knew a woman with eyebrows that met like that, but she'd shaved out the middle every few days.

The boy pulled a '49 green Ford up beside the Chrysler, turned off the ignition, and got out. "If you'd left him alone," he said, "we'd done be thirty mile up the road."

Clearwater was squatting, changing license plates on the Chrysler. He said, "I don't want to hear no more about it." He caught the boy's eye. The boy, tapping his fingers against his thigh, looked away. If he could learn when to keep his mouth shut, thought Clearwater, and how to think ahead, he might could still turn out with some kind of maturity and style.

From the trunk of the Ford, Clearwater retrieved eight license plates from eight different states; his photo album; a canvas bag containing a hunting jacket, two .38 pistols, masking tape, rope, and cigarette lighters; and a suitcase of clothes with a stash of jewelry and cash stored beneath false sides. He placed his things in the roomy Chrysler trunk, hid the license plates behind the trunk lining, and then waited until the boy put his things in next to the spare tire.

Only then did Clearwater, with a handkerchief, clean the blood specks from his glasses.

They drove both cars out of the woods and onto a two-lane blacktop. They were a few miles north of Albany, Georgia; and the boy, driving the Ford, followed Clearwater for about fifty miles, until they stopped near a crossroads called Little Leaf at a used car lot lit with a string of white lightbulbs where they sold the Ford for two hundred and fifty dollars to a man wearing red suspenders who said business was slow. The boy said, "Well, the Lord always provides." Clearwater had asked him not to talk.

Before daybreak they stopped just outside Aiken, South Carolina, at a motor court that had a palm tree beside a neon sign. Clearwater remembered from decades earlier a neon rooster in the window of a music joint in Knoxville.

After a day in Saluda and a day in Newberry they had stolen two expensive cars, sold them, rested a few days, and started out again.

As they drove north of Chester, South Carolina—a cold sunset outside, the fine heater running inside—Clearwater admired the dashboard of the Chrysler. The car felt heavy. He liked the solid sound of the doors closing. He liked that it was black and shiny. He would keep it, and hide half his stash inside the door panels. And the radio had a good sound: powerful and solid.

"Why don't we just rob a store?" asked the boy.

"That's not a good idea right now—or hardly ever."

"I know about being careful. I ain't never been caught but oncet."

They passed houses whose interior lights, yellow through pulled shades or white through glass, were just coming on.

"How many times you been caught?" asked the boy.

"I ain't been caught, but I've been with people who were."

"*When* they got caught?"

"Right before."

"How'd you get away?"

"I just did."

"How many people you shot?"

"Just that one. And you saw how it was self-defense." Except the one before that, thought Clearwater, and the one before that and . . . He wondered why his lips and then his chin always tingled when he shot somebody. Sometimes his chin went numb.

He started changing stations on the radio to see if he could find a preacher preaching. It was Wednesday night, and he might pick up a prayer meeting somewhere. He liked to listen to the way some radio preachers got all worked up. He liked to hear all that passion up against a world that, he now knew, no kind of belief about God or Jesus could ever change one whistle. He had once believed, but all that was gone—like a precious child who died on him, died with some kind of vengeance. He stopped the dial on a station that was playing—by God, yes—Roy Acuff singing "The Great Speckled Bird." He felt an ache in the hollow of his chest. "Do you know who that is, singing?" he asked.

"Nope."

They listened to the rest of the song.

The boy was eating a banana. Clearwater had trouble with the way the boy would peel only an inch or so and nibble. And how could somebody with their head out their ass not know about Roy Acuff?

"Why don't you just peel the whole thing and eat it?"

The boy tucked his chin and looked at Clearwater with shiny dark eyes from under his swing-bridge brow. "I eat it like I want to. I was taught not to touch the thing itself."

"That's Roy Acuff. We played music together. He used to love to fistfight." Those days were before everything got washed away like a house on a mud slide. There had been no pleasure since then but what he took for himself, to make up for what had got taken away.

"The boy rolled down the window and threw out his banana peel. They were driving by a wide, bare field that seemed almost snow white in the cold gloom just before dark. The boy thought maybe he could feel Clearwater needing to talk but not being able to. He was that way every now and then, and the boy despised that kind of condition. "Did I tell you my daddy shot hisself."

"No." Clearwater didn't believe him.

"He couldn't get help for his visions. He was bad to drink. My mama was in the garden picking tomatoes when he done it in the living room—with his feet propped up."

"That's too bad."

"She had to be somewheres."

"I was talking about your daddy."

They slowed for a blinking red light.

"So you ain't even heard that car wreck song that Roy Acuff sings?" asked Clearwater.

"No. I ain't ever been around many radios. Did you hear about that whole family that got shot after a car wreck?"

"I did. I knew that guy."

"The Misfit. Did they ever catch him?"

"Not that I've heard."

"How'd you know him? I bet he was something."

"We worked together some, but he was too nervous for me. I wished I had his teeth. He had real fine teeth."

"I wished I had about anybody's teeth."

After about a month, with the boy changing his name so much, Clearwater started calling him Preacher because the boy said that in order to really sell Bibles you had to know everything about Moses and Jesus and all them.

Clearwater kept him on into summer because he hadn't come across anybody any better, and he'd learned to avoid him a good bit of the time, even while using him. Preacher liked his new name, and didn't seem to mind being avoided as long as he could keep selling a few Bibles here and there. They'd worked up into Maryland and were working their way back south.

They'd been in the little crossroads town of Drain, North Carolina, for three days. It was hot and the town felt lazy. North of the railroad track that ran through town were big white houses with columns, maybe thirty or forty in all, and about three miles north a road conveniently doubled back so that they could first head north in case they were seen, then cut through and get back on Highway 301 headed south. During those first three days, Clearwater had checked several possibilities more lucrative than cars; and after his investigations he'd picked their mark—something different: a house where a doctor had his office and lived with his retarded son.

A maid came in the daytime. It looked lucrative because the doctor didn't bank in Drain or up in Boltonville, and he did abortions. There had to be a well-stocked safe in his house.

They separately checked into the Sir Walter Motor Lodge, an office and nine one-room cottages near the town limits sign. After driving through town and deciding on the Sir Walter, Clearwater had let Preacher—all dressed up and carrying his valise and suitcase—out of the car a ways from the lodge. As usual, Preacher was to avoid Clearwater until Clearwater gave the sign: two rocks on the back bumper of the Chrysler. That meant a meeting in Clearwater's cottage just after dark.

Preacher entered the Sir Walter about twenty minutes after Clearwater, signed in as Morris Poindexter, pulled a Coca-Cola up out of cold water in the drink box, and asked the desk clerk, a man with a sore on his mouth and pockmarks on his face, if a Bible was kept in the office for visitors.

The man said, "You don't see one, do you?"

"Well no, but with a Bible in sight, Christians like me would be happy about doing bidness here, and would spread the word. And I'll be happy to sell you one—that's my bidness—I carry red, blue, or traditional black, with the message of eternal life between the covers."

"Me and my wife can't afford no Bible. We had to let go our desk clerk, and we got one colored woman to clean the cabins and she's sementy-se'm years old. Course, she can outwork both of us."

"Some thinks the Lord rewards hard work," said Preacher, "but it don't mean a whittle 'less you been washed in the blood of the lamb."

The man said something and laughed.

Preacher walked to the road after leaving his suitcase in his room. It was hot and humid even though the sun was behind dirty clouds. He set down his valise and was ready to thumb a ride when he saw across the road, about thirty yards down, a vegetable stand—under a funeral home tent with white-painted plywood boxes all around. The paint was thin enough to expose the plywood. A big handpainted sign read COLLARDS, TURNIPS, WATERMELON, ECT.

From a distance he saw a woman or girl sitting in a chair beside a set of hanging scales. He picked up his valise and headed toward her.

When he got close he saw she was a big, healthy, blond, curly-headed girl with a thin dress that seemed to show her skin beneath. Hair ringlets stuck wet to her forehead it was so hot. She wasn't all that pretty right in the face, but there was something about her he liked—a kind of plumpness. He bought three peaches and introduced himself as Aaron Samuels. She said she was Marleen Dunlap, and he didn't talk long about Bibles before he realized that she was lonesome and not interested in the Bible at all; so he loosened his tie and took off his coat and asked if he might sit for a short spell in the other chair—she said yes—and he told her a little about his heart condition and asked her if she might want to come over to his room that night and see his collection of exotic cards. She said she couldn't do that, that she was bound to stay with her mama and daddy or grandma most of the time until she was twenty-one in three months, but if he had time, would he come by the next day and she'd show him a book from England that you could open and castles would pop up. He said he wasn't sure how long he was going to be around, but he *would* like to spend a little time with her, so sure, he'd make time.

On that second day she showed him the book under the tent during a brief afternoon shower, and that night they met in the woods—she was afraid to come to the motor lodge—down a path behind the vegetable stand. She even brought along a blanket and rub-on mosquito repellent. He brought along a pocket flask of whiskey, a flashlight, and his cards, and it turned out that she was delicious, in some ways more so than he'd hoped. She didn't protest about anything as long as he used a preventative, so after his joy making, he felt safe in baring his soul. He told her that actually he was not a Christian *yet*—in case she had that impression—but sold Bibles because it made him a good living, that he'd already saved over nine hundred dollars in less than a year. He was inter-ested in the business side of most anything, he said. He had gone to business school but had had to drop out because of his heart condition, which cured up on its own, and he didn't know if the cure had been a miracle or not. He was actually an agnostic, he said. And she told him that her mama and daddy had not gone to church since the church had brought them food one Christmas and made her daddy mad, but that she believed in God. She said they'd been Reformed Presbyterians, and what was an agnostic; and when he told her it was somebody who didn't know which way to lean, she said she guessed maybe she could be one of those, too. He then asked her to marry him and she said yes and he prom-ised they'd run away to get married in Dillon, South Carolina, as soon as his car got fixed up in Boltonville, and that they would come back and he would continue to sell Bibles in the surrounding area while they lived at home with her mama and daddy until they had children, and then he'd give up traveling and they'd move into a mobile home or, if he had the money, a small brick home. He said he really liked that brick pattern where there was a black brick along about every tenth red one. And he told her he wanted to get into some kind of business where he wouldn't have to mislead people about his own soul. He said he might like to sell cars.

Preacher couldn't believe his luck. She was a big happy girl, all sexed up, and she loved to giggle and rub his feet and didn't com-plain or ask any questions. It seemed like he was mighty lucky lately, especially if Clearwater would go ahead and get this big money job under way.

It would be their last job together because he'd decided to leave Clearwater. He had thought working for Clearwater would be a big step up for him. But the man was always overplanning, and sad, and cleaning his fingernails with his little two-blade Case. Preacher had seen a second set of keys to the Chrysler. After his cut from this one more job, he'd make his move.

On the afternoon of the third day the two rocks showed up on the Chrysler bumper. Preacher knocked on Clearwater's door just after dark. Clearwater let him in. He looked around the room. There was a bed, table, two chairs, and a pitcher and a bowl of water—like his room, except the bedspread was green instead of brown. Clearwater's canvas bag and other things were against a wall. On the table was an open road map, two hand-drawn maps, and a grocery sack with something in it. Clearwater had placed two pillows against the head of the bed; he sat down with his back against them and stretched his legs across the bed. He was wearing thin black socks. "Don't see that girl no more," he said. "That's a stupid move—to get mixed up with somebody while you're working. Wait until you're on vacation."

"I got to have some regular life things."

"Not while you're working for me, unless you want to work her into the plan — and there ain't no room for her in the plan I'm about to lay out."

Clearwater knew that something bad was going to have to happen to Preacher to get him over his connections to other people. "Have a seat. Beside the maps there."

Preacher took a seat and looked for the second set of keys or where they might be kept.

"What you looking for?"

"Nothing. Why? What would I be looking for?"

"I don't know. That's why I asked. You get overeager."

"I just don't want to be around here when people are supposed to start getting their Bibles in the mail."

"I wouldn't worry about that. This job is going to be pretty good, I think. We're going to get another car—the doctor owns a Cadillac—and a good deal of cash, the way I figure it. The first thing you need to do is memorize the escape routes and the side road turnoffs I got drawn on there—a copy for you and one for me. In case of a slipup. We can head south out of town and keep that way, or west then around to south, or north then south. There shouldn't be any problem; but if we get split up, meet me Saturday at noon at the first gas station after the town limits sign down in Laurinburg."

Preacher looked on the big road map for an easterly route — or southeasterly. That's what he'd do. Route 421. He looked at the coastline where 421 led to: Carolina Beach. He could live there for a while, go swimming in the ocean.

"What the hell are you looking at?" said Clearwater.

"The map."

"I'm talking about the one I drawed. You just need what I drawed. We'll do this gig tomorrow night or maybe the night after, as I see it. But first we got to go to a baseball game tomorrow and set it up. And we got to do some rehearsing."

"Rehearsing what?"

"Get the clothes outen that bag."

Preacher went for the canvas bag.

"No, not that bag. "That's my hunting stuff. The paper bag on the table there."

Clearwater had decided that during the opening of the safe, he would ask Preacher to stand guard outside. He would then hide a good deal of the money. Later, he'd split a portion with Preacher, give him the Cadillac if the money was good enough, and say he was retiring. He needed to head to another part of the country, before his luck ran out—or maybe actually retire.

The baseball team from Drain, the Drummers, was playing the Summerlin Nomads. The ball field rested in a bottom about a mile outside the Drain town limits.

Clearwater had learned that the doctor dropped off his son, Randy, at home ball games on Thursdays while he made house calls and that Randy always sat at the third base end of the second row in the old covered wooden grandstand behind home plate.

Clearwater and Preacher entered the grandstand at ground level and spotted him. Nobody sat near him. His round face sat on wide shoulders, and his brown hair was cropped short. A crescent scar showed through the hair over his left ear. He wore overalls with Sunday school attendance medals and men's service club buttons pinned to the front. He looked at the game through his brown eyes so big and lazy they reminded Preacher of a cow's eyes. The two entered Randy's row. Preacher, leading the way so he could sit beside Randy, had on a gray dress with little pink flowers, a black derby hat that didn't seem big enough, red lipstick, and a brown wig under the hat. His head bobbed around, and his lips were clamped together in a sort of silly grin.

A few innings later, the doctor, a small man dressed in a white shirt and tie, stood at the grandstand entrance and motioned for his son to come with him. Clearwater felt confident that the doctor was surprised and happy to see that a man—from Summerlin probably—had chosen to have a young woman, apparently delayed in development, sit with his son. The doctor motioned for his son to come; and Randy stood, looked down at Preacher, and reached his hand awkwardly toward him. He then slowly shuffled over to and down the center steps of the grandstand. A few people, over their shoulders, looked at Randy and then at the strangers, and then back to the game.

Clearwater caught up with the doctor and Randy at the doctor's car, introduced himself as Major Frank Arnold, just separated from the army because of kidney problems, and after a short friendly conversation explained quietly that the girl, Roberta Smith—his niece by his oldest sister—was pregnant by either her father or a cousin and needed an abortion, if at all possible, before they returned to Summerlin.

The doctor told Major Arnold where he lived, and said to bring Roberta to his house that night at eleven.

Preacher, dressed as the girl, was to be at Clearwater's cabin at ten-thirty with all his things packed and ready to go. When he got to his own room after the ball game, late in the afternoon, he did not sit tight as Clearwater had told him to do. Rather, he got out of the dress and wig, washed off the lipstick, put on his Bible-selling clothes, and started for the vegetable stand.

She was sitting at her place, reading a book.

"Whatcha reading, Sweetie-pie?" he asked. He loosened his tie.

"A paperback."

"I know that. What's the name of it?"

"*Blood at Stirrup Creek*. It's a Western. How come your lips are rosy?"

"I just ate a plate of beets. They're good for my heart. So they say. I keep a can around."

Clearwater, loading his canvas bag into the Chrysler, saw them.

Preacher told Marleen about his supply of paperbacks up at his uncle's in Virginia, where he was hitchhiking to that night to pick up his car that was finally fixed, and that he'd be by tomorrow as soon as possible, probably before dinner, to pick her up so they could head out to get married and then go on their honeymoon to Silver Springs, Florida. He had sold his quota of Bibles and then some, and did she reckon she might could come on over to his cabin after dark for a little roll in the hay before he headed out? She couldn't, she said. She had to sit with her grandma who had the blind staggers, but maybe they could find a place to pull off the road the next day. Preacher said for sure, and kissed her good-bye. As he walked away, he was wondering if he should go back and say something else—but he didn't know what that would be.

Outside his cabin, he noticed that the door was open a few inches. He stopped, thinking about what all he had that could be taken. The door opened, and Clearwater stood with a red face thrust forward. "Why the hell can't you follow instructions?" he said.

"Why come you're in my room?"

"Get the hell in here."

Preacher stepped back, but Clearwater stepped forward and ushered him in—a fierce grip to the elbow—and once inside the door, turned him around and pushed him onto the bed. "Get dressed and stay in the goddamn room until it's time to go. Like I told you."

"You shouldn't be pushing me around. You ain't my daddy."

Preacher hoped they'd get a lot of money—because he was moving on at his first chance.

•••

Wearing the dress, wig, hat, and lipstick, Preacher walked along the back alleyway toward the doctor's house. Clearwater, carrying his canvas bag, walked beside him. They'd parked, as instructed, behind the church nearby. It was a hot night. Preacher felt sweat drops rolling down his underarms. Clearwater pushed open a tall metal gate, and beyond that, off to the side, stood a garage with a light over the door shining down on a cream-colored Cadillac that sat outside the garage.

On the screened-in back porch Clearwater pushed a doorbell button; from inside came a sound like a telephone ring.

The door opened almost immediately. The doctor was dressed in a white jacket with a stethoscope in the front pocket and holding a cup of coffee that released a trace of steam. "Come in, Major. Roberta. Come right in."

"Doctor. How you doing?"

"Fine. Come right in."

"She don't talk," said Clearwater, "but she's got a real sweet disposition. I got some of her things here in the bag. She likes her teddy bears and a blanket."

"Come on through to my study," said the doctor. They were in a large kitchen with counters and cabinets all the way around. They walked through a breakfast room, a sitting room, a living room, and then into a study with books lining the walls. There, on a coffee table in front of a couch, sat a beveled glass pitcher of ice water and two glasses. "Have a seat there on the couch and have a drink of water if you like." The doctor sat in a big leather chair across from the couch. "I'll explain the procedure."

The room looked like an expensive hotel lobby to Preacher. The couch seat was soft. He imagined a safe behind a picture somewhere, opening to stacks of green money.

Clearwater leaned forward slowly, opened his canvas bag, pulled out his snubnosed .38 and pointed it at the doctor. "We won't be needing any abortion, doctor. But we do need to have your safe open, and we'd like you to do that as quickly as possible."

"Is this a joke?" asked the doctor. His face held a half smile, but also a look of new knowledge.

"That's for damn sure," said Preacher. He took off his hat. "Man oh man. That's for damn sure."

"Be quiet," said Clearwater.

The doctor put his hand to his head. "You must be actors."

"We ain't actors; were bidnessmen," said Preacher. He wanted to get in a little humor.

"Be quiet," said Clearwater.

A sound came from a door behind the couch. Clearwater looked quickly while holding the gun on the doctor. It was the son. He was dressed in blue pajamas and held a small teddy bear around the neck. He was trying to talk.

Clearwater bolted up and moved to where he could see everybody at once.

Preacher sat still, and then when he saw that Randy was coming for him, he stood, stepped over the coffee table, stopped between the doctor and Clearwater and pulled off his wig. "Look," he said to Randy, "I ain't a girl." Randy kept coming, his big brown cow eyes open wide in surprise and delight. Clearwater moved again— to cover the doctor. Randy gripped a large quantity of cloth on the long sleeve of the dress. He was smiling and making grunting noises like a hog.

"Sometimes he's difficult," said the doctor.

"Now'd be a bad time for that," said Clearwater. He didn't want any more movement in the room. "Just stand there and be still," he said to Preacher. "Let him hold your sleeve. Doctor, you need to open your safe. Right away."

"And ast him to turn me loose," Preacher said to the doctor.

"I said be quiet," hissed Clearwater.

"Mr. Arnold," said the doctor, still seated, "if that's your name, I don't have a safe."

"You got to have a safe. You don't bank in town or in Boltonville."

"I invest my money in stocks. My maid delivers all my cash to a financial advisor—every Friday. There is no safe. I can show you the paperwork, the stock market paperwork, over there in my top desk drawer." He stood.

"Sit back down! And you, too," he said to Preacher. "Sit on the damn couch." He motioned with the gun. He felt truth in the room. It was seeping in like smoke.

Preacher moved back around the coffee table with Randy attached to him and sat. Randy stood, holding the arm, which was raised as if Preacher had a question for a classroom teacher.

"Let's just leave," said Preacher.

"Shut up."

Clearwater walked to the desk drawer, opened it, and pulled out a handful of papers; he looked at them as he held the gun on the doctor. Three to four hundred dollars deposited somewhere every week. "Medical Services, Incorporated" was the damn account name. He felt a tightening in his chest.

"There is no safe," said the doctor, "and I'm expecting another client shortly."

"Well, then you work too damn fast, don't you?" said Clearwater. This was falling apart. They needed to cut and run. "Where's your cash on hand?"

"In the bottom left drawer there, in two envelopes, and you're welcome to it."

"Go get the car," Clearwater said to Preacher. "Maybe there's some silver and some other stuff."

"Where's the keys?" said Preacher. He was seeing the ocean. He could head out on his own. Tonight. Now.

"Under the floor mat."

With Randy attached, Preacher opened the back door to the warm night. They stepped onto the back porch, moved through the screen door, the gate, and down the dark alleyway. Only then did Preacher realize he'd picked up the canvas bag on the way out.

Randy's feet dragged as he loped along. Preacher tried to jerk his arm away. He thought about dropping the canvas bag, but no, it was heavy—something important might be in there. Randy held on. "Damn you, turn loose," said Preacher.

Randy said, "Orrriff."

The Chrysler faced the rear of the church. He knew he had to leave quickly, even if it meant taking Randy a little way and then . . . He led Randy to the passenger side. "Get in," he said. "I'll drive." Randy let him loose and got in the car. Preacher looked again down the dark alley and then out to the street. Hell, Clearwater would get the Cadillac and the silver and what not, all that. He got in behind the steering wheel, dropped the bag between him and Randy, found the keys, started the engine, and turned on the headlights, which lit the far wall of a Sunday school classroom inside the church. Drawings by children. One had a lot of red in it. He drove from behind the church, onto the street, and stopped in front of the doctor's house. The engine was so quiet. Lights were lit behind drawn curtains.

"OK, get out!" he said to Randy. He motioned with his hand.

Randy looked at him through his big cow eyes, made a sound, and slipped toward him. "Don't touch me!" He pushed the canvas bag toward Randy and felt something hard. He unzipped the bag and reached in. There was a jacket and, sure enough, a pistol. He could shoot Randy—in the foot, maybe, but down the road somewhere. No blood in the car. He slowly and quietly moved the car away from the curve. Damn, which way? Where was his map? The plan was to circle north and head south, but he needed to head southeast — on 421.

The doctor sat in his big seat in the study. Clearwater stuffed the envelopes into his pockets and asked for the keys to the Cadillac. The doctor pulled them from his pants pocket.

"Toss them on the couch," said Clearwater. He picked them up. "OK, stand up and walk in front of me." His bag was gone. Preacher had taken the bag to the car. Damn. They could have put silver in it. They still could. They would leave the doctor and Randy tied up. He needed his bag. In the kitchen he opened a silver chest and stuffed his pockets and shirtfront with knives, forks, and spoons.

They walked out onto the back porch — Clearwater behind the doctor. He looked for the Chrysler at the gate. He realized what had happened with the kind of delay one feels in seeing a tree fall far away and then hearing it. He strode quickly to the open gate and looked down to where the car had been parked. "That son of a bitch."

The doctor called out, "Randy. Randy?"

"He stole my car. My things." Anger was in him like icy winds.

The doctor was talking. "Randy couldn't steal—"

"The goddamn *Bible* salesman, not *Randy,* stole my car—and everything in it."

"Randy!" called the doctor, louder.

Clearwater looked at the doctor, thought it through. "Come in the garage here with me, Doctor. I, I need you to show me where the light switch is." His chin was beginning to tingle.

The boy couldn't remember how to get on Highway 421, unless if he crossed the railroad track, followed it, and then once out of town turned back across the track.

He had crossed the railroad track the second time and now saw a RESUME SAFE SPEED sign. He pressed on the gas pedal. He reached into the bag. He'd do what Clearwater was always talking about. He'd think through and plan exactly the best way to get shed of Randy. Randy was looking out the window. He pulled up the hem of his dress and put the gun in the waist of his pants, like in the cowboy movies. Tall pines lined each side of the highway as if leaning in from the top. He turned on the radio. Clearwater would come after him, but he'd never guess southeast. He pressed the gas pedal, watched the needle move to sixty, turned the radio dial and stopped it when he heard a familiar sound. It was that great speckled bird song. "Do you know who that is?" he asked Randy.

Randy turned and looked at the Bible salesman.

"That's Roy Acuff. That's 'The Great Speckled Bird,'" he said to the big eyes.

They were in a curve to the right—drifting over the middle line—when headlights appeared in their faces as if risen up from the ground. Preacher swerved right but couldn't avoid the side-swipe, which ricocheted the Chrysler like a glancing billiard ball. He saw the ditch coming, and just before he stomped the brakes he heard a loud tree-automobile collision somewhere behind him.

With some effort he got his door open. It made a loud scraping noise. He stood on the asphalt, his heart racing. He had to leave quickly. There was a bright moon lighting up the road in both directions. He opened the back door and grabbed his suitcase and valise. Randy's door was against the ditch bank; he was sliding across the front seat toward the steering wheel. Back down the road only one headlight was shining from the car that had hit the tree—shining upward at a sick angle like a spotlight. Smoke and dust drifted through the beam. He unbuttoned and stepped from the dress and threw it toward the ditch. Randy was out of the car and shuffling toward him.

He jumped the ditch, just out of Randy's reach and ran into the woods, stumbling, holding to his valise and suitcase, not feeling the briars through his pants. He fell, felt for the pistol, which was still there, got up and stumbled along in the moonlight until he burst into a field, his throat dry, and looked straight ahead, over a distant tree line and up into a full bright moon that bore into him like a lone headlight in a tunnel. He found a tree, sat down, leaned his back against it, and looked up at a gray white cloud running along, lit from behind.

He heard Randy coming. I'll just sit still, he thought. This is the place to wait and let him go by me.

He looked back toward the sounds. Where the hell did he get a flashlight? he wondered. Was that *Randy*? He moved to the side of the tree away from the flashlight, now shining here and there as if lighting up the entire woods. He pulled out the pistol, cocked the hammer, held it in his hand under his pants leg. The flashlight was beside him, then in front of him, shining in his eyes, right there in front of him so he could see nothing but the light.

"You made a big mistake, boy," said Clearwater. His voice sounded garbled somehow.

"I was coming back for you," said the boy. He heard a pistol hammer click. "Wait! Please. Just tell me about Roy Acuff. I just heard that song. Just tell me about what it was like. Tell me. just sit on that stump and tell me."

Clearwater looked into the face shining up at him, the pale face and red-rimmed eyes, lipstick, the eyebrows coming together. Where was that stump?

The boy pulled the trigger, saw flashes from both pistols, heard two shots boom, felt a bullet slam into the tree beside his head— it was as if he'd shot at himself. He fired three more times, then stood and fired again. The body lay still beside the lit flashlight. He looked backward, deep into himself, and couldn't think of who he was.

Clyde Edgerton is the author of nine novels, including *Walking Across Egypt* and *Lunch at the Piccadilly*. He teaches creative writing at UNC-Wilmington, where he lives with his wife, Kristina, and their children.

KRISTINA EDGERTON

*T*om *Franklin called me and said that he and William Gay were putting together an anthology of short stories that paid tribute to Flannery O'Connor. Would I write one? I said yes, and then started thinking about what do to. Two of my favorite characters in literature are the Bible salesman in "Good Country People," and the Misfit in "A Good Man Is Hard to Find." I decided if I could put those two characters together that would be fun. But that would be cheating. So I decided to create characters inspired by these two, and then to put them together in a* *story that would be, in a sense, a tribute to Flannery O'Connor. The result is "The Great Speckled Bird." After writing the story, I saw further dramatic possibilities with these two characters, so I wrote a novel. In the process of writing the novel I found that I had to change the characters and their relationships somewhat. The novel is called* The Bible Salesman.

BACK OF BEYOND

(from *Tin House*)

When Parson drove to his shop that morning, the sky was the color of lead. Flurries settled on the pickup's windshield, lingered a moment before expiring. A heavy snow tonight, the weatherman warned, and it looked to be certain, everything getting quiet and still, waiting. Even more snow in the higher mountains, enough to make many roads impassable. It would be a profitable day, for Parson knew they'd come to his pawnshop to barter before emptying every cold-remedy shelf in town. They would hit Wal-Mart first because it was cheapest, then the Rexall, and finally the town's three convenience stores, coming from every wayback cove and hollow in the county, because walls and windows could not conceal the smell of meth.

Parson pulled his jeep into the parking lot of the cinder block building with PARSON'S BUY AND SELL hung over the door. One of the addicts had wanted to sell him an electric portable sign last week, had it in his truck bed with a trash can filled with red plastic letters to stick on it. The man told Parson the sign would ensure potential customers noticed the pawnshop. "You found me easy enough," Parson replied. His watch read eight forty and the sign in the window said, "9:00 to 6:00 Tuesday through Saturday," but a gray decade-old Ford Escort had already nosed up to the building.

The car's windshield had been hit by something, a rupture in the glass spreading outward like a spiderweb. The gas cap a stuffed rag. A woman sat in the driver's seat. She could have been waiting ten minutes or ten hours.

Parson got out of his truck, unlocked the door, and cut off the alarm. He turned on the lights and walked around the counter, placed the loaded Smith & Wesson revolver on the shelf below the register. The copper bell above the sill tinkled.

The woman waited in the doorway, a wooden butter churn and dasher clutched in her arms. Parson had to hand it to them, they were getting more imaginative. Last week the electric sign and false teeth, the week before that four bicycle tires and a chiropractic table. Parson nodded for the woman to come on in. She set the churn and dasher on the table.

It's a antique," the woman said. "I seen one like it on TV and the fellow said it was worth a hundred dollars."

When the woman spoke Parson glimpsed the stubbed brown ruin inside her mouth. He could see her face now, sunken cheeks and eyes, furrows pruning the pale skin. He saw where the bones, impatient, poked at her cheeks and chin. The eyes glossy but alive, restless and needful.

"You better find that fellow then," Parson said. "A fool like that don't come around often."

"It was my great-grandma's," the woman said, nodding at the churn, "so it's near seventy-five years old." She paused. "I guess I could take fifty for it."

Parson looked the churn over, lifted the dasher and inspected it as well. An antiques dealer in Asheville might give him a hundred.

"Twenty dollars," Parson said.

"That man on TV said—"

"You told me," Parson interrupted. "Twenty dollars is what I'll pay."

The woman looked at the churn a few moments, then back at Parson.

"Okay," she said. She took the cash and stuffed the bills in her jeans. She did not leave.

"What?" Parson asked.

The woman hesitated, then raised her hands and took off her high school ring. She handed it to him, and Parson inspected it. "Class of 2000," the ring said.

"Ten," he said, laying the ring on her side of the glass counter.

She didn't try to barter this time but instead slid the ring across the glass as if the ring were a piece in a board game. She held her fingers on the metal a few moments before letting go and holding out her palm.

By noon he'd had twenty customers and almost all were meth addicts. Parson didn't need to look at them to know. The odor of it came in the door with them, in their hair, their clothes, a sour ammonia smell like cat piss. Snow fell steady now and his business began slacking off, even the manic needs of the addicted deferring to the weather. Parson was finishing his lunch in the back room when the bell sounded again. He came out and found Sheriff Hawkins waiting at the counter.

"So what they stole now, Doug?" Parson asked.

"Couldn't it be I just come by to see my old high school buddy?"

Parson placed his hands on the counter. "It could be, but I got the feeling it isn't."

"No," Hawkins said, smiling wryly. "In these troubled times there's not much chance to visit with friends and kin."

"Troubled times," Parson said. "But good for business, not just my business but yours."

"I guess that's a way of looking at it, though for me it's been too good of late."

Hawkins took a quick inventory of the bicycles and lawn mowers and chain saws filling the room's corners. Then he looked the room over again, more purposeful this time, checking behind the counter as well. The sheriff's brown eyes settled on the floor, where a shotgun lay amid other items yet to be tagged.

"That .410 may be what I'm looking for," the sheriff said. "Who brought it in?"

"I think you already know," Parson replied.

"Maybe, but I need confirmation."

"Danny." Parson handed the gun to the lawman without saying anything else.

Hawkins held the shotgun and studied the stock a moment. "My eyes ain't what they used to be, Parson, but I'd say them initials carved in it are SJ, not DP."

"That gun Steve Jackson's?"

"Yes, sir," the sheriff replied, laying the shotgun on the counter. "Danny took it out of Steve's truck yesterday. At least that's what Steve believed. Seems he was right."

"If I'd known it was Steve's, I'd not have taken it," Parson said. "I figured it came off the farm."

Hawkins picked the shotgun off the counter and held it in one hand, studying the weapon critically. He shifted it slightly, let his thumb rub the stock's varnished wood. "I'm going to take this back to Steve," he said. "I can talk him out of pressing charges."

"Don't do that as a favor to me," Parson said. "If his own daddy don't give a damn he's a thief, why should I?"

"How come you to think Ray doesn't care?" Hawkins asked.

"Because Danny's been bringing things to me from the farm for months. Ray knows where they're going. I called him three months ago and told him myself. He said he couldn't do anything about it."

"Doesn't look to be you're doing much about it either," the sheriff said. "I mean, you're buying from him, right?"

"If I don't he'll just drive down to Sylva and sell it there." Parson looked out at the snow, the parking lot empty but for his and Hawkins's vehicles. He wondered if any customers had decided not to pull in because of the sheriff's car. "You just as well go ahead and arrest him," Parson said. "You've seen enough of these meth addicts to know he'll steal something else soon enough."

"I didn't know he was on meth," Hawkins said.

"That's your job, isn't it," Parson replied, "to know such things?"

"There's too many of them to keep up with. This meth, it ain't like other drugs. Even cocaine and crack, at least those were expensive and hard to get. But this stuff, it's too easy." The sheriff looked out the window. "This snow's going to make for a long day, so I'd better get to it."

"So you're not going to arrest him?"

"No," Hawkins said. "He'll have to wait his turn. There's two dozen in line ahead of him. But you could do me a favor by giving him a call. Tell him this is his one chance, that next time I'll lock his ass up in jail. Tell him that." Hawkins pressed his lips together a moment, pensive. "Hell, he might even believe it."

"I'll tell him," Parson said, "but I'll do it in person."

Parson went to the window and watched as the sheriff backed out onto the two-lane and returned to the town's main drag. Snow stuck to the asphalt now, the jeep blanketed white. He'd watched Danny drive away the day before, the tailgate down and truck bed empty. Parson had known the truck bed would probably be empty when Danny headed out of town, no filled grocery bags or kerosene cans, because the boy lived in a world where food and warmth and clothing were no longer essentials. The only essentials were the packs of Sudafed in the passenger's seat as the truck disappeared back into the folds of the higher mountains, headed up into Chestnut Cove, what Parson's father had called the back of beyond, the place where Parson and his brother, Ray, had grown up.

He placed the pistol in his coat pocket and changed the OPEN sign to CLOSED. Once on the road, Parson saw the snow was dry, powdery, which would make the drive easier. He headed west and did not turn on the radio.

Except for two years in the army, Ray had lived his whole life in Chestnut Cove. He'd used his army pay to buy a farm adjacent to the one he'd grown up on and had soon after married Martha. Parson had joined the army as well but afterward went to Tuckasegee to live. When their parents had gotten too old to mend fences and feed livestock, plant and harvest the tobacco, Ray and Martha did it. Ray had never asked Parson to help, never expected him to, since he was twenty miles away in town. Parson had not been bitter when the farm was willed to the firstborn. Ray and Martha had earned it. By then Parson owned the pawnshop outright from the bank, had money enough. Ray and Martha sold their house and moved into the farmhouse, raised Danny and his three older sisters there.

Parson slowed as the road began a long curve around Brushy Mountain. The road soon forked and he went left. Another left and he was on a county road, poorly maintained because no wealthy Floridians had second homes on it. No guardrails. He met no other vehicle, because only a few people lived in the cove, had ever lived up here.

Parson parked beside Ray's truck and got out, stood a few moments before the homestead. He hadn't been up in nearly a year and supposed he should feel more than the burn of anger directed at his nephew. Some kind of nostalgia, but Parson couldn't summon it and if he had, then what for? Working his ass off in August tobacco fields, milking cows on mornings so cold his hands burned and reddened—the very things that had driven him away in the first place. Except for a thin ribbon of smoke unfurling from the chimney, the farm appeared forsaken. No lowing cattle huddled against the snow, no TV or radio playing in the front room or kitchen. Parson had never regretted leaving, and never more so than now, as his gaze moved from the rusting tractor and bailer to the sagging fences that held nothing in, settled on the shambling farmhouse itself, then turned toward the land between the barn and house.

Danny's battered blue and white trailer squatted in the pasture.

Parson's feet made a whisping sound as he went to deal with his nephew before talking to his brother and sister-in-law. No footprints marked the snow between house and trailer. Parson knocked on the flimsy aluminum door and when no one answered went in. No lights were on and Parson wasn't surprised when he flipped a switch and nothing happened. His eyes slowly adjusted to the room's darkness, and he saw the card table, on it a half dozen cereal boxes, some open, some not, a half gallon milk container, its contents frozen solid. The room's busted-out window helped explain why. Two bowls scabbed with dried cereal lay on the table as well. Two spoons. Parson made his way to the back room, seeing first the kerosene heater beside the bed, the wire wick's muted orange glow. Two closely lumped mounds rose under a pile of quilts. *Like they're already laid out in their graves,* Parson thought as he leaned over and poked the bigger form.

"Get up, boy," Parson said.

But it was Ray's face and torso that emerged, swaddled in an array of shirts and sweaters. Martha's face appeared as well. They seemed like timid animals disturbed in their dens. For a few moments Parson could only stare at them. After decades in the most cynical of professions, he was amazed that anything could still stun him.

"Why in the hell aren't you in the house?" Parson asked finally.

It was Martha who replied. "Danny, he's in there, sometimes his friends too." She paused. "It's just better, easier, if we're out here."

Parson looked at his brother. Ray was sixty-seven years old but he looked eighty, his mouth sunk in, skinny and feeble. His sister-in-law appeared a little better off, perhaps because she was a large, big-boned woman. But they both looked bad—hungry, weary, sickly. And scared. Parson could not remember his brother ever being scared, but he clearly was. Fear marked his face like something etched with a knife. Parson and his wife, DeAnne, had divorced before they'd had children. *Lucky for that,* Parson thought, for it had precluded any possibility of his ending up like this.

Martha had not been above lording her family over Parson in

the past, enough to where he'd made his visits to the farm rare and short. "You missed out not having any kids," she'd said to him more than once, words he'd recalled more than once when Danny pawned a chain saw or posthole digger or some other piece of the farm. It said much of how beaten down Martha appeared that Parson mustered no pleasure in recalling her words now. *You can't even call it forgiveness,* he thought.

He settled his eyes on the kerosene heater emitting its feeble warmth. "Yeah, it looks to be easier out here all right," he said.

Ray licked his cracked lips and then spoke, his voice raspy. "That stuff whatever you call it, has done made my boy crazy. He don't know nothing but a craving."

"It ain't his fault, it's the craving," Martha said, sitting up enough to reveal that she too wore layers of clothing. "Maybe I done something wrong raising him, petted him too much since he was my only boy. The girls always claimed I favored him."

"The girls been up here?" Parson asked. "Seen you like this?"

Martha shook her head. "They got their own families to look after," she said.

Ray's lower lip trembled. "That ain't it. They're scared to come up here."

Parson looked at his brother. He had thought this was going to be so much easier, a matter of twenty dollars, that and relaying the sheriff's threat. "How long you been out here, Ray?"

"I ain't sure," Ray replied.

Martha spoke. "Not more than a week."

"How long has the electricity been off?"

"Since October," Ray said.

"Is all you've had to eat on that table?"

Ray and Martha didn't meet his eyes.

A family photograph hung on the wall. Parson wondered when it had been put up, before or after Danny moved out. Danny was sixteen, maybe seventeen in the photo. Cocksure but also petulant, the expression of a young man who'd been indulged all his life. His family's golden child. Parson suddenly realized something.

"He's cashing your social security checks, isn't he?"

"It ain't his fault," Martha said. "It's the craving."

Parson still stood at the foot of the bed, Ray and Martha showing no indication of getting out. They looked like children waiting for him to turn out the light and leave so they could go to sleep. Pawnbrokers, like emergency room doctors and other small gods, had to absolve themselves of sympathy. That had never been a problem for Parson. As DeAnne had told him several times, he was a man incapable of understanding another person's heart. "Like you were given a shot years ago and inoculated," she had said that morning she left.

"I'll get your electricity turned back on," Parson told his brother. "Can you still drive?"

"I can drive," Ray said. "Only thing is, Danny uses that truck for his doings."

"That's going to change," Parson said.

"It ain't Danny's fault," Martha said again.

"Enough of it is," Parson said.

He went to the corner and lifted the kerosene can. Half-full.

"What you taking our kerosene for?" Martha asked, but Parson did not reply. He left the trailer and trudged back through the snow, the can heavy and awkward, his breath quick white heaves. Not so different from those mornings he'd carried a gallon pail of warm milk from barn to house, wanting to leave this place as far back in childhood as he could remember. *Inoculated.* Yet there was Ray, loving this land, never wanting to leave this cove.

Parson set the can on the lowered tailgate and perched himself on the hitched metal as well. He took the lighter and cigarettes from his coat pocket and stared at the house while he smoked. Kindling and logs brought from the woodshed littered the porch, no attempt to stack it.

It would be easy to do, Parson told himself. No one had stirred when he'd driven up and parked five yards from the front door, no one had even peaked out a window to see who it was. Why would they bother to move if he just stepped on the porch and moved around a bit, quietly soaked the logs and kindling with kerosene, and saved the last gallon for the back door? Hawkins would put it down as just another meth explosion caused by some punk who couldn't pass a tenth-grade chemistry class. And if others were in there, they were people quite willing to scare two old folks out of their home. No worse than setting fire to a woodpile infested with copperheads. Parson finished his cigarette and flicked it toward the house, a quick hiss as snow quenched the smoldering butt.

He eased off the tailgate and stepped onto the porch, tried the doorknob, and when it turned, stepped into the front room.

A dying fire glowed in the hearth. The room had been stripped of anything that could be sold, the only furnishing left a couch pulled up by the fireplace. Even wallpaper had been torn off a wall, perhaps in some belief that it too could be sold. The odor of meth infiltrated everything, seemed coated to the walls and floor.

Danny and a girl Parson did not know lay on the couch, a quilt thrown over them. Their clothes were worn and dirty and smelled as if lifted from a Dumpster. As Parson moved toward the couch he stepped over rotting sandwich scraps in paper sacks, candy wrappers, spills from soft drinks. If human shit had been on the floor he would not have been surprised.

"Who is he?" the girl asked Danny.

"A man who's owed twenty dollars," Parson said.

Danny sat up slowly, the girl as well, black stringy hair, flesh whittled away by the meth. Parson looked for something that might set her apart from the dozen or so similar women he saw each week. It took a few moments but he found one thing, a blue four-leaf clover tattooed on her forearm. Parson looked into her dead eyes and saw no indication luck had found her.

He turned to his nephew. "Got tired of stealing from your parents, did you?"

"What are you talking about?" Danny said. His eyes were light blue, similar to the girl's eyes in that they were bright but at the same time dead. A memory from elementary school came to Parson of colorful insects pinned and enclosed beneath glass.

"That shotgun you stole."

Danny smiled but kept his mouth closed. *Some vanity still left in him,* Parson mused, remembering how the boy had preened even as a child, a comb at the ready in his shirt pocket, nice clothes.

"I didn't figure him to miss it much," Danny said. "That gas station he owns does good enough business for him to buy another."

"You're damn lucky it's me telling you and not the sheriff, though he'll be up here before long, soon as the roads clear."

Danny looked at the dying fire as if he spoke to it, not Parson. "So why did you show up? I know it's not to warn me Hawkins is coming."

"Because I want my twenty dollars," Parson said.

"I don't have your twenty dollars," Danny said.

"Then you're going to pay me another way."

"And what's that?"

"By getting in the truck," Parson said. "I'm taking your sorry ass to the bus station. One-way ticket to Atlanta."

"What if I don't want to do that?" Danny said.

There had been a time the boy could have made that comment formidable, for he'd been broad-shouldered and stout, an all-county tight end, but he'd shucked off fifty pounds, the muscles melted away same as his teeth. Parson didn't even bother showing him the revolver.

"Well, you can wait here until the sheriff comes and hauls your worthless ass off to jail."

Danny stared at the fire. The girl reached out her hand, let it settle on Danny's forearm. The room was utterly quiet except for a few crackles and pops from the fire. No time ticking on the fireboard. Parson had bought the Franklin clock from Danny two months ago. He'd thought briefly of keeping it himself but had resold it to the antiques dealer in Asheville.

"If I get arrested then it's an embarrassment to you. Is that the reason?" Danny asked.

"The reason for what?" Parson said.

"That you're acting like you give a damn about me."

Parson didn't reply, and for almost a full minute no one spoke. It was the girl who finally broke the silence.

"What about me?" she asked.

"I'll buy you a ticket or let you out in Asheville," Parson said. "But you're not staying here."

"We can't go nowhere without our drugs," the girl said.

Parson nodded at her. "Get them then."

She went into the kitchen and came back with a brown paper bag, its top half folded over and crumpled.

"Hey," she said when Parson took it from her.

"I'll give it back when you're boarding the bus," he said.

Danny looked to be contemplating something and Parson wondered if he might have a knife on him, possibly a revolver of his own, but when Danny stood up there was no handle jutting from his pocket.

"Get your coats on," Parson said. "You'll be riding in the back."

"It's too cold," the girl said.

"No colder than that trailer," Parson said.

Danny paused as he put on a denim jacket. "So you went there first."

"Yes," Parson said.

A few moments passed before Danny spoke.

"I didn't make them go out there," he said. "They got scared by some guys that were here last week." Danny sneered, something Parson suspected the boy had probably practiced in front of a mirror. "I check on them more than you do," he said.

"Let's go," Parson said. He dangled the paper bag in front of Danny and the girl, then took the revolver out of his pocket. "I've got both of these things, just in case you think you might try something."

They went outside. The snow still fell hard, the way back down to the county road now only a white absence of trees. Danny and the girl stood by the truck's tailgate, but they didn't get in.

Danny nodded at the paper bag in Parson's left hand. "At least give us some so we can stand the cold."

Parson opened the bag, took out one of the baggies. He had no idea if one was enough for the both of them or not. He threw the packet into the truck bed and watched Danny and the girl climb in after it. *No different than you'd do for two hounds with a dog biscuit,* Parson thought, shoving the kerosene can farther inside and hitching the tailgate.

He got in the truck and cranked the engine, drove slowly down the drive. Once on the county road he turned left and began the fifteen-mile trip to Sylva. Danny and the girl huddled against the back window, their heads and his separated by half an inch of glass. Their proximity made the cab feel claustrophobic, especially when he heard the girl's muffled crying. Parson turned on the radio, the one station he could pick up promising a foot of snow by nightfall. Then a song he hadn't heard in thirty years, Earnest Tubb's "I'm Walking the Floor Over You." Halfway down Brushy Mountain the road made a quick veer and plunge. Danny and the girl slid across the bed and banged against the tailgate. A few moments later, when the road leveled out, Danny pounded against the window with his fist, but Parson didn't look back. He just turned up the radio.

At the bus station, Danny and the girl sat on a bench while Parson bought the tickets. The Atlanta bus wasn't due for an hour so Parson waited across the room from them. The girl had a busted lip, probably from sliding into the tailgate. She dabbed her mouth with a Kleenex, then stared a long time at the blood on the tissue. Danny was agitated, hands restless, constantly shifting on the bench as though unable to find a comfortable position. He finally got up and came over to where Parson sat, stood before him.

"You never liked me, did you?" Danny said.

Parson looked up at the boy, for though in his twenties Danny was still a boy, would die a boy, Parson believed.

"No, I guess not," Parson said.

"What's happened to me. It ain't all my fault," Danny said.

"I keep hearing that," Parson said.

"There ain't no good jobs in this county, you can't make a living farming no more. If there'd been something for me, a good job I mean."

"I hear there's lots of jobs in Atlanta," Parson said. "It's booming down there, so you're headed to the land of no excuses."

"I don't want to go down there." Danny paused. "I'll die there."

"What you're using will kill you here same as Atlanta. At least down there you won't take your momma and daddy with you."

"You've never cared much for them before, especially Momma. How come you to care now?"

Parson thought about the question, mulled over several possible answers. "I guess because no one else does."

When the bus came, Parson walked with them to the loading platform. He gave the girl the bag and the tickets, then watched the bus groan out from under the awning and head south. There would be several stops before Atlanta, but Danny and the girl would stay aboard because of a promised two hundred sent via Western Union. A promise Parson would not keep.

The Winn-Dixie shelves were emptied of milk and bread but enough of all else remained to fill four grocery bags. Parson stopped at Steve Johnson's gas station and filled the kerosene can. Neither man mentioned the shotgun now reracked against the pickup's back window. The return trip to Chestnut Cove was slower, more snow on the roads, the visibility less as what dim light the day had left drained into the high mountains to the west. Dark by five, he knew, and it was already past four. After the truck slid a second time, spun, and stopped precariously close to a drop-off, Parson stayed in first or second gear. A trip of thirty minutes in good weather took him an hour.

When he got to the farmhouse, Parson took a flashlight from the dash, carried the groceries into the kitchen. He brought the kerosene into the farmhouse as well, then walked down to the trailer and went inside. The heater's metal wick still glowed orange. Parson cut it off so the metal would cool.

He shone the light on the bed. They were huddled together,

Martha's head tucked under Ray's chin, his arms enclosing hers. They were asleep and seemed at peace. Parson felt regret in waking them and for a few minutes did not. He brought a chair from the front room and placed it by the foot of the bed. He waited. Martha woke first. The room was dark and shadowy but she sensed his presence, turned and looked at him. She moved to see him better and Ray's eyes opened as well.

"You can go back to the house now," Parson said.

They only stared back at him.

"He's gone," Parson said. "And he won't come back. There will be no reason for his friends to come either."

Martha stirred now, sat up in the bed. "What did you do to him?"

"I didn't do anything," Parson said. "He and that girlfriend wanted to go to Atlanta and I drove them to the bus station."

Martha didn't look like she believed him. She got slowly out of the bed and Ray did as well. They put on their shoes, then moved tentatively to the trailer's door, seemingly with little pleasure. They hesitated.

"Go on," Parson said. "I'll bring the heater."

Parson went and got the kerosene heater. He stooped and lifted it slowly, careful to use his legs instead of his back. Little fuel remained in it, so it wasn't heavy, just awkward. When he came into the front room, his brother and sister-in-law still stood inside the door.

"Open the door," he told Ray, "and help me get down the steps with this thing."

The two men navigated the heater down the steps and Parson carried it the rest of the way. Once inside the farmhouse he set it near the hearth, filled the tank, and turned it on. He and Ray gathered logs and kindling off the front porch and got a good flame going in the fireplace. The flume was not drawing as it should. By the time Parson had adjusted it a smoky odor filled the room, but that was a better smell than the meth. The three of them sat on the couch and unwrapped plastic wrap from the deli sandwiches,

Parson eating one as well. They did not speak even when they'd finished, just stared at the hearth as flame shadows trembled on the walls. Parson thought what an old human feeling this must be, how ten thousand years ago people would have done the same thing on a cold night, would have eaten, then settled before the fire, looked into it and found peace, knowing they'd survived the day and now with fire and food in their bellies could rest.

Martha began snoring softly and Parson grew sleepy as well. He roused himself, looked over at his brother, whose eyes still watched the fire. Ray did not look sleepy, just lost in thought.

Parson got up and stood before the hearth, let the heat soak into his clothes and skin before going out into the cold. He took the revolver from his pocket and gave it to Ray.

"In case any of Danny's friends give you any trouble," Parson said. "I'll get your power turned back on in the morning."

Martha awoke with a start. For a few moments she seemed not to know where she was.

"You ain't thinking of driving back to Tuckasegee tonight?" Ray asked. "The roads will be dangerous."

"I'll be all right. My jeep can handle them."

"I still wish you wouldn't go," Ray said. "You ain't slept under this roof for near forty years. That's too long."

"Not tonight," Parson said.

Ray shook his head. "I never thought things could ever get like this," he said. "The world, I just don't understand it no more."

Martha spoke. "Did Danny say where he'd be staying?"

"No," Parson said, and turned to leave.

"I'd rather be in that trailer tonight and knowing he was in this house," Martha said. "Knowing where he was, if he's alive or dead." She spoke to Parson's back as he reached for the door knob. "You had no right."

Parson walked out to the jeep. It took a few tries but the engine turned over and he made his way down the drive. Only flurries glanced the windshield now. Parson drove slowly and several times had to stop and get out to find the road amid the white blankness.

He finally gave up after a mile and stopped the jeep. The clock on the dashboard read one thirty. Parson cut off the engine, wrapped himself in the quilt Danny and the girl had huddled under earlier. The engine might not start again, he knew, but to drive farther would mean getting stuck in a ditch or tumbling off a cliff. He spent the night there, turning the heater on occasionally, letting warm air take hold before cutting it off and drowsing again. When the morning came he drove on, making his slow way back to Tuckasegee, back home.

Ron Rash is the author of three novels, three books of poetry, and three collections of stories. His latest novel, *Serena,* will be published in fall 2008. He has won NEA fellowships in poetry and fiction, an O. Henry Award, and the James Still Award from the Fellowship of Southern Writers. He teaches at Western Carolina University.

MARK HASKETT

*M*eth is the most sinister drug I know of—inexpensive, easily made, incredibly addictive—and it has been especially rampant in rural regions such as southern Appalachia, the place where all my work is set. My stories and novels almost always start with a single image, and "Back of Beyond" started with a man driving back to where he'd grown up. I knew he didn't want to go, but I also knew he felt he had no choice. For me, the story is most concerned with the obligations of family, and how those obligations can bring about salvation as well as destruction.

Merritt Tierce

SUCK IT

(from *Southwest Review*)

Suck it is Danny's favorite phrase, which he employs as a general greeting. Sometimes he inflects it as a question: *Suck it?* Directed at a female, it might often be appended: *Suck it, sista.* This is only for staff members, of course; our patrons will more likely get an egregiously enthusiastic *What's up, my brother?* accompanied by a handshake/backslap combination. (If you're one of his friends you might receive a more sincere *What's up, my fucking brother?*) Egregious enthusiasm is Danny's trademark—he can transmit his buzz and momentum to anyone at will. This is called charisma. His charisma—any charisma, I suppose—is entirely performance, yet in being never more or less than a performer he somehow remains endearingly genuine. He might embrace a beautiful woman, kiss her on both cheeks, escort her to the bar—*What do you like, sister, what do you want? Cosmo? Martini? Chardonnay? Tequila? Tongue kiss? That's what I thought—Ethan, get my lover here a glass of Mer-Soleil, thank you brother—Good to see you, love—*and as soon as he spins around to answer your question mutter *Dirty whore, suck it.*

Almost every question must be brought to Danny, because it's his restaurant. These people want a booth instead of a table, ask Danny. You want Friday off this week, ask Danny. The guy said his steak looked more medium than rare and he wants a different one, better check with Danny. Music's too loud, lights are too low, the room's too cold, tell Danny. You want to go to Silver City, ask Danny—he's king there and she'll fuck you for real in a back room at his word. You want tickets to the game or an eight o'clock reservation at Tei Tei, which doesn't take eight o'clock reservations—Danny will work it out for you. You need a bump, ask Danny—but not until after service, he never starts till almost everybody's out of the building.

Most nights he gets it from the undocumented Mexican and Salvadoran bussers and dishwashers. The Mexicans are usually from Guanajuato, some from Yucatán—the Yucas have a reputation for being lazy, the Guanajuatans for being easygoing and hardworking. Sometimes on his day off Danny comes up to the restaurant, ostensibly to check on us and grace the regulars with his presence like a politician, but he's also there to pick something up. He'll say to me *Pablo working? Get me sixty?* and I'll say *Okay boss.* I pick up a stack of dirty plates and silverware and head into the dishroom, where I unload them and then hold up three fingers for only Pablo, who is polishing Bordeaux glasses, to see. He nods with his eyes. A few minutes later I'll come back to wash my hands or run some stock out to the line and he'll discreetly slip me a tiny square package, three twenty-bags wrapped up tight in a piece of paper towel. I'll wait for Danny to come find me, or sometimes he'll ask me to put it under a Le Volte bottle. The Le Volte is a Chianti in the uppermost corner of the French/Italian wine bin wall; I'm too short to reach it, so I have to climb up on a chair without being seen. If he pays me I pass the three twenty-dollar bills along to Pablo—back in the spring he used to ask me to front it for him and bring it to him somewhere, like Zaza or the alley behind the Stoneleigh P. I rarely have money I don't need to spend immediately on something or other, so sometimes I had to borrow from someone else to get it for him. The first few times he gave me extra cash when he paid me back, which I think was supposed to seal me into the whole thing, but since I quit using I've just been asking the bussers for it. They know it's for him, and somehow he knows I don't want to front it anymore, so he settles up with them when he's back in the restaurant. I hate this arrangement, because I'm both too timid and too interested in protecting my income to beg off, and the bussers are barely making a living as it is. They live in one-bedroom apartments with five other people and share broken-down cars and every one of them has a morning job in a different restaurant.

Lately they've been coming down harder on me. There's something wrong with Pablo's eyes; he has kind of a flat face, like you see in the pictures of fetal alcohol syndrome victims, and his pupils are strange. The top half of each is a cloudy blue, and the bottom half is an opaque dark, so when he stares at me and says *Tellen, tellen Danny que necesita pagar, tellen Danny he pay, okay? Ten. Diez.* I feel disarmed by his aberrant, unreadable gaze. He tells me in Spanish, then in English, then he holds up how many fingers to make sure I get it.

My friend Calvin says they're going to start cutting it worse for him, that even though he's their boss they won't tolerate it. We agree that he makes too much money to do it like this, that if he wants it he should just pay for it. Either give me the cash or get right with them straightaway.

Suck it is his favorite, but not by much—we joke that he has Tourette's syndrome, and I wouldn't be surprised if it were true. He might be looking over the seating chart for the night, trying to puzzle out how he can possibly fit another six-top in at seven-thirty, and run through a litany like *suck it shit fuck cock'n'balls shit fuck fuck fuck fuck suck it.* He might hang up the phone after sweetly giving a stranger detailed directions and declare *filthy cunt whore suck my cock may I help you?*

Every night he makes snap public-relations decisions with a ferocity that is unquestionable and an accuracy that is never less than dead-on. He is a fast-talking Italian fox from Yonkers who can get his way with anyone, can make any Mur[1] feel like a VIP, and thus

---

1. *Mur* is a term that denotes any individual "we don't know." A *Mur* is just a regular customer, no one deserving of special treatment. This fairly benign significance is the standard, though it might also be used more pejoratively, to indicate that the individual is a nobody, a chump, a tool—all of

has been the general manager of a multimillion-dollar-grossing fine-dining steakhouse since he was twenty-four.

However he is blowing his crystalline mind four square inches of shittily cut cocaine at a time, night after night. The urgency in his voice when he calls up the restaurant on his days off to ask me to get it for him—well, last night all he said was *Four. Now.*

Danny's appetite is the spirit of the place: the excesses of an entire microculture are concentrated in his one body. We are accustomed to businessmen arriving with clients whom they want to impress, we are accustomed to those businessmen spending our weekly incomes on several bottles of fine wine alone, we are accustomed to a per-person average that can linger fatly around three hundred dollars. We are accustomed to Danny's binges, his unbelievable gluttony. He routinely fucks women in the restaurant—once there was a pink lacy thong on the floor by the trash can in the office on a Sunday, and he came up with Rob and some other guy who looked exactly like Rob. They were already out of control with their high and they were there for me to get them some more. Danny told them my name and they said *Ooooh!* and looked at me as if they cherished me, because he must have told them earlier who was going to help them along. While they were crashing around the office, laughing and pushing and glowing and shrieking, Danny told me and the wine manager Dave how he had fucked this one girl by the trash can last night (above the thong on the floor, he re-enacted his thrusting), and how he then

---

which in turn signify primarily an absence of wealth. Example: "Honey-love, would you please take those *Murs* by the candles to 27 [table number], and that's with Chris [server]." I once inquired about the etymology of *Mur,* and Danny said that he and his buddy Rob, who is the general manager at our sister restaurant Il Castello, used to know a guy named Murray when they were kids growing up in Yonkers. Murray was a social misfit, soft or naïve in some unforgivable way that inspired them to refer to any such person as a Murray, and later simply a *Mur.*

fucked her friend in the same place. I guess that one wasn't wearing underwear, or kept it on.

There is a kind of partying undertaken by people of my age and station on birthdays, or on other momentous occasions such as the losing of a job. The kind of partying that leaves one wrecked for days, and sometimes literally close to death. The kind of partying that concludes with the unconscious body of the individual being arranged by any remaining friends in such a way that it can be trusted not to aspirate vomit. This is the kind of partying that lingers so badly it causes one to leave off for another year or so. This is also the kind of partying that Danny rips through several times a week.

He was in the hospital last month. No one could remember a day when Danny didn't come in—in seven years he's never been out sick. He's been in all fucked up, for sure, but he maintains better than most people who aren't fucked up, so a hush came over us when they said he was in the hospital. They said it was something with his stomach, that he'd had unbearable pains and his dad convinced his friend Bobby to drag him to the emergency room, where they gave him great quantities of morphine. I asked my friend Calvin, who knows everything I know about Danny and more, if, when one got to the emergency room like that, one told the doctors that one was severely addicted to cocaine and alcohol. He was out only the one day; the next day he was back, drinking flavored water instead of the four or five cokes he habitually downs during the shift. On the third day he had returned to his usual pace. I saw him in the back talking to Pablo.

He is the chief exhibitionist in the house. Our ladderback chairs have a decorative hole in the top rung, and late one afternoon I came around the corner of the bar and saw he'd stuck his cock through the hole there. Just to shock me or anyone else who walked by. Somehow he knows which girls can handle this and which can't.

Other guys imitate him sometimes. Once Big John told me that he let his dick hang out underneath his apron all night, and because he's about 6'3" when he was standing at his tables his junk would rest on the tabletop, hidden behind the apron. Then last Sunday I was in the office before the shift started, talking to Rich, the maître d'. Vegas John walked in to ask me if he could pay me to do his alcohol seller-server recertification for him. I said yes, so he was writing down his information for me, and behind his back Rich unzipped his pants and pulled it out. He wadded it up in his hand and waited for Vegas John to turn around. But before Vegas turned around, Anna walked in the door of the office. I don't know how Rich did it fast enough, but he covered it with his hands as if he just had his hands in his lap. The real reason she didn't see it probably owes more to the fact that she would never expect to see it than Rich's expediency.

They call her the church lady because she's devout and attends Dallas Theological Seminary. She has a virginal seriousness about her, an inability to offer corruptions that excludes her from much of what passes for humor in the restaurant. She's young and very sincere. She seems fragile to me in a way that I used to be fragile and I treat her a bit coldly for reminding me of it. She'd need a deep and abiding context for sex, and I'd secretly like to need one too, but I tried to fuck that out of myself. An effort my restaurant obliged.

Danny and his roommate like to fuck the same women. Joe Ambrogetti is the Cuban-Italian chef at Il Castello. He is short, bronze, and beautiful, and though he's only thirty-four, the stubble atop his round head is pigeon-colored. His full lips hold still underneath a gaze that's pruriently curious, and a tattooed sun circumscribes his navel. One Saturday night I sucked him off at the bottom of the back stairs behind Cosimo, the nightclub affiliated with our restaurant. I was there only because one of the owners, Mr. Michael Lissandri, brought me over from the steak house in his Porsche; it was Mike himself who got me the job in February.

Lissandri philandered. But first—he came into the Sunrise Café, one of the two restaurants I was working in that year, a few mornings a week for breakfast. We fought over him, whoever else was on the breakfast shift and I, because he always tipped fifteen dollars, which worked out to be 160 percent of his nine-dollar tab. He ate steel-cut organic oatmeal with no brown sugar and soy milk on the side, followed by four egg whites scrambled with spinach and tomatoes. He drank water only, with a straw. He didn't say much to us and always had the paper with him. He was a native New Yorker and Mets fan; I think he read nothing but the sports section. Often he talked and fast-talked on his mobile phone all during his breakfast.

When Jamie started waiting on him he put the paper down. She was new, a yoga instructor from Woodstock, in town to save money by living with her folks so she could take a trip to India to develop her practice. Mike liked her—we all did, she radiated bliss and vigor. He flirted with her and told her she ought to come over to his restaurant, he'd set her up in the bar over there. She turned him down because she didn't want to work nights, but she was recently divorced and more than ready to embrace her new freedom, so we wondered how he was in bed, if she should try to go out or get in with him.

One Sunday Mike came in with his sometime companion, Laura, at the peak of brunch service. The Sunrise Café was not a well-run restaurant and as the strongest server I often took six or seven tables at once. From ten AM till about one in the afternoon I'd feel like I was continuously on the precarious edge of a sheer food-service cliff. What heroics I performed to get people their fucking brunch. Mike and Laura sat down on the patio that morning—I had never seen him in on the weekend, or even during the volume part of any weekday. I already had a half-dozen booths in the lanai going, but as I flew past them he said *Can you take care of us here?* I said *Absolutely.* I rang his food in and miraculously it was on the table five minutes later. That day he left me twenty dollars, a raise.

The following Tuesday I woke up and knew he'd be coming in. (I have a sense, which my daughter has also, about some things; usually about insignificant things. Once I decided in the shower to wear this purple shirt—I visualized it and she heard me somehow. She came to me in the bathroom and said she wanted to pick out my shirt. I looked into her eyes, which are the pure glittering blue of a sky far removed from any inhabited place, and thought about my purple shirt. She went to my closet and I followed. She reached up above her head and grabbed its sleeve.)

That morning I woke up in my shithole apartment in the warren of Latino complexes near Park Lane and Greenville Avenue. Black mold on one wall and in six months I had never cooked a meal there because it would have seemed de facto contaminated. I woke up and knew Mike would be coming in, so with my Sunrise Café T-shirt I put on some makeup and my grandmother's lapis bead necklace. I didn't usually bother with makeup at 6 AM, but I wanted a different life. I wanted to ask him soon, before the memory of my Sunday service dissipated.

When I dropped the check I said *I have a question for you.*

Okay, he said, and sat back. I said *I was wondering if you had any openings in your restaurant.* He said *Sure, I'll hire you. Come in on Friday, I'll tell Danny to get you going.*

Easy as that.

So after I had been there a month I guess he decided he wanted to try me out, and on a Saturday night he put his hand on my elbow and said *I heard you were gonna buy me a drink at Cosimo.* I said *Oh?* He said *Come with me.* I told the closing manager that Mike wanted me to go with him, and I was abruptly granted amnesty from sidework, which didn't exactly do much for my standing with the rest of the waitstaff. I got into Mike's Boxster and he told me I had to take off my vest and tie before we went in, so I left them in his car, along with my phone. At the club he schmoozed Dallas's most expensive, meticulously produced women, periodically coming back over to bump against me in my dirty dark gray button-down work shirt. When the lights went up at last call, he was gone, my phone and uniform with him. I don't know if he ditched me because he found something better—likely—or because he saw me with Joe—also likely. It was several weeks before I ended up at his palatial Highland Park house.

While he was stroking the glamorous ones I was meeting Joe. He opened his fly in the middle of the dance floor and let his penis hang out underneath his shirt, which concealed it, though not completely. It was an interview. It was a question about me, which I answered by grabbing it. The music thrummed so loudly he had to say in my ear *What are you doing later?* I said *What are you doing now?*

We went out the back door and down the stairs. At the bottom of the stairs he held his beer in one hand and took mine with the other. I went down on him and got him off before three minutes had passed. We went back upstairs and he told me his phone number, which I remembered and borrowed a phone to call when I found myself stranded at 2 AM.

I took a cab to his and Danny's condo. Inside we did lines and fucked. Ambrogetti is the only guy I know who can fuck on coke. Everybody else it makes limp. The worst is, they're horny and limp. They want you to work hard on it but it never responds. I stayed up all night with Joe and Danny and two other guys who took turns with me.

And so on. In about three months' time I had sex with approximately thirty different men, who worked for or patronized my steak house, the bar next door, Il Castello, and Cosimo. Three managers, one owner, one sous-chef, one busser, one bartender, a dozen servers and as many customers, the latter group including a preponderance of surgeons and athletes. They began to say about me *She don't play* and *She's for real.* They meant *She's not like other girls—if you want to fuck her you can, just say so.* Once I was turning my cashout in, getting ready to leave for the night, and a server I hadn't yet been with asked me if he could buy me a beer next door. I said *Do you want to fuck?* He chuckled, taken aback, and said *No, I just want to buy you a beer. You know, hang out and talk and stuff, that's all.* I said *Oh. No, that's okay. Thanks though.* In the days afterward I heard this story repeated while people were folding napkins or polishing silverware, and it became a totemic tale about me that people distributed to new servers.

Calvin was my confessor—every afternoon I'd tell him about the new ones and spare no detail, be it of ugliness or danger. He would call me out, question my judgment, show me a worry I wanted to feel for myself. I didn't hide from Calvin how much I pretended. Pretended to like it, pretended to want it, pretended to have orgasms. He didn't understand and I couldn't explain. It had something to do with love and something to do with grief. It was just this: I'd be down on the floor sometimes, picking up fallen chunks of crab cake near some diamond broker's shoe, with my apron and my crumber and my *yes, sir, certainly, right away,* and I'd feel impaled by the sight and feel of the half-eaten crabmeat because it wasn't his fine sandy hair and it wasn't that place on her shoulder, right up against her neck, that smells like sunlight. *I am not a mother,* I'd think as I walked to the trash can. *You can fuck a lot of people,* Calvin would say to me, *and still enjoy yourself. Make it about you, about pleasure. At least make it safe.* But it wasn't about pleasure; it was about the opposite of pleasure. It was about abandoning myself because I had abandoned them. It was about punishment and exile: some kinds of pain make fine antidotes to others. So when they gave me their numbers and they were old and I'd seen them with hookers, I said yes.

And so on. One rainy night in April Danny took me into the office—he had to kick another manager out with a look—and bent me over the desk. My head knocked the phone off its cradle. He said *I think Joe's waiting for you in the Sterling Room.* I went into the Sterling Room and Joe bent me over. Joe went back to his date in the bar, and later she was so drunk she let him fuck her at the host stand. All the customers were gone, but Justin and I watched. Andy Vanderveer took a picture with his camera phone. That was one of my highest-grossing shifts, too—while I was getting fucked by the general manager and his best friend I had probably twenty-five covers running in the bar. I think I made around six hundred dollars that night. After Joe fucked his date I carried her out to the car. I'm not a big woman — I weigh about 115 pounds and I'm 5'5". I was wearing a cocktail dress and heels, but I picked her up in my arms like a baby and put her in the front seat. Her name was Indica, a breed of marijuana plant.

When I'd puff it was so much easier to get down. I used to imagine a small tribe of aborigines living inside me, representative en masse of my true identity, and I always knew they thought me reckless whenever I'd end up in some dark place with some feral soul. I liked to smoke them out, to puff and puff until I got them all up in the hills so I could do whatever I was doing and they'd be unaware. For example, the ex-pro who stood almost seven feet tall and came into the bar in May. His enormous cock was the size of a rolling pin and not nearly as domesticated. He measured me in the restaurant: when I delivered his salad he said *Whyntcha sit here fo a minute* and pulled me down on his lap. I guess he judged my ass adequate and we met later at Zaza, where I slammed determinedly the shot he bought me, to demonstrate that I was not afraid of whatever debasement awaited. He noted this and nodded to the bartender for another as he said *Like a champ, huh? Baby have one more, it'll help.* In the corner of a dark parking lot we lit a blunt for more help. Eventually I felt that haze come between me and the natives, the little people inside, so I was separated from their judgments and they were protected from my actions for a while. He said *What's up. You okay? Ready? I'm 'onna give it to you.* Inside the truck he fucked me in the ass, and his cock took up so much room in me it seemed logistically impossible that he'd done it. Like if you heard a school bus drove into a pup tent.

That could have been the last. After that one I wanted to say to my indigenous selves *This is fine, here's good, this is far enough. We'll camp here for the night and make our ascent in the morning.* But I didn't, and one June night at the bar next door Brendan pimped me out. He told me to go outside with his friend James. We got into my car and James told me to suck his dick. What reluctance I felt at the sight of his slack penis flopped over on his thigh. (By that time the natives didn't linger. They just slipped out the back of me quick and let the fire door slam.) When it got hard he wanted to fuck, so I got in the passenger seat underneath him. There were servers and kitchen guys in the parking lot drinking after work and I'm sure they all saw the car rocking. I was thinking it might be over soon when the passenger door opened and Brendan stood there, watching his friend fuck me. He got right down in my face and poured a Modelo Especial all over my head and neck. He said *That's right you like it you're such a slut. He's fucking you good isn't he.* I said *Shut the door Brendan* and wiped beer out of my eyes while James continued to fuck as if he were oblivious. Brendan slapped my cheek and said *Shut up shut the fuck up.* I said *Okay* and stared at him impassively. James fucked. Brendan opened the back door of the car so he could reach me better because the seat was reclined. He poured beer on me and hit my face and called me a bitch and hit my face, and I thought about my children sleeping in their bunk beds half an hour away. I wondered who was in the top bunk tonight and which pajamas they were wearing. After James got out of me and out of the car I quit using drugs and started parking in front of the restaurant so that when my shift was over I wouldn't have to walk past anyone who might offer me a beer, a drag, or a bump, or tell me they wanted their duck sicked.

Yesterday Danny walked through the mother station—what we call the area in the back where we make tea and coffee and prep bread baskets—singing *Fuckin shiiiiiiiit, fuckin shiiiiiiiiit* to the tune of the *Rocky* theme. He went into the employee bathroom, where he shaves every day before service while conferring with one or the other of his inner circle. When he came out he said, as he adjusted his tie, *Fuckin suck my balls, bitches. I'm starvin.*

He strides lankily through the main dining room around 5 PM every day, half-dressed in his suit trousers and a Yankees T-shirt. He sees everything. He can tell if you're chewing gum from all the way across the cavernous dining room, which we keep so dark we have to give the guests flashlights to read the menu. He hates it when you don't make sure there's enough room to work around your tables—at the height of dinner service sometimes you have only six inches of space between chair backs, and the path from the kitchen line to the tables in the back becomes labyrinthine if not unnavigable. Danny will walk past your five-top and say *Sister-love, would you please scoot this fucker a cunt-hair to the right so we don't dump mac-n-cheese all over the fat-ass in seat two?*

Miguel Loera will be sending out the mac-n-cheese when dinner service starts, but right now he's talking to one of the other servers about Chivas, the fútbol team favored and followed by most of our kitchen staff. Miguel runs the kitchen line for Chef. He is a magician, he never fucks up. He calls me Maestra, because I sometimes wear *lentas* that make me look bookish. I call him Miguelito or Maestro. He always leaves the second button on his chef's coat unbuttoned, for luck. When I first see him in the afternoon as I walk past the kitchen I'll catch his eye and pat my heart, where that button rests on his coat, in a gesture of solidarity. Yesterday he asked me if I had a good time with my family for Easter. *Did you find eggs?* he asked. *You kids look for little huevos?* I said *Yes, we looked for little huevos. Did you look for eggs?* I asked. *No,* he said, *I no look. Ah,* I said, *but did someone look for your little huevos? Yes,* he said with a grin, *someone find my little huevos and they eat them.*

When he calls me to run food he always says *Maestra, don't hate me, you take one mash and one mush to twenty-three please.* Or *Maestra, ¿sabes que te amo, verdad?, I do anyting for you, just do this one poquito ting for me please.* Sometimes he sneaks me a crab cocktail at the end of the night because he knows I love it, the tender jumbo lump crabmeat lightly dressed with lemon and parsley, a bit of cocktail sauce on the side.

Often the Mexicans ask me if I am *enojada,* or *¿Porque estas Mari?* they wonder. *¿Que te molesta, Mariquita?* It's because I'm perpetually lost in thought and wear a sunken, anxious face. I say *No, I'm not mad. I'm not sad either. Nothing's bothering me.* Miguel asks me *Maestra, what are you tinking about? He doesn't love you anymore?* I say *He never loved me.* Miguel tells me that last year the woman he loved was pregnant with twins, his first children. For no discernible reason she decided to have an abortion and she left him. He tells me he couldn't work, he would cry while he was running the line every day, every night he would get so drunk. He kept trying to quit but Danny wouldn't let him. He says to me *And now, Maestra, I'm fine. See? Look at me. I want to die then. But now—what can you do? Stop tinking about it, tinking is no good for you.* I say *Okay, Maestro, claro, you're right. No mas thinking.*

He's right, it's important to buck up every night and breathe deeply and be happy for the people so they'll want to believe you when you call the $140 Kobe filet the best beef in the world and promise it will melt in their mouths. You have to stay bright to get them on a bottle of Caymus or Cakebread, you can't be lurking in the back of your melancholy head. Sometimes I think this is why Danny says *Suck my balls* whenever I walk past him—it's spoken with the utmost affection and the utmost defiance. When he says *Suck it* he's saying *It's a circus, honey-love, so fuck those motherfuckers.* And when my retort is *Get it out* I'm saying *Here we are being hard and relentlessly dazzling in spite of whatever shit.* We are saying to each other *If you have an affliction, any remorse or anguish, eat it, drink it, snort it, fuck it, use it, suck it, kill it.*

————————

Merritt Tierce lives in Dallas, where she works as a legal assistant for a class-action securities-fraud law firm. At night she turns into a server at a fine-dining steak house, and she also invests many hours as the president of a local nonprofit reproductive rights organization. She is currently cowriting a play about abortion that will debut in Dallas in 2009. "Suck It" was her first published story.

*T*he fancy restaurant where I work attracts a parade of celebrities, libertines, sharks, and charlatans who get all the attention in real life, so I wrote an upstairs/downstairs story to restore balance in the universe. A friend of mine once told me he'd been advised caution when dating a woman who worked at a restaurant, because "in restaurants everyone sleeps with everyone and everyone's addicted," which is how the downstairs came to be so dirty. "Suck It" imagines the front-of-house burlesque as only a backdrop for the back-of-house gothic, where all kinds of unseen people work out their own appetites for salvation and self-destruction.

R. T. Smith

WRETCH LIKE ME

(from *Virginia Quartely Review*)

In the hospitality of war we left them their dead to remember us by.
—Archilochus

*T*he soldier kneeling in the wet gully has ceased his rocking and sobbing, though the claw-pronged limb reaching over him keeps trembling in the breeze, its shadow shaking. It's an oak branch, and its wet-gold leaves are among the first to burnish with the season. The man is grime-faced and hatless, no more beard than a peach, his eyes gray and stunned nearly silver. His blue tunic is soiled and torn at the shoulder, where Du Pre's saber kissed him in the fray. We have watched over this New Yorker since last night, and a weary-faced Garland says the man's collarbone is broken. He's a buck private green as creek moss who just followed orders, factorylike, but he is one of Kilpatrick's new Shadows. His saddle-mates have killed too many of our friends, and he knows the musketoon poised at his ear is cocked, the trigger finger eager to be finished with all this.

We are traveling too light to accommodate a prisoner, and we don't feel kindly toward any of these Yankee mudsills, no matter how addled or inept they seem up close. We've seen their deeds. The sky is rank and smudged with their aftermath. Pure demons, and they drive us to acts of shame.

Last night the prisoner opined to Garland how he found in singed

*weeds a shell-shot Rebel drummer not more than a dozen years on this
earth with his front blown open like a butcher's display. The soldier said
he could see the red beating heart as the boy whispered "Lordy God" and
died. Our captive claimed he tried to ease the boy over. Suffer the little
children. Everybody gets baptized in the blood. It's out of my hands.*

*The morning's first rays are spangling, and the wheeling birds have
found our handiwork again. They get bolder with each feast, their feath-
erless heads red as the raw wounds they delve. We splash the dregs of
what we call coffee on the embers as the sun clears the rise where we can
make out ruins of a torched plantation, the big house, sheds and barns
all rubbled. The chimneys dark as pillars of ash. Time to shadow off
ourselves and seek the column. It's a suffering world. "This flesh and
heart shall fail," the grace song says, and I repeat it in a whisper as I
sling my kit over the makeshift pommel. The camp apostle would say it's
all a vale of tears.*

*I am in the saddle and out of the ravine, ready to hunt where Wheeler
and his staff broke their fast, when I hear the roar of the musketoon. Eye
for an eye, but it is not Christian business, none of it. What could we do
but embrace their ways? The horse snorts and champs. He doesn't care
for the slaughter smell trailing behind us like spoor.*

*This is a place where deer would nuzzle and browse at a kinder time,
where rabbits would slumber and hungers of the spirit might be fed. A
vee of geese is arrowing eastward in the clabbered sky. How fine it would
be to rise and flee with them. How splendid to be delivered and redeemed.
Best to stifle that, though. Best to heel my mount and leave the misgiv-
ings behind, mourn my companions at the gallop. If somebody has to beg
mercy for all this at the Last Reckoning, his name in Hell is Sherman.*

Dreaming back now, I could almost believe it was the horrors I
beheld, rather than a lead pellet, that knocked my left eye into darkness. In the fall of '64 the rivers were burning, rails snarled around
pine trunks, homes and barns and churches black as Christy's
Minstrels, the burdened people streaming pathetic along the
roads. Torched bales and gangrene gave off a stench like the pit of
Gehenna. Who were the monsters behind it—the laws of nature

repealed, milk of kindness spoiled, even warfare a set of ruined rules? Stirrup jerky and biscuit, skillygalee and hominy, reloading on the run. The smell of horse sweat and smoke kept us dizzy, a poor excuse for righteous avengers. Our only hymns were rackety bugles or cannon blasts. Sortie and demonstrate, raid and rebuke.

We were keeping owl hours, saddle sleep if any. Maps and the long glass, scouts in and out, always somebody coughing hard or falling behind with the scours. Any hickory might shield a sniper. Any knoll could conceal a score of horsemen. Caution and dispatch, hide and seek. Outside Fentry we halted at a sweet spring. Fighting Joe Wheeler spat his plug and turned to offer me the gourd: "Bible Job had no more reason to grumble than us, Goddamn it, Major, but at least we've got powder and chuck and a barrel of hard spirits. Any well-versed God must take up our side." A dedicated honey man, he was ever seeking after bee signs—some said because his beloved was called "Deborah"—but by then the flowers were long gone. Need be, he could live without sweetness or bacon. He was just sixteen hands high and weighing one twenty, hair ever-tousled, the boy general, a saucy talker, thrice shot, over a dozen horses gone to meet their maker under his saddle. "Damn this" and "shit on that." He was a terror, our best thing left.

We had hit Kilpatrick's mob near Sylvan Grove at dawn. A quick breach. We exploited it full force. It was "Let her go, Gallagher," and the pukes showed their backsides. Kils escaped, but we captured his braided hat and camp kit. A day and a night. At Waynesboro we fought the Federals' barn fires and their repeating Spencers till dark. Our dozen bugle boys went down, every one. Kils torched the bridge over Buckhead Creek, but we patched it with church pews and pushed hard till the niddering buttermilk rangers stampeded headlong into their own infantry. Other days went their way. Sharp work, flummoxed fury. We rode on.

Atlanta was two hundred acres of ash behind us. Wick-black chimneys at every turn. Georgia was already howling, as Lazarus and his wolves headed to the sea. He chewed a cigar even in his sleep, Dame Rumor sang, the bastard who once had claimed to love the South. Lazarus to us, risen from the insane. They had sent him home to Ohio as mad but summoned him back, madness being much the fashion. Now he was blindered as a mill mule, pushing his horde east, muttering, "Saltwater, saltwater." Nothing to stop him now but pitiful militia and us, Wheeler's Desperates. Thin as crickets, mean as hornets but twice as busy, we had flanked him at Dalton, stood our ground in Kennesaw's inferno. We learned from lightning how to strike and leave only singe and sorrow. Hit and run, harry and sting. Our numbers were not great. Garland Rutledge was still with me, Marichal Wilkes, Big Buck Cooperman, Champs Du Pre, but we lost the Soames boys at Griffin in one volley. A ball cut my collar there. John Sparrow lost an ear. Dozens of horses went down wailing like the damned, thrashing and bloodspray everywhere. We buried the Soamses at the depot with hardtack lids to mark their rest, names and dates carved on the front, PILOT BREAD stamped on the back. Lean times, desperate measures, the season turned frosty and bleak.

Garland was practical, the first to shred the pages of Cooke's *Cavalry Tactics* for tinder. He had been with Wheeler since Chickamauga, but he was reared up in Spalding County, so this was his ground. He had purpose. The blue demons thought themselves Thrones and Seraphs. They were setting the Lost Tribes free, their tabloids boasted, and we were no more than Satan's spawn, soiled knights for the Kingdom of Chains.

"We'll teach them manners," said Garland. "Reap evil will they? We'll put a nick in the scythe."

A slashed country, braised and gloomed. In the railroad beds, they'd prized up the irons, heated and bent them like hairpins around jack pines. "Where's your Jesus now, Taddy Sherburne?" Garland was fuming. "Where's your sword of the Lord? Trust Fighting Joe, dry powder and Mr. Sharps, but Sweet Jesus is obsolete or sleeping. Let's be Hell." He spurred his Tennessee and galloped toward the stench.

• • •

It was a camp revival that sparked my appetite for scripture and incited the wags to snipe at me with rough humor. If we'd had a graceful God back in Carolina, my folks had scarce been acquainted with His ways. There was a Bible in the pantry and one dinner blessing: "Keep the plow wing sharp and the mule safe from snakes, our Father. Amen." But they say the whiz of Minié balls can teach you devotion. When Cam Hatley fell at Peachtree Creek, I was altered. On picket before dusk, just lighting our pipes, he was bragging on a jug of molasses he'd scrounged. Then I heard the howl of a shell, felt gust, and nearly half Cam was gone. I was talking to a belt buckle and bloodspray. I didn't talk long.

That night the End of Time Man showed up in a caravan, Testament in his fist. He was no agent for the gold road of Heaven. Raw-boned, tall, rough as a cob. "The Whirlwind is near," he shouted from the wagon tongue. "Get ready, get ready!" He balanced easy as a bird. "Prepare your eternal soul for the pain and the glory." In the flicker of a brazier, he gave rant and brimstone a flavor even Sherman's butchers hadn't summoned, but he promised solace, and I needed some. I let him wet my head with springwater the horses had likely pissed in, bade him bless my sinful hands. He said, "Praise be. You're safe now, boy," and winked. Since then, I'd tried to "Lord-is-my-shepherd" on the march and read the tracts by firelight. Many of the hymns in *The Times in Which We Live* I studied till I'd got them by heart and worn the booklet almost to shreds. Garland showed me no mercy. Marichal was worse.

"Joe Wheeler's fool, Jeff Davis's fool and now Jehovah's. Parson Parsnips! You'll be a man of the cloth before we know it, Sherburne. And won't your little wifey be proud. Now pray me up some sheep stew and a glass of nockum stiff. A warm wench from the flesh farm. Pray us fresh horses, old son. Put your faith to use." I took it in the spirit of my newfound humility, rank aside. We all had more than enough paradox already, trying to get a mind around loving neighbors while hating the Yankees enough to gut them, and I was desperate to preserve some of the man Maggie had pledged yes to under the arbor just after Manassas.

Two nights later big Buck invented the cowbell ruse, and I was up to my wrists in eye-for-an-eye again, hoping Jesus would set aside "Thou Shalt Not" and excuse my occupation, though I knew I'd be too ashamed ever to tell it back home.

We'd get close enough to smell their hish and hash, a few of us bellying through the bramble, and when we found a sweet spot, the decoy would clang the bell gentle till some of Lazarus's jack-ass foragers could start to picture ribs sizzling. They'd dispatch a pilgrim or two to come seeking the stray offering, and we'd hold the Arkansas toothpick up before a man's eyes just after we showed it to his throat, his own breath rasp the last note he heard. Thou Shalt Not, I know, but think of Joshua and young David. The ruse worked four times before word rippled through their ranks. Soon they were shooting at any bovine sound.

When Lazarus turned his eye on Savannah, still prosperous as a wedding cake on the coast, Jeff Davis in his wisdom announced the whole Union force would flounder like Napoleon in Russian winter. They'd starve and freeze, suffer and limpdick it home just like the French fools, but Lazarus sent Jeff a note on Yankee wiping paper, just the two words: "No snow."

Both sides needed to believe they were fighting God's ordained war. We were protecting native ground—cornfields, sisterly virtue, and the right to say, "We step out of your Union." The Lincolnites were wiping away an abomination, enslavement of a stolen people. By '64 I'd sure seen enough lashed backs and shackled urchins to admit they had an argument, but back in Buncombe County the only slave I knew up close was Aeneas Beedle, and he always sported horehound sticks in his pocket and a big-foot dobbin to run errands for Doctor West. By the time I saw cotton bottoms and regiments of sad stoop-overs aching in the autumn rows, Lincoln had sent his saviors over our threshold. My personal heart's opinion was, "Go home, mill monkeys, and then we'll discuss this other matter." Three years of blaze should have been enough to educate any imbecile. Hell, three months would more than teach a man.

The Soames brothers had come to Bragg's muster with a body servant all shuffle-step and *yassuh, boss*. They loved him like a whipped dog, but no better. Cam had confessed his own family had a dozen and treated them "decent," but he said slaving was a rewardless practice, so they hired smallholders to sucker their tobacco and shell their corn. Results about the same. Out in the world there is no end of questions and ample evil for both sides. What happened to the twelve I never asked.

We fought the blue jackets because they were our enemy and because Lazarus meant to burn a rift in Georgia. His rear guard cut the well ropes and stole the buckets, pissed on the salt licks and shit in the weirs. No more conscience than a crow. His bummers murdered every stock animal they couldn't wolf down and nailed silver services to trees for target practice, poured sorghum in pipe organs. They shot anything resembling a dog for being kin to slave hounds. Here is what Back-from-the-Grave told the papers: "I will scorch this land till its residents feel a permanent night has fallen upon the ground and clung to it." I dreamed him with a bottle of cask-aged how-come-you-so? and a cigar glowing and smoking like a brand.

As Sandy Chavis lessoned me over one breakfast of guineas, it was easy to believe whatever favored the coloreds cursed us directly. After all, Lazarus had arrived to raise them and flail us down. *Set my people free* was his command and provided excuse for rampage, though even before the Ebenezer Creek confusion, I could see the way truth was all stewed up with fraud, the Devil's work. Some Yankees just came south for a big Barnum show, the swag and permission to relish arson. "The goose question," as parlor society named slavery, well, it wasn't what made factory men take up arms. As I saw it, they came foremost to seize our land, so I donated a small plot to each hoplite I could fell and prayed forgiveness.

One evening Captain Wilkes and I were on vidette outside Macon, and we happened upon a yellow-toned wench sitting by a willow spring at twilight, dressed as fetching as Lola Montez herself, her hair in an apple-hued rigolette, a flowery umbrella in her hands. When we came rattling up, rifles and tack banging the saddletree, she didn't raise a glance to see if we were blue or butternuts.

"Gal," called Marichal. "You, nigger gal." She finally issued just a sigh, but she was so don't-carish in her finery, we might as well of been squirrels. I leaned hard into her face and said, "What ails you, Liza?"

"Well . . ." But when she dropped back to a mutter, I sharpened up my voice.

"Well, young marsters, ain't no profit to try twisting it all into sense. Don't sort out straight no more than a red snake."

"Speak plain, gal."

Then she stuck out her feet, bare and bleeding. "Jubilo come. Horns a-blasting, big men with killing swords and feathers in they hats, they come march on through like a blue-sky storm with wagon guns and flags, cast out the marster's old ways, give us the freedom and set us to dancing a Jordan reel. Two days they roast hog, prance about, promise us pretties and snuggle us gals in the hay, then the whole bunch button up and head on toward the sun's come-rise. Next day, they dirty drag-tail buckra spill into our camp, haul off the free nigra men to use they shovels. Last one come through the farm steal my field hat and shoes, then ride off whistling that 'Dixie' with Missy's peacock slung over the mule back."

She had set out after her footwear, but being a house gal she lacked the soles for such a trek, and now her feet were raw as steak shambles. I thought it a woeful tale and wished for solutions, a pair of charity boots, but we had a rendezvous to keep.

Marichal spat dry and said we should put them out of their misery, all Ham's issue, but I answered she had not invaded us, just another weed in the sickle's path, little different from ourselves. He had a blindness of his own woven deep into the otherwise fine instincts of a golden soul.

• • •

Kilpatrick and Wheeler had dueled for half a year from Tennessee on down till Kils had taken a ball at Resaca and was packed back home, but they couldn't hold him from the grand farce. He'd long been a gaslights man for the sham pleasure of it and liked to strike poses, take curtain calls, and curse Lee and Lincoln in one windy speech, theatrical fashion. Now he was the prompter for a swarm of locusts. "I am pure Harry on a raid." he boasted to *Harper's Weekly.* To break the Confederacy's back, they would not leave chick nor child unmolested. It was his men who'd broken into the playhouse in Atlanta and looted off the costumes. They cut the fool at Cassville in pantaloons, capes, and helmets, as on a lark.

That Cassville fight was the first day I ever glassed him up, despite the covey of white-glove staff trying to shield him. They were dolled up as Turks and queens and such theater exotics, but I spied him in those mutton whiskers and a frogged coat with more braid than wool. Joe Wheeler hated the man, his brags and lies, and when I directed the general to their command position, he ordered up our jackass gun to loft a shell in that vicinity. The two had been at West Point, and General Joe said in the case of that tuck-tail son of a bitch chivalry did not apply. "That pig pizzle wouldn't have the sense to rub down a frothy mule nor piss with the wind. It's a long taw, but give that barrel full elevation, kiss it for distance and see if we can break his frolic." If the Yankee thought this was all a fox hunt, we'd show him teeth, give him a snarl. Shortfall, somewhat, but their horses reared and startled. We saw them shit and scamper.

Running reconnaissance after the Yanks hunkered down in Atlanta, the Soames boys and I had come on a file of civilians pulling their goods on Indian-style travois. A pert young woman with too many freckles was swearing with every step, so Garland hove to and asked could he be of service.

"They are turning out our dead in the cemetery," she answered, "tossing blessed bones to make room for their own fallen. It is sacrilege." This through rillets of tears.

The Soames boys worked themselves into a frenzy, cussing Lazarus and pledging to go on private raid that night. Even their servant John was wild with it by darkfall. He doted on those boys, and when the one barrage took them both, I offered him their personals and said, "Go home or go North, John. Likely you're free. Thank Jesus." He joined the shovel brigade instead, throwing up works, and I never saw him after that to find out exactly why. But Sherman, the resurrection man, the grave robber: now he was primed to lick our skillet clean. God forgive me, but I would sink to anything to stop him.

Before long, I was dreaming him as a game rooster, all spurred and cockerel-surly, his head a flame that raged across the state, like he was dreaming back at me, all waste work and incendiary. I could picture him strutting under bloody clouds, his boots turning frost to cinders as he strode. He was waving a map of Carolina big as a bedsheet, and I was crawling through an endless woods to warn my Maggie. I could feel the pressure of his mind. Then I would wake in a sweat, the taste of ditch water on my tongue. It was all turning personal.

Wheeler said to hurt him, to clip his wings. Every time, whether with Garland or Zeke Mapple, I volunteered for advance guard, against Jesus' rules or not. I thought I was learning how the righteous are meant to smite. The Assyrian had fallen wolfish on the fold and should be thrashed and rendered sightless. Sometimes, we'd come on a Yank just sent to his Maker, somebody's darling, his face all ghast and nasty, and Wheeler's orderly Stowbridge would put another shot up his ass, to sign the message, so to speak. It wasn't Christian, but I started to reckon it wasn't altogether wrong.

We had our own disputes, as if invaders weren't ordeal enough. On bivouac, those rare evenings out of the saddle, we'd debate customs of engagement and the war's mainspring and cause.

One evening Marichal advanced the idea we were justified in any act designed to rid our rightful land of trespassers. If you could think it, he said, the Almighty had lent His stamp. "Assassination of generals, poisoned wells, snakes flung into their camp. Delilah spies or playing scorn songs at them like an Irish harper. Anything. And don't go righteous. Your God, Taddy, comprehends our plight and licenses whatever we can conjure."

He was a lean, straw-headed Alabamian with a brow red as a russet potato. You couldn't help but like him for his shroudless spirit and craving for jest, though he was the most bloody-minded. He would cut you half his plug, though, or take blame for others' errors, Samaritan-like. He'd come back for me when my horse stumbled at the scurry by Harris's gin, the lead hot and hailing. I was so mammocked, I didn't know up hith from yon and stumbled about like a child. Out of the smoke he came of a sudden on that ghost horse, his open hand reaching out and my name on his tongue. That act alone purchased him my tolerance and admiration, though I saw his scapegoating of coloreds as half-sighted, at best.

Garland picked his teeth with a twig and praised all partisan procedures. "What I hold most high, gentlemen, is the boy who will force slow toxin down his pet duck when the foragers come close, or Zora Fair of Oxford, who blacked her face and lurked into Atlanta to map Sherman's works. She is a paragon, sirs. We should all be so zealous."

"But what of the wounded, Lieutenant? Surely you sponsor mercy there. You know of Jesus in the garden and that Roman's ear." I couldn't resist.

But Garland was adamant. He tossed a pebble off into the dark, and his face was serious as canister. "They don't want the inconveniences we provide, they should not wander down here. We are not obliged to be hospitable, and we will give their injured quarter when it is offered to our women and children. Our by-God dogs. This Lazarus wants to put the living under the earth and spill out the buried. I say, the man commits to swapping the dead and the quick about like chess pieces, let him brace for all havoc. Every plague we can muster. Woe betide." He hawked and spat a bloody missile into the flames.

As always, Marichal had to introduce the slaves. He lit an old turd of a cigar and jabbed it into his mouth, an organ we scarce had ever seen, due to his thicket of whiskers.

"As I see it, it is your son of Ham who introduced savagery into this whole damned matter. Once we seen what the Nat Turners and their ilk enacted up in Virginia, the whole ante was raised. Lacking that, us whites might have arrived at a compromise." He went back to whittling slivers into the fire, his anger transferred to his wrist.

Du Pre laughed like a jackal, his big shoulders shaking. "It's always the niggers for you, Wilkes. I speck you'll soon inform us that John Brown himself was truly a brown man bleached off to pass scrutiny and buy rifles."

"If not brown, then black to the heart, anyways."

"And what of you, Parson Sherburne? Do you also take mutinous slaves for your models and conduct yourself a notch more brutal to follow their example?" Du Pre, playing with me again.

I needn't answer, as Garland would not let the rein fall slack. He leaned close, nearly touching brows with Du Pre. "Some men are inclined to depravity by misbirth or Yankee raising, though most of us have the aptitude but lack the appetite. We act the fiend out of responsibility, Wilkes, to avenge our damaged nation, our honor, our sovereign God-given rights."

"Here, here," added Wilkes. "Duty. And to reclaim our chattel, but you, Reverend Sherburne, can you with your new-got religion be fierce for the sake of Georgia?"

I had only time to mutter, more at the dying cookfire than my companions, "I reckon." Little did I know how in two days' time circumstance would provide ample answer, but the horn blared "Boots and Saddles," saving us from further disputation. Cursing and kicking, we debouched, and when I gave my new horse the quirt and spur, he leapt across the trickling branch. He was a spirited Irish Draught I called Festus at the suggestion of the End-of-Time apostle. "One of the judges," he said, "a right-thinker." A strong haunch and lean gaskin, a thinking animal. He had a white hourglass feathering his breast, but his hide was black as a Bible.

The next afternoon Garland and I were deployed as skirmishers, our end of the line wending through a scorched peach orchard. On a northward ridge I saw a lone figure at the quick march and motioned to bring up the glass. A fine mist was blowing too hard to make out details through the scarified lens, so we thought it best to investigate and put the heel to our mounts. Up close, we found an old colored man in deaconish habiliments, a grain sack over his shoulder.

"Captains."

"Uncle. You from nearbouts?"

"Nassir. I was of the Joliets up by Madison. Them Gen'l Baird and Sherman come through a-burning, and the everywhich of us scampered hither and skither. Come morning, I was discombobbed and lost, so all I knowed to do was follow 'em, they smell."

"So you're an emancipated?"

"Just unattached, I speck."

Garland stood in his stirrups and surveyed the landscape. We could see a few of our advance down by the stream, but no blue ahead. Even the sky seemed uniform gray, but in the distance, no matter which way you turned, smoketrees rose.

"What's in the poke, uncle?"

"Just my pones of cornbread. Seemed like the kitchen door the best one to skitter out." I counted just three dark teeth in his smile.

"Pass on."

As we rode along, I remembered aloud. "Lazarus said he'd scalp this swath so bad a crow passing would have to tote his own provisions. Likely that uncle is one of those he meant."

"If he was the genuine article I'd shoot him and start a pie. Wilkes might do it anyway."

"We've already had a-plenty of those, and why any nursery-rhyme king would order up crow pie lies beyond my reckoning, unless he was King of Georgia."

"That would mean Joe Brown, if a governor is akin to a king."

"No, that would refer to Lazarus, and he's crowned himself king of the Dead Land. I expect Wheeler means to let him sample the taste of blood and grue before this week concludes."

The dust of our column to the north was sharpening the sunset, so we turned our nags and cantered back toward our own kind.

Next night, we would truly cut loose from the civilized for the first time since the cowbell ruse, and I had to image myself as Gideon to forge an effective outlook. Marichal had set the pace, for I figured that he'd met the old refugee when he offered us extra rations: "Cornbread all around."

Recognizing the poke dangling from his saddletree, I stepped up to speak, but Garland touched my arm and shook his head.

"Fortunes of war, Taddy. Let it be."

The next morning Sergeant Zeke, galloping pell-mell back from a scout, caught me filling my drum canteen from the first wet well in days. He swung off without pulling his gelding to a stop. I'd ridden with him in the actions at Lovejoy and Rough-and-Ready, and I knew from his red face he was in full pique. His usual forage hat was missing, his scabbard empty and eyes big as a horse's.

"Rape and murder, Major. Lazarus has got no shame. It ain't quadrilles and reels no more, I'll tell you. You'uns got any quinine left? I'm feeling swimmy." His eyes seemed not working as a team.

"Take a deep pull of air," I said, though that always meant the smell of burning, "and you can quaff some of this sweet water. So Lazarus has snaked back and struck out again?"

"You've hit the bull by the eye, son. Howard, you know, but most specific Kils' First Division. They swept some of Joe's infantry he'd put on commandeered swaybacks, but later a few of our run-offs found a little farm nestled secret-like in a vale. A couple of old non-slavers had held three sons back from this nasty business, but they were quick to offer Joe's lads aid and comfort, two daughters cleaning wounds and wrapping bandages, the mama beating biscuit, boys tending the horses. A nice little spread, pigs and chickens, a couple Dutch milkers. I don't know how the blue columns missed them, but our boys found it a haven. They were lollygagging half a day, not even bothering with pickets. I guess everybody's desperate for a spell of relief.

"An hour after they traipsed off, Kils' First came on in force, rushing the farm from all sides, barrels blazing. Not a question, not a by-your-leave. They locked the women in the smokehouse and strung the men up in an apple tree. Apple fruit falling down while the men rose, drums and fife driving 'The Dead March' to a jig."

"Hanged them, Zeke?"

"Sure enough. Tongues dangling out, faces blue as damsons. Strangled sons and sire, milked the cows, filled a wagon with chickens and loot, then shut the razorbacks into the house and burned it."

Worse than Herod's minions prowling for firstborns. "And?"

"The officers went off with the wagon and the cows, the one girl says."

"Which girl?"

"Onliest one left. Louandy, they say. Other died, and the mother was shot when she tried to stop the raping. Taddy, it was awful to hear: wolves had the gals spraddle-tied on wagon wheels, treading them like brood hens, one and then the other."

Trying not to think of Maggie, I slung the canteens over my pommel as I mounted. "How much lead have they, Zeke? Can we catch up before they rejoin their column?"

"If'n we don't spare the spur."

"Company's over yonder bluff. Let's ride."

We called that kind Shadows because they were kin to the night. We didn't know whose license they carried—Kils or Hitchcock or Lazarus himself—but they were no more soldiers than wild curs. Faces painted demon-like, one old darkie told us, they were showing us the savage path. Keen to overtake them, we drove our mounts to a lather.

At the farm, the bodies were laid out with arms crossed, except the old daddy, who was a hunchback and wouldn't straighten. The one young woman was weeping in torrents, her mother and sister covered with horse blankets. I left a grave detail. How could God allow it? How might a man ever make his wife understand what he'd seen? I wondered. Jesus wept. We dashed on till dusk.

"They're fifty," Du Pre reported back, "having an evening feed by a quick little river. Pickets out, but no sharp guard. I do believe they've been sipping some strong wet goods, as they're lax and boistery. Moonlight coming and going through clouds. They've staked their horses and spitted chickens. Muskets stacked. Two miles. I love it when idiots travel in a pack."

We were just over twenty strong—Sharps, three repeaters, pistols and steel. Mustering all the reserve I could to cloak my rage, I said we could pick at them, cut and run, or just swarm in direct at all hazards. Not thinking military or Christian, I had seen Wheeler race into such a fight yelling, "Kill the scabby-tongued whoremongers," and I'd watched the End-of-Time rise to full fury when scolding drunks for scorning the Gospel. Borders blur. I was champing at the bit, not hearing anything inside me saying "No."

"I'd wager we'll take the bushwhackers in a sweep," said Garland.

Wilkes had blood fire in his eyes, no restraint. "Liberators my ass. Desecrators, Taddy. Criminals. This is bigger than war, and numbers hardly matter. It's End Time now and you know we can fight like bulldogs when it comes to scratch. You know God wants us to set things right." Looking at his face, no man would doubt it.

I had orders to monitor Kils' forage parties and harry them but not to open a pitched fight that would cost more than we could afford. All at my discretion. But I was losing the mood to be discreet by quarts and gallons.

John Scott and I went in with Du Pre, cat-walking, then on

our bellies to the top of the bluff. The sky had cleared off and the rain had ceased. We were inside their pickets and could only whisper, but the camp we saw downslope was without discipline, their fires high and racket higher, boots off and jugs passing. The moon hadn't showed itself for a spell, but there were stars in the sky and in the river, which rushed on like hot black glass across the cold night.

Scott was a good scout with sharpshooter's gray eyes and cold blood. He reached out his hand to indicate their deployment.

"Mighty damn sure of theyselves, Major. Like a picnic."

"A picnic with Spencers. No telling what's in the wagons."

"Ripe, Major. Lax and napping." And he was on the mark. An owl whooed from a treeline. I didn't know if it was courting or hunting, but I whispered back, "It's our omen, John. Let's mischief their festivities."

Scott placed the three troopers with repeaters to the south. The river would block the east, and we'd come in the other two ways. Already we'd worked quittance on a pair of their pickets and gained two more Spencers. We'd have surprise, position and vinegar. I thought, "The sword of the Lord and Gideon."

When we were deployed, shucked of anything but killing implements, Wilkes asked the honor of going in first, quiet-like, in one of their uniform coats. He and Harold Leary in full masquerade, laughing like the other Yankee tipplers, swinging a jorum and bluffing the sentry's challenge. I told the cadre, "These raiders are not soldiers. Send them straight to Canaan."

A battle is all whirl and hot breath like the weather in Hell. Even a skirmish. Anybody with sense will reel against it and be hang-back at first, but you get used to the music quick. When the puzzle starts to fit, you learn to lose yourself. At night, though, it's worse. You can't be sure how long it will be all a-swirl. As we eased in, a big picket smoking a pipe said, "What the Samuel Hell?" and one of our riders shot him through the middle. I hardly recollect the next details. Whirligig and scramble. Wilkes and Leary slung some stacked carbines into the water and commenced to shoot.

Some of the Yanks recovered quick, and it was hot work. We yelled like gamecocks, then bore down in a file, and I never thought again of Gideon till a big blur knocked me from my horse. Festus rushed on, and both pistols went flying into the dark, so I was on the ground, rolling. Rocks and roots. I had naught but my little belly gun to face the fray.

As I righted myself, running and stumbling were general amid the smoke and river mist. I could hear our new Spencers raking them where the waters forked. One wagon was ablaze, and I figured everybody on a horse was ours, but the cookfires and flashes from weapons were too unsteady to judge, and what moon showed was slight and cloud-scumped. The general blur came at me again, and I could see a big Yankee in a coat emerging from the fracas. He had a farrier's hammer in one hand, a pistol in the other. Tall as a cornstalk, beard red as pepper. Then an officer drew alongside him, and I saw them both looking straight into my eyes, but just as I figured this my faretheewell, I saw the outlines of a gang of plunging horses over their shoulders, their teeth gleaming and hide sheen picking up whatever light would flare like lantern beams striking a stack of anvils. The glory of their nostrils! Somebody behind them was driving the Federal mounts right at their masters, and they were coming as demons, bucking and snorting. The pair demonstrating against me sensed it, too. As they cut and ran, the sudden smell said one of them had shit, and I could see Wilkes waving a blanket to encourage the stampede. The hammer man had dodged left, and he got off a hasty shot that passed my ear like a hornet, but I saw the blanket swoop over him, and when Wilkes turned his big horse, he had the saber out, and then it was wet and the Yank was on all fours like a hog.

I have seen men perform prodigies in the heat of the hunt, but nothing to match Wilkes. He galloped the officer to the ground and, ignoring the dropped weapons and surrendering arms, shot the man through the neck with his boot gun, then caught a horse by the bridle and led it over. I loved him most at that juncture.

"Climb on, Taddy. The assholes are scrambling. They're ours."

So a second time this poor gump was lifted from the fray by an angel.

About the time I got a leg over the horse, a wagon with Hale rockets caught fire and sent missiles whizzing, and by their light we could see the remaining Yankees making a stand in a runoff ditch. Garland held our riders at bay and said, "Let the fireworks die off. We know how to pick blackberries in the dark."

In a few minutes the Yanks were crying for quarter in general alarm as balls rattled through the brush and found them, but our boys had no interest in recess. One soldier was whimpering as he handed his Spencer to John Scott, who turned it about and shot the man full in the face. I was glad it was still too dreamy-gloamy to register the details. Blindness has its virtues.

What I could see and hear were the dead and injured horses all about, heads and legs thrusting skyways with the fires agleam behind them. The Yankees had fired into the stampede and found the panicked animals easier to hit than us. No doubt we shot some, too, and I saw one muley-looking brown struggle to its feet, shaking like a wet terrier, but then its legs spraddled, and it collapsed in a braying heap. I looked for Zeke to put them from their misery, but he was down. And Harold. Scott carried out the order, but I knew we'd suffered bad losses. I didn't want to hear the count.

The camp was ours for the ransacking, but we couldn't be sure how long before the commotion would bring a relief squadron, so we heaped up what we couldn't carry quick and put the torch to it, the flames licking higher than the riverside willows, while Munce Bratton's squad salvaged some of the roasted chickens. When I saw them, I realized how scratchy my belly was with hunger, and my lips were dry as bark. One cart turned out to be full of leathered books, and though you can't eat them, I ordered the crates separated. Before anybody could follow up a stray spark caught purchase on the paper, and they went up as well, just more waste. I was finally asking after our casualties when Marichal touched my shoulder.

"A decent prize, Taddy. They had a brigadier. Didn't get his name."

In the shine of the fire and the half-moon now out of the clouds, I saw him raise his hand, which was holding by the hair a mangled head, beard all matted with blood and soil. Even in the dark, I saw as much detail as I wanted, like some picture of Goliath.

"Like I said, didn't receive a proper introduction. I hoped it might be Smith Atkins."

"Burn it," I said. "Burn it all."

I couldn't but wonder was this the "fountain filled with blood" our column's apostle loved to fill his cool tenor voice with.

The men were still racing about, seeking the last skulkers along the river, and two of them were using horses to drag bodies about the bonfire. I had never seen my veterans so taken with the fever, but it seemed, in that strange light in the wake of the owl's call and the Yankees' crimes, as just as any decree ever handed down. I had but one concern: we had to ghost off by cockcrow. If we were to steal a moment's rest, it had to be far from this position, or we would all be crow food.

"Du Pre," I sang out, "find us a ford."

Breaking out of the woods and onto a farm road an hour later, we headed east, dripping wet, squinting at a red moon low in the soapy sky.

Three days later our Joe Johnston's sappers had hacked and blazed the bridge over Ebenezer Creek to fluster Lazarus, but Buell's Jersey engineers strung quick pontoons, while their General Hawkface Davis strung a cordon to detain on the near side the great multitude of displaced coloreds trailing their saviors. Our scouts had seen the to-do, and John Scott said the tag-alongs were massing on the west bank, mostly old folks, gals, and young 'uns pacing around scared or just hunched in the icy squall while their liberators crossed over, Ohio conscripts looking hard over their shoulders, skittish, nearing panic themselves, wary of our ruthless ways. When our vanguard snaked through the cypress swamps to the bridge site, we saw hundreds of coloreds milling about and the last of the Federals holding back the mob with bayonets fixed. "Aha," said Du Pre, his arm sweeping in grand presentation. "Behold the true face of manumission."

Wilkes grinned like a sheep-killing dog around his dead cigar: "On occasion, I applaud the suitably cruel." Sensing his blood was up, I shook my head and wondered what next as I muttered a prayer for guidance: "Lead us not into temptation."

I could see our horses' wet breath in the drizzle, mist billows from their nostrils like cannon smoke, their fetlocks clotted with dried mud. Festus gave a shiver to shake off the water, then pranced a bit sideways. The rain kept raining. Even this far from any recent sparkfest, the taint of old smoke was conspicuous and charnel amid the first smells of autumn. Every man jack of us was sodden and desperate for rest, but this was not the time for such wishes.

Riverside sycamores stood leafless and ghost-like, peeled to their winter bones, and the live oaks hung with ringlets of Spanish moss like manacles. Not exactly our native ground. Gnarled cypress, cedar, palmettos, and salty cordgrass testified we were nearing the sea Lazarus lusted for. The throng of abandoned vagrants gathered in their calico and sacking gave off their own smell I could just catch from the bluff: it was a battle smell, an old familiar, the sweet stink of fear. A fair few wore coats of Federal issue blue, trousers of kersey, but not a one was a soldier. The rabblement was milling more animated, confused, and fog off the rain-swollen water lent its own haunted flavor. Despite sunrise, the place was silver and black—skeleton trees, char—and the shimmer of the water was like new tack leather that's been spat on.

We were under a dozen at the vanguard, but the coloreds must have reckoned our whole column was close enough to mount an assault, and here they were, hemmed up, liberated but wholly unprotected. Valley of the Shadow. For them, we might as well be bonafide demons. For me, they were the darkness of smoke upon the land. They were ghosts shaped from night's deepest hours, and I wanted them to cross and get out of our business. Was this throng the cause of it all? I thought, "Stamp Thy image on my heart," and wanted to muster charity, but my heart would render only ashes. I intended no harm but could not cease being anxious to have them permanently gone. Equal in God's sight, maybe, but still somehow at the genesis of things, the bone of contention. Gone, that's all I wanted.

Directly, the Federal engineers got nervous and strutted about howling orders. When they cut their pontoons free to haul them over, the contrabands, realizing they were to be stranded, let loose high panic, as if Moses had come to the Red Sea and left a tribe behind to deal with angry Egypt. Whatever they screamed or begged separate, the one shrill of their predicament rose like a choir of the damned. For agony, I have never heard it exceeded.

One granny in her rocking chair atop a plunder wagon turned west and pointed hard in my direction. I could see how large her eyes were gaped open, and her mouth as she hollered, "Dez dare, de Reb sojurs. Mercy Jesus."

From the rise where I leaned forward on my saddle, I could detect them edging toward the swift water, beckoning to the last blue coats beyond the deep, their gestures frantic, their words unanswered. From where I sat they might have been dolls or even some midnight phantasm. It was mid-December, their number in the hundreds, and as the bluebellies began to turn away and enter the trees, one by one, the howling coloreds started to abandon dry land.

At first, they eased or leaped into the current, old men and women, gals with their babes in arms. You could see they knew little of swimming, but the crowd at the back was pushing, not able to reckon what was the holdup, and those up front were trying to enlist logs and even slight limbs for floating. Some few were decked out in fine rummage, probably snatched from attics or chifforobes, but most were in blue rags with hats like something off scarecrows. They were weighted down with bundles, and the lion's share that went into the river struggled with the rush and swirl but were pulled under. A child in a daffodil frock, a woman whose gingham was green as leafing laurel, a grandpappy in a livery coat red as blood. "At Hell's dark door we lay." The notes of that song climbed through me, and I nearabout said them aloud. Maybe I did, and I felt the heart go out of me. The daffodil child bobbed up once more and was gone.

Then it came over me that it was likely the simple sight of us setting the match to their fright, and I was ashamed. There I sat on Festus, leg cocked over the saddle now, wind tickling the turkey feather in my hatband, my hilt and bridle and gun trimmings flashing in the dim light as murderous metal. What was I but Nightmare poised for their destruction? What were we all but Revelation horsemen, locked in the center of their eyes and champing to rampage down? In terror, the mob pushed up to the banks and by ones and pairs into the cold water, which splashed silvery where they entered but quickly closed.

"Colonel Goode," I called back. "Sir, might we withdraw and lend some calm to this scene? We are like unto ghouls as they see us. The contrabands will not be crossing today at any event. No use in us roosting here, now that the Lazarus legion has slipped us."

He leaned to the right and cocked his head, as he did when pondering, then removed his slouch hat and pulled his sleeve across his brow.

"Yes, Major Sherburne, call in the point riders. We mean no slaughter to even the lackeys that worship Lazarus. I would prefer to engage instead with the shitpoke soldiers who marooned them there. Hell of a note. Not our trumpet. Pull back. We will renew our discourse with those blue scoundrels on the other shore."

Du Pre was reined in beside me, and as I swiveled to pass the order, I caught the shock in his eyes, then turned in time to see Marichal's red face, merry and wild. He had wheeled about and was facing me, his horse rearing as he whipped his saber from its scabbard and shouted, "Kill the niggers! What a chance! Kill them all!" Again he wheeled his roan toward the river and gave it the spur. He was hatless, his flaxen curls flying behind like a dancer's ribands. I felt a twine tighten on my heart.

"No." My voice was weak with the moment and the damp, so I forced a second try, "Marichal, no." I was too stunned to do aught else but draw my Colt and raise it, as I shouted—"Wilkes, you Wilkes"—but he heeded me no more than a lark. He had executed a perfect moulinet and was leaning steep, as if the naked blade pulled him toward the melee ahead, and I could see the contraband had glimpsed him, as their ant-like movements suddenly increased and more rushed straight into the river. I reached with my thumb to cock the pistol, thinking "no, no, no," but my whole hand was trembling, and I discharged high into the pelting rain.

Then I saw his head snap back and bloom like a rose, even before I heard the cracking rifles and saw smoke puffs rising across the river. Kilpatrick's rear guard had swung to action. True to discipline, we swiftly dismounted and made answer with our Sharps, while cries of dire agony rose from the shore below, and more coloreds—dozens now, a hundred—entered the water snarling between the banks.

We could see some Yanks had dropped their rifles and were trying to pull swimmers to safety. They reached in branches and threw ropes. Some felled saplings to provide a ladder over the rapids, and we did not aim at them. Most of the coloreds who entered just threw themselves in, though, trusting to Providence, but no divine mercy was granted, and you could see their heads bobbling in the water still tack-brown and silvery with some trick of shadowed light and deluge. It was all chaos and scramble, and nothing we yearned to touch. I tried not to picture old Aeneas Beedle in the bunch, but his face kept ghosting up before my eyes.

Billy Goode said, "Pull back," and waved his plumed white hat, but even as we left the wraiths to die or prosper, I could still hear Marichal's "Kill all," and—much as I had seen and even acted myself since Chattanooga and Atlanta—I was unsteady in my saddle and tasted the vomit as it rose. In an hour we went back in force, flanks covered, skirmishers out in a fan, half dismounted, the rest ready to surround or engage. The Yankees were one. Some col-oreds had skedaddled into the swamp, but most were huddled about their wagons and pelf, ignoring the rain, resigned, eager to plead for our mercy. I found Wilkes' body undisturbed, our only casualty, and while our companions herded slaves off or fished out some of the drowned, we spaded a grave in sandy earth and placed him down at a distance from the dead coloreds he so de-spised. Garland and I piled a cairn of stones licked clean as cobbles, though the woods were so hunted out no rooters were likely to probe. I said some scripture over him, trying to find the right tone, words like "dwell in the house of the Lord forever," but they felt empty, coming from me.

"Ebenezer." It means "stone of help" in the Hebrew tongue, and Marichal's end was the stone I carried badly. Wheeler, with his boastful notion of arithmetic, claimed we corralled two thou-sand runaways that evening and returned them to rightful own-ers, but who believed that? The country was waste and rife with decay. Planters were dispersed or too meagerly supplied to tend to themselves, and did we have time to perform escort duty with Lazarus in full frenzy and hammering the gates of Zion? Their General Davis was said to guarantee we'd butcher our captives, but mostly we just turned them about face and scolded, "Get you gone. Beg forgiveness of your masters, Judas." We'd seen how their train could slow a column, and now they were so pitiful, we could scarce accommodate such an anchor. I handed out two boxes of hardtack and gave a sobbing pappy Marichal's blanket, but nothing more. Leading my companion's roan away from the catastrophe, I felt no trace of God in me and wondered if I could manage to re-light the wet wick of Christian charity the preacher had once kindled. I reckoned his end-of-time warnings had come too late to save one such as myself.

Soon we were swept back into the big tempest. Millen, Bristow, along the Ogeechee. Savannah fell, while a night ruse permitted Hardee with his now-mongrel command to escape north toward

Lee. So Lincoln received that year his sweet Christmas gift from Lazarus. As for us, we limped northward, riding jockey weight, still fit and feisty, despite all accidents of battle, most of us hoping to meet Lee and make another stand, but Johnston used the cavalry mostly as file closers sweeping our rear ranks to discourage or shoot skulkers. It had come to that shameful duty. At times, I was thankful Marichal was not present to endure it.

The heart for it was out of me by then, which is why I let my guard down outside Bentonville where a Yankee sniper up in a young sweetgum like some Nicodemus opened up with a scatter charge, and I went down. Mostly I was scarred about the face and neck, but of course that left eye would be dark forever. When I finally walked out of the hospital, the whole circus was ended, Kirby Smith the only big Reb still in the field. A bald doctor nearly short as a circus midget handed me my boots and explained how to clean the socket and why I should keep it patched against the elements. Crossing the empty street toward the corral, it struck me like a slap in the face: I had been on a camp bed for some forty bleak days, and not one prayer had risen on my lips or in my heart, no matter how often I thought of home or the general horrors or the melee at Ebenezer. There's a song hung on that word, too: "Here I raise my Ebenezer." A stone, yes, but it also means your standard, though I didn't have so much as a scrap of flag left to fly. I would have to find Him all over again, I thought, but this time delving with just the one eye.

I soon ran into Garland who was headed west, and he said Du Pre was gone back to New Orleans to marry a cousin. We three had been scorched but not consumed, like the three Hebrew boys in the furnace, though I couldn't cite a reason for us to be spared. Garland had seen Wheeler, too, shackled and cussing. Surrender didn't much alter his vocabulary. Fighting Joe. His story was just starting, if you follow events. He'd wind up in Congress.

I straggled on home slowly and saw more waste and sorrow than even the one eye could stand, but Maggie was safe, our acres untouched by the war. We made our crop and I built a cradle, so we were looking forward and hopeful. Maybe I thought it was over, but it comes back at night. It takes me by the scruff and hauls me limp and will-less to a particular November ravine.

It's the morning after a wild fight, and the men are finishing with the fresh graves. The clang of spades on stones, the smell of clay, that other smell. We are still licking our wounds and winding our watches, and the buzzards have come for their rations. They circle and light and sup on the fallen Yankees as if they thought themselves the chosen tribe. That boy with the shoulder, with no hat and the fish-silver eyes, has pissed himself and I am the ranking officer in the squadron. I could say just leave him, but four of our own have fallen, and the turned dirt is mounding up as sorrow's souvenirs. I could say just bind him on an extra horse and we'll bequeath him to the column by noon. Not practical, I know. I could at least pronounce "forgive our trespasses" over him or "bright shining as the sun" and order them to dig another hole. He keeps shaking like a colt, his eagle buttons catching the first sprays of light. He keeps whining, "his heart beating, I tried to help," but I've given the order only I can alter and am riding off. Let the cup pass from me. Sunshafts in the pine needles, the report of the weapon, wind whipping the cold trees, gallop sound of my horse's hooves. I give him the spur.

I can still see the boy's face, hear his damp breath. Small scar over his nose. Silvery pupils. His features give way to the floating daffodil frock in Ebenezer Creek, the empty face of a child pointed toward Heaven, the screams like Hell's choir. And Wilkes' accusing eyes.

I should want to go back and reverse it, save the boy, pass on the mercy of Jesus my Shepherd, but hard as I try, lying here in the still bedroom with enough floor space to fit eight rough coffins, I come up empty, unforgiving, unwilling even in the heart to change my command. And now I have become that shapeless cry in the wilderness, though my mind labors to summon the song: Dangers, toils and snares. Blind but now I see. Just words now, just animal murmurs as they issue from me, the milk of pity soured. And there's also the other voice: Spur the Irish horse till his flanks bleed. Do your duty: red thoughts, red deeds. Wolf back at the wolves

till blood is the general weather we tenant. The voice I've come to know
as mine. Lamb of Jesus, revenant avenger. Poor Marichal, poor pitiful
savage human race. And alone in darkness, the sinner, half-sighted
survivor sweating cold in his own bedclothes, remnant wretch like me.

R. T. Smith's stories have appeared in *The Best*
American Short Stories, The Pushcart Prize, The
Best American Mystery Stories, and four previous volumes of *New Stories from the South.* His
fiction collections are *Faith, Uke Rivers Delivers,*
and the forthcoming *Tastes Like Chicken,* and
his newest book of poems is *Outlaw Style.* Smith
lives in Rockbridge County, Virginia, and edits
Shenandoah for Washington and Lee University.
He has served as Alumni Writer-in-Residence
at Auburn University, Philips Family Distinguished Professor of
Rhetoric at Virginia Military Institute, and Sara Lura Matthews Self
Distinguished Writer-in-Residence at Converse College.

I'*d been working for some time on a cycle of stories about a fictional*
Lexington, Virginia, sheriff named Blaine Sherburne, and the more he
thought about the legacy of his father, the more I felt a need to invent him,
too. I felt certain the elder Sherburne, a horse dealer most of his life, had been
in Wheeler's cavalry near the end of the Civil War, so I began to imagine
him striving to rescue some decency from the savagery of those times. With a
valise of books (Burke Davis, Shelby Foote, Sherman himself) on that phase
of the war, I set out for a month in Ireland with my wife, whose tolerance was
crucial to the making of this story. We stayed in a house outside Kilkenny,
and almost every afternoon I went into the west-facing bedroom and stared
at the distant round tower, the wheatfields and fences and roads, the active
sky, until it all blurred into blasted and piney Georgia. I wrote the people
down as I saw them, with not a little assistance from my troubling dreams.
I was on something of a mission, too, to discover more about the notorious

desertion by Sherman's rear guard of the freed slaves at Ebenezer Creek and how a man like Thaddeus Sherburne might have seen it. I just kept hammering at the question, "How can one keep a good heart in such times as those?" I know it has something to do with forgiveness, but the overall equation remains a mystery.

Karen E. Bender

CANDIDATE

(from *Ecotone*)

It was four thirty in the afternoon, and Diane Bernstein knew that the phone was about to ring. She had just paid the babysitter, the third one to quit this month, extremely polite when she quit, blaming it on other issues—sorority functions, heavy schoolwork—as though the boy had not unnerved her at all. When Diane had walked through the door, Liza, the baby girl, fell into her mother's arms, weeping so hard she began to choke. The boy, Johnny, was curled up in his bed, rocking himself, for he had scratched the babysitter in a fury ("I had wanted to play the radio," she said, "and he just went insane") and the young woman had shut him in his room. Why hadn't Diane found a better babysitter? It was not a question she allowed herself anymore. She had long stopped worrying about forgiveness, of herself or others. When the therapist had told her, again, that it was not her fault, she laughed; everything was her fault; everything was everyone's fault. "Even if it was his fault," she said, meaning her husband, to the therapist, "what would it matter? He's gone."

Diane had to figure out who to comfort first: the two-year-old, Liza, who clung to her, frantic with love, unwilling to peel herself from her mother after their long day apart, or Johnny, curled up, a knot of frustration in his bed. "They're cute kids," the babysitter called back, apologetically, pulling her long sleeves over the scratches the boy had given her; clutching her fifty dollars, she got into her Jeep and drove off.

Diane had spent the day working in the remedial writing lab of a private university in the Southeast. She hunched in a dimly lit cubicle with the undergraduates, glossy, overfed children who drove SUVs that were gifts from their parents and who could not correctly use a comma. Their essays were supposed to address the presidential election, and involved passionate, ungrammatical declarations stating why the Republicans should win. *Lazy people should not get my tax mony,* they wrote, or *I dont want any gay agenda on my family. Marriage is between a man and a woman.* That day, Diane sat with a young woman dressed like a prostitute, her pink Spandex halter top stretched across her breasts. Her hair was styled in two pigtail braids. The girl smelled of the beach, of coconut and salt. She had written a diatribe about how the United States should not only take over Iraq but Saudi Arabia, Egypt, Russia, and Japan, as revenge for Pearl Harbor. It was an extremely long and angry run-on sentence.

"Do you worry about how other countries might respond to this?" asked Diane.

The girl glared at her. "The terrorists want to kill me," she said.

The girl's previous paper had recorded her frustrations about her parents' divorce, the insensitivities of her superiors at Wal-Mart, the cheap gifts her boyfriend had given her. It had been a more interesting paper, though it still lacked consistent punctuation.

"The terrorists would come to Briar Wood College?" Diane asked, before she could stop herself.

The girl's eyes narrowed. Then, as though concerned about her grade, she smiled and said sweetly, "You're just from the North," she said, which was true, though "the North" seemed to imply anywhere slanting north or west; Diane had moved here from Seattle.

Diane closed her eyes; the school where she worked had raised tuition too many times, and faculty had been cautioned not to discuss the election with the conservative students. They lurched about campus, students and teachers, ignoring each other's pins and T-shirts. She had done what she could: covered her car in bumper stickers and stuck yard signs in her lawn that were later torn down.

Now, at home, Diane thought it was best to unplug the phone. Then she would not have to decide whether to answer it. The father, who was now residing in Florida, was not supposed to call at this hour; he was supposed to only speak to the children in the morning, for his voice upset them when it was time for dinner and bed. She carried the girl up to the boy's room and sat on his bed. The children both fell upon her. Liza put her head on Diane's leg and closed her eyes, quiet; her breathing became calm. The boy did not like to be touched, but was generally soothed by coloring in squares in black and yellow. She gave him crayons and paper and he sat up, filling each box in with extraordinary love.

Diane listened to the silence in the room and envied the girl's belief that she had been rescued. It was an acute misunderstanding between parents and children, one which sometimes comforted her, but also felt like a joke. She sat in her son's bedroom and was overcome by loneliness so crushing it was hard to breathe. Her girl's tiny hands fumbled to grab her mother's waistband, and Diane was still as the girl gripped her, as though Diane was waiting to be pulled to a safe place.

Someone was knocking at the door. Diane jumped up, holding Liza, and she and Johnny ran to the door. She opened the door and found a man in a crisp white shirt and navy pants standing on the other side of it. He held out his hand as though slicing the air in two.

"Hi there," he said. "Woody Wilson here. Running for state legislature. I want to represent you."

Before he said his name, he was just an ordinary stranger, standing there, slim, brown-haired—a salesman of encyclopedias or cleaning equipment—with the belligerent, trudging optimism of someone who went door to door. After he declared his name, she hated him. This shift in feeling was so abrupt that her heart felt like an emptied balloon. His face seemed to glow the way a famous person's did, as though it was an accident that he was walking around on earth. He lived most fully on the newspaper ads and billboards all over town. *Woody Wilson, Republican for North Carolina State Senate.*

"And what's your name?"

"Diane," said the boy.

"Man," the girl said, looking up at Woody Wilson.

It was late afternoon. The house smelled like a rotten melon. The afternoon was weighted toward night. The golden light already held an undertone of darkness. Diane had read what he stood for and she hated all of it. It would be so simple, so luxurious to slam the door on him! But she did not. His eyes were clear and blue as a baby's. Her heart began to march as though she had been waiting for him.

"Diane, can I have just a moment of your time?" he asked. He kept smiling, but his face was red from the heat. "I can see you're a family person." He stepped back and began to arrange the plastic vehicles scattered across her front porch. He put Big Wheel behind sedan. "I have a family, too. How old are your kids? I have two, eight years old and five." He laughed, brokenly; it almost sounded as though he was weeping. "I've come to ask for your vote, Diane," he said. "I am for family. We are what make America great." He swept his arm toward her in a grand, appropriating gesture; she stepped back from him. "What does your family need? If you want more money in your wallet, I have the answers. If you want better schools, I can answer that, too."

She tightened her arm around Liza's waist. She knew that her ideas were opposite to his in everything that made up a political belief. "And how are you going to make the schools better?" she asked.

He heard the blade in her voice; his eyes narrowed. The pale, clapboard houses behind him seemed to be melting in the heat. "Good question, Diane," he said, speaking quickly. "We want to bring faith back to our schools. Every child should be allowed to pray. No cost to the taxpayer." His words sounded a little breathless.

"Pray to what?" she asked.

He blinked. "I'd say Jesus," he said. She was silent. "But it's a free country," he said. He sounded hesitant on that one, she thought. He tapped a rolled-up leaflet against his hand.

"I believe in separation of church and state," she said, crisply.

He nodded vigorously, as though by making this movement they would be in agreement. The optimism in the gesture was ridiculous, almost moving. But then he handed her a leaflet. "Some folks may say it's hard to know whether to choose me or my opponent, Judy Hollis. So I wanted you to know this."

Did you know that JUDY HOLLIS is a lesbian?
That she is bringing her gay agenda to Raleigh?
Vote for WOODY. FAMILY VALUES.

She looked at the ad and her heart began to pound faster. She had seen it earlier that day, in the local newspaper. She set the baby down; she'd heard enough of the hate masquerading as more congenial agendas.

"Diane, our campaign is getting the word out," he said. "Judy is bad news for our state."

"Because she's gay?" she asked.

"Yes," he said. "We don't want them coming here. I stand for values, Diane, family values. You know what I mean—"

"No, I don't," she said. "I don't want to hear this bullshit. Just stop."

Woody blinked but did not move. The boy glared at Woody Wilson as though he were an animal the boy wanted to eat. He regarded most men who were tall with brown hair this way—it was the simplest way they could describe their father. The boy lay on the floor and rolled from side to side. Why did they work, the ways he tried to comfort himself? He rolled and screeched and turned; they were strategies which adults found amusing at two but now made them look away. The girl gazed at him. The girl's love for the boy poured out of her; she could not help herself. She stretched herself on top of him. She screeched and tried to lick his lips. "Stop!" the boy roared, trying to push her off. She clutched his foot as he tried to crawl away from her. Diane plucked the girl off the boy and set her on the couch, where the girl began to scream.

"Please," Woody Wilson said, "let me say—" His face went white. Then he toppled forward onto her living room floor.

The girl let out a piercing shriek of delight, as though the man was entertaining them. The boy jumped back, his hands pressing his ears. "Stop!" he bellowed. He rolled into a ball on the floor.

Woody was lying facedown across Diane's hardwood floor. He seemed as incongruous as a whale washed up on a beach; she looked down at him, afraid. Diane lightly tapped his shoulder, then she rolled him over. His shoulder was soft as an avocado. He had recently had a breath mint and his breath was medicinal.

"What'd he do?" yelled the boy.

She jumped up and grabbed the phone off a side table. Woody's eyes opened, and he was staring at them.

"I'm calling a doctor," she said.

"Don't call anyone. I don't want them to know." His presence on billboards made the mundane facts of his humanity strange and troubling. His forehead was pink, with creases in it like clay. There was golden hair on the backs of his hands. He touched his eyebrow; a dark bruise was forming. She was afraid of him, which translated into a great and useless pity. She rarely pitied anyone but herself now, so that superiority was somewhat enjoyable.

She left the front door open. Moths flew in. Woody Wilson put a hand on his forehead. "Ow," he said. He took a deep breath. "Exhaustion. That's what the doctor said. Nothing wrong at all. He said if it happens, sit down for a few minutes, take some breaths, and keep going. I have to keep going."

"Okay," she said, reluctantly. She felt vaguely afraid of being blamed.

"I don't know what happened," he said. "But when I feel strongly about something, sometimes I see black. I feel my heart churning. Perhaps the Lord is telling me something. Ow," he said, softly.

What did he mean, the Lord told him things? She sat in her cubicle every day, convincing her students: Evidence. A clear and organized argument. Sometimes she heard herself ranting about evidence, concrete examples, and she felt herself sweating, pathetically, with her own zealotry. He rubbed the bruise on his forehead. She went to the kitchen and brought him an ice pack. He sat up and pressed it to his face.

"Why are you running for office?" she asked.

"He told me to do this. Woody Wilson. I will stand for values. Speak out. The town needs to know your name."

Through the open front door the clouds were knitting together in a searing, bright sky. She could see the houses on their lawns, each life parceled out into its plot of land, the determined, clipped order of flowers and shrubbery. There were two registered Democrats on her street that she knew of, and four Republicans. They went in and out of their houses, shaving their lawns, picking up their newspapers, remarking on the weather. They would all walk into the voting booths, educated and uneducated, intelligent and dumb, and their votes would be worth the same. They sat, diligently filling in bubbles on paper, and, she thought, because of the voters' impulsive, careless yearnings, wars started, debts soared, the land grew barren, and their great-grandchildren would starve.

The bump on Woody's head was growing larger and darker. It made Diane ashamed, as though it somehow implied something sinister about her. The phone began to ring. Her husband felt most lonely around dinnertime. He did not love them, but did not know who else to call.

"I'm sorry," said Woody Wilson. His right foot tapped on the floor like a rabbit's. "A minute. I'll be on my way." He paused. "Does it look very bad?" he asked.

"I don't know," she said. "Maybe you should keep the ice on it."

The phone rang ten times and then stopped.

"Thank you very much, Diane," he said. He tapped his fingers on the floor rapidly. "I'll just be here a second. I'm a person who does best when he's busy. No one can say I don't have plans."

"All right," she said. "While you're here, I just have one question," she said, suddenly breathless. "Why do you hate so many people? Why so intolerant? I just want to know."

"I do not hate them," he said. "Listen. I am trying to help them from leading lives of so much pain—"

"Why do you assume that people who are not like you are in pain?" she asked.

"I know a lot about pain," he said. "My momma died when I was eight," he said briskly. "My father had to work three jobs. He was always tired. He was so tired he fell asleep on elevators, between floors. I had to get a job working a paper route when I was a small boy. I worked hard. I worked my way up, the good days and the bad. Hard work and faith, that's what got me to college, law school, where I am today."

He recited his litany of pain solemnly, as though it were a prayer. Everyone was competitive in terms of their pain. Whose pain was the worst? Did it matter more that Woody's mother had died when he was young or that Diane's husband had left the family? Was a troubled, problematic child a worse pain than infertility? What about the fact that Diane's hours working as a remedial composition instructor had been cut in half, the sudden eczema that spread across her skin, how did that weigh in compared to diagnosis with cancer, losing your family in a war, fearing that you might not make love to another person again?

"You were lucky you succeeded," she said. "Some people don't."

"It was not luck" he said sternly. "It was faith. Let me tell you something. A few months ago, before I decided to run for office, I was waking up one morning and I swore I saw a pitbull rush toward the bed. It wanted to eat me. It had a huge, pink mouth. It had been waiting for years for me. It was probably a dream, but it looked real. I said 'Jesus' and it disappeared."

The boy noticed Woody's bag of buttons and stickers. He began, methodically, to take them out and count them. The phone rang again.

"Don't you need to answer that?" Woody asked.

How did anyone know the right way to live a life? Diane's husband, at forty-five, had begun to feel pains in his chest. The pains were nothing, the doctor said, but anxiety, but her husband felt, abruptly, the slow, inevitable closing of his own life. He had awakened one night, damp and trembling, after dreaming that Johnny had his hands around his throat. In the dream he had peeled his son's hands off his throat and risen up, free, into the sky. She had these feelings too, for she had had her own disappointments—it had not been her dream to berate undergraduates about commas, for one thing—but she was going along with what was given them, and when she tucked the children in she had not thought there was anything else to do. But suddenly her husband believed that their family was killing him. He was almost gleeful in this, a solution. He was a large, healthy man, but after this dream, he began visiting doctors, checking not only his heart, but his lungs, his kidneys, his skin. He said that something was dirty in his blood. No doctors found anything. He searched the Internet for remote adventures; he logged onto sites that described trips into mountains, forests, deserts barely developed by human hands. He said he wanted to go somewhere clean. His home office—he was a freelance reporter for a variety of computer magazines—was papered with posters of Tibet, mountains white, iridescent with snow.

This business had intensified shortly after the doctor had explained to Diane and her husband that testing had placed their son on the autism spectrum. The boy, he said, loved rules so intensely it could be difficult for him to get married or live with someone. He might be tormented in public school, so make sure to explain his issues to the teachers. He could receive therapy to help him understand when another person was happy or sad. On the bright side, the boy would be proficient at math.

After they had heard this, her husband asked her to drive the car home. She stared at the shiny, broad backs of the cars in front of them. His silence made her aggressively talkative.

"I don't know if he was the best guy," she said. "We could see someone else."

He sat, hunched, arms wrapped around himself as though he were freezing.

"Don't you have anything to say?" she asked sharply, in the tone she sometimes used, despite herself, with the children.

He glanced at the dashboard. "We're low on gas," he said.

The phone stopped ringing. She counted; this time it took twenty rings. Woody lowered the ice pack. "Someone wants to talk to you," he said.

"No," she said. "Actually, he doesn't."

The boy looked up. "There are fifty-eight Woody Wilson buttons in your bag," he said.

"Really?" said Woody. "There are, I think, one hundred eight signs all over town. Yard signs, billboards. I drive around counting them. My wife, Tracy, helped me put up the signs. She did a good job. It was a good day for her." He pressed the ice pack to his head and closed his eyes. "I am her rock," he said. "I am her anchor in troubled water."

The hope in his face, his desire to be seen in this role, made her look away.

"You are your husband's rock," he said eagerly. "I can see it." He picked up the ice pack again. "My wife used to work in real estate," he said. "Did I tell you? She sold a house three blocks away." He paused. "She was very happy," he said. "We had wine and steaks at the Port House." He was staring at his shoe with the frozen gaze of someone banishing other thoughts from his head. Then he quickly looked at her. "And what kind of work does your husband do?"

"I don't really know anymore," she said.

She did not yet know how to answer this. Should she say he was dead? "He left six months ago," she said. Telling Woody was practice, she told herself. She hated other people's pity; their sympathy, she felt, was a way of flattering themselves. She tried to laugh, a hollow, cheerless sound—why? She did not want him to be afraid of her. She was certainly afraid of herself. "That was him on the phone."

"I'm sorry," he said.

A month before her husband had left, she had told him that she was picking up some milk at the supermarket and had checked into a motel instead. It was a one-story chain motel with a small aqua pool, one she had often passed and wondered who frolicked inside there, and this time she put her own key in the door. She had no idea what she would do in the room, as she was not meeting anyone there, but she bought a bag of chips from the snack machine, walked into room twenty-seven, and sat on the bed. She ate each chip slowly, trying to make the bag last a while. The room whitened with light every few seconds from the passing cars. She undressed and looked at her naked body in the mirror over the dresser. She did not look much different than she had ten years before; that was before she had met her husband. The fact that she did not look different seemed absurd. She lay on the bed. She tried to imagine an alternative life that she could have, but her fantasies were surprisingly clichéd: tipping champagne glasses in a fancy restaurant in a hotel, floating on a gondola on golden water. Why did she think these things would give her the feelings she wanted? She lay in the dim room and understood that her longing would never end. She lay in the darkness for half an hour. Then she got dressed and went home.

"When I'm feeling troubled," said Woody, "I let Him in my heart. I put myself in the hands of the Lord."

"What does that even mean?" she said. "What hands? What are you talking about?"

"I call his name when I cannot take another step." He looked at her as though she would understand this. "Do you ever feel that, Diane? Who do you call when you cannot take another step?"

She called Dr. Dawson, a woman in her sixties, who had a doctorate in clinical psychology. They sat in a drab, spare room in a mirrored office building, and Diane talked for fifty minutes to this woman who had red hair that was stiff like a meringue. The woman laughed at her jokes, listened when she cried, was quiet when Diane yelled at her. Occasionally Dr. Dawson would tell Diane facts about herself, such as the fact that she had enjoyed math as a child, or her own desire to write erotic poetry; somehow, these facts were always disturbing. But Diane never wanted to leave that room when the hour was up, not even for what relief she had gained during that hour, but the mere hope of it.

"I call Dr. Dawson," she said.

"What does *she* say?" he asked.

"She tells me that I am not my parents," she said.

"Who else would you be?"

"I don't know," she said.

He laughed carefully. "Have you thought why you have not given God a chance to mend your heart—"

"I'm my own responsibility," she said. "Now I don't have to act out the failings of my own parents. I am responsible for my own future. I know I can rely on myself." What did all of this mean? Did it mean simply getting up in the morning, driving the boy to school, handing the daughter to the babysitter, making sure they all had enough to eat, sitting in her cubicle for the appointed number of hours, driving home? What was that? Did it mean she could make herself happy? "So your wife sells real estate," she said lightly.

"She did until a year ago," said Woody.

He put down the ice pack and stared at it. When he looked up, he stared through her, as though another person was simply a clear window to some better view. "She won't get out of bed. She stays there with the curtains shut. She says the light hurts her hair," he said.

She looked at Woody Wilson, the blazing whiteness of his shirt, the way his hair was parted very neatly in the middle. She imagined him standing in front of the mirror that morning while his wife lay silent in the dim bedroom, drawing his comb tenderly through his hair. "I'm sorry," she said. "It sounds hard."

"Hard," he said, and laughed, a sad laugh. "Life is hard. But you know, marriage is a sacred union."

"Fine," she said, thinking that this was what she resented most of all, the lack of specifics, the cheerful vagueness, "but, you know, I think that each person has to give something."

"I give her my devotion," he said, sitting up, excited, ready for a debate. "She does the best she can. I wake up in the morning and sometimes I look at her face, and I just want to know what she is thinking. I tell her she needs to go to church. God will help her." His face was naked, a boy's face, the pale, terrible lids of a child. "I want people to see that I'm trying. I want people to say that Woody Wilson was a good man."

A few weeks before her husband had left, Diane had heard him crying at odd moments: when he was in the bathroom shaving, when he was in the garage taking in the trash. His crying was soft, private, not meant for her or the children, and each time she came upon it she felt both wounded and enraged. He never wept with her but away from her, and she knew that this meant she was not supposed to comfort him. One night, during this time, she had woken up and made his lunch for him. In the dark kitchen, she had put a peanut butter sandwich, an apple, a string cheese, and a cookie in a brown bag and left it on the counter. The next day, he took the bag to work and when he came back, he said, "I took your lunch today. Sorry."

She was suddenly ashamed of her gesture. "I know you did," she said, and they were both more familiar in this, the feeling of deprivation, their quiet, growing anger toward each other. The next morning, when she had woken up, that same lunch was on the counter; he had made it for her. She had wept, and had begun to eat it slowly; after a few bites, she stopped. He would be leaving soon; they both knew this. She sat in the empty kitchen and wondered at the point of these gestures, their ultimate selfishness.

The phone was ringing again. Woody clapped his hands over his ears. The boy suddenly stood up and went into the kitchen. The girl wandered off to join him. There was the scream, "Stop!" by the girl followed by the boy yelling, "Give it!" and then the sound of a body falling in the kitchen. "Oh no," Diane said. She ran into the kitchen. She heard the candidate stepping behind her.

The boy had the girl pressed to the floor with his body. She was coughing. He was trying to unpeel her tiny closed fist. "Give it!" he, growled.

"I want it!" screamed the girl.

"Get off her!" Diane yelled at the boy. She grabbed his thin shoulders and tried to shake him off, but the boy would not move. "Now!"

Diane imagined how Woody Wilson saw them, the disheveled middle-aged woman in the putrid kitchen, wrestling with the enraged son who was stronger than she was. Legislate against this, she thought. The girl opened her mouth to bite the boy's hand.

Woody grasped the boy's hands. "Let go of your sister," said Woody quietly.

"She stole it!" screamed the boy.

Woody held a hand out, as though to calm the air. "Now wait, everybody," he said. "Wait." He reached into his pocket to pull out a Woody Wilson sticker. "I'll trade you." He handed the girl his sticker. "Vote for me." The girl grabbed it. She was already possessed of a startling rage, as though she foresaw the difficulties her own beauty, her brother's rantings, and her father's fumblings would bring her. When the girl stared at someone, as she did at her brother, Diane saw how she would someday regard a lover, the assumption that the other would feed some endless hunger inside of her. She gazed at Diane with the same expression, and Diane whispered to her, ashamed before its vastness.

The boy broke away from the girl. Woody pressed the boy's sticker back into his outstretched hand. The boy turned away from him and hunched over his sticker. It had the green, smiling face of Shrek on it.

"Where'd you get this?" Woody asked the boy.

"At school. They called my name in the cafeteria," the boy said. "I heard my name. They said it like this: John. Nee. Bern. Steen. They chose me. They said I could go home. The lady gave me this when I walked out. She said hold this and go right to the car. I held it the whole way."

Diane remembered this from the day before, the first time she had picked up her son by car at school. The car riders waited for their mothers in the cafeteria, while their parents, in cars at the traffic circle, told their names to the pickup coordinators, who called their names on the walkie-talkie. "Johnny Bernstein," Diane had said to the coordinator. She imagined her son's name floating over the loudspeaker in the cafeteria, where the children were sitting on long steel benches. She pictured all the children, Johnny and Keesha and Juan and Christopher and Sandra and the others, hunched over the tables, waiting to be summoned back to their lives. How many times in their lives would they sit like this, waiting to be called—for work, for love, for good fortune or bad, for luck or despair? What joys or sorrows would each of them be chosen for? She wished she could see how her son hurried down the dingy, dim brown public school corridor, how he walked to the doors that burst open to the afternoon light.

She was relieved when she saw him coming to her car; it was as though he had just been born. "What happened?" she asked. He had told her the same thing: "They said my name like this." Her son cupped his hands together and spoke into them: "John. Nee. Bern. Steen." He said these words with awe, as though they had been spoken by the voice of God. She watched his face in the rearview mirror, blank but suffused with a new brightness, and she wanted to touch his young face and feel what hope was in it, but she simply drove on.

Now Woody leaned toward the boy. "John. Nee. Bern. Steen. You did a good job," Woody said.

The boy nodded at Woody's correct pronunciation. "Yes," he said.

"Your parents will be proud," Woody continued.

"My father calls in the morning," Johnny said. "I hear him, but I don't see his face."

"He must miss you," said Woody. Stop, she thought. Don't pity him. Woody rolled up his shirt sleeves. He bent so he was looking into the boy's face. "Johnny," said Woody, "I know how you feel. When I was a boy, I woke up and the house was quiet. No one called me. Johnny, I didn't have a mother. My father was at work long before I got up." He ran his hand through his hair. "I dressed and got myself to the bus stop. I rode the school bus. I waited for it to pick me up. Some days it took a long time. Sometimes I said my name, too. *Woody Wilson.* I said it over and over. *WoodyWilson. WoodyWilson.WoodyWilson.* There was a bar beside the bus stop. Sometimes a couple men would be sleeping in the doorway. They looked dead. They smelled terrible. Johnny, I said my name so many times it was like a prayer. *Woody Wilson,* I said, *you are not those men. You are yourself.*"

His voice had become quieter as he spoke to Johnny. The boy gazed at him, strangely lulled. She felt the little girl grab her leg and Diane touched her hair. How many more moments would Woody speak to her son? And how had her life come to this, hoarding minutes of kindness doled to them by strangers who knocked on her door? She wondered if this would be the future texture of their lives, this hoarding, and she wished Woody Wilson would leave, but also appreciated the fact that someone else was in the room. She looked away from his pale, thin hair, his shirt rolled halfway up his pinkish arms. She was suddenly afraid that her son would ask him to stay.

But the boy suddenly turned his back to Woody, squatting over his stickers with a fierce expression. "Johnny?" Woody asked. "Are you all right?"

"I don't care," said the boy sharply. "Guess what? I don't care."

She did not know what would comfort him; she barely knew what would comfort herself.

"Well," said Woody. "Hey." His voice broke a little, and he laughed, a hearty, rehearsed laugh. "Well, you never know what will work with kids, what will help them. Never hurts to try, right, Diane? Got to keep trying?"

He touched his hair as though to check that it still existed, that he was all here. He wanted to be reassured, and so did she, and for what? They were soft, graying, halfway to their deaths. They both knew that no one could understand another person's love, parent or child's; they both knew that everyone would die alone.

"Okay," she said carefully, and shrugged.

"Thank you," he said.

The tinny sound of the "Star-Spangled Banner" burst into the room. It was Woody Wilson's cell phone. Woody's face assumed a stern expression as he held it to his ear. "Yes. Still on Greenfield. Yep." He turned it off. "Well," he said. "Time to go."

He picked up his briefcase. "Thank you for your hospitality, Diane," he said brightly. The politician's voice burst out of him as though he were on the radio; he seemed almost surprised to hear it. He smiled as he had in the billboard, holding out his hand. "Goodbye," he said.

"Goodbye," she said, shaking his hand, the firm, remote grip of a stranger. She felt his pulse jump in his hand and it startled her; she let go and stepped away.

Standing on Diane's front porch, Woody Wilson slipped his briefcase under his arm. The bump on his head was dark and monstrous. "What should I tell people?" he asked. "How did this happen?"

"I don't know," she said. "Tell them you tripped."

"Yes," he said, brightening, as though delighted by the idea of simplicity. "I just tripped."

Silence bore down on them; there was nothing more to say. Woody Wilson hurried up the sidewalk to the next house, lifting a hand to knock on the door. Outside, the sunlight was dying. His lips were moving; she believed that he was murmuring his name. She heard the phone begin to ring again. Quickly, she stepped out the door into the cooling, pink air. She looked at the names of all the candidates stuck into the green lawns. They sat, arranged in rows under the sky, fluttering in the low wind. She stood for a moment, reading the names displayed there; then she turned and went back into the house.

———————————

Karen E. Bender's novel, *Like Normal People,* was a *Los Angeles Times* bestseller and a *Washington Post* Best Book of the Year. Her short fiction has appeared in *The New Yorker, Granta, Zoetrope, Ploughshares, The Harvard Review, Story;* has been anthologized in *Best American Short Stories and Best American Mystery Stories;* and has won two Pushcart Prizes. She has received grants from the Rona Jaffe Foundation and the National Endowment for the Arts and is coeditor of the anthology *Choice.* She teaches in the creative writing department of the University of North Carolina at Wilmington and is finishing *Refund,* a collection of stories, and *Allegations,* a novel.

The seed of this story began with an actual election for state legislature in our city of Wilmington, North Carolina. The Republican candidate, who portrayed himself as the "Family Guy," sent out a mailing outing the Democratic candidate, who is gay. The Republican mailing was shocking in its bigotry, and its insinuations that because of this person's sexual orientation, she would not stand up for "family values" in the state

legislature. Happily, there was general outrage at these tactics, it backfired, and the Democratic candidate won. But as a writer, I wanted to know why the Republican candidate would hold these anti-gay values, and where does the narrow-minded thinking of the Evangelical right come from? Is it, ultimately, a way to deal with chaos and sorrow? I wrote this story in an attempt to figure this out.

David James Poissant

LIZARD MAN

(from *Playboy*)

I rattle into the driveway around sunup, and Cam's on my front stoop with his boy, Bobby. Cam stands. He's a huge man, thick and muscled from a decade of work in construction. Sleeves of green dragons run armpit to wrist. He claims there's a pair of naked ladies tattooed into all those scales if you look close enough.

When Crystal left him, Cam got the boy, which tells you what kind of a mother Crystal was. Cam's my last friend. He's a saint when he's sober, and he hasn't touched liquor in ten years.

He puts a hand on the boy's shoulder, but Bobby spins from his grip and charges. He meets me at the truck, grabs my leg and hugs it with his whole body. I head toward Cam. Bobby bounces and laughs with every step.

We shake hands, but Cam's expression is no-nonsense.

"Graveyard again?" he says. My apron, rolled into a tan tube, hangs from my front pocket, and I reek of kitchen grease.

"Yeah," I say. I haven't told Cam how I lost my temper and yelled at a customer, how apparently some people don't know what over easy means, how my agreement to work the ten-to-six shift is the only thing keeping my electricity on and the water running.

"Bobby," Cam says, "go play for a minute, okay?" Bobby releases my leg and stares at his father skeptically. "Don't make me tell you twice," Cam says. The boy runs to my mailbox, drops to the lawn cross-legged and scowls. "Keep going," Cam says. Slowly, deliberately, Bobby stands and sulks toward their house.

"What is it?" I say. "What's wrong?"

Cam shakes his head, "Red's dead," he says.

Red is Cam's dad, though I've never heard him call him that. "Bastard used to beat the fuck out of me," Cam said one night back when we both drank too much and swapped sad stories. When he turned eighteen, Cam enlisted and left for the first Gulf war. The last time he saw his father, the man was staggering, drunk, across the lawn. "Go, then!" he screamed. "Go die for your fucking country!" Bobby never knew he had a grandfather.

I don't know whether Cam is upset or relieved, and I don't know what to say. Cam must see this, because he says, "It's okay. I'm okay."

"How'd it happen?" I ask.

"He was drinking," Cam says. "Bartender said one minute Red was laughing, the next his forehead was on the bar. When they went to shake him awake, he was dead."

"Wow." It's a stupid thing to say, but I've been up all night. My hand still grips an invisible steel spatula. I can feel lard under my nails.

"I need a favor," Cam says.

"Anything," I say. When I was in jail, it was Cam who bailed me out. When my wife and son moved to Baton Rouge, it was Cam who knocked down my door, kicked my ass, threw the contents of my liquor cabinet onto the front lawn, set it on fire, and got me a job at his friend's diner.

"I need a ride to Red's house," Cam says.

"Okay," I say. Cam hasn't had a car for years. Half the people on our block can't afford storm shutters, let alone cars, but it's St. Petersburg, a pedestrian city, and downtown's only a five-minute walk.

"Well, don't say okay yet," Cam says. "It's in Lee."

"Lee, Florida?"

Cam nods. Lee is four hours north, the last city you pass on I-75 before you hit Georgia.

"No problem," I say, "as long as I'm back before ten tonight."

"Another graveyard?" Cam asks. I nod. "Okay," he says, "let's go."

Last year I threw my son through the family-room window. I don't remember how it happened, not exactly. I remember stepping into the room. I remember seeing Jack, his mouth pressed to the mouth of the other boy, his hands moving fast in the boy's lap. Then I stood over him in the garden. Lynn ran from the house, screaming. She saw Jack and hit me in the face. She battered my shoulders and my chest. Above us, through the window frame, the other boy stood, staring, shaking, hugging himself with his thin arms. Jack lay on the ground. He did not move except for the rise and fall of his chest. The window had broken cleanly and there was no blood, just shards of glass scattered over flowers, but one of Jack's arms was bent behind his head, as though he had gone to sleep that way, an elbow for a pillow.

"Call 911," Lynn yelled to the boy above.

"No," I said. Whatever else I didn't know in that time and place, I knew we could never afford an ambulance ride. "I'll take him," I said.

"No!" Lynn cried. "You'll kill him!"

"I'm not going to kill him," I said. "Come here." I gestured to the boy. He shook his head and stepped back. "Please," I said.

Tentatively the boy stepped over the jagged edge of the sill. He planted his feet on the brick ledge of the front wall, then dropped the few feet to the ground. Glass crunched beneath his sneakers.

"Grab his ankles," I said. I hooked my hands under Jack's armpits, and we lifted him. One arm trailed the ground as we walked him to the car. Lynn opened the hatchback. We laid Jack in the back and covered him with a blanket. It seemed like the right thing, what you see on TV.

A few neighbors had come outside to watch. We ignored them.

"I'll need you with me," I said to the boy. "When we're done, I'll take you home." The boy was wringing the hem of his shirt in both hands. His eyes brimmed with tears. "I won't hurt you, if that's what you think."

We set off for the hospital, Lynn following in my pickup. The boy sat beside me in the passenger seat, his body pressed to the door, face against the window, the seat-belt strap clenched in one hand at his waist. With each bump in the road, he turned to look at Jack.

"What's your name?" I asked.

"Alan," he said.

"How old are you, Alan?"

"Seventeen."

"Seventeen. Seventeen. And have you ever been with a woman, Alan?"

Alan looked at me. His face drained of color. His hand tightened on the seat belt.

"It's a simple question, Alan. I'm asking you: Have you been with a woman?"

"No," Alan said. "No, sir."

"Then how do you know you're gay?"

In back, Jack began to stir. He moaned, then grew silent. Alan watched him.

"Look at me, Alan," I said. "I asked you a question. If you've never been with a woman, then how do you know you're gay?"

"I don't know," Alan said.

"You mean you don't know that you're gay, or you don't know how you know?"

"I don't know how I know," Alan said. "I just do."

We passed the bakery, the Laundromat, the supermarket, and entered the city limits. In the distance, the silhouette of the helicopter on the hospital's roof. Behind us, the steady pursuit of the pickup truck.

"And your parents, do they know about this?" I asked.

"Yes," Alan said.

"And do they approve?"

"Not really."

"No. I bet they don't, Alan. I'll bet they do not."

I glanced in the rearview mirror. Jack had not opened his eyes, but he had a hand to his temple. The other hand, the one attached to the broken arm, lay at his side. The fingers moved, but without purpose, the hand spasming from fist to open palm.

"I just have one more question for you, Alan," I said.

Alan looked like he might be sick. He watched the road unfurl before us. He was afraid of me, afraid to look at Jack.

"What right do you have teaching my son to be gay?"

"I didn't!" Alan said. "I'm not!"

"You're not? Then what do you call that? Back there? That business on the couch?"

"Mr. Lawson," Alan said, and here the tone of his voice changed and I felt as though I were speaking to another man. "With all due respect, sir, Jack came on to me."

"Jack is not gay."

"He is. I know it. Jack knows it. Your wife knows it. I don't know how you couldn't know it. I don't see how you've missed the signals."

I tried to imagine what signals, but I couldn't. I couldn't recall a thing that would have signaled that I'd wind up here, delivering my son to the hospital with a concussion and a broken arm. What signal might have foretold that, following this day, after two months spent in a motel and two months in prison, my wife of twenty years would divorce me because, as she put it, I was full of hate?

I pulled up to the emergency room's entryway, and Alan helped me pull Jack from the car. A nurse with a wheelchair ran out to meet us. We settled Jack into the chair, and she wheeled him away.

I pulled the car into a parking spot and walked back to the entrance. Alan stood on the curb where I had left him.

"Where's Lynn?" I said.

"Inside," Alan said. "Jack's awake."

"All right, I'm going in. I suggest you get out of here."

"But you said you'd drive me home."

"Sorry," I said. "I changed my mind."

Alan stared at me, dumbfounded. His hands groped the air.

"Hey," I said, "I got a signal for you." I gave him a hitchhiker's thumbs-up and cast it over my shoulder as I entered the hospital.

I wake and Cam's making his way down back roads, their surfaces cratered with potholes.

"Rise and shine," he says, "and welcome to Lee."

It's nearly noon. The sun is bright, and the cab is hot. I wipe gunk from my eyes and drool from the corner of my mouth. Cam watches the road with one eye and studies directions he's scrawled in black ink across the back of a cereal box. He's never seen the house where his father spent his last twenty years.

We turn onto a dirt road. The truck lurches into and then out of an enormous waterlogged hole. Pines line the road. Their needles shiver as we go by. We pass turn after turn, but only half of the roads are marked. Every few miles we pass a driveway, the house deep in the trees and out of sight. It's a haunted place, and I'm already ready to leave.

Cam says, "I don't know where the fuck we are."

We drive some more. I think about Bobby home alone, how Cam gave him six VHS tapes. "By the time you watch all of these," he said, "I'll be back." Then he put in the first movie, something Disney, and we left. "He'll be fine," Cam said. "He'll never even know we're gone."

"We could bring him with us," I said, but Cam refused.

"There's no telling what we'll find there," he said.

Ahead, a child stands beside the road. Cam slows the truck to a halt and rolls down the window. The girl steps forward. She looks over her shoulder, then back at us. She is barefoot, and her face is smeared with dirt. She wears a brown dress and a green bow in her hair. A string is looped around her wrist, and from the end of the string floats a blue balloon.

"Hi, there," Cam says. He leans out the window, his hand extended, but the child does not take it. Instead, she stares at his arms, the coiled dragons. She takes a step back.

"You're scaring her," I say.

Cam glares at me, but he returns his head to the cab and his hand to the wheel and gives the girl his warmest smile. "Do you know where we could find Cherry Road?" he says.

"Sure," the girl says. She pumps her arm and the balloon bobs in response. "It's that way," she says, pointing in the direction from which we've come.

"About how far?" Cam asks.

"Not the next road but the next. But it's a dead end. There's only one house." She flails her wrist and the balloon thunks against her fist.

Cam glances at the cereal box. "That's the one," he says.

"Oh," the girl says, and for a moment she is silent. "You're going to visit the Lizard Man. I seen him. I seen him once."

Cam looks at me. I shrug. We look at the girl.

"Well, thank you," Cam says. The girl gives the balloon a good shake. Cam turns the truck around, and the girl waves good-bye.

"Cute kid," I say. We turn onto Cherry.

"Creepy little fucker," Cam says.

The house is hidden in pines, and the yard is overgrown with knee-high weeds. Tire tracks mark where the driveway used to be. Plastic flamingos dot the yard, their curved beaks peeking out of the weeds, wire legs rusted, bodies bleached a light pink.

The roof of the house is littered with pine needles and piles of shingles where someone abandoned a roofing project. The porch has buckled, and the siding is rotten, the planks loose. I press a fingernail to the soft wood and it slides in.

Our mission is unclear. There's no body to ID or papers to sign.

Nothing to inherit and there will be no funeral. But I know why we're here. This is how Cam will say good-bye.

The front door is locked but gives with two kicks. "Right here," Cam says. He taps the wood a foot above the lock before slamming the heel of his boot through the door.

Inside, the house waits for its owner's return. The hallway light is on. The AC unit shakes in the window over the kitchen sink. Tan wallpaper curls away from the cabinets like birch bark, exposing thin ribbons of yellow glue on the walls.

We hear voices. Cam puts a hand to my chest and a finger to his lips. He brings a hand to his waist and feels for a gun that is not there. Neither of us moves for a full minute, then Cam laughs.

"Fuck!" he says. "That's a TV." He hoots. He runs a hand through his hair. "About scared the shit out of me."

We move to the main room. It too is in disarray, the lamp shades thick with dust, a coffee table awash in a sea of newspapers and unopened mail. There is an old and scary-looking couch, its arms held to its sides with duct tape. A pair of springs pokes through the cushion, ripe with tetanus.

The exception is the television. It is beautiful. It is six feet of widescreen glory. "Look at that picture," I say, and Cam and I step back to take it in. The TV's tuned to the Military Channel, some cable extravagance. B-2 bombers streak the sky in black and white, propellers the size of my head. On top of the set sits a bottle of Windex and a filthy washcloth, along with several many-buttoned remote controls. Cam grabs one, fondles it, holds down a button, and the sound swells. The drone of plane engines and firefights tears across the room from one speaker to another. I jump. Cam grins.

"We're taking it," he says. "We are so taking this shit."

He pushes another button and the picture blips to a single point of white at the center of the screen. The point fades and dies.

"No!" Cam says. "No!"

"What did you do?" I say.

"I don't know. I don't know!"

Cam shakes the remote, picks up another, punches more buttons, picks up a third, presses its buttons. The television hums, and the picture shimmers back to life.

"Ahhh," Cam says. We sit, careful to avoid the springs. While we watch, the beaches at Normandy are stormed, two bombs are dropped, and the war is won. We're halfway into Vietnam when Cam says, "I'm going to check out his room." It is not an invitation.

Cam's gone for half an hour. When he returns, he looks terrible. The color is gone from his face, and his eyes are red-rimmed. He carries a shoe box under one arm. I don't ask, and he doesn't offer.

"Let's load up the set and get out of here," Cam says. "I'll pull the truck around." I hear a glass door slide open then shut behind me. I hear something like a scream. Then the door slides open again. I turn around to see Cam. If he looked bad before, now he looks downright awful.

"What is it?" I say.

"Big," Cam says. "In the backyard."

"What? What's big in the backyard?"

"Big. Fucking. Alligator."

It *is* a big fucking alligator. I've seen alligators before, in movies, at zoos, but never this big and never so close. We stare at him. We don't know it's a him, but we decide it's a him. He is big. It's insane.

It's also the saddest fucking thing I have ever seen. In the backyard is a makeshift cage, an oval of chain-link fence with a chicken-wire roof. Inside, the alligator straddles an old kiddie pool. The pool's cracked plastic lip strains with the alligator's weight. His middle fills the pool, his belly submerged in a few inches of syrupy brown water, legs hanging out. His tail, the span of a man, curls against a length of chain-link.

When he sees us, the alligator hisses and paddles his front feet in the air. He opens his jaws, baring yellow teeth and white fleshy gums. Everywhere there are flies and gnats. They fly into his open mouth and land on his teeth. Others swarm open wounds along his back.

"What is he doing here?" Cam asks.

"Red was the Lizard Man," I say. "Apparently."

We stare at the alligator. He stares back. I consider the cage and wonder whether the alligator can turn around.

"He looks bored," Cam says. And it's true. He looks bored, and sick. He shuts his mouth, and his open eyes are the only thing reminding me he's alive.

"We can't leave him here," Cam says.

"We should call someone," I say. But who would we call? The authorities? Animal control?

"We can't," Cam says. "They'll kill him."

Cam is right. I've seen it before, on the news. Some jackass raises a gator. The gator gets loose. It's been handfed and knows no fear of man. The segments always end the same way: *Sadly, the alligator had to be destroyed*.

"I don't see that we have a choice," I say.

"We have the pickup," Cam says.

My mouth says no, but my eyes must say yes, because before I know what's happening, we're in the front yard, examining the bed of the truck, Cam measuring the length with his open arms.

"This won't work," I say. Cam ignores me. He pulls a blue tarp from the backseat and unrolls it on the ground beside the truck.

"He'll never fit," I say.

"He'll fit. It'll be close, but he'll fit."

"Cam," I say. "Wait. Stop." Cam leans against the truck. He looks right at me. "Say we get the alligator out of the cage and into the truck. Say we manage to do this and keep all of our fingers. Where do we take him? I mean, what the hell, Cam? What the hell do you do with twelve feet of living, breathing alligator? And what about the TV? I thought you wanted to take the TV."

"Shit. I forgot about the TV."

We stare at the truck. I look up. The sky has turned from bright to light blue, and the sun has disappeared behind a scatter of clouds. On the ground, one corner of the tarp flaps in the breeze, winking its gold eyelet.

Cam bows his head as if in mourning, "Maybe if we stand the set up on its end."

"Cam," I say. "We can take the alligator or we can take the television, but we can't take both."

Electric-taping the snout, Cam decides, will be the hard part.

"All of it's the hard part," I say, but Cam's not listening.

Cam finds a T-bone in Red's refrigerator. It's spoiled, but the alligator doesn't seem to mind. Cam sets the steak near the cage and the alligator waddles out of the pool. He presses his nostrils to the fence. The thick musk of alligator and reek of rotten meat turn my stomach and I retch.

"You puke, I kick your ass," Cam says.

We've raided Red's garage for supplies. Lying scattered at our feet are bolt cutters, a roll of electric tape, a spool of twine, bungee cords, a dozen two-by-fours, my tarp and, for no reason I'm immediately able to ascertain, a chain saw.

"Protection," Cam says, nudging the old Sears model with his toe. The chain is rusted and hangs loose from the blade. I imagine Cam starting the chain saw, the chain snapping, flying, landing far away in the tall grass. I try to picture the struggle between man and beast, Cam pinned beneath five hundred pounds of alligator, Cam's head in the gator's mouth, Cam dragged in circles around the yard, a tangle of limbs and screams. Throughout each scenario, the chain saw offers little assistance.

Cam's hands are sheathed in oven mitts, a compromise he accepted begrudgingly when the boxing gloves he found, while offering superior protection, failed to provide him the ability to grip, pick up, or hold.

"This is stupid," I say. "Are we really doing this?"

"We're doing this," Cam says. He swats a fly from his face with one pot-holdered hand.

There is a clatter of chain-link. We turn to see the alligator nudging the fence with his snout. He snorts, eyes the T-bone, opens and shuts his mouth. He really is surprisingly large. Cam's parked the pickup in the backyard. He pulls off his oven mitts, lowers the gate, exposing the wide, bare bed of the truck, and we set to work angling the two-by-fours from gate to grass. We press the planks together, and Cam cinches them tight with the bungee cords. The boards are long, ten or twelve feet, so physics is on our side. We should be able to drag him up the incline.

We return our attention to the alligator, who is sort of throwing himself against the fence, except that he can only back up a few feet and therefore build very little momentum. Above his head, at knee level, is a hand-size wire mesh door held shut by a combination lock. With each lunge, the lock jumps, then clatters against the door. With each charge, I jump too.

"He can't break out," Cam says. He picks up the bolt cutters.

"You don't know that," I say.

"If he could, don't you think he'd have done it by now?" Cam positions the bolt cutters on the loop of the lock, bows his legs, and squats. He squeezes, and his face reddens. He grunts, there's a snap, and the lock falls away, followed by a flash of movement. Cam howls and falls. The alligator's open jaws stretch halfway through the hole. All I see is teeth.

"Motherfucker!" Cam yells.

"You okay?" I say.

Cam holds up his hands, wiggles ten fingers.

"Okay," Cam says. "Okay." He picks up the T-bone and throws it at the alligator. The steak lands on his nose, hangs there, then slides off.

"It's not a dog," I say. "This isn't catch."

Cam puts on the oven mitts and slowly reaches for the meat resting in the grass just a few feet beneath all those teeth. Suddenly, the pen looks less sturdy, less like a thing the alligator could never escape.

The cage shakes, but this time it's the wind, which has really picked up. I wonder whether it's storming in St. Petersburg. Cam should be at home with Bobby, and I almost say as much. But Cam's eyes are wild. He's dead set on doing this.

Cam says, "I'm going to put the steak into his mouth, and when I do, I want you to tape the jaws shut."

"No way," I say. "No way am I putting my hand in range of that thing." And then this happens: My son walks out of my memory and into my thoughts, his arm hanging loose at the elbow. The nurse asks what happened, and he looks up, ready to lie for me. There is something beautiful in the pause between this question and the one to come. Then there's the officer's hand on my shoulder, the "Would you mind stepping out with me, please?" Oh, I've heard it a hundred times. It never leaves me. It is a whisper. It is a prison sentence.

I want to put the elbow back into the socket myself. I want to turn back time. I want Jack at five or ten. I want him curled in my lap like a dog. I want him writing on the walls with an orange crayon and blaming the angels that live in the attic. I want him before his voice plummeted two octaves, before he learned to stand with a hand on one hip, before he grew confused. I want my boy back.

"Come on!" Cam shouts. "Don't puss out on me now. As soon as he bites down, just wrap the tape around it."

"Give me your oven mitts," I say.

"No!"

"Give me the mitts and I'll do it."

"But you won't be able to handle the tape."

"Trust me," I say. "I'll find a way."

We do it. Cam waves the cut of meat at the snout until it smacks teeth. The jaws grab. There's an unnatural crunch as the *T* in the T-bone becomes two *I*s and then a pile of periods. I drape a length of tape over the nose, fasten the ends beneath the jaws, then run my gloved hands up both strands of tape, sealing them. Then I start wrapping like crazy. I wind the roll of tape around and around the jaws. The tape unspools from the roll and coils in a flat black worm around the snout.

When I step back, the alligator's jaws are shut tight and my hands shake.

"I can't believe it," Cam says. "I can't believe you actually did that shit."

The alligator's one heavy son of a bitch. We hold him in a kind of headlock, arms cradling his neck and front legs, fingers gripping his scaly hide. It's a good twenty feet from cage to truck. We sidestep toward the pickup, the alligator's back end and tail tracing a path through the grass. Every few feet we stop to rest.

When we drag, the alligator's back feet scramble and claw at the ground, but he doesn't writhe or thrash. He is not a healthy alligator. I stop.

"C'mon," Cam says. "Almost there."

"What are we doing?" I say.

"We're putting an alligator into your truck," Cam says. "C'mon."

"But look at him," I say. Cam looks down, examines the alligator's wide green head, his wet Ping-Pong ball eyes. He looks up.

"No," I say. "Really look."

"What?" Cam's impatient. He shifts his weight, gets a better grip on the gator. "I don't know what you want me to see."

"He's not even fighting us. He's too sick. Even if we set him free, how do we know he'll make it?"

"We don't."

"No, we don't. We don't know where he came from. We don't know where to take him. And what if Red raised him? How will he survive in the wild? How will he learn to hunt and catch fish and stuff?"

Cam shrugs, shakes his head.

"So why?" I ask. "Why are we doing this?"

Cam locks eyes with me. After a minute I look away. My arms

are weak with the weight of alligator. My legs quiver. We shuffle forward.

I didn't give Jack the chance to lie. I admitted guilt to second-degree battery and kept everyone out of court. I got four months and served two, plus fines, plus community service. Had that been the end of it, I'd have gotten off easy. Instead, I lost my family.

The last time I saw Jack he stood beside his mother's car, showing Alan his new driver's license. They reclined like girls against the hood but laughed like men at something on the license: a typo. "Weight: 1500." I watched them from the doorway. Jack kept his distance, flinched when I came close.

Alan had helped me load the furniture. With each piece, I thought of Jack's body. How it hung between us that afternoon, how it swayed, how much like a game wherein you and a friend grab another boy by ankles and wrists and throw him off a dock and into a lake.

Everything Jack and Lynn owned we'd packed into a U-Haul truck. I was not meant to know where they were going. I was not meant to see them again, but I'd found maps and directions in a pile of Lynn's things and had written down the address of their new place in Baton Rouge. I could forgive Lynn not wanting to see me, but taking my son away was a thing I could not abide.

I decided I would go there one day, a day that seems more distant with each passing afternoon. And what would Jack do when he opened the door? In my dreams, it was always Jack who opened the door. I would open my arms in invitation. I would say what I had not said.

But that afternoon it was Alan who sent Jack to me. Lynn waited in the U-Haul, ready to drive away. Alan gestured in my direction. He and Jack argued in hushed voices. And finally, remarkably, Jack moved toward me. I did not leave the doorway, and Jack stopped just short of the stoop.

What can I tell you about my son? He had been a beautiful boy, and standing before me I saw that he had become something different: a man I did not understand. His T-shirt was too tight for him, and the hem rode just above his navel. A trail of light brown hair led from there and disappeared behind a silver belt buckle. His fingernails were painted black. The cast had come off, and his right arm was a nest of curly, dark hair.

I wanted to say, "I want to understand you."

I wanted to say, "I will do whatever it takes to earn your trust."

I wanted to say "I love you," but I had never said it, not to Jack— yes, I am one of those men—and I could not bear the thought of speaking these words to my son for the first time and not hearing them spoken in return.

Instead, I said nothing.

Jack held out his hand, and we shook like strangers.

I still feel it, the infinity of Jack's handshake: the nod of pressed palms, flesh of my flesh.

The rain arrives in sheets, and the windshield wipers can hardly keep up. I drive. Cam sits beside me. He's placed the shoe box on the seat between us. His arm rests protectively against the lid. The alligator slides around with the two-by-fours in the back. We fastened the tarp over the bed of the truck to conceal our cargo, but we didn't pull it taut. The tarp sags with water, threatening to smother the animal underneath.

Cam flips on the radio and we catch snippets of the weather before the speakers turn to static.

". . . upgraded to a tropical storm . . . usually signals the forma- tion of a hurricane . . . storm will pick up speed as it makes its way across the Gulf . . . expected to come ashore as far north as the panhandle . . . far south as St. Petersburg. . . ."

Cam turns the radio off. We watch rain pelt the windshield, the black flash of wipers pushing water.

I don't ask whether Bobby is afraid of storms. As a boy, I'd been frightened, but not Jack. During storms Jack had stood at the win- dow and watched as branches skittered down the street and power lines unraveled onto the sidewalks. He smiled and stared until Lynn pulled him away from the glass and we moved to the bathroom with our blankets and flashlights. It was only then, huddled in the dark, that Jack sometimes cried.

"We should go back," I say. "The power could be out."

"Bobby's a tough kid," Cam says. "He'll be fine."

"Cam," I say.

"In case you've forgotten, there's a fucking alligator in the back of your truck."

I say nothing. Whatever happens is Cam's responsibility. This, I tell myself, is not your fault.

Thunder shakes the truck. Not far ahead a cell tower ignites with lightning. A shower of sparks waterfalls onto the highway. Cars and trucks are dusted with fire. Everyone drives on.

I don't know where we're headed, but Cam says we're close.

Cam, I think, after this, I owe you nothing. Once this is over, we're even.

"If it's work you're worried about," Cam says, "I'll talk to Mickey. I'll tell him about Red. He'll understand if you're a little late."

"It's not Mickey I'm worried about," I say. I don't say, *Mickey can kiss my ass.* I don't say, *You and Mickey can go to hell.*

"Look," Cam says, "I know why you're pulling the graveyard shift. Mickey told me what you did. But this is different. This he'll understand."

I recognize the ache at the back of my throat immediately. The second I'm alone it will take a miracle to keep a bottle out of my hand.

"Take this exit," Cam says. "At the bottom, turn right."

I guide the truck down the ramp toward Grove Street. The water in back sloshes forward and unfloods the tarp. Alligator feet scratch for purchase on the truck bed's corrugated plastic lining.

"Where are you taking us?" I ask.

"Havenbrook," he says. I wait for Cam to say he's kidding. But Cam isn't kidding.

•••

The largest of the lakes cradles the seventeenth green. Cam's seen gators there before, big bastards who come ashore to sun themselves and scare off golfers. I've never golfed in my life and neither has he, but Cam led the team that patched the clubhouse roof following last year's hurricane season. He remembers the five-digit code, and it still works. The security gate slides open, and we head down the paved drive reserved for maintenance.

No one's on the course. Fallen limbs litter the greens. An abandoned white cart lies turned on its side where the golf-cart path rounds the fifteenth hole.

Lightning streaks the sky. The rain has turned the windshield to water, and sudden gusts of wind jostle the truck from every direction. I fight the steering wheel to stay on the asphalt. Even Cam is wide-eyed, his fingers buried in the seat cushion. The shoe box bounces between us.

We reach the lake, but the shore is half a football field away. The green is soggy, thick with water, and already the lake is flooding its banks. The first tire that leaves the road, I know, will sink into the mud, and we'll never get the truck out.

"I can't drive out there," I tell Cam. I have to yell over the wind and rain, the deafening thunder. It's like the world is pulling apart. "This is the closest I can get us."

Cam says something I can't hear, and then he's out of the truck, the door slamming behind him. I jump out, and the wet cold slaps me. Within seconds I'm drenched, my clothes heavy. All I hear is the wind. I move as if underwater.

As soon as Cam gets the tarp off, the storm catches it and it billows into the sky like a flaming blue parachute, up into the trees overhead. It tangles itself into the branches, and then there is only the *smack-smack* of the tarp's uncaught corners pummeled by gusts.

Cam screams at me. His teeth flash in bursts of lightning, but his words are choked by wind. I tap my ear and he nods. He motions toward the alligator. We approach it slowly. I expect the animal to charge, but he lies motionless. I check the jaws. They're still wrapped tight. This, I realize, will be our last challenge. If he gets away from us before we remove the tape, he's doomed.

I'm wondering which of us will climb into the bed of the truck when the gator starts scuttling forward. We leap out of the way as hundreds of pounds of reptile spill from the truck and onto the green. The gate cracks under the weight and swings loose like a trapdoor in midair, the hinges busted. Then the alligator is free on the grass. We don't move, and neither does he.

Cam approaches me. He makes a megaphone of his cupped hands and mouth and leans in close to my ear. His hot breath on my face is startling and sudden and wonderful in all that fierce cold and rain.

"I think he's stunned," Cam yells. "We've got to get the tape off, now."

I nod. I am exhausted and anxious, and I know there's no way we'll be able to lug the alligator to the water's edge. I wonder whether he'll make it, if he'll find his way to the water, or if this fall from the truck is the final blow, if tomorrow the groundskeepers will find an alligator carcass fifty yards from the lake. It would make the *St. Petersburg Times* front page. A giant alligator killed in the hurricane. Officials would be baffled.

"I want you to straddle its neck," Cam yells. "Keep its head pressed to the ground. I'll try to get the tape off."

"No," I say. I point to my chest. I circle my hand through the air, pantomiming the unraveling. Cam looks surprised, but he nods.

Cam brings his hands to my face again and yells his hot words into my ear. "On my signal," he screams, but I push him away.

I don't wait for a signal. Before I know it, I'm on the ground, my side hugging mud, and I'm digging my nails into the tape. My eye is inches from the alligator's eye. He blinks without blinking, a thin, clear membrane sliding over his eyeball, then up and under his eyelid. It is a thing to see. It is a knowing wink. I see this and I feel safe.

The tape is harder to unwrap than it was to wrap. The rain has made it soft, the glue gooey. Every few turns, I lose my grip. Finally, I let the tape coil around my hand like a snake. It unwinds and soon my fist is a ball of dark, sticky fruit. The last of the tape pulls cleanly from the snout, and I roll away from the alligator. I stand, and Cam pulls me back. He holds me up. The alligator flexes his jaws. His mouth opens wide, then slams shut. And then he's off, zigzagging toward the water.

He is swift and strong, and I'm glad it is cold and raining so Cam can't see the tears streaking my cheeks and won't know that my shivering is from sobbing. Cam lets go of me and I think I will fall, but instead I am running. Running! And I'm laughing and hollering and leaping. I'm pumping my fist into the air. I'm screaming, "Go! Go!" And just before the alligator reaches the water, I lunge and my fingertips trace the last ridges and scales of tail whipping their way ahead of me. The sky is alive with lightning, and I see the hulking body, so awkward and graceless on land, slide into the water as it was meant to do. That great body cuts the water fast and sleek, and the alligator dives out of sight, at home in the world where he belongs, safe in the warm quiet of mud and fish and unseen things that thrive in deep green darkness.

Cam and I don't say much on the ride home. The rain has slowed to an even, steady downpour. The truck's cab has grown cold. Cam holds his hands close to the vents to catch whatever weak streams of heat trickle out. "We have done a good thing," Cam says, and I agree, but I worry at what cost. We listen to the radio, but the storm has headed north. The reporters have moved on to new cities: Clearwater, Crystal Springs, Ocala.

"There was this one time," Cam says at last. "About five years back. I spoke to Red."

This is news to me. This, I know, is no small revelation.

"I called him," Cam says. "I called him up, and I said, 'Dad? I just want you to know that you have a grandson and that his name is Robert and that I think he should know his grandfather.'

And you know what that prick did? He hung up. The only thing Red said to me in twenty years was 'Hello' when he picked up the phone."

"I'm sorry," I say.

"If he'd even once told me he was sorry, I'd have forgiven him anything. I'd have forgiven him my own murder. He was my father. I would have forgiven everything.

"Do you know why I got all these fucking tattoos? To hide the fucking scars from the night Red cut me with a fillet knife, and I'd have forgiven that if he'd just said something, anything, when he answered the phone."

Cam doesn't shake or sob or bang a fist on the dashboard, but when I look away, I catch his reflection in the window, a knuckle in each eye socket, and I'm suddenly sorry for my impatience, the grudge I've carried all afternoon.

"But you tried," I say. "At least you won't spend your life wondering."

We sit in silence for a while. The rain on the roof beats a cadence into the cab and it soothes me.

"You know, I served with gay guys in the Gulf," Cam says, and I almost drive the truck off the road. A tire slips over the lip of asphalt and my side mirror nearly catches a guardrail before I bring the truck back to the center of the lane.

"Jesus!" Cam says. "I'm just saying they were okay guys, and if Jack's gay, it's not the end of the world."

"Jack's confused," I say. "He isn't gay."

"Well, either he is or he isn't, and what you think or want or say won't change it."

"Cam," I say, "all due respect. This doesn't concern you."

"I know," Cam says. He sits up straighter in his seat and grips the door handle as we pull onto our block. "I'm just saying it isn't too late."

We pull into the driveway. Cam jumps out of the truck before it's in park. The yard is a mess of fallen limbs and garbage. Two shutters have been torn from the front of the house. The mailbox is on its side. Otherwise everything looks all right. I glance down the street and see that my house is still standing.

When I turn back to Cam's house, what I see breaks my heart in ten places. I see Cam running across the lawn. I see Bobby, his hands pressed to the big bay window. His face is puffy and red. Cam disappears into the house, and then he is there with the boy, he is there on his knees, and he pulls Bobby to him. He mouths the words *I'm sorry, I'm sorry* over and over again, and Bobby collapses into him, buries his head in Cam's chest, and my friend wraps his son in dragons.

I watch them. They stay like that for minutes, framed by window and house and darkening sky. I watch, and then I open the shoe box and look inside.

I don't know what I was expecting, but it wasn't this. What I find are letters, over a hundred of them. About a letter a month for roughly ten years, all of them unopened. Each has been dated and stamped RETURN TO SENDER, the last one sent back just a week ago. Each is marked by the same shaky handwriting. Each is addressed to a single recipient, Mr. Cameron Starnes, from a single sender, Red.

And I know then that there was no phone call, no forgiveness on Cam's part, that Cam never came close until after the monster was safely out of reach.

I stare at the letters, and I know who it is Cam wants to keep me from becoming.

I pull out of Cam's driveway. I stop to right Cam's mailbox, then I tuck the shoe box safely inside. I follow the street to the end of the block. At the stop sign, I pause. I don't know whether to turn right or left. Finally, I head for the interstate. There's a spare uniform at the diner, clean and dry, and if I hurry, I won't be late for work.

But I'm not going to work.

It's a ten-hour drive to Baton Rouge, but I will make it in eight.

I will make it before morning. I will drive north, following the storm. I will drive through the wind and the rain. I will drive all night.

———————

David James Poissant's stories have appeared in *Playboy, The Chicago Tribune, Willow Springs, The Chattahoochee Review, Redivider,* and in the anthology *Best New American Voices 2008.* He has won the *Playboy* College Fiction Contest, the AWP Quickie Contest, the George Garrett Fiction Award, second prize in the *Atlantic Monthly* Student Writing Contest, and was a runner-up for the 2006 Nelson Algren Award. He is currently a PhD candidate at the University of Cincinnati.

RANDI MOODY

*S*ometimes *I take extensive notes before beginning a story. Other times, as with "Lizard Man," the story evolves in the writing from a single, unformed idea. Looking through a notebook, I see that the hastily scribbled impetus for "Lizard Man" was this: "Two brothers drive north to recover the remains of a dead brother. Also, somehow, an alligator." In the telling, the brothers would become friends. The dead brother would become a dead father. The story, as it turned out, was never one of brothers, but of fathers and sons, the strained father/son relationships between Cam and his son, Cam and his father, and the narrator and his son. Once I accepted this, writing "Lizard Man" became a matter of entwining these three narratives with the central storyline, that of Cam and the narrator and the very strange day that they share.*

Fun fact: This story was composed mostly at Waffle House. This was when I lived in Tucson, Arizona, and a hectic schedule left me little time to write. I carved out midnight to 3 AM, five nights a week, for writing, and, as not much is open past midnight in Tucson, I often found myself working at a lonely little Waffle House off the interstate that bisects the city. The place was quiet and well lit, and the service—what with, most nights, my pretty much being the only customer—was impeccable. It was a place like this that I imagined for the story's narrator when I made him a short-order cook at an all-night diner.

Daniel Wallace

THE GIRLS

(from *Land-Grant College Review*)

You could always tell the ones he liked the best.

"So, Rachel," he'd ask me, casual as you please. "About how old is she?"

He'd be watching her walk away in the beam of the headlights, after a long and mostly silent ride. For a moment she'd be lit up like a star. She'd turn to wave and my dad would get another look at her ambitious chest, but mostly we had this long look at her butt as she walked down her driveway and paused at her back door, either fishing for a key or waiting for a parent to open it for her. Then she'd wave again, and we'd pull away, going home.

"How old?" he'd ask again.

"My age," I'd invariably say, because how great an age difference are you going to find in ninth-grade girls, the pool from which my friends were chosen?

"Fourteen," he said, almost in a whisper.

Fourteen woke my father up. When we were twelve and thirteen he never asked anything about them, only directions to their homes. He'd keep the radio low on a station he liked, and you could hear him listening to it, tuning me and my friends out as he drove his one way once or twice a week.

But when we turned fourteen something happened to him— and to us—that shook him out of his sleep. Until then he had been more of a part-time parent. I mean you could count on Mom for

most things all of the time, but Dad—who worked (he sold pho-
tocopiers), and when he wasn't working looked to be recovering
from it—Dad was there for a certain number of hours a day, usually around dusk during the week, afternoons on the weekends.
And there were only certain things you asked him for, things like
money and rides and, occasionally, permission. But asking him
wasn't usually productive, because he wasn't around enough to
know what was permissible, and the things he said were okay
sometimes weren't, and I suppose that's why I asked him at all,
knowing what Mom's answer would have been all along.

Roused from his sleep, though, he was an inquisitive, clumsy
giant. Even so, I don't think anyone would have noticed the change
but me; even Mom might not have. It was the situation we were
in that made me able to notice, the two of us together in the small
space of the car, the routine travel back and forth from our house
to the girls'; it was in this very specific circumstance that I was able
to see—hard to describe what it was, really. But I saw it, this thing
growing inside him like a bud. And I just watched it grow.

"Fourteen," he said again, shaking his head.

"She's mature for her age," I said.

"I'll say," he said. Then, catching himself, glancing at me sitting
still beside him, my face glowing briefly in a street lamp, "She's a
very well-spoken young lady."

"Whatever."

At a stoplight he tapped his fingers on the steering wheel, eyes
roaming through the dark world outside.

"So, did she just move here?"

"Andrea Nichols?" I said. I couldn't believe this. "I've known
her since I was in third grade!"

"Andrea? That's Andrea?"

"That's Andrea."

Dad had this thing where in moments of mild surprise he would
breathe in deeply through his nose: this is what he did now. In,
then out. He was quiet for the rest of the way home, turning things

over in his head. It wasn't until we were pulling into the driveway
that he spoke again.

"I remember her now," he said.

I took a look at myself in the mirror that night. I had a long
one on the back of my bedroom door, and I would close the door
and lock it and take off my clothes—all of them, except for my
socks—and look at my body. I'd been doing this for the last two
years, ever since I came to realize my body's stubborn sameness,
its fear of change. I tried to put a space of time between my looks,
so something would have a chance to happen, somewhere.

But tonight there was no change at all. Nothing. I don't think
I even qualified as having a figure yet, though if I were being op-
timistic I'd say there were indications of a shape to come. I tried
to be positive about it, I really did. But my breasts were like tear-
drops, and my hips barely rippled at all. Not much there, but then
that wasn't the point: the point was who was doing the looking.
I simply gazed at what was me and did that thing my father did:
breathed in deeply through my nose. Then out.

That summer we started carpooling a lot. Dad would take a load
of us to a movie, then someone else would pick us up, or the other
way around. Mom stepped in occasionally when it was impossible
for him to be there—he did have to work, after all—but he was an
eager parent in this regard. He kind of became known as the guy
for that. When every other parent failed, there was always my dad,
ready and willing to take us wherever we wanted to go. I think I
saw him more in the car than I did at home, and if I'm exaggerat-
ing it's only by a little.

He liked all of my friends—Andrea, Robin, Ellen, Jennifer—and
they liked him back. He had this very well-modulated persona, he
knew when to back off, when to laugh, when to ask a question.
At home be crawled into his cold fatherly shell, radiating a kind of
general dissatisfaction with everything. But riding around with

my girlfriends he was Mr. Personality. Sometimes I just shook my head in wonder and disgust.

Of course, he about jumped out of his skin when I asked him if he wanted to chaperone a bunch of us girls to the roller-skating rink for a party one Friday night. You'd have figured there was no better way for a thirty-nine-year-old man to spend a Friday night. He didn't scream or dance or anything. But when my father was interested, really interested in something he raised his left eyebrow, just that much; he couldn't help it. And so even though he didn't act excited, I knew when I saw that eyebrow rise he viewed this as the Ultimate Treat.

I thought it sucked. I was through with skating rinks, and now for some reason Robin wanted her party at a skating rink, and I didn't know if I could stand it. Everything at a rink is dirty, and sticky, especially the bathroom door handle, and then these really vulgar boys who come from way out in the county—the same guys who like to hang out at the mall—skate up beside you and try to get your phone number. So yes. I was really looking forward to it.

In the car that night my father smelled like a candy bar.

"Where to, Pumpkin?" he asked, not looking at me but over his shoulder, backing out. I almost didn't answer because of him calling me Pumpkin. It's what he called me when I was a little girl, and I don't think I'd heard the word used that way for a decade. So I gave him a look and breathed in deep.

"Well," I said. "We have to pick up Ellen, Andrea, and Jennifer. Robin's going in another car. I'm not sure what the best way is."

"Where's the rink?"

"Durham," I said. "I think. Jennifer has directions."

"Okay. Then I'd say Jennifer first, Ellen second, and Andrea third. Sound good?"

"Fine with me."

"Then off we go."

Off we went! At Jennifer's house he honked the horn once,

lightly. I offered to go in after her but he said we could wait a minute: he wanted to see her come out and walk the walk without any possible obstruction from me. His tiny blue eyes peered through the dusty windshield. He had to squint when she finally came. Breathing in and out in short nervous bursts, I thought he might have a heart attack—seriously, it occurred to me. He was that much into it. Jennifer's T-shirts all were about a size too small: her breasts ballooned out of them almost comically. Her hips made a kind of rolling motion when she walked, as if she were dancing. We watched her, my father and I, Jennifer walking toward us in the haze of the orange summer sun. Ellen, the next stop, was a disappointment I'm sure: she was waiting on the curb by her mailbox when we drove up, and slipped in the backseat so quickly he had to turn around in his seat, craning his neck, for a glimpse of taut tanned thigh. She had tight blue shorts on and at the cuff her legs suddenly seemed to just pop out, like dough overflowing in a pan. They exchanged warm smiles and we drove on.

Andrea, of course, was last, but hardly least, in my father's book. She was first and foremost in his mind; a vision of her was a kind of gauze through which everything else flowed. It was true what he said that time: Andrea didn't look fourteen. She could have been twenty, I guess, if you didn't look too close or deep into her eyes. If you just looked at the outline, though—the hair, the chest, the butt, the legs—she looked old enough. Her legs seemed as long as my whole body, and not skinny, either—they had a real, full shape. The three of them in the backseat together certainly filled it up; whereas my little straw body in the front seat by my father only accentuated the empty space I seemed to surround myself with. I was next to invisible.

"Andrea!" my father bellowed as she climbed in. "Welcome."

"Hi, Mr. Lockhart," she said. She was quiet for a girl her size. You just expected more out of her, is what I mean. "Thanks for the ride."

"No problemo," he said.

"Mucho gracias," she replied, ha ha ha, and off we went.

Oh, how I wish I could have thrown myself through the window! I absolutely hated them all—my father, my friends, all of them. As the girls chatted prettily with him, a noise in my ears grew and grew—a white noise, like static. I blocked them out. I sailed away. Any lunatic in the world can stare straight away bug-eyed out the windshield, and that's what I did, creeping down into myself for a better comfort. But occasionally I picked up a transmission.

And how many thousands of boyfriends do you girls have between you? he asked them.

Boys! said Andrea.

They suck! Jennifer said.

Ha ha ha ha ha ha!

Lost in my own space, I watched trees and telephone poles zip by, fences, mailboxes, flowerbeds. Up close the world was a pleasant blur.

Some time went by. I slipped out of my zone, and tuned in to the chatter.

"I'm not sure these are the best directions, Jennifer," my father said, slowing for a light. He stared at the piece of paper Jennifer had given him, frowning. Shook his head. He was on the edge. This is the sort of daddy I was used to.

"Are we lost?" she said.

"I hadn't wanted to use the word," he said, "but I think so, yes."

A chorus of groans, sighs.

"Robin's going to kill us," Andrea said. Already it was the end of the world. You could hear it in her voice.

"How far—."

"I—I have no idea where we are," he said, semi-stuttering. "These directions—I don't know. Some rights are supposed to be lefts, some lefts rights. I mean, I've lived here all my life and I've never even been in this part of town before."

Looking around us, we too realized how far we were from our destination, and what a strange piece of the world we had ended up in. We were at an intersection, and there was a gas station there and a supermarket and a video rental, but they were different than the stores we were used to, with different names on the front and different-looking people coming in and out of them. The light turned green and a car behind us honked: they knew we weren't from there. My father pulled into a gas station as if to escape.

"I'm asking for directions," he said, working at keeping that lilt in his voice, but he was straining. He breathed in, then out. "Be right back."

I watched him walk up to the guy there, hands in his trousers, trying to be cool. But he couldn't pull it off: there was something insulated about him, unfamiliar and uncomfortable with the ways of the world. He was not used to getting dirty, talking to gas station attendants and such.

He was a dork, a grown-up, professional dork.

The girls in the back registered as much.

"I can't believe he got us lost," Jennifer said. "Those directions were perfect."

"Shit for brains," Andrea said, laughing, and the car laughed with her—my chuckles preeminent.

"I don't know. The directions probably sucked," Ellen said through her laughter. "Remember the time you got us lost getting to Tim's house?"

"That was not my fault!" she said.

"Whatever."

We were awed by the extent of our removal from our native terrain.

"Where in God's asshole are we?" Andrea said. "I mean, look at this place."

"This is like, another country."

"Somebody help us!" we cried, happier seeming now—speaking for myself, anyway—than we had been the whole trip.

By the time my father got back the laughter had subsided, and he had revived.

"We're actually not too far out of our way," he said, smiling at the bevy in back. "The skating rink's just a few blocks down this street here."

"Good work, Mr. Lockhart," Andrea said.

"Bravo," said Ellen. "You're our hero."

As we drove the last few blocks, buoyed as I was by that bout of honest, derisive laughter, I wondered if the skating rink would be a fiasco after all. I could overlook the grime, I supposed; and there were some cute boys there, sometimes. I was a pretty good skater too; actually, I could fly as fast as anybody. So I was trying hard to look on the bright side of things when we pulled into the parking lot.

I shouldn't have bothered. It was a dump, a converted barn with a neon sign—RICK's RINK—tacked on the side. White paint peeled off in scaly sheets. There was a car in the parking lot sitting on big blocks of cement, no wheels at all. It was almost scary. It made you wonder what kind of person Rick was.

"This is definitely not it," Andrea said, sort of painfully.

"It's gotta be," my father said. "There's not another rink around."

"I can't believe Robin would have her party here," Ellen said. "Look at this place."

"Hey. It's probably a wonderland inside," my father said. "Let's give it a chance. Right, Pumpkin?"

That's when I wanted him to die. To gasp for air, turn blue, then purple, grasp his neck with his hands and slump forward onto the steering wheel. Pumpkin, he said. By such seemingly small and thoughtless disclosures a future is suddenly darkened. I heard Pumpkin on the lips of my friends, playfully at first but occasionally with a mind to hurt; I heard Pumpkin muttered softly, and then like some unrestrained virus making its way through school, Pumpkin, to the girls who were not my friends, and to the boys, until I was finally and utterly Pumpkin, forever and ever.

Thank you, Daddy.

He looked at me. "Did I say something?" he said.

But by then we were out of the car, hovering around the doors, unsure of the wisdom of moving much farther afield before we banded together as a group. My father made a point to lock the car, and then we followed him, like ducks, through the pot-hole-filled parking lot to the door of Rick's Rink, which had a picture of a clown painted on the front. But even the clown looked some-how scandalous and leering to me, as if beneath the thin veneer of chalky white face paint was an unshaven and greasy-fingered molester of girls.

"See?" my father said once we got inside. "Nothing to be afraid of. It's just a good old-fashioned family-style rink."

And he was right. Maybe it was a bit scuzzier than some others, but otherwise not much was amiss. There was the snack bar with the sad-looking woman serving behind it, there were the brightly colored chairs and tables, the video games, and the rink itself, thick with boys and girls, moms and dads, circling, spinning, falling on their asses. There really didn't appear to be much more room out there. Andrea's breasts would take up a whole lane on their own, I thought, and Ellen's thighs—make way!

Robin wasn't there, of course. I knew, as I think the rest of us knew, that we had come to the wrong rink, and that Robin and the rest of her friends were somewhere else, probably not waiting for us anymore because, you know, the party must go on. Mean-while, we were still lost—only we had decided to pretend not to be. Dad did most of the pretending for us. He told us if Robin had the same directions he did she was probably lost now too, and that she'd be here soon. So he led us up to the stand where we gave them our shoes and rented our skates, and we sat together, lacing up. He hung back, leaned against a pole, and watched us. That was his job, of course, and he was feeling mighty lucky that it was, too. Keep an eye on those girls. Never let your eyes off those girls. He didn't. Jennifer looked up and he smiled. He was happy, but I don't think he included me in the feeling: I existed just beyond the edge of his gaze. There was a sheet of reflective metal along the base of the wall beside me, and as I leaned over lacing up I saw myself, all wavy and distorted, larger than I was in real life, billowing, grotesque—a slight improvement, I thought, over the real thing that was me. The real thing that was me disappeared too easily. The thing in the metal, though horrifying, demanded your attention, couldn't be ignored.

I wish I had this as a mirror on the back of my door, I thought.

And so we skated, round and round. But the boredom set in fairly quickly. The boys there were nothing to look at, and the floor was cracked in places, and a sense of something larger was missing. There was no party here; it was just us, a few girls, skating in circles, pretending. I was willing to put up with the feeling until the time came to go, but the rest of them weren't, I could tell. Something needed to happen.

"Doesn't your dad skate?" Andrea asked as she rolled up beside me. "He looks so lonely over there."

I glanced his way—so did Andrea. He smiled and waved. He was sitting with his legs crossed, drinking a coke, just having the time of his life. If only I could have told her what he was thinking, as he watched her and the rest of them parade around in front of him. But I couldn't give words to it, even though I knew.

"He doesn't skate," I said. "He doesn't do much physical activity like that."

"You call this physical?" She laughed. "It'd be a blast to see him give it a try."

"I really doubt he'd be up to it," I said.

But that wasn't the answer she'd been looking for. She skated away, moving gracefully past a mother and her crying child, until she caught up with Ellen and Jennifer. They conferred briefly, and in a spontaneous giggling girlish rush sped from the rink to his table. Andrea and Jennifer each grabbed an arm while Ellen tugged at his shoes, finally pulling them off to expose his damp, blue-socked feet. He pretended to object, gazing wide-eyed at the perpetrators, gently trying to free himself from their weak grasps, but he was smiling (and blushing!) throughout the entire procedure. By the time Ellen got back with the skates they had released him, but he had submitted to their wishes by then, lacing up without any further prompting, though they stood above him, arms crossed, smiling wickedly.

"I'm going to need some help here," I heard him say as he stood, flailing with his arms like a flightless bird. Jennifer and Ellen were there for him, thank goodness, and they led him from his chair to the metal bar that circled the rink. He gripped it, unsure of any footing at all.

"I'm not sure this is such a good idea," he said. He glanced at me and shrugged his shoulders, rolled his eyes, like *Can you believe these crazy gals?*

"Where's your sense of adventure, Mr. Lockhart?" Andrea asked him.

"I think I left it at home."

"It's fun," Ellen said. "Give it a try."

"We'll help," said Jennifer, as she and Andrea each took an arm. "We're old hands at skating, Mr. Lockhart. Nothing to worry about. As soon as you get the technique down you'll be fine."

But my father was hopeless. Without Andrea and Ellen holding his arms he wouldn't have moved two feet. As it was he appeared to be in a continuous act of falling, saved time and again by the practiced hands of my lovely friends. His own hands brushed against their hips; falling, or almost falling, he clutched their shoulders, their sides. I skated past two or three times, and each time he was touching a different part.

My poor dad.

I circled by them a couple of times, then the next time slowed down.

"Looks like he's about ready," I told them.

They had gone around the rink once already. He appeared to still be grappling with the most basic of mechanics; nothing was working the way it was supposed to. I backpedaled a few feet in front of them, moving with an ease meant to mock. I held my hands out to him.

"Come on, Daddy," I said. "You can do it!"

"I think he needs another lap around," Andrea said.

"With his helpers!" Ellen said, and they laughed, steadying the clumsy monster as best they could.

"Well, he looks ready to me," I said, arms still open wide for him. "What do you think, Dad?"

"I don't know," he said. "I am feeling a bit unsteady."

"You know what you always say," I said. "We don't know what we can do until we try."

And that did it: the decision was made. He straightened up; the girls released their grip. They guided him for a moment, but as soon as he moved toward my hands they let him go, disappearing into the river-world of skaters all around us. Almost miraculously, he stayed erect. Tall and proud, he was skating! I was only a few feet away from him, and was there to catch him if he fell. But as he moved closer to me I glided farther away, and so the distance between us was constant. He lumbered comically onward for a few seconds, somehow managing to stay upright, as though with equal parts of uncertainty in his arms and legs and mind he was able to achieve a kind of quirky balance.

But the most uncertain thing about him was his eyes: they were open, and scared, like a child's eyes. I'd never seen him scared be-fore. I'd never thought of him as being scared, or imagined that he ever was. But here, in this strange building with indoor ice, he didn't know where he was going, or if he could stay up long enough to get there. I knew the feeling. He was alone now with only me to help him, and his thoughts and feelings shone plainly through his eyes.

Can I trust you? His own daughter. He couldn't trust his own daughter. And he knew why, too. He knew why.

I stopped skating, and let the distance close between us. But as his hands approached mine I let our fingertips just touch—and I pulled them back. I thought he'd go right down, face first to the floor, but he didn't. He kept coming at me, moving by one impossible lurch after another, thrashing the air with his arms, finally catching up and bringing me to him in a kind of bear hug, clutching me pressed hard against his chest—and we both went down, together.

"Pumpkin!" he softly whispered as we fell. Pumpkin, he called me, like when I was his girl.

Daniel Wallace is the author of four novels, most recently *Mr. Sebastian and the Negro Magician.* His work has been translated into twenty-five languages and is included in the curricula of high schools and colleges throughout the country. This is his third appearance in *New Stories from the South.* He lives in Chapel Hill, North Carolina, with his wife and son, where he's a Distinguished Professor of English at the University of North Carolina.

My father's brother was named Waylon, Waylon Wallace, and looking back now you have to wonder if it was that name—Waylon—that changed things. If he had been named Gary or Lee or Jack or Danny (like his brother), would he have turned out the way he did? Because Waylon was the Bad Egg. While my father struck it rich in the import/export business, traveled around the world in sleek private jets, and could say "How much is that?" in seven different languages, Waylon never left Moab, Alabama. He dropped out of high school, got married, had a few kids we rarely saw, was obstreperously drunk, and shaved almost once a week whether he needed to or not. When something untoward happened in Moab (pronounced mow-ab*), it usually had something to do with Waylon. He either did it, or he was with the person who did.*

So the part he plays in this story is, my father bought him a skating rink. Waylon was forty-one or forty-two. No one would hire him to do anything anymore. No one trusted him, not even with a lawn mower. Maybe especially with a lawn mower. My father made an "investment" in his brother, as he put it. He was showing Waylon he still had faith in him. He bought the

Moab Skating Rink and Waylon became the skating rink manager. This was his big chance to turn things around. But he didn't turn things around; he burned them down, falling asleep one night in the office while smoking a cigarette. The rink didn't even last a year.

But the part he plays in this story is, our whole family went down there for the Opening Night. And it was something. Lynyrd Skynyrd blaring from the ancient sound system, balloons and streamers everywhere, free hot dogs to the first hundred people. It wasn't even eight o'clock before Waylon was out there, skating. He was too drunk to stand upright, but with skates on he could fly along with the best of them, constantly appearing to fall, and then miraculously not, over and over and over. He was having the time of his life. He doesn't really play a big part in this story at all. But that's the way stories are written sometimes.

Jim Tomlinson

FIRST HUSBAND, FIRST WIFE

(from *Five Points*)

It was Jerry Cole's ex-wife, Cheryl, who lifted the drugs, which were already illegal anyway. She boosted them from this fat pill lady who manages Hilltop Green Assisted Living. As Jerry waited outside behind the wheel of his rust-bucket GMC piece-of-crap pickup truck parked at the curb, as he sat there imagining how good things would be now that his luck was finally changing, Cheryl's chrome beautician cart came careening down Hilltop Green's front walk like a runaway Peterbilt. Cheryl herself followed close behind, the shoebox stash tucked under her arm for anyone with eyes to see.

She handed the box through the window, stowed the cart in back, and climbed in. Three times she slammed the door, harder each time, until finally it latched. Her face was all wadded up with stupid worry, was it right or was it wrong, this thing they were doing. He lifted the lid and grabbed three bottles out, read the labels, then pushed them close to her face. See? he said, pointing to the people's names, the dates. Isn't it just like I told you? They're dead, aren't they, long ago dead, if they were ever alive, if they aren't someone's made-up names.

Cheryl's eyes got teary. Okay, she said, okay. He said, There's no way Fat-Ass reports this stuff missing. You just relax, babe. Her fists burrowed into her lap. Okay, she said again, and she wiped her cheek on his shoulder. Don't be like that, he said. She said, I'll try Jerry, really I will.

While he drove, Cheryl pawed through the jumble. She picked out bottles, shaking each one like a baby's rattle. She read labels out loud to him, sounding out the syllables of the chemical names. Jesus, she said, I don't recognize none of this stuff.

No problem, Jerry said, feeling juiced now that they were on the interstate. We'll get us a D.A.R.E. book, he said, sort it all out, what we can sell, what to flush.

Jerry, she yelled. Slow down! He was changing lanes, passing cars on both sides. The pickup vibrated, shuddered, the steering wheel numbing his hands. The speedometer needle was waggling a blur around eighty. He backed off the gas, downshifted, and dropped back to legal speed.

He'd had to let Cheryl do the actual swiping, even though she wasn't cut out for it. She worked at Hilltop Green, came and went all the time, fixing old people's hair in their rooms. She had natural access, which Jerry considered important for successful burglary. That's also how, in the first place, she came to be poking around the manager's room, how she happened upon that shoebox hidden high on a closet shelf. Cheryl had always been the kind of person who liked to look at other people's stuff. She'd open drawers and touch a few things, maybe try on shoes or jewelry, check out what's in the medicine cabinet, dab ointment, maybe sniff some perfume. That's all, though. Jacking those pills would never cross her mind, not in a million years. Jerry had to help her see that shoebox for the opportunity it was.

Even though she was the one who took the pill lady's stash, Jerry was the one who got caught. It happened when he tried to broker the Lorcet. His buyer, this muscle-bound freak with a bullet-shaped head and a dragon tattoo glommed onto his jugular, turned out to be a cop, his killer tattoo a fake. A Lexington TV reporter called Jerry a regional drug lord. A station cameraman shot video of him in his orange jail jumpsuit, leg-chains dragging as he waddled up the courthouse steps. The station ran the tape on the newscasts at six and eleven. Cheryl rented a VCR, and she tried to record it so he could see. The piece-of-crap machine screwed up, though, taping some revivalist preacher instead, a completely different channel.

While Cheryl's trial got delayed and delayed, Jerry got convicted and served eight months at Blackburn Correctional Facility. It felt like eight years. The day he was to get out was also his thirtieth birthday, which he took to be some kind of sign. When he woke up that last prison morning, his mind was filled with thoughts of change, of setting off in new directions. He thought maybe he'd start an herb farm on five acres his cousin Shuey owned. Or he'd fence those acres and raise emus, raise them for meat, sell it to restaurants. Or maybe he'd get into ginseng, what Shuey called "sang." The stuff grew wild in Daniel Boone National Forest, old stuff, premium stuff. Foreigners paid small fortunes for a wild-grown root shaped like an animal, a duck, a horse, or maybe a hog. Sang just grew out there, grew in plain dirt, knuckles of the stuff like shallow nuggets of gold, a waiting fortune for someone with ambition to find it. As he lay on his bunk, Jerry could almost feel it in his fingers, smell the soft, musty earth as it crumbled away to reveal the root's shape. His wasted months at Blackburn were ending today. His life was starting again. This time he'd get it right.

Cheryl had rented a motel room not two miles from Blackburn's main gate. She'd decorated it with yellow balloons and rainbow streamers. She bought the fancy Kroger cheese and cold cut platter and laid it out on one bed, a washtub of ice and beer stationed at the foot. She even baked his favorite strawberry jam cake. Two blocky number candles were stuck in the coconut frosting, a three and a zero. As soon as they got to the room, Cheryl lit the candles, shut the drapes, and switched off the lights. She started singing a birthday song, the one the Beatles sing, while performing a cheerleader-style dance in the flickery light. As she did, Jerry inched over to the beer tub. Kneeling there, he uncapped his first bottle since forever, brought its cold lips to his, and pointed the bottom to the swirly motel ceiling. His mind started thinking about riverboats on the Ohio. Did they run in winter when weather got too cold to dig sang? He wondered about their casinos, what they looked for in card dealers, if a felony conviction would hurt someone's chances.

Where are you? Cheryl asked, her face near his, the smell of her bubblegum everywhere. She was still breathing hard from the dancing, but the song was over. Who? Jerry asked. Where? He looked behind him, lifted a bedspread corner, stood and looked all around as though someone else might be there. He lurched toward Cheryl and poked a hand at her ribs. She dodged, squealing, her elbows tucked for protection. He said, That really was great, babe, just great, the song. He grabbed an armload of her then and wrestled her onto the bed. He pinned her there, blowing mouth-farts across her soft, surging belly. A taste like herbs was slick on his lips and tongue. Changing his life, he decided, could wait one more day.

The candles melted down. Their flames grew wide and flickered and blistered the frosting. A sugar char smell filled the room, sweet like campfire marshmallows. Jerry rolled off the bed and blew out the blaze. As he lay back down, he said, Marry me. I did, she said. Haven't we had this talk, Jerry, maybe eighty-nine times? Monkey-like, he scrambled across her. Then marry me *again*. He said it as if it were something totally new. Never, she said. His lip pouted out, and he made a whimpering sound. She combed his hair with her fingers and kissed his neck. You'll always be my first husband, she said.

They were kids when they married. Later Jerry had another wife, six months, that one a real mistake. She's somewhere in Iowa now, she and the twins. After Jerry, Cheryl had two husbands, the last one, Fenton, a real bastard. One night a couple years into that marriage, she called Jerry's house, waking him, her words all mush-mouthed. Fenton, the son of a bitch, had been beating on her for no good reason, threatening her, sticking the barrel of his fancy pistol in her mouth like it was his dick. Jerry got there fast. He caught the guy scrambling out the back door, got his gun away and creased his skull with it. With his bare fists he busted up Fenton's face. Cheryl packed up what was rightfully hers, and they loaded it all into Jerry's pickup. They left Fenton on the kitchen linoleum, unconscious and bleeding a puddle. Jerry drove her back to his place and unloaded her stuff into the bedroom that used to be theirs.

Cheryl calls herself a three-time loser when it comes to marriage, says it with a quick smile whenever talk heads that direction. She doesn't mean it, though, not really. It's instinctive, like turning with a punch to take away some of its sting.

Jerry's better than most about hitting her. He rarely does, and then it's because of some incredibly stupid, unthinking thing she's done. And it's never with fists. Never. That's nothing compared to the good things he's done, like getting her away from Fenton. One time he gave her this absolutely perfect making-up present, a calico kitten that she named Myrtle. And now, his refusing to finger her about the drugs, even when they offered probation if he'd just testify against her. Cheryl doesn't know what love feels like, not for sure. Her history is too messy for certainty about that. But on his best days Jerry does the sweetest things anyone's ever done for her. She likes how it makes her feel, and she thinks maybe that feeling is love.

She puts her spiral notebook in her purse for her meeting with Suggs, the lawyer assigned by the court. Usually they meet in his courthouse office, which he shares with four other public defenders. She thinks of it as an office of stalls—milking stalls, toilet stalls, small stalls, hardly room for someone to yawn. On the phone, Suggs said to meet him for breakfast this time, the restaurant across the street, Habeas Cibus. She's seen the place, but she's never been inside. A foreign name like that and crowds of men in striped suits make her antsy. She worries about what to wear, if the place has rules about that. A dress to be safe, she decides. Not a new one, though. Something she can wear to work afterwards and not worry about dye or chemical spots. An hour ago she got a call, an urgent shampoo-and-set job waiting downstairs at Rodell-Ward.

She slips a light blue, flower-print dress over her head and buttons the front in the mirror. She thinks she's pretty enough, although sometimes she thinks maybe she got pretty too young. She wishes she were brighter when it comes to people, understanding what they do and why. She has this sense that everyone else was born knowing some secret thing that they're not allowed to tell her. In her notebook she writes quotes, snatches of things people say that sound intelligent, scribbling them down like clues.

Suggs is sipping coffee in a corner booth, file folders stacked beside him. One folder—it's hers, she sees—lies open on the table, its long pages flipped open, rolled over the top, and tucked under. The lawyer's necktie knot is tugged loose. The wide end lolls across the papers like a second tongue. He's writing, making check marks on the page with his fat ink pen. As Cheryl slides into the booth, the pillow seat breathes cold air on her legs. The lawyer quits what he's doing, and he caps his pen with a snap. He laces his fingers together and tucks his elbows tight against the paunch of his gut. Cheryl tries to cross her legs, bangs a knee beneath the table. Suggs steadies his sloshing cup. Leaning forward, he says, Good morning, Miss Riffle. There's a bourbon breeze in the air.

Cheryl tries to read what's under his fist-ball. She asks, Is that my case?

Indeed it is, he says. His kind of word—indeed. His face gives her nothing.

Let me guess, she says. The judge has to delay us again. Am I right?

Suggs flips her file closed, pats the worn cover like somebody's shoulder. He says, The judge wants this one cleared up. He thinks it's dragged on much too long.

Heat rises in Cheryl's neck. After all, they're the ones who kept delaying, kept making excuses, kept putting it off. She won't say it, though, not to Suggs. The court made him her lawyer. It's confusing, though, because he's not hers, not really. Jerry says Suggs probably fishes with the judge, that they're best buddies behind her back. More times than she can count, Jerry's hunches turn out true.

A waitress comes over and refills the lawyer's cup. She's a slip of a girl, tall and young, her forehead freckled and acne-spotted. She's pregnant—six months, maybe seven—the bulge of her belly hugged tight by a denim skirt. She sets the coffeepot down, pulls a pad from her pocket, and stands near Cheryl, a pencil stub pinched between nail-bit fingers. She asks, Can I get you something?

Coffee, Cheryl says, looking at the pot. And a Pepsi and a fried honey bun. The girl repeats it, and when Cheryl says, That's right, she writes it down. There's a jittery tension in this girl. She feels familiar to Cheryl, like someone she used to be. As the waitress starts back to the kitchen, she drops her pad. She has to stoop sideways picking it up, fumbling it twice before getting a grip and standing again. A few seconds later, she's back at the table. Red-faced, she snatches up the coffee pot she forgot. As she leaves, it occurs to Cheryl that this girl might be the kind of person who could be her friend.

Suggs blows across his coffee and slurps a noisy first sip. He says, Don't you go reminding the judge about who stretched things out.

I won't, Cheryl says. Lord knows, I'm in no rush to do prison time.

Suggs says, Let's not get ahead of ourselves, young lady. You got a lawyer here, don't forget.

She can see she's hurt his feelings. Considering he isn't billing her—she couldn't pay, couldn't afford a hired lawyer, but still, considering that he'd never so much as sent her a bill—she tries extra hard to not disrespect him. She knows how it hurts, fixing hair for free at the county home, getting yelled at by people who don't know better. That's part of the deal. But their relatives, the ones who should still have manners? That's ignorant, plain-and-simple.

So what if Jerry is right? Maybe Suggs does bass fish with the judge. Still, she wouldn't want Suggs thinking she's ignorant that way.

I know I've got me a lawyer, she says. She reaches across and touches his hand. You're a good lawyer, too, she says. She has no way to know that, not really, no lawyer to compare him to. Still, it seems the right kind of thing to say.

He straightens, clears his throat. Listen, Miss Riffle, he says. If we go to trial, they have to prove this case. You understand that? They have to prove your involvement with that shoebox of drugs.

I'm the one lifted it, she says, like me and Jerry. . . .

Suggs slaps the table. Did I ask you who took it? Did I ask you that? She hates feeling scolded, hates how it puckers her insides, how it brings tears to her eyes for everyone looking to see. She turns toward the wall, hides her eyes with a hand.

Cheryl, he says. Miss Riffle.

She draws in an unsteady breath and turns back toward him again. His face has a pitying look. It's a look she can't stand. She studies her fingers, pinches the knuckle skin, taps each nail, rubs her thumb on the sensitive center of a palm, pressing hard.

Suggs says, We have several ways we can go with your case. You need to tell me what you want, though, so I'll know how to proceed.

Her brain feels strangely cluttered, yet empty, filled with lots of nothing. She says, What I want?

He says, What you want. His eyes look straight into hers, and she imagines he can read everything in there, can see the mess she is.

I want, she says, not knowing what comes next. I want things to go back like before.

Suggs asks, Before what?

She feels the tears again. This time she can't stop them. She searches her purse for a tissue. The lawyer hands her a napkin, which she takes and turns away.

When Cheryl turns back to Suggs, having finally gotten hold

of herself, her coffee, Pepsi, and fried honey bun are there on the table. She's got her own napkins now, and she uses one to wipe her face, to catch the last sniffle under her nose. I'm such a mess, she says.

He looks into what's left of his coffee. It's okay.

I'm sorry, she says.

It's okay, he says again. He picks up the folder. Flipping pages, he asks, Have you ever been evaluated?

A laugh escapes her, and she can't understand why. Evaluated? She says. Sure. Yes. All the time. Is that what you're doing now? She asks. Evaluating me? He's smiling at her, but it's not a real smile. It's not in his eyes.

He gathers up folders and stacks them on his lap. Let me talk to Judge Hawkins, he says, run something by him.

You're leaving?

He says that his next appointment is waiting two booths away. Stay here as long as you want, Suggs says. Take your time. Finish your breakfast. Bring me the check when it comes.

The parking lot at Rodell-Ward is full. Cars are parked down the street, both sides, both directions. Black limousines line the circular driveway. Their tiny green bumper flags flutter like spring leaves in a breeze. Several smokers cluster on the porch, a sunny place, talking. Cheryl drives past the stately old house and circles to the alley behind the place.

The backyard is overgrown, the path shaded by enormous live oaks. Beside the basement door, she puts down her shoulder bag, takes out a sweatshirt, and tugs it on. She shoves the right sleeve up to her elbow, reaches up and searches with a hand deep among the damp trumpet vines. Out front, the smokers' low banter floats through the air like spoken tunes. In the rough stones, Cheryl's fingers find a tiny alcove, and there the key that Mr. Rodell left for her. She unlocks the door, turns the oval brass knob, and silently opens the door. Inside, she switches on the lights.

The girl waits for Cheryl in a pea-green room, a room with a double door. It's a cold room with a sour kind of hospital smell, small like a prison cell. The girl lies waiting there, waiting on a bright metal table. She lies covered head to toe on the table, covered by a sheet the same color as the walls. Cheryl lifts the sheet, pulls it back to see the lifeless face, the shoulders, narrow, bare, the neck jogged oddly to one side, an impossible angle for a neck. The girl looks young, eleven or twelve, her skin a nutmeg color. Although her eyes are closed, a mildly surprised look is on her face. Her full lips seem poised to speak. Her untroubled forehead reflects the room's sickly green light. Her black hair has red-dyed streaks in it. Maroon tips, too. Cheryl touches the hair, rolls a few strands between finger and thumb. It's straight and shiny, but matted now. No injuries to work around. That's good. An arcade photo of the girl, alive and mugging for the camera, is tucked beside her head. Cheryl picks it up. She's younger in the photo. Her hair, not as long, is clipped in tiny bow barrettes. When he called, Rodell told her, Cheryl, you get all that red out you can. Her Momma wants it natural black.

Overhead, the upstairs floorboards creak—people standing, people shifting foot-to-foot, people filing past another someone's coffin, their voices a low murmuring, a rolling kind of sound.

Cheryl looks around, searching for paperwork. She doesn't want to know how the girl died. It doesn't matter anyway, not now. She doesn't want the dreams, either, the ones that come from knowing. She only wants a name, what to call this girl, how to think of her as she does her hair. She wishes now she'd thought to ask Rodell about a name.

She pulls the sheet back and folds it onto itself at the end of the table. The girl is long-boned, slender. Her nail polish matches the streaks in her hair. She has a slight swell of breasts, narrow hips, first signs of private hair. Last signs. She's eleven at most. Maybe ten. Her frail chest is sunken and still. Her knees are knobby, boy-like, scabbed. One knee is slightly bent as if, walking, she'd died mid-stride.

My name is Cheryl, she says out loud. She touches the soles of the girl's feet, the tender white skin of the arches. She runs a finger along her ankle and calf, past a knee, up a slender thigh. She touches the girl's hand, the fingers cold and stiff, and she imagines how it would feel, this child holding her hand like a mother's.

I'm Cheryl, she says again. I'm here to fix your hair. She leans close, her ear near the girl's lips, and she listens for a secret. In the stainless steel table, she sees side-by-side two reflections, sees parts of two faces, one cheek, one ear each, falling hair black and light brown on bright metal, one eye alive and open, one closed.

The shampoo smells like apricots. In her hands the suds feel thick and warm. She works the lather in. The girl's head moves slightly side-to-side. Cheryl rinses, and the suds drain away on the tilted table, drain down plastic tubes to plastic jugs below.

When she looks at the tangle of tubes below that table, Cheryl feels a pang low in her abdomen. She thinks of her own tubes, remembers the pair of dark-faced granny women, their treatments, the gnawing ache for days down there. She was just fourteen then, and still the women said she'd come too late. The root cures hadn't worked, they said, dishonesty in their eyes. Infections, they said, the word like spit on their lips, the devil's own worst kind. She'll bear no children now, they told her mother, not in this life. Amen, her mother answered, and she counted out ten-dollar bills into their waiting hands.

Jerry kicks at the cinderblock with his muddy boots, trying to loosen the clods stuck deep in the treads. Rust-colored mud shapes—diamonds—fly out and disappear among the trumpet vines. From heel to toe, he scrapes the soles on the block's gritty edge. After wiping his hand on the back pocket of his jeans, he grips the oval brass doorknob. Silently, he opens the door.

Inside he hears a sound, the whine of a hairdryer. It comes from a room off to his right. He's never been in this place before, not in the basement. Upstairs, yes. Never down here, though. It feels like trespassing, like burglary must feel. He moves quietly. The air feels clammy against his skin. Its sour smell makes him want to burp. He cracks open the double door. Cheryl's back is turned to him, three steps away. He'll step in behind her and before she sees him, before she even knows he's there, he'll clamp his hands on her ribs, dig them in sharp and deep, scare the b'jesus out of her. As he inches the door open, she switches off the hairdryer. The sudden silence is a roar in his ears. A hinge squeaks. She hears, gasps, turns. Her hand flies to her mouth too late to catch a small scream.

I knocked, he says, opening the door fully now.

Don't you ever, she says.

He says, You didn't answer.

The hairdryer, she says, like it's her fault.

He sees the black hair now, the face, the shoulders, the sheet. And who is this?

Cheryl's hand is on his chest, pushing. Out! She says. Now!

He's stronger and stubborn when he wants to be, and he wants to be now. Was he hurting anything? No. Besides, he has reason to be here. He grabs her wrist and pushes it aside, pushes her aside, and goes over to the table.

Jerry, get out!

He lifts the sheet, stoops and looks under it. She's just a kid, he says.

With small fists Cheryl punches his shoulder. So help me, Jerry, she says. You've got no right.

He backs away, hands up, backs to the door. What killed her? he asks. Cheryl pushes him, and this time he lets her, stumbling back into the hall.

She says, You don't belong here.

He asks, You got any idea what time it is?

You'll get lunch when I get home, she says. Fix a sandwich if you're hungry.

Your lawyer called, he says. That's why I came. That was the reason, he says, if you must know, why I came all the way out here. Jerry turns then and starts to leave.

Wait, she says. She grabs his sleeve. What'd he say?

That jackass judge wants to see you today. One o'clock. He wants me there, too.

Cheryl's face takes on its confused look. Jerry wonders if he's saying too much, talking too fast for her peanut butter brain. He shows her his wristwatch, pushes it up close to her nose. Almost twelve-thirty, babe, he says. She doesn't answer. He says, What it means is we've got thirty minutes to get there. Hurry up and finish Miss Stiff.

She says she'll be five minutes, that she's putting final touches on the girl's hair, the red streaks and maroon tips.

As soon as Jerry walks to the water fountain, Suggs comes over to where Cheryl is sitting. He says, Tell your boyfriend to keep his mouth shut once we get inside. It's a useless thing to tell Jerry, she knows, but she says, Okay. They're in the courthouse hallway, waiting on hard wooden benches. And you, Suggs says, remember you only answer what you're asked. Nothing more.

She nods.

I'll call when we're ready, Suggs says, and he goes into the judge's office. She thinks of the girl on the table, how she's lying there dead in this world, her hair whatever color her mother or a stranger, a hairdresser she never knew, decides it should be. Cheryl hasn't stopped thinking of the girl, not once since leaving her there.

Jerry comes back. His footsteps sound hollow in the marble hall. He plops down on the bench, pushes close beside her and straddles his legs. His knee nudges hers. He says, Let me show you something. From his pants pocket, he pulls a root. It's shaped like three fingers joined by a large knuckle. Tendrils stick out of the thing everywhere. She covers it with her hands.

That's ginseng, she whispers.

Not just any sang, he says, pulling it free. See that shape? Don't it look like an elephant?

She doesn't think so, but it's not something to argue about. Where'd you dig it?

He whispers, Boone Forest, over by Spivey. Spent the morning scouting around.

It's illegal, she says, digging sang there.

He slides it back into his pocket. Can't no one prove where it came from, he says. Besides, you know what foreigners pay for wild-grown sang that's animal-shaped?

Jerry, she says, I want nothing to do with that.

Suit yourself, he says.

Cheryl can tell by his voice he's hurt. He may sulk about it, but she's not going along with this scheme, not while she's looking at jail. Jerry stands and stuffs his hands in his pockets. He hunches his shoulders to his ears, and he wanders down the hall. He's still standing there studying the photos on the wall a minute later when Suggs comes out and calls them into the judge's chambers.

Judge Hawkins sits pushed back from his desk. He isn't wearing his robes, just pants and white shirt and starry blue necktie. He looks shorter now, wide, his face loose like bread dough. A lawyer named Embry sits to one side. He's the gourd-shaped one who prosecuted Jerry before. Jerry gives him his dagger look. He doesn't say anything, though, not yet.

Judge Hawkins has more files than Suggs. They're stacked on his desk. He says, Let's get on with it.

Embry says, Your Honor, the Commonwealth has offered to drop several charges against Miss Riffle, in exchange for a guilty plea on count six of the indictment.

Hawkins flips pages, adjusts his glasses. And count six is what? Yes, here, second-degree drug trafficking. These were prescription drugs?

Suggs says, Yes, Your Honor.

Cheryl fights the urge to explain, to tell that she's the one who stole them in the first place, a shoebox full, that she deserves as much jail time as Jerry, maybe more.

The judge says, Mr. Suggs tells me there are circumstances. He's talking to Embry, but he glances at Jerry, too. Jerry's got the root elephant out of his pocket. He holds it low, below the desk so the judge can't see. He rubs it with a thumb like he doesn't even care.

Embry says, Your Honor, we're prepared to recommend probation for Miss Riffle, two years, with a stipulation that it include behavioral evaluation and counseling.

Jerry jumps up. That's bullshit, he says. He waves the root like a floppy finger.

The judge says, Sit down, son. Put a sock in it.

Jerry says, Two years? I only got eight months.

Cheryl's on her feet. She grabs his arm, pulls him back to his chair. Probation, she whispers. The guy said probation.

Jerry's chest shrinks like a balloon taken out in the cold.

Cheryl says, I can keep my jobs? Then, remembering what her lawyer said, she clamps a hand over her mouth. She mouths a *sorry* to Suggs and sits back in her chair.

Suggs says, I'll confer with my client. We'll let you know.

I want this case cleared today, Hawkins says, standing. Five o'clock.

Embry stands, too, and says, Paperwork will be on your desk in an hour, Your Honor, ready for Miss Riffle's signature.

We'll talk in the hall, Suggs whispers to her. Jerry, you too.

What a circus, Jerry says when they're outside. Cheryl knows he's fed up about something. Tell me this, he says to Suggs. Why drag me down here, make me sit next to the bastard who sent me away. I've done my time. I never need to see him again.

Cheryl wishes he hadn't come, for his sake and for hers.

Suggs says, You both need to understand the options. There's a strange look on Suggs' face, one Cheryl can't figure out.

Jerry says, There's no contest. She'll take the parole.

It's probation, Suggs says.

Jerry says, Okay, probation. She can tell he's pissed about her lawyer playing big shot with him.

The thing about probation, Suggs says looking straight at Jerry, is she can't be having contact with convicted felons.

The hall goes silent.

Jerry says, They can't do this. Can they?

Cheryl says, Me and Jerry, we live together.

You're not married, though, Suggs says. Not now.

That makes a difference? she asks.

To the law, it does, Suggs says.

Cheryl finds a bench and sits. If I take their probation, she says, I've got to move out?

Suggs comes over and sits sideways by her. No contact means no contact, he says. His eyes are steady on hers. She wonders if he's working some kind of telepathy.

I don't know, Cheryl says, her mind a complete swirl.

Suggs says, Think about it. Talk it over, you two. He looks at his watch and says, Their offer's good till five.

The woman who seats them at Habeas Cibus reminds Jerry of the prosecutor, Embry, the way she looks at them. She leaves them with menus and water. All Jerry wants is something to eat, something sweet and syrupy, something solid and wholesome to nourish him. Waffles, maybe, and blueberry syrup. He's had enough of weasel words, enough slanted options, enough of getting shoved from seventeen different directions. He can tell Cheryl is thinking. She hasn't said one word since they crossed the street.

The waitress, a skinny kid with scads of ripe acne on her face, comes over. She's pregnant as hell and her ring finger is naked. The girl ignores him and smiles at Cheryl, who says, Back again, as if the girl's taking attendance with her pencil and pad.

Jerry orders the waffle and coffee, Cheryl a double cheeseburger, Pepsi and fries. When he gets back from the men's room, their drinks are already there.

It's not fair, Cheryl says, peeling paper off her straw.

Damn straight, he says. He bongos the table, the chrome edge with his hands. We can't, he says, we just can't let them run our lives.

Damn straight, she says back at him. She pokes her straw into the Pepsi and ice cubes, stirring and tinkling the drink.

It gives Jerry a good feeling inside, hearing her say it. He's always thought of her as someone special, this first wife of his.

Babe, he says carefully, watching her face. Say we did get married again.

No! she says. She's not fooling about it now.

I'm just saying, he says, just saying if we did. What could they do then? Think about it, Cheryl. They'd be screwed. What could they do?

She says like a groan, Jerry, I can't. You know marriage never works for me.

He says, Maybe this time.

She laughs like it's a sad joke, and she says, Every time, I'm miserable.

He says, That was before.

Jerry, I can't, she says. Don't ask anymore.

He takes out the ginseng root, makes it hop across the paper placemat, makes it look at its reflection in the steel napkin dispenser. His mind is working on something. He catches himself humming. You tell me what then, he says.

I don't know, she says. Her eyes start to go wild. We'll go somewhere, she says, but she says it like she doesn't really believe it herself. We'll pack and move, not tell anyone, Somerset maybe or Louisville.

He laughs at her. You think they won't find you? You look for work, and you're in their computers. They'll find you, and now you're in for serious prison time. An idea is breathing inside him now, alive and wanting out.

Cheryl says, Then *what*? You tell me.

He says, Guess. She can't. He thinks and then says, Here's a hint. It's right in front of you. She isn't even looking now. He says, It's right under your nose.

Cheryl's eyes are empty. She doesn't have a clue in that head of hers, not one idea. Like always, he's the one left to do the real thinking.

The food comes, his waffle, thinner than the menu picture, a ball of butter sliding off. There's a tiny shot glass of blueberry syrup, not nearly enough. Her burger is open, surrounded by curly fries. Before she can slather on ketchup, he grabs one to try.

Okay, Jerry says when the waitress leaves. Here's what we do. We take this crap they're giving us, and we make us some lemonade. Your sister living in Richmond? We say you're living with her.

Cheryl's head tilts bird-like. She's interested. But I'm not?

Jerry says, That's the beauty. We're camped out together in Boone Forest, the two of us, and we're digging a fortune in sang. This piece here, the one I dug this morning? Twenty-five bucks, maybe thirty. This guy I know, he'll buy all we can dig. Just imagine, two of us living out there every day. We're moving around. Can you imagine it? We're moving around, and we're digging a fortune right out of the ground.

Cheryl twirls a curly fry like a corkscrew streamer and flips it into her mouth. He can tell she doesn't get it yet, doesn't see the beauty of his plan. She says, It's illegal, digging sang in a national forest. Right?

He says, Anyone asks, we say we're campers. We'll even get a legal camp permit. We'll hang it up on our tent. Our sang stash, we'll hide it up a tree for when the rangers come poking around.

She says, There's millions of acres out there.

He says, Millions of trees.

In her face, Jerry sees the splendor of his idea, how it fills her with new hope, fills her head-to-toe with glorious possibilities. That last morning lying on his Blackburn bunk, his intuition had been right.

Cheryl closes her hamburger and flattens it with her palm and takes a bite. And Myrtle, she says through the food, imagine her out there catching a million crickets and cicadas and mice, bringing them all proud to show me.

Jerry says, Any fool knows you can't take a cat to live in the forest. A dog, maybe yes. Cats aren't like that.

She puts the burger down, wipes ketchup from her lips with the back of her hand. She says, Myrtle has to come, too. I'm all she's got. We can put her on a leash or zip her in the tent. Either way, she's got to come.

Jerry takes his fork and knife and rips the waffle into dry, ragged pieces. He says, I don't know about you, Cheryl. He says, Here I do all this for you, do it all so we can stay together. And you? You complicate things. You make up roadblocks like nothing in this world matters but you. He pushes his plate away, suddenly sick of the food. He drops his fork and knife on top and pours syrup over everything. He tips the shot glass upside-down in the mess, and he squishes it to make his point.

Cheryl straightens, sits schoolteacher stiff, and she stares at him, really stares. He knows he's gotten to her, even though she's not crying yet.

Miss Pizza-faced Waitress decides to come by right then and ask so sweetly is their food okay. They're trained to ask, he knows, so they'll get a decent tip. But he can tell for a fact that this has more to do with what's going on, the discussion about the cat. She's got this know-it-all look spread across her festered-zit face. Not for one minute does she fool Jerry. The little sneak is showing them up in this backhanded sort of way.

You want a tip? he asks straight-faced. She looks surprised, doesn't answer. Here's a tip, he says. Buy yourself some maternity clothes, he says. And get yourself a husband, too. Fast.

The girl whirls around and goes. Jerry glances over. Cheryl's face is frozen into a weird kind of mask. She doesn't get the joke, which any fool with a sense of humor would. She isn't even trying. Instead, she tilts the napkin dispenser, and she stares at her reflection until the mask starts to melt. He tries to think how to explain it to her, how it's funny, what he said to the girl about a tip. Cheryl tosses her napkin. It lands on the table like a parachute. Right away she grabs it again. Her brain, he thinks must be melting, too.

We don't even know her name, Jerry, she says. She slides out of the booth, and before he can say, Hey wait, she chases after the waitress, who's already halfway across the room. It occurs to him then how birdbrained women can be, how amazingly strange, women like his first wife and this waitress.

She catches up with the girl. Even though their backs are turned his way, Jerry would lay odds the waitress is bawling. Sure enough, Cheryl hands the girl her napkin to use on her face. For a minute they stand right there. People coming and going from the kitchen have to walk around them. Cheryl and the girl have their heads together, almost touching as they talk. Cheryl scribbles in her notepad. She rips out the page, folds it several times, and she gives it to the girl, who squeezes it in a fist.

Jerry drinks his coffee, and he looks around the booth for his sang root. He moves dishes, shoves aside the napkin dispenser and ketchup bottle, runs a hand along the seat's gritty vinyl crease, pushing the hand as deep as he dares. He stands and pats his pockets twice around. Nothing. He gets down and looks under the table. The root shaped like an elephant is nowhere. Jerry swears, and he slams a fist on his thigh. People turn to look. Their stares feel like ants all over his skin. He sits again, drinks his coffee, thinking.

When Cheryl finally comes back, Jerry starts to tell her about the sang root, how it's lost. She straightens the mess on the table, stacking things. She's not really looking for it, though. That much he can tell. We should go, she says when she's finished. She bites her bottom lip the way she does when she's getting ready for something. Jerry doesn't move. I looked everywhere, he tells her, and I can't find the damn thing. Cheryl doesn't answer. She seems different now, an odd version of herself, different in a troublesome kind of way. Jerry feels a new tightness in his head. He says, The sang root is nowhere. He moves closer to her. It's gone, he says. Vanished. As he tells her this, she fools with her fingers, examines her hands on the table, the dye-stained knuckle skin, her ragged fingernails, the necked-down places where rings used to be. Not once does she look up at him. He wishes she'd just cry and be done with it, if that's what she's working up to. What she's doing instead feels too much like being alone.

———————

Jim Tomlinson's debut collection of stories, *Things Kept, Things Left Behind,* won the 2006 Iowa Short Fiction Award. His work has appeared in *Five Points, Shenandoah, Bellevue Literary Review,* and elsewhere. Recipient of a 2008 NEA Fellowship, Jim lives and writes in rural Kentucky.

GIN PETTY

I often clip bits from magazines and newspapers, things that snag my interest and might belong in a story. One such clipping—an item about a local judge's ruling against cohabitation by two convicted drug thieves—so intrigued me that it stayed tacked to my office bulletin board for months. Get married or don't associate—those were the options the judge handed down. It seemed a wonderful quandary, a dilemma that deserved worthy characters. In time, Jerry and Cheryl showed up.

I wrote and revised the story many times. Jerry told the earliest version. Not surprisingly, it lacked any sense of redemption or grace. Later Cheryl told the story—at least she tried to—her many limitations getting terribly in the way. Then I enlisted the help of a somewhat chameleon narrator. He took over, with Jerry and Cheryl still influencing how things are told. That arrangement seemed to open up the story and give it much-needed depth. In the end, "First Husband, First Wife" turned out to be more about those two characters than about the judge's ruling that first sparked the story. And that's as it should be.

Bret Anthony Johnston

REPUBLICAN

(from *Ploughshares*)

A section of the newspaper, rolled into a tight cone and flaming at the top, stuck out of the cook's ear the first time I saw him. This was early June, in Corpus Christi, Texas, when I was sixteen and had been hired as the delivery driver for La Cocina Mexican Restaurant. The cook was sweating. He sat cross-legged on the stove in the kitchen, eyes and fists clenched, with two waitresses beside him. One of the women was dribbling salsa into plastic to-go cups. The other fanned the blue-black smoke away from the cook's face with a laminated menu.

The night before, I'd called about the ad in the paper and was told to show up the next morning for an interview. My father made me wear his pink tie, his only tie, though I'd just expected to fill out an application and learn that I lacked adequate experience. Aside from helping out at my father's pawnshop, I'd never held a job. But there'd been no paperwork at La Cocina, no discussion of previous employment. The owner asked if I had a valid driver's license, a reliable car, any moving violations or outstanding warrants. She asked if I was an honest person, and I said, "I try to be." The answer seemed to surprise and please her, as if I'd solved a riddle that had stumped other drivers, then she told me to go into the kitchen and ask if there were any orders yet. She also told me to tell the cook that if another customer complained about the menudo tasting like beer, she'd call immigration.

When the waitress fanning the smoke saw me, she said, "Bathroom's down the hall.

"I work here," I said.

The cook's head was parallel to the floor, the smoke from the newspaper ribboning toward the grease-blotched ceiling. He wore a mustache and a V-neck T-shirt. A half-empty beer bottle sat next to him on the counter; he reached for it without opening his eyes and brought it into his lap. The kitchen smelled of cilantro and eggs and burning ink.

I said, "Mrs. Martinez just hired me."

"You're white," the other waitress said. Her eyebrows were penciled on. Both of the women looked tired to me, fierce and old. She said, "*Ay dios mio*. Affirmative action at La Cocina."

The cook mumbled something no one understood. The flaming newspaper made me think of the downtown curio shops where old women rubbed oil on your palms to predict your future.

The cook said, "Am I being fired again?"

"Fired," the waitress said, eyeing the burning newspaper. "Now he's a comedian. Now he's Cheech and Chong."

"I'm the new delivery driver," I said. "My name's Julian. Everyone calls me Jay."

"Julian," the cook said. "Julian, what kind of car do you drive?"

"A Cadillac," I said. The waitresses glared at me. I saw that the one holding the menu was a lifetime younger than I'd originally thought. It occurred to me that she was the other woman's daughter. My father's tie suddenly felt tight around my neck. An hour earlier, he'd tied it on himself in the mirror, then loosened the knot and slipped it over my head. Now I wished I'd left it in the car. I said, "It's a convertible Fleetwood.

"The King of the Cadillac line," the cook said.

"Exactly."

"Julian, when I own this restaurant—"

"Ay dios mio," the older waitress said and took her tray of salsa cups out of the kitchen. Her daughter rolled her eyes and started fanning the smoke again. Her hair hung in thick spirals, her nails were glittery vermilion. She said, "Carlos, Jay's worked here for two minutes and already you're starting with your fantasies."

Carlos raised the beer to his lips and awkwardly tried to sip without disturbing the newspaper in his ear. I wanted to ask why it was there, but also wanted to act unfazed, like I encountered such things daily. When Carlos couldn't manage a drink, he extended his arm behind him and emptied the bottle into a pot of simmering menudo.

"Julian," he said, when I buy this restaurant, you'll deliver tacos by limousine."

The Caddy was cream-colored, a 1978 Brougham. Whitewalls, chrome, power windows, locks, and mirrors, and leather seats and a retractable antenna. Even at thirteen years old, the Fleetwood wasn't a car my family could normally afford—my father drove a Datsun pickup, my mother a Chevy hatchback—but an old woman had pawned it, and when her loan expired, my father brought the keys home. Things had already soured in their marriage by then, but my mother had always coveted a convertible, and my father knew her boss drove one, so he must have hoped that a luxury sedan could turn things around for our family, deliver us to a different destiny.

He was the manager of Blue Water Pawn, and he believed everything you'd ever need would eventually float through the pawnshop doors. My mother's opal earrings and pearl necklace, her espresso machine and electric range and Tiffany lamps, my ten-speed bike and computer, my cordless phone and bowie knife and Nikon camera, all of it had once belonged to someone else, and either the owners or the people who'd robbed them had sold the stuff to Blue Water for pennies on the dollar. My father once paid twelve bucks for an acoustic guitar that had belonged to Elvis Presley, and he gave it to my mother for one of their anniversaries.

I'd been forbidden from telling my friends about the guitar, but I regularly bragged about it. Sometimes I lifted it from its fur-lined case and strummed its strings.

That the Cadillac came through the pawnshop surprised everyone except my father, and for a while that surprise buoyed my parents. Every couple of weeks they soaped the car with sponges and waxed it until their reflections emerged in the hubcaps. They took it to open-air restaurants on the Laguna Madre, and on weekends they drove into the hill country with the top down. When they returned, the seats were littered with pine needles and mesquite leaves, the floorboards dusted with sand like confectioner's sugar. Once, they stopped at a rest area outside Austin and had someone snap a photo of them with my Nikon. They're wearing sunglasses, leaning on the Fleetwood with the tawny hills rolling into the horizon behind them; the landscape looks like a solemn, arrested wave, and studying the picture closely, you can almost sense that my mother is poised to tighten her scarf around her hair and walk out of the frame for good.

On the second anniversary of the night she moved to Arizona with her boss, my father calmly walked outside and cut the Fleetwood's ragtop into ribbons with my bowie knife. When he came back in, he said, "Pop quiz."

Ever since I'd started high school he'd been quizzing me: Name the capital of Delaware. What was the shortest war in history? Who invented wallpaper? When I botched the answers—I'd never answered one correctly—he'd say, "Time to hit the books." My father had his GED.

I couldn't tell if he knew I'd watched him shred the vinyl, so I tried to act casual. I was also worried he'd ask me about my mother. She called me every other month, but sometimes my father answered before I could reach the phone. I hadn't heard from her in a while, so we were both anticipating her call.

I said, "Ready, professor."

"Tonight's prize is a 1978 Fleetwood Brougham, the King of the Cadillac line."

I didn't know what he'd done with my knife. Maybe he'd stabbed it into the steering wheel or one of the whitewalls. My father twirled the keys around his finger. He'd been trying to unload the car for two years.

He said, "What's the beginning of wisdom?"

I knew the answer immediately. A bronze plaque with the words engraved on it hung in his office at Blue Water. I said, "The beginning of wisdom is the acquisition of a roof."

"Touchdown," he said and chucked me the keys.

Later that night I walked by his bedroom and heard him crying. His door was closed, but his sobbing was hard enough to carry into the hall. His room wasn't the one he'd shared with my mother—he'd converted the master bedroom into a storage space and pushed his bed into our old study—though when I pictured him, I couldn't help imagining the furniture as it had been before she left. I saw my mother's vanity under the shuttered window, saw my father trying to muffle his weeping with one of her tasseled pillows.

"Jay," he said through the door. "Jay, are you out there?"

"Just returned from my maiden voyage, professor."

For a moment I thought he hadn't heard me, thought maybe I hadn't spoken at all. Then he said, "I left the paper on the counter."

I wondered if this was a new kind of quiz. I said, "Ready, professor."

"Roofs cost money. I'd say it's time you found gainful employment."

"Right away," I said. I thought he'd say something more, or that I would, maybe *I love you* or *Thank you* or *I'm sorry Mom hasn't come home,* but finally I just walked into the kitchen and read the classifieds. I called La Cocina because a delivery job would afford me more time in the Caddy.

When I'd worked at Blue Water, the man who stocked the Pepsi machine would brag about free lap dances when his route took him to the Landing Strip out by the airport, and a customer—a young guy who delivered newspapers and always pawned his fishing rod—said he'd twice happened upon a married couple having sex in their front yard, but most of my deliveries went to construction sites or businesses where women wore suits and bifocals: banks, other restaurants, a fabric store, a podiatrist's office. Mornings were our busiest time, and there was usually a lunch rush, but by mid-afternoon our phone stopped ringing and Mrs. Martinez tallied our receipts. I swept and watered the potted ivies and ferns behind the cash register.

At the end of my first week I asked Melinda—who *was* Alma's daughter and a year older than me—why we didn't stay open for dinner. She said, "The only ones that come after lunch are wearing suits."

She was wiping down the tables before I flipped the chairs and balanced them on the Formica. When Melinda leaned over to spray the surface, I saw a butterfly tattoo on the small of her back.

"Suits? You mean, businessmen?"

"*Health department* suits," she said. "If we fail another inspection, they'll chain the door."

Before I'd left with my last delivery, Carlos had been chasing a roach around the kitchen, swatting at it with a menu. The stove was gummy with caked-on lard, and I'd watched Alma drink from the milk jug before pouring a glass for a customer. I said, "I guess a flaming sports section in the cook's ear could be considered unsanitary."

"*Aire de oído*. Like an ear infection. The smoke draws it out," she said.

"I know. My father—"

"How do you afford that car?" she interrupted. She was scrubbing the seat of a booth, trying to remove dried enchilada sauce. There were no more chairs to upend, so I was just waiting, watching her butterfly. She said, "Carlos says you sell drugs, Mama thinks you have a trust fund. I haven't asked Mrs. Martinez because she's all pissed."

"How do *you* think I afford it, Melinda?"

She plopped herself into the booth and looked me up and down. I tried to puff out my chest, and hoped she wouldn't notice my ears, which I knew turned red when I got nervous. She sucked in her cheeks, pursed her lips, squinted. Alma rolled a bucket and mop into the kitchen.

Melinda said, "You sell Avon. No, you mug old ladies. No, you're a hot-rodder. You won it in a midnight drag race."

"Close," I said, trying to sound serious. I remembered what my father told our neighbor when he asked about our new riding lawnmower. "I won it in a poker game."

She laughed so loud that Mrs. Martinez poked her head out of the office and whipped off her glasses. "Melinda, have you started making the hot sauce?"

"*Ya mero,*" she said. After Mrs. Martinez closed her door, Melinda said, "So, drugs or trust fund?"

Why I answered her the way I did is still a mystery to me. The words surprised me as much they did Melinda. I said, "The car was my mother's. She died two years ago. I inherited it."

Melinda squinted at me again, studied me in a softer way than before. I was waiting for her to react—to accuse or curse me, or start laughing again—when Carlos began singing in the kitchen. It was a Spanish song I'd heard playing on his transistor radio earlier that morning. Melinda continued assessing me. I stared at my shoes, at the restaurant's chipped linoleum.

Sliding out of the booth, she said, "Losing that pink tie after your first day was a good call. You look more like yourself now."

"You just met me," I said.

"Does that matter?" she said.

"Maybe not."

"You're cute," she said. "Especially when your ears turn red."

I never repaired the roof on the Caddy, and after a month of delivering tacos, I'd forgotten my father had ruined it. Summer in Corpus is glomming. Thick, viscous heat, and there's no rain unless a hurricane is churning in the Gulf, so I just left the top down. I enjoyed smelling the baking asphalt, the far-off briny bay. When I saw someone I knew, I saluted them from behind the wheel. Or I turned up the stereo and pretended not to recognize them.

In July, Mrs. Martinez catered a wedding in Portland, the little shrimping town across the ship channel. It took me two trips to deliver all the food—two hundred enchiladas, vats of beans and rice, and bags of flour tortillas that I had to stash in the trunk. (A bag had flown out of the backseat on my first trip. When the wind lifted it into the night, it looked like a jellyfish swimming in black, black water.) By the time we'd set up the buffet it was ten o'clock. I'd thought I might drive Melinda home, but she had to serve coffee to the guests. She said, "If you stay, you can ask me to dance."

"I don't know how to dance," I said.

"Then stay and you can ask me *not* to dance."

I spent the next hour pacing outside the reception hall, pretending I'd just married Melinda. I stole glances at her serving flan and leaning down to ask if people wanted decaf or regular, and the simple fact of her knowing my name amazed me. The prospect of meeting her after dessert sent my heart kicking. I wondered if she was a virgin, if she knew I was. I almost vomited into a pot of azaleas.

When I looked up, Mrs. Martinez was standing over me, telling me to drive back to Corpus and make sure Carlos had locked up. The last time he'd been in charge of closing, he'd polished off a fifth of tequila and pushed each of the refrigerators into the dining area. She said, "Next morning, what do I have? Rotten food and a cook in the hospital with a hernia."

"Can Melinda come with me?"

Mrs. Martinez touched my cheek. She said, "Sweet Jay. Melinda just left."

As I drove back, moonlight marbled the slatey sky, and the bay under the Harbor Bridge stretched out like an endless expanse of deep, rich soil. I imagined Melinda riding beside me, her long hair whipping around us. I heard her small laugh that always reminded me of a sparrow bouncing into flight. With the Caddy coasting along Ocean Drive, I could almost feel Melinda reaching for my hand across the smooth seats. I'd only kissed one girl at a homecoming party, and I'd been too nervous to enjoy it. Our teeth knocked and scraped together, and her mouth tasted of meatloaf and wine coolers; after a few minutes of kissing, she fell asleep and I tiptoed out of the room, feeling simultaneously relieved and despondent. I thought Melinda's mouth would taste of cinnamon. "Melinda," I said aloud. "My Mexican lover."

I thought nothing of the few fat drops of rain that pelted me, nothing of the first thunderclap or the shudder of pink lightning or the heavy, muscular-smelling air that precedes a storm. But within a mile, rain was bouncing off my dashboard and drenching the seats and pooling under the accelerator. The windshield wipers sprayed the water back into my eyes and face, and the Fleetwood fishtailed around corners. Out of dumb instinct, I flipped the switch to raise the roof. The hinges lurched and moaned, a low steel-on-steel grinding like a hurt animal, and eventually the jagged strips of wet, ruined vinyl slapped down against me. I was a mile from home, but with the blurring rain and the wind pushing water over my windshield, I could only inch forward. I had to pull over when I couldn't see the lanes. The ragtop draped over my shoulders, like I'd gotten stuck in an automatic carwash.

When I unlocked our front door, the phone was ringing. I'd heard it when I was hustling up the slippery driveway, but I'd figured it for the sound of traffic sloshing by. My father's antique grandfather clock—another boon from the pawnshop—was about to hit midnight. For a beat, I allowed myself to believe Melinda was calling, but I knew better. In two years, my mother had never grasped the time difference between Corpus and Phoenix.

When I picked up, I heard, "Julian. This is Carlos, the cook from La Cocina."

I hadn't even said hello. I'd almost fallen trying to answer before the phone woke my father, and I was shivering in my soaked clothes. A puddle formed around my shoes.

"Is everything okay, Carlos?" With the storm, I'd forgotten to check the door at the restaurant.

"I'm calling to say we've never had a better driver. When I own the restaurant, I'm going to give you . . ." His voice trailed off, and it sounded like he was knocking a bottle against his forehead, trying to jog the word he wanted. I thought he might say *promotion* or *raise,* but he said, "A trophy. When I own La Cocina, I'm going to give you the blue ribbon."

My teeth wouldn't stop chattering. I said, "Thank you."

"Julian," he said, "the true reason I'm calling is for a small favor."

A ride, I thought. Through the front window, I could see the Fleetwood parked by the curb. In the streetlamp's amber glow, with the rain streaming over its body, the car looked immaculate and reposed. The upholstery was getting ruined, and I was to blame, but seeing the car like that, I felt an inexplicable pride.

Carlos said, "What I need, what I really need, is for you to bring me an accordion."

"An accordion?"

"This is life or death. I truly need this instrument," he said. "I wonder if your mom or dad plays the accordion, Julian. Maybe they have a spare."

"We're not a very musical family," I said.

"Because here's my idea," he said, then took a long pull from his drink. "When I own the restaurant, we'll have girls posing by the door in Santa costumes. They'll wave in customers. Or maybe they'll be naked except for Santa hats, and they'll play carols on accordions."

"The health department might frown on that, Carlos."

He knocked the bottle against his head again, then drained it and dropped it in the trash. I heard him pop a top with a bottle opener. Sounding suddenly sober and grim, he said, "Julian, you're right. Even with pasties, we'd be in trouble."

"Unfortunately."

"You're an idea man, Julian. Manager material. When I'm the boss—"

The line went dead. I was about to call Carlos back when my father said, "How was the old girl tonight?"

I didn't know how long he'd been behind me. He was leaning against the sink, wearing pajama pants and no shirt. The scar where he'd had his gall bladder removed looked like a centipede on his stomach. I said, "That was Carlos, from work."

"The cook calls you at midnight?"

"He was drunk. He wants an accordion. I told him to check Blue Water."

My father wasn't listening. He was peering over my shoulder, seeing the Fleetwood in the rain. Wet tallow leaves were stuck to its hood like leaches. The tattered roof looked like a busted garbage bag.

Our air-conditioner cycled on. I crossed my arms over my chest, which only made me colder.

My father said, "Pop quiz."

"Ready, professor."

He fixed me with his eyes again, then averted them to the car. He said, "What happens when a yacht fills with water?"

The question seemed deceptively easy, so I considered each word individually. Yacht. Fills. Water. But I couldn't think of any answer beyond the obvious one. I said, "It sinks."

"Touchdown," he said. Then he left me alone, trembling.

Carlos had gone outside after the phone went dead; he thought lightning had struck the shopping center; the floor and walls had jolted, like an earthquake. But there'd been no more lightning, just gusts of wind that blew the rain sideways and sent shallow waves rippling over the dark parking lot. He was about to return to the restaurant when he saw the downed telephone pole, then after he shelved his hands over his eyes, he recognized the car smashed under it, heard its weak, droning horn, and saw the headlamps shining dimly through the darkness. The driver was a college student named Whitney Garrett, and if Carlos hadn't carried her to his truck and driven her to the ER, she might've died.

I'd taken the morning off to bucket out the Caddy's floorboards, but that afternoon Carlos recounted everything. He was frying flautas, dancing around the kitchen with his spatula and beer. He said, "Cook saves princess, earns handsome reward."

"How handsome?"

"Julian, by the looks of Mama Garrett, I won't need to borrow your accordion again."

"Carlos, I don't own an accordion."

He slid the flautas onto the plate, spooned on extra rice and beans, then rang the bell for Alma to take the order to her table.

Carlos said, "*Yet*. You don't own an accordion yet."

But the reward never came. Days, then weeks, passed after he saved Whitney Garrett, and still Carlos heard nothing. He called me every few nights to talk to me while he drank. He asked if I'd enroll with him in classes to become a rodeo clown, and another time he told me the story of catching himself in his trouser zipper and getting stitches. He said, "Julian, that's happened to me *twice*, so please be careful." He told me that as a boy he'd wanted to be a mariachi singer, that his father had owned a monkey that smoked cigarettes. He talked about how he'd spend his reward money—he planned to buy La Cocina as well as a shrimp boat and recording studio, to outfit Alma with a new wardrobe, to send Melinda to college. He asked if I could think of why Mrs. Garrett would promise to visit the restaurant, but hadn't.

"Maybe she's planning something really special," I said.

"If someone saved my daughter, I'd give them the keys to my house. I'd send thank-you cards every morning. I'd call every night and sing them to sleep."

"Why does Carlos always talk about buying the restaurant?" I asked Melinda. We were eating a late lunch and trying out one of his new recipes. When he brought out the plates—steak picado in a taco shell bowl—he'd said, *In my restaurant, this dish goes on the menu. The Melinda and Julian Special.*

Melinda dabbed her mouth with a napkin and stared out the window, thinking. Puddles of heat radiated on the sidewalk, the grass across the street was as dry and blond as hay. I felt lucky to be in the air-conditioning, eating food that tasted of beer. The phone rang, and Mrs. Martinez answered, then walked the order into the kitchen. This was my favorite time of the day to look at Melinda, when her lipstick had worn off and her ponytail was loose. I imagined her looking this way just after waking. I wanted to stay in that booth forever.

She said, "Because Carlos is an optimist, like you."

"Like me?"

"He's always jabbered about owning a restaurant. For years he played the lottery, before that it was bingo. Now he thinks this girl's mother will be his ticket. Carlos thinks money will fall in his lap if he just waits long enough."

"And me? What am I waiting for?"

She took a long drink of sweet tea, crunched an ice cube. She said, "Me."

Mrs. Martinez ambled across the restaurant and handed me a bag of taquitos. She said, "To Beechwood Nursery, on Padre Island. Vamos, before the causeway gets bumper to bumper."

After she'd left I stood and looked down at Melinda. I said, "If I wait long enough, will something happen?"

She took a bite and chewed slowly, staring at me and smirking. "Do you think Carlos will ever buy La Cocina?"

As often as he'd mentioned it, I'd never really considered that possibility, and realizing that I didn't have an answer puzzled me. I felt shamefully confident that he'd never hear from the Garretts again—a month had passed—but that alone didn't preclude him from owning a restaurant. I said, "I hope so."

"Me, too," she said. Then she winked at me. "Plus, if he gets his own place, he's naming it *Melinda's.*"

I thought she was joking, but then it clicked. I said, "You're Carlos's daughter?"

"Stepdaughter," she said.

Then, before I could stop myself, I said, "Melinda, I lied about my mother. She's not dead. She left my father to live with a lawyer in Arizona."

She took another bite, and my palms went clammy. Mrs. Martinez started feeding her plants behind me, though I could feel her leering at us. The phone rang again. I knew I needed to leave before I got stuck with another delivery, but my feet were rooted, like I'd stepped in drying cement.

Finally, Melinda said, "So it all makes sense."

"What does?"

"Your father," she said. "He's another optimist."

Driving to the nursery, I thought about this, my father being an optimist. He threw horseshoes alone in our backyard and listened to Bach suites while tinkering at his workbench. He read books about surviving divorce, and maybe because a book advised it, he'd started writing in a diary that he hid in his nightstand. I'd read a few pages, but then guilt swamped me, and I returned the notebook to its hiding place. He'd lectured me on responsibility because I'd ignored the ragtop, and when I told him about Carlos saving Whitney Garrett, he said, "I hope she *wanted* to be saved."

Roundtrip, the delivery took me two hours because the causeway had clogged with civilians leaving the Naval Air Station after their shifts. By the time I made it back to La Cocina, the health inspector had come and gone. The restaurant was empty, the door locked. The CLOSED notice and our failed inspection were posted in the window like new, elaborate menus.

At home, my father was watching *General Hospital*. He sometimes watched soap operas before work, maybe because my mother had watched them. The shows always left him cross. When he saw me, he clicked off the television and asked if I'd been messing with Elvis's guitar again.

I *had* been in his closet, twice in the last week, but I hadn't played the guitar. I'd just wanted to see it. I'd started thinking that my father only kept it around to punish himself, and holding the case, I felt sorry for him, and furious; I wanted to cut the strings in half, bash the guitar against the concrete.

I said, "I lost my job today. The health department shut us down."

My father levered himself from his recliner, set the remote control beside the lamp. He said, "Maybe now you'll have time to work on the ragtop."

I nodded. I felt my ears going scarlet.

"So, have you been fooling with the guitar?"

"No," I said.

"It's a collector's item, Jay. I shouldn't have to remind you how much it's worth. When I gave it to your mother, she—"

"Professor," I interrupted, "have you seen my bowie knife?"

I drove by two and three times a day, testing the lock and pressing my forehead to the window. The restaurant was like a diorama, and the longer I was kept out, the more I wanted back in, the more I felt that I'd never worked there at all. I loitered in the parking lot, hoping Carlos or Melinda would happen by, but they never did, and nothing ever changed. The notice stayed on the door, the chairs waited to be lifted onto the tables. Through the windows I watched the leaves of Mrs. Martinez's plants wilt and fall to the floor. Eventually, a moving crew carted the booths and tables and refrigerators onto a flatbed trailer; two weeks later, a wig store opened in our space.

When the phone rang one evening, I expected to hear Carlos's slurred voice on the line, but my mother said, "Do you hate me as much as your father does?"

Outside, I could hear him tightening a bolt with his drill. I remembered watching him thrash the ragtop, hearing him cry in his bedroom. In his journal, he'd written, *I hope Jay never loves someone the way I love you.* I said, "He doesn't hate you."

"That's a surprise," she said. "Your father, he's a—"

"An optimist," I said. I liked saying that, liked how it made me think of Melinda.

"An optimist. That's sweet of you. You're a good egg, Jay," she said. "Do you know when I think about him most? Around an election, when everyone blabs about Democrats and Republicans. Remember? *Republican.*"

Every pawnshop has a code that it uses for pricing—a ten-letter word with no repeating characters—and Blue Water's was Republican. Each letter represents a numeral (R is 1, E is 2, all the way through 0), so pawnbrokers can openly discuss how much to buy or sell merchandise for without betraying anything to customers. My father had taught us the code years before, so when he said he'd paid I-N-N for the Caddy, I knew he'd bought it for seven hundred. I'd tried to explain the code to Carlos one afternoon, and he said, "Julian, you shouldn't discuss politics at work."

My mother said, "I loved hearing the pawnshop guys talk that way. It excited me, a language you didn't hear if you didn't speak it. I still size things up like that. I'll think, Do I want to pay A-L for a blouse? Is an espresso really worth B? Is R-N-N-N too much to send in my Jay's birthday card?"

"I never got a birthday card," I said.

She went quiet. I listened to the static crackling on the line, to my father putting away his tools in the garage. He'd been working out there for hours each evening, and I'd been dodging him.

My mother said, "Maybe my calling was a bad idea, maybe I'll let you go."

"I'm glad you called," I said.

"That's nice to hear," she said and started crying a little. Once she'd composed herself, she said, "So, the check's in the mail, as they say."

"Thank you."

"And Jay, when you get your money, treat your father to a fancy restaurant. Or, one night when he's not expecting it, bring him home a steak and asparagus. That's his favorite meal, and he'd like you showing up with it."

Outside, our automatic garage door started closing. The light on the driveway diminished, diminished, diminished, and I heard my father run water to rinse his hands with the garden hose.

I said, "I'll deliver it in a limo."

For the two years between my mother's leaving and my father giving me the Cadillac, he intentionally left the keys in the ignition and the doors unlocked. He said he wanted someone to steal the car so he could file an insurance claim. I'd believed him at the time, but after La Cocina closed, I found myself thinking more about it and doubting him. He'd never put an ad in the paper or a FOR SALE sign in the window, so I suspected that he wouldn't have reported the car stolen or tried to claim any money; I think he wanted the car gone, but couldn't bear to get rid of it. My father, I think, was an idealist.

I worked at Blue Water until school started up again. I loaned thieves and addicts money for mounted javelina heads and leather jackets and leaf blowers; I sold stolen pistols to cops and widows and preachers. I listened to men lie about women and fishing, brawling and hunting, and my father taught me how to study a diamond through a jeweler's lens, to see how its imperfections determined its beauty. He quizzed me on how much to pay for solitaires, how low to sell princess cuts. We spoke in code. We skirted the topic of the Fleetwood's roof. In September, the heat relented and troughs of cooler air brought bands of rain in from the Gulf. If I saw thunderclouds carpeting the sky through Blue Water's windows, I'd run into the parking lot and cover the Fleetwood's interior with a tarp. I weighted the corners with barbells someone had pawned, and after the rain dispersed, I wadded the tarp into a ball and shoved it in the trunk.

One Friday night—Blue Water's busiest because everyone needs loans for the weekend—I pulled out my tarp and uncovered a bag of tortillas from the wedding Mrs. Martinez had catered in Portland. The tortillas had slipped under the spare tire and were fuzzy with gray mold. My stomach went whispery, my ears burned. I wanted to throw the bag into the street or on top of the pawnshop's roof, but I left it where it was and slammed the trunk shut and drove home.

The phone was ringing when I got to the house, but I didn't answer it. My father had barged into Blue Water's parking lot as I was accelerating away, and I didn't want to hear how I'd disappointed him again. He called a second, third, and fourth time, but I only stared at the receiver, unable to will myself to answer. *He'll tell me I'm irresponsible,* I thought. *He'll say I lack discipline.* When I finally picked up, his voice was tight and deliberate. "Stay there, he said. "We need to break bread."

"Will do, professor."

Five minutes later he called back. I answered by saying, "Still here, professor."

"Julian? This is Carlos. Maybe you remember me. I used to work—"

"Where are you?" I asked. Then I was out the door.

They lived in a section of Corpus called The Cut, a neighborhood crowded with rusted, broken-down cars and dirt lawns and boxy tract houses. If the stop signs hadn't been stolen, they were spray-painted with looping gang tags. White-shirted men anchored street corners; women sat on porches and rocked crying babies. A German shepherd lunged against a chain-link fence as the Caddy crawled by, and the air was tinged with mesquite smoke, someone barbecuing or burning branches. A young girl was pinning wet sheets to a clothesline. The streetlights were flickering to life when I saw her, and in the darkness, it looked like she was raising long flags of surrender.

Carlos was doing figure-eights on a BMX bike in the middle of his street. He looked like a child learning to ride without training wheels. When he saw me, he laid the bike on the curb and sauntered to the Fleetwood. He'd holstered a beer bottle in each of his front pockets, and he gave one to me. We leaned against my rear bumper, watching the night sky thicken.

"A toast," he said. We raised our bottles. "To La Cocina. May she rest in peace."

He'd been working day labor, taking the bus across town each morning and waiting outside Home Depot until someone hired him to clear brush or build a fence or fix a toilet. Melinda had started school again, and Alma was cleaning houses. No one had heard from Mrs. Martinez. That day, Carlos had helped a crew dig up a Country Club yard and install a sprinkler system; he'd worked for fourteen hours, then called me when he came home. He finished his beer and lobbed it at a trash can, missing by a foot. He held his arm in the air like a basketball player after a jumpshot, and I smelled his sweat. The odor wasn't foul, just that of a body after a day's work. It smelled vaguely of La Cocina, of the last summer.

"A wig store moved into our old space," I said. "It's kind of sad, I guess."

He nodded twice, shoved his hands in his pockets, and stared into the darkness. I guessed he'd visited the restaurant, too, and was remembering the old days, but he said, "If I owned a wig store, I'd have full-bodied mannequins instead of the little heads. I'd leave them naked except for the wigs. That way, when there were no customers, I'd have something to look at besides hair."

"No health code violations in that," I said.

Down the street a man pushing a rickety snowcone cart argued with a teenager. The teenager whistled a hard, sharp whistle, and the man trundled away. I took a drink of my beer and tried to think of a way to ask if Melinda was home.

"Julian, driving the King of the Cadillacs out here was maybe not your best idea," Carlos said. "Two weeks ago, they shot a deaf guy because they thought he was making gang signs with his hands."

I'd heard the story at Blue Water. After the shooting, my father took each of his pawnbrokers aside and told them to be vigilant about background checks before selling guns. But standing with Carlos, I wasn't scared, and I hadn't been afraid navigating the streets. The world seemed random and unknowable to me, but not utterly cruel, not terrifying. Sometimes circumstances put you face to face with people you never thought you'd see again, and with that possibility in mind, you could make a life.

"Pop quiz," I said to Carlos. I'd turned around and was unlocking the trunk. I said, "Why did I rush over here tonight?"

"Julian, if I owe you any money—"

"You don't," I said. "Guess who I ran into."

I took my tarp out of the trunk. I'd handed Carlos my beer, and when I looked up at him, he was scratching his head with it. He said, "Julian, I'm not so good at tests."

"Mrs. Garrett. Whitney Garrett's mother," I said. "She came to La Cocina trying to find you. I was up there, looking in the window."

Carlos swigged from my beer, then swallowed hard and swigged again. He said, "Julian, are you fucking with Carlos?"

"She wanted to thank you for saving her daughter. She wanted to give you your reward," I said. I lifted the case from my trunk and clicked open the latches. In the violet moonlight, the strings shone like spun silk. The fur-lined case looked like a jewelry box.

I said, "For you, Carlos."

"A guitar," he said.

"It used to belong to Elvis Presley," I said. "It's worth—"

"She must have known I love music. Maybe I said something at the hospital."

"Probably," I said. "You were probably trying to take her mind off the accident.

"Carlos knows how to comfort the ladies." He admired the guitar at arm's length, then held it close and strummed an open chord, then another and another. When the notes died away, I suggested he sell the guitar and put the money toward starting his own restaurant. He said, "Julian, I'll never sell this."

"Where are we going?" Melinda said from behind us.

She'd climbed over the door and into the driver's seat of the Fleetwood. Behind the wheel, she looked exhausted and beautiful, just as she had on the day she'd told me Carlos was her stepfather.

"Field trip in the Fleetwood!" Carlos sang.

He jogged around the front of the car, strumming his strings. He set the guitar on the backseat first, then lowered himself in beside it. I sat in the passenger seat. I must have ridden that way when my mother owned the car, but I couldn't recall ever sitting there before. With the night sky starless and heavy above us, those days seemed part of another boy's life. I didn't know what to say, and had I spoken, I wouldn't have recognized my own voice.

Melinda fixed me with her eyes. I thought she was waiting for me to pass her the keys, but even after I did, she kept looking at me.

"Hey, you," she finally whispered. Then she winked and cranked the ignition.

She hung a U-turn and wound her way out of The Cut. She headed straight for the freeway and floored the gas once she hit those clean wide-open lanes. She took the car to speeds I never would, the speedometer needle trembling toward eighty, eighty-five, ninety. The streetlamps whizzed by like comets. Carlos was strumming and singing in the backseat, but I could barely hear him over the engine and the air whooshing around the windshield. Melinda's hair swirled wildly, and the scent of her honeyed shampoo wafted. It seemed we were floating.

I'm not sure when I realized she was driving to La Cocina, or when I realized she didn't know the restaurant was gone. Maybe I knew it when she exited the freeway doing sixty and it felt slow as walking. Maybe it was when she braked at an intersection and the speed had left her giddy enough that she leaned over and kissed me so hard and long that drivers behind us laid into their horns. Maybe it was when I looked back, worrying Carlos would be angry, and found him fast asleep, cradling the guitar. Or maybe I realized it when the night sky opened and the rain poured. Before I could stop her, Melinda flipped the switch to raise the roof. I thought of how disappointed my father had been by my neglecting the ragtop and how I'd been avoiding him because it shamed me, too. With the rain drumming on the hood and streaking the glass, I thought of him finding the house empty tonight. I'd never disobeyed him like that before, but now I thought he'd forgive what I'd done, maybe even approve of it. As a new pristine ragtop eased down and the rain grew quieter and quieter, I saw my father working those many nights in his garage: He's stretching the vinyl taut over the roof's ribs, riveting the corners, oiling the hinges. He's listening to the intricate music of longing and weeping when he must. He's watching the clouds. He's waiting and waiting, whiling away the hours until a storm gathers and his son can appreciate the painstaking labor of hope, the coded, sheltering lessons of sorrow.

STEPHANIE DIANI

Bret Anthony Johnston is the editor of *Naming the World: And Other Exercises for the Creative Writer* and the author of *Corpus Christi: Stories.* His stories have appeared in *New Stories from the South: The Year's Best,* 2003, 2004, and 2005 editions, and in 2006 he received a National Book Award honor for young writers. He is currently the Director of Creative Writing at Harvard University and can be reached on the web at www.bretanthonyjohnston.com.

*T*his story took me ten years to write. I wrote a draft of it in 1997, a draft I liked but found unsatisfying, then filed the story away in a folder with the name "Carlos" written on the tab. For the next decade, I worked on other projects while Carlos hibernated in basements in Ohio, Texas, Iowa, and Michigan, a garage in California, and another basement in Massachusetts. Every so often, I'd scribble an idea onto a scrap of paper and slip it into the Carlos folder, but as much as I liked the character *and the promise of the first draft, I never revised it. Maybe I liked the story's potential so much that I was afraid to ruin it. Then, in 2007, I got a really nice and flattering letter from a magazine editor asking for a story, and because I was waist-deep in a novel and had no stories in the works, and because I'd always remembered liking parts of "Carlos," I pulled the file out of the drawer and went back to work. The editor finally didn't take the story, though I didn't know that until I saw his magazine on the stands and "Carlos" wasn't in it, which was, you know, awesome. But then Don Lee and Andrea Barrett liked it, and so I'm almost as grateful to that first editor for "rejecting" the story as I am to them for taking it. I owe Don a trip to Hawaii and I owe Andrea a miniature dachshund for their support and enthusiasm.*

One more thing: Although this is most certainly a work of fiction, the cook is inspired by a man my friend Bill used to work with in Texas. Every afternoon after Bill got off his shift at the restaurant, he would call and tell me what trouble the cook had caused that morning. Bill would always close by saying, "So put that in one of your little stories." Much of what he told me didn't make it into the story, but plenty did. I hope he approves, and I hope Carlos does, too.

Mary Miller

LEAK

(from *The Oxford American*)

There's a leak, I told him, it's right over my bed. He didn't
believe me. I was a girl.

What's it look like? he said. He was reading cartoons. When he
found a good one he'd pass the paper across the table, tell me to
read it. He'd say, Here, take a look at this, and I'd laugh, but I never
thought they were funny. It was just the two of us and things had
been difficult since I'd grown breasts. They came between us. He
wouldn't let me sit on his lap anymore.

It looks like a bull's-eye, I said.

How many rings?

Several, it's pretty big and it's getting bigger.

I need to see it, he said, before I call the roofer and get an esti-
mate. Later, after lunch, I followed him upstairs to my bedroom.
It's a leak, he said, his hands on his hips. He had salad dressing on
his shirt, a wet spot where he'd tried to rub it off. I could see his
chest hairs. It was like looking through a porthole. And there's one
here, too, he said, pointing to a long thin one like a comet's tail, or
the streak left behind by an airplane. I used to have a friend who
put her hand over her heart every time she saw an airplane, but she
switched to private school and I didn't see her anymore.

You didn't tell me about that one, he said. What about in the
other room? Go look.

I went. I knew what a leak looked like now.

I don't see anything, I called.

I'll call the roofer, he said. Bill has a guy.

What'll happen if we don't get it fixed?

The ceiling'll fall in, he said, and I reminded him that it was right over my bed, on the side I liked to sleep because I didn't like sleeping by the door, even with it locked, because I was afraid of intruders.

He went back downstairs and watched men hunt turkeys on television. He had a little wooden box he practiced on. When his friend Bub called, he started cleaning his gun.

Aunt Pat lived next door. She barely did anything but sit on her couch all day long and wait for Uncle Bill to come home. I'd go over there and play with her dog because I didn't have a dog. I wanted a dog but my father said we weren't dog people.

I sat on the steps while Li'l Baby looked for a gumball. She only liked the ones with stems. When she found a good one, we went back inside and she chased it around the living room while Aunt Pat clapped and said, Oh Li'l Baby, get it! Get it, Li'l Baby! She told me she collected them on her walks and planted them all over the backyard like Easter eggs.

Why don't you invite a friend over? she said. She was always asking about my friends. What were their names? Did I want to invite one over? Was I popular? I got the feeling she didn't know why anyone would want to be my friend, and when I did invite someone over she acted like the girl was doing everybody a big favor.

I don't feel like it, I said.

You're too young to not be feeling like things, she said.

I didn't know what to say to that. Li'l Baby flipped over on her back and stuck her legs in the air like an armadillo, dead on the side of the road.

She wants you to scratch her stomach, Aunt Pat said.

I scratched but my fingernails kept getting hung up on her nipples, so I rubbed. Her belly looked like the inside of a shell. You could press your ear to it and hear the ocean.

When do y'all leave? she said.

We were going to Florida, like we did every year. We stayed in a house on the beach and ate seafood and went to the outlet malls, but my father wouldn't let me go in the water because once I got caught by a riptide and almost drowned and after that I got stung by a jellyfish and after that my mother died. Neither of us wanted to go, but we did it to show somebody something. Lately I'd felt like tossing myself down the stairs and letting my father clean up the mess. It was kind of like that.

Saturday, I said.

Where are y'all staying?

The same place we always stay.

A house?

It's yellow. There's an RV park nearby with a lot of old people.

That'll be nice. Maybe you'll make a new friend. Bill never takes me anywhere. He's so cheap, you wouldn't believe how cheap he is, she said.

Everybody knew how cheap he was. Our ladder leaned against their house. He always needed to borrow a battery or shotgun shells or he couldn't find his saw.

Li'l Baby shredded her gumball, tore the stem off, so we went back outside and I sat there while she searched for another.

Bub brought his fat kid and donuts over on Saturday morning. He forgot we were leaving, or he didn't know. My father didn't tell him anything. They wore their camouflage and went out into the woods and got drunk, but they kept to themselves.

Sometimes they'd take me and the fat kid fishing but I never caught anything. You could be sitting right next to someone and the fish went to them every time. There was a trick to it. I figured they wanted me to figure it out for myself but I didn't want to think about fish, their gills and jelly eyes and the way they flopped about in protest while dying.

My father wanted a boy, like the fat kid, who was named Darrell.

You could clonk him on the head and teach him to shoot guns and skin animals and, as long as he didn't turn out to be faggot, things were easy.

Hey, Pocahontas, Bub said. Where's your dad?

In his study, I said, getting ready to go.

Go where?

The beach.

Oh.

Yeah.

Well, that'll be fun.

The fat kid sat at the table and asked if we had any milk. My father came out of his study and clonked him on the head. Then he sat and opened the box of donuts. I got the milk out of the refrigerator and four glasses, passed them around. I'd recently learned to thaw meat and boil eggs. My father bought me a five-ingredient cookbook and kept the refrigerator stocked with ground beef and chicken and I had to find something to do with it. Mostly I combined the beef with ketchup and onions and shaped it into a loaf, and the chicken I cut up and sprinkled with salt and pepper. He wanted me to fry things but I was afraid to fry.

The kid had his own personal bag of donut holes. He reached his hand in and popped them into his mouth one at a time.

I think this milk is bad, the fat kid said to me.

I'm not in charge of the milk.

My father picked up the gallon and said, June thirteenth. Still good.

Bub and the fat kid left and my father followed me upstairs and asked me questions: Did I pack swimsuits, my toothbrush, T-shirts? Did I pack the beach towels? Did we have any sunscreen? What was the difference between sunscreen and sunblock and suntan lotion?

I thought about the time my mother told me I better take a bath or I wasn't going to Florida because I didn't like to take baths and sometimes she had to threaten me and I took one and went to sleep but then she heard the water running in the middle of the night and found me in an inch of cold water and my father made her feel terrible about it the whole way down.

I'm pretty sure sunscreen and sunblock are the same thing, I said. Suntan lotion is if you want to get a tan.

I don't want to get a tan, he said.

Okay.

You can get a tan if you want.

Okay.

We better get going here pretty soon.

I zipped up my suitcase and he carried it down the stairs and out the door to his open trunk. Then he put his suitcase in, a cooler full of Cokes.

Why don't you run over to Pat's and remind her to get the mail? he said.

I walked.

Aunt Pat, he said, was flighty. Aunt Pat was my mother's people. His people didn't come around. They were spread out all over, Arkansas and New Mexico and California, which made them easier to like. He had a sister who traveled the world on a boat with her sea-captain husband. She sent us things through the mail: statues of Buddha, first-edition books, turquoise bracelets. We gave them away to poor people, who had less use for them than we had.

I knocked and Uncle Bill opened the door. He handed me a plate of cookies Aunt Pat made and winked and I reminded him to get our mail and then I turned around and walked back to the car. I could feel him watching me. I looked back and he held up a hand but he didn't lift the corners of his mouth. He was a deacon at our church. I tried not to hold it against God. It wasn't God's fault that all the sick people in the world latched onto Him.

She's going to get the mail? he said. My dad was crazy about the mail. He was also crazy about our property line. If someone parked in front of our house, he took down their license plate.

I told Uncle Bill.

Cookies, he said. What kind?

Looks like some kind of nut.

Hand me one, he said, backing out. I peeled the Saran Wrap off and gave him a broken one. Chocolate chip and pecan, he said, holding it up. I like Pat. That Pat's a good woman.

She's always acting like I don't have any friends.

You have friends.

Not that many.

You've got lots of friends. What about that little bowlegged girl?

She goes to the academy now.

Since when?

Since last year.

Oh, he said. Phyllis is your friend.

Phyllis lived around the corner. She was allergic to the sun. When I went over to her house we sat in the dark and played with dolls but mostly I watched the circles under her eyes grow. We were too old to play with dolls but Phyllis hadn't heard. She was homeschooled.

If you've got one true friend that's all you really need, he said. I didn't know where he'd heard that load of crap but I'd heard it, too. It seemed like a bad idea, narrowing your options down to one.

Let's don't talk about it anymore, I said.

We stopped at Shoney's for lunch. The lady led us to a booth and my father sat down but then he got up to use the bathroom and the man at the next booth had no companion so we were facing each other. The man was wearing a red T-shirt with a tattoo creeping out of the neck of it. He smiled at me with straight white teeth and I looked away and then my father came back and sat down and I scooted over so he blocked the man.

I'm not really that hungry, I said.

You better eat. Who knows when we'll stop next.

I knew when we'd stop next, at five o'clock, for supper, but I said okay and ordered chicken fingers and my father ordered the catfish with greens and macaroni and cheese and cornbread. While we waited, there was nothing to say but he felt the need to talk, which meant he asked me questions he already knew the answers to. I didn't ask him anything. I could see straight through him. The red T-shirt man stood and opened his wallet, laid a bill on the table. He showed me his teeth for the last time and walked out to his VW.

He looked so small and hunched over behind the wheel.

Our food came and I made myself eat because my father was disappointed when I didn't eat. He probably catalogued my needs in his head, checked them off one by one: food, water, shelter, love.

The people got trashier the farther south you went.

We pulled into a gas station in Navarre Beach and my father pumped gas while men toted cases of beer to their trucks. They smoked without hands and had wiry arms the color of old ground beef. Enormous women in tight clothes leaned against phone booths and parked cars, like they couldn't be bothered to hold themselves up anymore.

When we got to Panama City, I rolled down the window and breathed in the heavy air. We stopped off at the office for a key and then drove to the house.

I went to my room, put my suitcase on the bed, and unzipped it. My clothes were jostled and hot. I checked the drawers to see if anybody'd left anything. Then I put my swimsuit on because the sun was still out. My swimsuit was last year's swimsuit. It was red with COCA-COLA written in cursive all over it. I tried not to ask for things because I was worried about money. I used to hear them arguing about it, where to put it, why there wasn't more of it.

I knew my father went to her grave to deposit flowers and I could see him kneeling there with his head bowed and I wanted to kneel beside him, but he wanted to protect me from death. He didn't know I could see it everywhere.

As soon as I got back, I went over to Phyllis's house. Her mother answered the door and called me Sugar, said Phyllis had been missing me something terrible. Then the phone rang and she left me standing in the open door. *Something terrible* got stuck in my head. I walked down the hall thinking, *Something terrible, something terrible*. Phyllis's room had yellow walls and a dresser with a row of things I wasn't allowed to touch: bath salts and body lotion and soap shaped like ducks, but she didn't use them because once you used them they were worthless.

We sat on her floor with a stack of magazines. I stuck my legs straight out and pressed my fingers into them to call attention to my tan, but she flipped through the pages of her magazine without looking up.

The tops of my feet got burned, I said, though the burn wasn't a burn anymore. It was a pretty red-brown color, same as my arms and legs.

Look at the ears on this one, she said. The girl was straddling a horse in a string bikini, her hair slicked back so she was basically eyes and ears and the places where things should have been. It wasn't unattractive. Phyllis wanted to be a model but she was plump and white with just the tiniest hint of a nose. I could see her in a pot of water surrounded by carrots and potatoes.

She's not too bad, I said.

You're right, I'd trade.

I want to swing, I said.

When the sun goes down I can.

My dad likes to eat at five o'clock.

Maybe you can go home and feed your dad and then come back and spend the night.

I can't, I said, because I didn't feel like waking up in her house and wondering where I was, and I didn't feel like sitting at the breakfast table with her brothers while her mother asked if I wanted this, or that, or more of this, like she would give anything.

So come back tomorrow.

Maybe.

I'll call you, she said, and you'll come back.

Okay.

You better come back.

I will.

She walked over to her dresser and selected the smallest duck in the family of ducks. Here, she said. This is the baby. You can have it if you come back tomorrow.

It would have been easier to stay had she not wanted me to stay so badly. I walked down the hall and let myself out but then I heard her mother say something so I opened the door and her mother said to come back soon and I said I would. I took a left out of her driveway and walked down her street and then I took a right and was almost to my house when a boy passed on a bike. He flung his hair and circled back and flung his hair some more. I turned up my driveway. When I got to the door, I watched him push his bike up the street a ways before hopping back on.

My father was grilling hot dogs. I sat at the table and watched as he took them off the grill with his fingers, one at a time, furious. We had tongs but he looked for ways to suffer over and above all of the ways already in place.

He set the plate of hot dogs on the table. There were eight of them and two of us.

Would you fix us a couple of Cokes? he said.

I put ice in the glasses while he got the ketchup and mustard out of the cabinet, the bag of buns. I checked the date smudged into the plastic to make sure they were still good.

After he finished his first one, he looked up at me and asked how Phyllis's was. I couldn't look at him. I looked out the window at the birds poking around the grass. A statue of a saint found lost things.

I don't like Phyllis anymore.

That's too bad. Phyllis likes you.

That doesn't mean I have to like her back.

No, it doesn't, he said. Then he told me to eat my hot dog and I told him I didn't like hot dogs and he said since when, and I told him that hot dogs were like eggs. I'd never liked eggs but he kept giving them to me and I kept saying I didn't eat them and finally I broke down and started eating them.

And now you like them.

I don't like them. I eat them.

He repositioned his fork, his glass, centered the plate on his mat.

In the morning, Aunt Pat called. My father answered and she told him to send me over. I'd go back and forth, fetching things.

She waved me in and we stood in her kitchen. There was a cuckoo clock and a framed picture of connected stick figures: IF MAMA AIN'T HAPPY AIN'T NOBODY HAPPY. There was a teapot and a grocery-store cake and Li'l Baby laid out on the floor. She hobbled over to me like an old lady and I picked her up.

Li'l Baby is pooped, she said. We went for a walk. I made a chicken casserole. Do you like chicken casserole?

It's okay.

Everything with you is always okay.

I wanted her to just give me the damn casserole and let me go home but she was going to take an interest in me first.

Your father tells me you're having problems with your little friend, she said.

Which little friend?

The neighbor girl.

There's no problem.

If there's a problem, you can tell me about it.

Okay.

So?

She can't go outside because she has this thing with the sun. She's allergic.

And?

And I like to go outside.

I'm sure you two can work it out, she said.

She gave me the casserole and told me to heat it for thirty minutes at three-fifty and serve it with a tossed salad and a loaf of

French bread. Sometimes she unfolded the arms from my chest. Other times she just put things in them. After my mother died she took me to J.C. Penney and bought me bras and I'd never really gotten over it, how she clutched my shoulders and told me I was spilling out all over the place.

I carried the casserole home and stuck it in the refrigerator. Then I found my father in his study with his shotgun on his lap. He'd been in the war, done something with radios, fixed them, or talked over them. It wasn't clear. Now he just broke down his gun and put it back together. Fish and deer were mounted on the walls and there was this smell like something rotting, but if I mentioned it, he'd say a rodent must have crawled under the house and died. The fish had plaques underneath them like birth announcements: weight and date and who was responsible.

What'd Pat want? he said.

A casserole.

She wanted you to make her a casserole?

No, she gave me one.

What kind?

Chicken.

Chickenshit, he said. I'm sick of chicken.

The phone rang. I walked into his bedroom and sat on the side where my mother used to sleep. Sometimes I peeled back the covers and got in, the sheets so cold and clean, and stayed there for hours. It was Phyllis. She wanted to know where her duck was and I told her it was my duck now and she asked where my duck was and I told her I was looking at it that very minute, that I'd just snapped its head off and now that it was ruined I could use it.

My mom made haystacks for you, she said.

I found her on the floor with her laundry basket full of dolls. The dolls were mostly pieces of dolls because we popped the legs off at the hip, and sometimes the arms. She selected one with a haphazard haircut and made her hoist herself up into the pink van and sit there, wishing she had legs. She pushed the van around in circles. Vroom, vroom, she said. We called it the Love Bus because we made the legless dolls get in the back of it and eat each other out.

I kicked off my shoes. Her mother brought in a tin of haystacks and set them at my feet.

Phyllis popped them into her mouth whole. Then she opened her mouth and laughed. It sounded like it came from a place she had no control over. It made me nervous so I got up and went to the bathroom and sat on the toilet pinching the skin on my stomach. I fingered a mole to the left of my bellybutton and another one above it and wondered what a mole was and why I had so many of them.

When her mother came back, the tin was empty except for a few loose straws, and since I was skinny I told her I must have been really hungry because I'd eaten nearly all of them, and she smiled and said she'd make more. She was glad I liked them. I was just a little wisp of a thing. Bless my heart. Her mother went out and one of her brothers came in, the smaller one. He was wearing a silver jacket with tabs on the shoulders so you could pick him up and toss him.

Hey, he said to me. I smiled. Phyllis shrieked. Her brothers weren't allowed in her room without permission, which she never granted. He put his palm on the flat of the van and pushed it as hard as he could into the wall.

I was certain that whatever was wrong with her she'd brought upon herself.

I went home and waited for the lightning bugs to show up. I used to catch them and put them in a jar and watch them blink themselves out, but now I just watched them. I saw the first couple of blinks and then I saw the boy come up the street. He got off his bike and dropped it on the grass and told me he had on a flame-retardant suit and he was going to light himself on fire. He struck a match and lit himself on fire, like he said he would, and he flamed up pretty good and then he flailed into the fence that divided our house from Aunt Pat's and a section of it came down and then he started rolling around while I sat there trying to mask my alarm and feeling like this was all my fault even though I'd done nothing wrong because this was clearly about me. I stood up and went inside but then I heard him scream so I looked out the window and saw that he'd managed to put himself out. He was in our grass on his stomach and I wanted it to be morning already so I could go over there and stand inside the outline of his body.

My father hadn't heard a thing. He was watching television. A man high up in the trees whispered into the camera. It was the first day of deer season, he said, so he wasn't going to get too excited.

We had a maid come three times a week. She had eleven children and her children had started having children. The circle of life, my father said, when we saw a bunch of lions kill an elephant on TV, or when Deloris had another baby. In the mornings, the bus would let off and all the black women would walk to the houses they belonged to for the next six hours, and then you'd see them strolling the little white babies up and down the street but they didn't love the little white babies, you could tell, they cared for them but they didn't love them, not like I imagined I'd love a little black baby.

When Deloris came in, my father went out. I sat at the table, looking out the window at a paunchy orange-bellied bird. Deloris moved her weight around the kitchen. She peeled off strips of bacon, cracked eggs.

She set the plate in front of me and I ate a piece of bacon but I didn't touch the eggs.

Eat them eggs, she told me.

I was sorry I'd ever eaten the first bite of an egg.

You is disappearin right before my eyes, she said, shaking her head.

I wanted to ride my bike but the tires were flat.

The boy who lit himself on fire was at the ditch, tying a rope to a blow-up raft. He dropped the raft in the water and we stood there and watched it bob. He asked where I thought it would take him and I said to the river and then probably to the ocean.

That's cool, he said. I checked to see if his eyebrows were singed, leaned into his hair to see if it smelled like burned peanuts.

Where'd you get that raft? I said.

I have a pool.

That's nice.

It's not so great, he said. You can come over and swim in it if you want, see how boring it is.

When?

Now.

I have to go home. Deloris is probably wondering where I am.

Who's Deloris?

My maid. I stood there for a minute waiting to see what he'd do but he didn't do anything.

So go home then, he said.

Deloris's kids called all day long. They called during *The Young and the Restless* when something good happened. They called for no reason at all. My father said black people were often purposeless like this. He said you could go to any government office and just see them hanging around, using the bathroom and drinking from the water fountain and eating up all the free mints. There was this black boy at school named Terrance who sat behind me. He poked me with the eraser side of his pencil and I wanted to turn around but I just let him poke me and say, Hey, hey, hey, hey, girl.

The phone rang. Deloris was upstairs, cleaning my tub. It didn't drain properly so all the dirty water stood at my ankles when I showered and nests of hair and grayish sludge gathered at the edges. It was Deborah. She was the only one whose name I could remember, but I pronounced it wrong. The accent was on the *bor*. I was always putting the accent on the *Deb*. Sometimes I asked Deloris to tell me the names of her children and she'd reel them off. The first seven had names that started with D.

I called for Deloris, and waited for her to pick up, and then I went outside and walked through the hole the boy made and knocked on Aunt Pat's door. As soon as I saw her stiff hair and green pantsuit, I regretted it.

Oh, Li'l Baby, look who's here! She passed Li'l Baby to me.

Aunt Pat was my mother's older sister but my mother had never had much use for her. By extension I didn't have much use for her but I kept finding myself at her door, looking for what I'd lost.

Are you hungry? she said. Let's go to lunch.

Okay.

You pick.

Ruby Tuesday?

The last time I went in there the service was terrible, you wouldn't believe how bad it was. I know this great little French place.

Okay.

Just let me grab my purse and we'll go, she said, and I stood there waiting for the second hand to get back around to the twelve: cuckoo, cuckoo, cuckoo. Li'l Baby jumped out of my arms and went to get her gumball. She tossed it and retrieved it and tossed it again. It wound up under the couch. She wouldn't go under things, or over them, so she just stood there barking.

Li'l Baby shit on the floor. That's what my father said when I mentioned her: That dog shits on the floor.

Aunt Pat's car was big and white with leather seats. There was nothing on the floorboards except an empty pill bottle rolling back and forth and I wanted to pick it up and put it in the glove box but I didn't. I moved as little as possible around her because she watched me so closely.

The little French place was full of old women. The girl led us to a table and I sat down while Aunt Pat visited with a group of women in hats. She pointed at me and I smiled and they gave me sorry looks so probably she was telling them I was her niece and my mother was dead and she was trying to do the best she could by me, but it wasn't easy because I was at that age. My mother used to sing at the retarded mass and I'd give them the same looks, like they were awfully sad and yet so brave! They had their own mass because they liked to get up on stage with the priest and take the microphone away from my mother and sing the same note over and over and that was all part of the show. It was their own special mass! So sad and yet so brave!

The women squawked from across the room, flopped their heads about on loose necks. Aunt Pat laughed and the women laughed and then she sat down across from me and unfolded her napkin.

So, she said. What're we having?

I don't know.

The quiche is good.

I don't like quiche.

What about chicken salad? You like chicken salad.

It's okay, I said.

Let's not be difficult, she said so brightly it made my teeth hurt. I wanted to be at home, on my mother's side of the bed where the sheets were cold and clean.

After lunch, we picked up Li'l Baby so we could drive her out to the country and a girl named Sue.

You're gonna get your hair did, Li'l Baby! Aunt Pat told her. She handed her to me; the dog rested her paws on my arm and I pinched at them. They were like tiny bear claws. I rolled down the window and stuck her head out. Her ears blew back and her heart beat so fast: bum, bum, bum, bum, bum, bum, bum. Aunt Pat yelled I was scaring her so I pulled her head in and rolled up the window.

On our way up the dirt drive, two country men stopped talking to watch us, a lawn mower between them. Sue came out of her trailer. She was small and young-looking but something about her was old. She was wearing an apron and smiling. Her hair stopped at her chin. She seems happy, I said. Aunt Pat said it was because she didn't have to pay taxes. We left Li'l Baby with her and drove around, stopping at a shop that sold candles and necklaces and things she called setabouts. She bought me a necklace I said I liked. It was beaded. I didn't really like it but I wanted to let her buy me something so I could see if she'd charge my father for every little thing.

After an hour we went back to pick her up. Li'l Baby looked especially bug-eyed and her lashes kept falling into her eyes. We told her how pretty she was, how special. She didn't seem to know what to make of herself.

Deloris was eating her lunch when I came in. It was two o'clock and soon she'd pack her bag and lumber down the driveway and up the street while I waited for my father. Every day, she made a big show of eating one sandwich and drinking one can of Coke, but I walked in on her eating all day long. She ate spoonfuls of peanut butter and slices of cheese on white bread and sugar cookies. Sometimes I counted the cookies just so I'd know how many she'd eaten because she'd been with us since I was a baby and she didn't love me any more now than she did then.

My father came home and put on his shorts and walked outside to pick up the trash cans. Then he came back in and told me to turn off the oven. I could eat the baked chicken tomorrow or throw it away for all he cared. It was a relief. Everything in the five-recipe cookbook tasted the same and if I used one of my mother's cookbooks, I'd have to make a list of things for him to get at the store and he had trouble getting things he didn't normally get. He'd come home missing the one item I couldn't do without, like the tarragon in the chicken with tarragon mayonnaise or the pineapple in the pineapple pork roast.

I sat outside with him while he drank his bourbon and Coke and watched the pigeons circle. They went round and round like they were on a track. The man who lived behind us kept them.

How come they always go back home? I said.

Because the man feeds them, he said, but I knew it was more

than that. Then he asked if I'd make the potatoes so I went inside and ran a couple under the faucet, stabbed them with a knife, and put them in the microwave. I went back out and waited for him to give me another assignment. He was a manager at a bank, and his job, he liked to tell me, was to make people want to do theirs.

He made me want to do a shitty job.

When the food was ready, we went inside and sat down.

I took my time dressing the meat with lettuce and pickles and mustard. I got up to get a slice of cheese from the refrigerator. Then I put it together before tearing it apart.

I was thinking you should go to the academy this year, he said.

That costs a lot of money.

You don't have to worry about money. Your mother left you money.

She did?

It'd be easier for me to take you in the mornings.

Okay.

You'd probably fit in better there anyway. The little bowlegged girl—.

Emily, I said, and I saw her standing on the soccer field with her hand over her heart as an airplane deposited its fluffy white strip across the sky.

The phone rang.

We looked at each other.

I told him not to answer it but he was incapable of letting a phone ring so he picked it up and said hello and hold on just a second, Phyllis, and handed it to me.

My dad's taking us skating, she said.

Twenty minutes later, I left my father in his chair with an ice cream cone. I hardly ever went out after dark. It was like falling out an open window.

Men swooshed past us skating backwards. They'd been planted there to show us how easy it was. Phyllis and I pumped away. She had on tight shorts, her legs thick and straight down to the ankle, and I hoped I wouldn't see anyone I knew because Phyllis was ugly and kids were liable to point this out. We skated together and then we skated apart to see who needed who more.

I was making the turn when she went down. She crawled over to the carpeted wall and lifted herself up. Her father put down his newspaper and smiled at her, brushed the hair from her face. I skated up beside her and asked if she was okay and she said she was and then I just stood there watching the two of them interact, how easy they were with each other. He wasn't afraid of her, of himself, what he might be capable of. He asked if we wanted something to eat and we said we did so he gave her a five-dollar bill and we went and stood in line and ordered French fries and Cokes, ate them while everyone was gearing up for the Hokey Pokey.

My father was asleep in his chair when I got back.

Dad? Dad, dad. You wanna get in bed?

He opened his eyes and told me he was getting up, but he didn't budge. I turned off the lights and climbed the stairs, slept with my bra on.

In the morning, there was Deloris standing over a skillet of bacon. I fixed a bowl of Fruity Pebbles and sat down. She put the plate of bacon in front of me and I watched the strips soak through the paper towel.

You has got to eat, she said.

I am eating.

You has got to eat somethin other than cereals.

She sat down and rested her chin in her hand. Then she got up and opened the ironing board. It made a loud sound of protest. She turned on the small black-and-white TV and talked back to it. I went upstairs and got back in bed. There was the bull's-eye and the long thin streak like a comet's tail. The roof hadn't been fixed yet. My father called the guy but he was busy until the first of August and my father hadn't bothered to call anyone else. I was hoping the ceiling would hold.

———————

Mary Miller's stories have appeared in *The Oxford American, Mississippi Review, Quick Fiction,* and *Black Clock,* and her flash fiction has been widely published online. Though Mississippi will always be home, she currently lives in Nashville.

I was spending some time at my parents' house when I noticed a leak on the ceiling. I told my dad about it but he didn't seem to believe me. I had to take him upstairs and show him. Shortly thereafter, I started writing the scene, but the voice was that of an adolescent girl. She had something to say, so I listened. After I got them to Florida, they didn't want to do anything (I can still see them shuffling their feet) so I put the story away, but then Phyllis showed up with her sun allergy and her row of duck-shaped soaps and I couldn't pass her up. People keep telling me the story is sad, but I don't think of it as sad and I don't think the narrator would view her life as particularly sad, either. On a final note: A boy really did come over to my house one night and light himself on fire. I was hugely flattered. I had been waiting to use that scene for a very long time.

Charlie Smith

ALBEMARLE

(from *The Southern Review*)

T he man, Jimmy Porcell, was a large fat man with freckles like impressions from rusty nailheads patted onto his face. I never felt kidnapped, not until he showed me the photographs. The photographs were of little boys. Boys laid out dead on narrow beds. The boys were naked and they lay on top of dark bedspreads with their hands folded over their private parts. "I'm a photographer," the man said. He had stopped his black Cadillac to pick me up.

We were a few miles down the road when he said, "I thought you were a boy."

"That's because I wear my hair short," I said, slightly scandalized, though I was the one who'd demanded that my brother cut off my wild black hair.

"Now I don't know what I want to do with you."

"I'm on my way to the beach."

"I suppose I can take you."

I'd been there before, many times, and remembered the way.

Out on the highroad I had only waited a few minutes for a car. I knew—it came to me lightly and swiftly—that I would go on to the next town, and then the next and the next, to see how far off I could get. The country extended away from me limitlessly, and this was its charm. Wherever I was, the ground simply peeled away continuously, headed elsewhere. The ocean would be no different. All of it was connected to itself, not a break in any of it.

And here came my first traveling companion.

He was a heavy man wearing a brown suit. His grizzled hair was like a thick hair cap set hard onto his head, appearing to make the sides of his face swell out; the freckles made him look as if he were playing at something. He drove with both hands high on the steering wheel.

"You want a drink?"

I said sure.

He reached in the back and brought out a soda, a cola drink, dark brown in the bottle, without a label, and handed it to me.

"You got a opener?"

He cursed and glared at me, half like he was making a joke, but not really, and said, "Now she wants a bottle opener."

He pulled a small church key from the breast pocket of his suit and holding the bottle against the steering wheel, as if he was afraid to let go of the wheel even with one hand, opened it. The soda spewed against the windshield and he lost control. The car lurched across the empty road and ran through the low grass into a ditch, bumping and slurring a ways before it came to rest. We sat there in silence. The bottle had fallen to the floor. The man was white-faced and his jaw chewed. I could see he was trying to get a grip on himself. I had experienced a surge of emptiness in my stomach. As if a hollow place had blown open. But then it filled back up. I was scared, but I thought I could move all right. We were stopped on a slant, driver's side angled down into the ditch. The air smelled of grass and fresh-turned earth, like a newly plowed field. The man took his hands off the steering wheel and looked at them. The palms were speckled pink like a baby's.

"I got to get out a minute," he said.

He opened the door—it still worked—and slid out, falling to his knees in the ditch. He pushed himself up and there were wet black circles on his knees. He looked scared, and sad, like he knew the worst was going to happen to him. I slid down and gingerly got out, slipping past the man, and holding onto the hood made my way around to the front of the car. I went up to the road to wave down a passerby, but nobody was coming. Far away a tractor turned in at a farm road, but it was two miles away if anything, and it continued hauling its dust cloud on up the road. I pushed back my hair in front, and a breeze tickled the fuzz where I had had my brother shave the back of my neck. Between my shoulder blades I could feel the sweat that must have come up when we wrecked. "You think you can get it out?" I called down to him.

"Like as not," he said in a mournful voice.

I walked a ways along the road and stopped. The fields, pale green at this time of year, stretching away, had a tightfisted, jumbled look, the hollows pressed hard against the swollen places, the grass wind-crawling as if tormented or caressed by swarms of bugs. I felt loneliness like a fever, taking me. I stayed still to feel what it would do. It was familiar and large and filled my body. Far across the fields a flock of crows settled into some pecan trees and lifted off again. They were doing something I didn't recognize. There was nothing much happening in any other quarter. After a while the man came up out of the ditch and joined me. "I guess we have to hitch a ride," he said. "You won't tell anybody about me, will you?"

"What is there to tell?"

"I don't know." He took out his handkerchief, spread it on the grass, and sat down. "I look funny to some people. Act funny, too. Sometimes people get the wrong idea about me."

"What idea is that?"

"That I'm up to no good."

I stepped up the road and came back. There were beggar's-lice on my sneakers. I sat down in the grass and began to pick them off. "What *are* you up to?"

"No good."

We both laughed.

He said his name was Jimmy.

"I know six Jimmies," I said.

"Everybody does."

I realized I would have to make everything up. That was how I would say it later, years from then, when the three Spanish detectives asked me what I could possibly mean by what I was doing. I got up and as if in passing—though it wasn't—touched the man on the back. He flinched. I liked that. He squinted up at me.

"Maybe a car'll come soon."

"Maybe not."

I crossed to the other side of the road. The road was a river I waded, and then I was on the far shore. He couldn't come after me, I reckoned that. He lay on his back whistling. I didn't recognize the tune but liked it. After a while a car came over the low rise to the south. It seemed at first to be coming through the grass. The man Jimmy got up before it reached us and began signaling. I didn't make any sign, but the car pulled up next to me. The man Jimmy, who was too fat for his own good, made a wobbling trot across the road. The driver of the car looked like a preacher because he was dressed in a dark suit on a weekday. He aimed his narrow, clever face at me and asked if I needed any help.

"I don't. But I think he does."

"You know where I can get somebody with a tractor to pull this car out of the ditch?" the man Jimmy asked.

"I can take you to the settlement."

"Well, if there's nothing else, that will suffice."

He piled into the front. "This is my niece," he said, indicating me as I got in the back. The back smelled like something had died there. I mentioned this to the driver, and he winced. "It was mice got in. A nest of them."

"How'd mice get in your car?"

"I didn't use it for six months, and they built a nest."

"Pugh!"

"We're on the way to the beach," Jimmy said. His voice sounded false and hopeful. I liked that, too, as I liked his wobbling little run. Then I could see in the distance a gap opening up through the woods. It was wide and blue, yellowish at the edges, and there were people riding on horses down it, approaching. I understood these were people from the past, entering the present in a stately and dignified way. For a while now I had brooded over the responsibility I had for my visions. Was I supposed to do something, take some kind of part? I couldn't tell, and nothing was asked directly of me, but I had a feeling that I was a participant and this worried me. For the moment I didn't say anything. The sun, which was keeping up a quiet existence behind clouds so pale they looked not like clouds but a new form of sky, rubbed through, and it shone so brightly on the pale green fields that I thought they were about to change into something else, but they didn't. The riders faded into the background. Often it was like this: nothing happening, no portents or revelations, just a sight seen and passed on from. On that side, too, the other side, heaven or hell or a far boundary land not discovered yet—how could anybody know what it is, I thought—there wasn't much going on.

We were headed away from the county seat. I didn't mind and felt aloof from what was happening. Then we came to the settlement, Rest Peak (country store, café and filling station combo, church, three houses at a crossroads), and the driver put us out. "I can't take you no farther," he said with a cross finality. We thanked him, both of us saying thank-you in unison—so it must appear we really were kin, I thought—and entered the café. There was no one inside, so we went into the store and a woman behind the counter directed us to the filling station, which we should have gone into first. There we found a man with a dumb handsome face who said he could pull us out with a tow truck, but not that second. We returned to the café and took a booth. It was there the man showed me the photographs.

"So you won't think I am some kind of mysterious person."

"I think these pictures are mysterious," I said. "You must either really trust me or be especially crazy to show me such a stupid thing." I said this because the pictures hurt and excited me and I wanted to conceal this.

"I do trust you," he said nervously. I could tell he had to show me the pictures. They were burning him up, I could tell. He had waited as long as he could. It was all not right, though I realized I could stand it. I was a little breathless. "Could I have a CoCola?" The man Jimmy signaled. I bent down and studied the pictures fanned out on the tabletop, without touching them. "They are holy," I said.

"Nah, nothing like that." Shuffling them up so the waitress wouldn't see.

"Wait . . ."

"In a minute."

I sucked the Coke until it hurt in my cheekbones. I liked the pain. The man fanned the pictures out, then closed them up, then fanned them out again. He probably did that when he was alone, sitting on a hotel bed, just staring. I probably would, too, I thought, and this embarrassed me.

"Why you turning red?" he said. "The snaps too much for you?"

"They almost are."

"I shouldn't carry 'em around, I know."

"It's really wrong."

I bent down close. The boy on top had light-colored hair and a big nose above a pointed little chin. He looked like he was sorry for whatever he had done.

"You said you took these yourself?"

"I did."

"Did people let you, or did you sneak in?"

"They pretty much let me. I used to work at the funeral home."

"Where was that?"

"Over to Scotland Neck." He picked up my Coke and started to swig from it, all in one swift motion, but then he set the glass back down. He rubbed the wet off his palms. "You collecting evidence against me?"

"I don't know yet. Well, yes, I am collecting evidence, but not necessarily against you."

"What were you doing walking out on the road?"

"Where you picked me up? I was looking for love."

"Hunh, hunh. How much'd you find?"

"You're getting personal now."

I was tired and didn't want to joke with this man. Then I wanted to be kissed. It came on me suddenly. There was a counter, or was it a bar, along one wall. Two men sat over there eating oysters another man behind the counter had shucked and set out for them on trays. They were drinking beer. I wanted a beer and something else I couldn't put my finger on.

"Excuse me," I said to Jimmy, then got up and went over to the bar.

"Can I sit here?" I said to the closest man, a stringy fellow in overalls and a hat with a blue patch on it. He had a pinhole eye that intrigued me.

"Sure," he said, and acted as if he would snug over on his stool to make room. I hauled up on my own stool and leaned over the counter. In a soft, engaging voice I said, "How much are those oysters?" to the stringy man, not looking at him as I spoke, just to see if he would get that I was talking to him and answer.

"Penny a piece. Ten cents a dozen." I caught him in the corner of my eye. "How about buying me one."

"Dozen? You like oysters?"

"Whenever I can get 'em."

"Give me a dime, Bob," he said to his companion.

Bob, who had black hair cut short as beard stubble, ducked his head into his shoulders. "You shouldn't be feeding oysters to a child."

"I can if I want to. And the young lady wants me to," he said, smiling at me. His pinhole eye took me in and sent me back out chilled like fruit from the icebox.

"Hey, mister," I said to the man behind the counter. He was skinny, too, but he had a warm, slightly slanted face.

"What you need?"

"Could I get a dozen oysters on credit?"

"Ain't you Mr. Trapnell Marks's little girl?"

"No."

"I think you are. You look just like him."

"What if I looked like President Hoover—you'd think I was his daughter?"

"He ain't got no daughter," the pinhole eye said.

"He does, too," Bob the companion said. "I heard her talk on the radio. What's her name, Rud?"

"Who?" the bartender, thus addressed, said.

"President Hoover's daughter—what's her name?"

"Hoover?"

"Nah. His daughter."

"He's daughterless," pinhole eye said.

"It's a shame," Rud said. "A man like that. He could use a good daughter."

"How about those oysters?" I said. I made smacking noises and licked my top lip.

"They look mighty good, don't they?" pinhole said. "Why would you want to starve a young girl, Rud?" he said, leaning slightly forward.

The bartender turned half away, scratching at a place below his left ear. "Her daddy, I know him; he won't pay for no oysters. Not if he didn't order 'em hisself."

I was angry now, and embarrassed. This was becoming an embarrassing day. "Wait a damn minute then." I scampered back to the booth and asked the fat man, Jimmy, for a quarter.

"What you want it for?"

"To get you to stop asking me questions."

"You don't have to be rude to me. I know I wrecked the car, but I didn't mean to."

"I'm sorry."

"Will you ride with me some more?"

"Probably not."

"That makes me feel terrible."

"If you had your car here right now I would."

"Would you wait till I bring it?"

"I can't do that, Jimmy."

"Why don't I get a room?" He pursed his lips, looked around, focusing sharply as if he was counting things.

"What for?"

"We could take a nap."

"OK."

He gave me a case quarter and got up to arrange for a room. They had rooms upstairs, up a box staircase in the back. I returned to the counter, where I offered the barman the coin. "I think I'd rather have a beer instead. How much is that?"

"It's a nickel. But I can't serve you no beer."

"It's not for me directly. It's for . . . my uncle."

"Who's your uncle?" pinhole eye said.

"That fat man who just went into the store."

"That man ain't nobody's uncle."

The barman eyed me assessingly. "Don't think he's yours." He turned away, then turned back. "Out at your daddy's place, y'all got—ah, I guess you do—y'all probably got ten phones."

"Yep. I mean, I don't know what you're talking about."

I felt hot now, tired, and wanted to rest somewhere, briefly, out of the light of scrutiny. I thought of the fat man pressing his face down upon mine. Would it weigh a lot? I said, "One of my other uncles weighs five hundred pounds."

"His brother?" the man Bob said, jerking a thumb.

"My uncle on the other side. He fell through his kitchen floor."

"Ate one chunk of sidemeat too many, huh?"

"It wasn't as funny as it sounds."

"Things rarely are," pinhole eye said.

A nervousness like a rash began to come on me. I hadn't meant to stretch the truth or to try to divert attention, none of that, and I had already done it several times. Was there something wrong with me? It was too hard to be among people. "I'll take that beer now," I said.

The barman wouldn't give it to me, but it was all right because as it turned out, the man Jimmy had a pint of still-run whiskey in his coat pocket. He showed it to me when we got up to the room. "Did you see how those men's eyes were following us?" he asked. "As if we might do something untoward."

"They didn't think we were who we said we were."

"Did you tell 'em anything?"

"I told them what you told me. But they didn't believe me."

"Gaa. Life's just a damn comedy. You want a drink?"

"I'll have a little one."

He splashed a bit into two glasses and handed one to me. "Best to you."

"And to you." I felt like crowing. The liquor tore my throat and I coughed hard, spewing it on the floor. "Damn."

He looked at me with avid eyes, then looked at the spots of whiskey on the varnished floor board. "You didn't swallow any of it."

"I couldn't."

"Try again."

I got it down this time by sipping. It tasted rusty and depleted, as if everything but the rasp had been boiled out of it. Then it slid across my stomach like an old woman rubbing herself, leaving a warm trail. It was all right.

I lay down on the bed and balanced the refilled glass on my chest. I pouched my shirt out to conceal the buds of my breasts, just last week appearing. They'd shocked me, but I hadn't let on to anyone, not even my sister out in San Francisco. "I'm not usually a calm person," I said.

"Me neither. I look like I ought to be—what with being fat and all—"

"People expect it."

"You're right, but I'm not. I'm nervous as a dog shitting razor blades."

I let this picture sink in, and winced. "All the time?"

He sat in the threadbare floral armchair, leaning over his knees. The posture squeezed him together in a puffy way. A look of pain crossed his face. "I look and long for anything that will unfluster me. You might say seeking the so-called Balm of Gilead is my permanent task."

"Have you made headway?"

"Well, this whiskey helps some."

"It's making me light-headed."

"That's good if you carry burdens."

"I'm eleven. I don't know what burdens I could be carrying." But I was lying; there were plenty of burdens. Probably I could off-load a warehouse full if I had to. All the visions for one. I started to say something about them, but stopped.

"We all got burdens—even children. Think of these little dead boys." He took the pictures from his coat pocket and shuffled through them, stopping here and there to study one.

The room's one window was fogged over with dust. The sun was turning it orange. A rooster crowed, the sound brassy then suddenly disengaging. It made me lonely.

He tapped a photo. "A couple of these boys I knew in life."

"How did you get so many?"

"This is several years' work."

"Taking those pictures makes you calm?" It wasn't really a question. I could see how it would. After you got over the shock—or maybe because of the shock. I set the glass on the table, stretched, and plumped up the pillow. "I want to take a nap," I said, though I didn't really intend to. I had a desire to go exploring, play a game of chance if I came on one.

"Could I lie down beside you?"

The way he said it—humbly, without sham—touched me.

"All right."

I scooted over to the side and watched him carefully settle his bulk. "I know I take up too much room," he said, turning his back to me. Up close I could smell his fusty, stale chicken-grease odor. I still thought I would ask him to kiss me—or, I thought, I still wanted to be kissed, suddenly very badly—but I couldn't bring myself to do it. I scrunched around to face him, then, abashed, swiveled quickly back. His body was humped and swollen and this unnerved me. Maybe he would crush me. Maybe he would do something worse to me, rise up whooping and ranting, shouting crazy things about God or the devil; or maybe he would start to cry and want to tell me secrets that he told to no one. Maybe I would stab him then, if I could find a knife somewhere. I wanted him to attack me so I could scream at the top of my lungs and tear his eyes out and leave the room bloody so people would come by for years and say to each other, *It was here that brave young girl fought for her life against a madman,* and then I wanted him to scrunch quietly around and tell me how he had once fallen in love with a hootchie-cootchie dancer who broke his sorry heart.

I turned away from the fat man and pressed my back against his, at first gently and then hard.

"Am I taking up too much room?" he asked.

"No. Am I pushing too hard?"

"Nah. It feels good. It's a long time since I had something solid pressed up against me."

That couldn't be true, but I knew what he meant. I started to tap his back, thinking I would ask him to kiss me, but just then a key rasped in the lock and the door swung open. Several men burst into the room. "Hold on there," the first one said. He was a khaki-clothed man I didn't recognize. Behind him were the two men from the bar and a couple of others I had seen before, but I didn't know where. I jumped off the bed in a hurry. The man Jimmy rolled onto his back and pushed partway up on an elbow. The first man had a gun, a pistol, in his hand, and he pointed it at the man Jimmy and told him to stay right where he was. "Don't move one inch," he said.

The other men fanned out in the room. There was a woman,

too, in the back, and she pushed up to the front, saying as she came, "It's all right, isn't it?"

"Y'all better get out of here," I said, disappointment showing in my voice.

"Oh, honey," the woman said—she was the woman from the store, wearing a man's straw hat—"you don't have to be scared now."

"I'm not scared. I'm mad."

The man Jimmy had covered his head with his arms, his wrists crossed over his forehead.

"Look at him cringe," the pinhole-eyed man said. He wasn't looking at Jimmy, though; he was looking at me. He might start slobbering any minute, I thought. I started at the men, with my fist raised. But I didn't know what I was doing. Before I reached them, in the short space inside the room that was painted light green and smelled of salt sweat, I lost track of what I wanted, in either that moment or any other, and so I stopped and stood there blinking at them, my head buzzing. A sadness came over me and I slumped down. "It's all right," the man with the gun said. "Get him off the bed," he said to the others. I watched as they hauled the man Jimmy up, put handcuffs on him, and rough-walked him out. "We were having an OK time," he said, looking at me as he passed. He didn't wink, but I wanted him to, wanted something that would make things a little better. I felt sorry for him and sorry for myself because I was too young to do anything.

They took me out, left me to sit with the woman in the store, and after a while the man with the gun—he was the deputy sheriff—drove me home. While I was in the store I stole a little mirror and a red-hot jawbreaker. It shocked me to do this, but I wanted to badly. The woman might have seen me take the jawbreaker—no, not might; she did see me—but she didn't say anything. I could see in her face that she wanted to—was about to—but just then the sheriff came in and said it was time to go. The woman shook her finger at me and I grinned at her.

"Where's Jimmy?" I asked.

"You won't be seeing that young man again," the deputy said. "Not before he's brought up on trial, that is."

"He didn't do anything."

"Well, he did for a fact—a lot of things."

"You better get on home," the woman said.

I could tell the woman didn't like me. It hurt me a little to be disliked, and I thought of putting the jawbreaker back, but I didn't have the strength to and I didn't really want to either. I couldn't tell exactly why I was acting the way I was. "I need to think about things," I said.

"You probably just better forget all this for now," the deputy said.

He took my hand in his, tenderly, like he wanted to do it especially, and walked me to the car. Outside I saw the sun was using sunbeams to feel its way through the dust thrown up off the road. Beams, I thought—girders, studs, rafters. The dust glittered, and then four small brown birds flung themselves in full flight through it, veering up over our heads and over the peaked roof of the filling station. I reared back a little, straightening my posture, glad to be alive, glad to be in such a honey-colored, sunshiny world. The rooster, over by the big gas supply tanks, crowed again.

On the way home the deputy asked me about what happened with the man Jimmy. Several questions. "At what point did he get overfriendly? At what time did he do something that made you feel uncomfortable? What did he do—exactly—that made you feel uncomfortable?"

"Aren't you being a little too personal?"

"I have to ask you. Jimmy Porcell has committed a crime—several crimes."

"I got slightly nervous when we went into the ditch."

"What? Did he make you go down there? What did he do?"

"He gushered a drink all over the car and lost control."

"You mean he went crazy?"

"No. I think he was just shocked. He happened to be driving the car at the time."

"Did he strike you at that point?"

"That man Jimmy? At which point?"

"The one where he lost control."

"How could he hit me? He was trying to hold on to the car. And he didn't want to hit me anyway." I was mortified that this man would think any traveling companion of mine would want to strike me. I wasn't an unpopular girl.

"He was drunk?"

"Not that I noticed. You know, I met a woman this afternoon who told me she was my mother's twin sister. I told her she was lying."

"Were you with Jimmy Porcell at that time?"

"No. I met that man Jimmy after I met the old woman. She was an old, old woman—my mam's not old like that. You can't be older than your own twin sister—not by that much."

"That's true. Now what did Jimmy Porcell make you do down in that ditch?"

I shifted into a silence, my eye caught—or something caught me—on a streak, bright silver and flowing like a river, but where there was no river I could remember. I was sad I wasn't going to the beach, wasn't, I realized, getting out of this county. Then I didn't want to get out; I was forlorn, as if something indispensable had been taken from me—*forlorn:* "The very word," Papa quoted, "was like a bell." I wanted to go home, to talk to Papa. I was scared right then to speak to Mama, a strange person who had a twin.

"You can whisper it in my ear, if you want to," the deputy said.

"Whisper what, exactly?"

"What Jimmy Porcell did to you down in that ditch."

"I don't have to whisper it."

"But you can if you want to. It's probably best if you did."

He shifted slightly in the seat, moving a little closer, and in-clined his head toward me.

I remembered what I'd felt; how an open space had appeared inside me, not a lonely place, exactly, though it felt like that at first, but a kind of sunny spot, lonely a little (you could say) because it was only me, only inside me, that it appeared—as the visions made me lonely in that way—but charming, too, and appealing; so that I found myself wandering away from the wreck, across the road that was like a river, and standing on the far side of it, dreaming really, my eyes following the flight of some crows in the distance that were rising and falling in the tops of pecan trees.

"You know how lonely you get sometimes?" No, that wasn't what I wanted to talk about.

"Does it make you lonely?"

"Does what?"

"This late experience. I'd imagine it would."

"Could we go get something to eat?"

"Wouldn't you rather go home?"

"I've had enough of home for today."

I didn't even know what I was saying. But I could say anything. I knew already that the world was unsure of what it really was, constantly changing itself, disappearing and reappearing in new and stranger garb. It had holes in it and avenues unmentioned by others I knew. I wondered if the deputy sheriff could see down leafy roads that were on no map.

He tapped the steering wheel.

"Where would you like to go? You want to go to the Patio for an ice cream?"

"Then could you take me to the orphanage?"

"You poor child."

"Take me somewhere where I can make a phone call."

At the Patio Drive-in I ordered a banana split made entirely with banana ice cream, hold the bananas. "Isn't it interesting," I said, "how you can love banana ice cream and hate bananas. Is that a bad sign?"

"No, it's all right."

"I'm feeling a little faint. Could we go over there under those trees, where that tire swing is?"

Beyond a fence line on the other side of the trees was the city cemetery: a sloping, bumpy expanse of sparse grass set with shaggy cedars. Some of my relatives were buried there. The descending sun seemed to be taking some of the usual color back, some of the grass and the weight of the headstones, too. I imagined riding across the cemetery on a horse, leaning down as I rode to pluck the flowers from the pots set on the graves. The deputy continued his questioning. He wanted to know what had happened. "It was nothing," I told him. "We got interrupted."

"Somebody saw you?"

I was tired of listening to this man. He sat on a leached cypress stump like on a commode, leaning over his elbows. His face had a peculiar jut to it, as if it were sticking out from itself, and his leaning made it seem bigger than it was. Halfway through the banana split I was full, but I made myself finish it by imagining that I was lost in a strange forest, alone, with only this to eat. Scout rations, I called such food at home, where nearly every meal I imagined myself out on the trail, lost or lonely, a wanderer, with only this rough homemade pemmican to eat. The man, Deputy Greeve, kept talking, but I had stopped listening. I made answers anyway and didn't really keep track of what I was saying. I continued to be alert, however, to slurs against the man Jimmy. I liked standing up for him. Probably tomorrow, if not in a minute, I'd feel the opposite. He was a sad man, misguided probably, but I could tell he couldn't help himself. I mentioned that he couldn't.

"Is that any reason he shouldn't pay for his crimes?"

"Do you think they have a phone here?"

"You want to talk to your people. That's a good idea. I 'spect they have one inside. But we can go over to my office after a while. I got one you can use. It's probably more private."

"OK, let's do that."

I felt a little sick to my stomach, but I liked the feeling, in a way. It was different enough to be something from another world, really, and it took my mind off some things that were beginning to trouble me. I couldn't say what these were, but they sizzled along inside me, little insinuations and tsks. I stood up, lengthily stretched, and then to my surprise, so swiftly that I did not feel any introductory nausea, leaned over and vomited. Everything came up. "Oh," I said, "oh," and swayed. The deputy was on his feet instantly and caught me, caught as well—oddly, I thought, even then—a little of the upsurge in his cupped hands. I backed away, dizzy somewhat, frail, seeing things.

He shook the vomit off his fingers—it was yellow—and the look in his startlingly blue eyes troubled me, even as my stomach kicked again and I brought up bitter squirts. Then I felt better. The look was gone from his eyes. He was too interested, I could see that clearly. But I felt paralyzed in a way, not sure of what to do. I had experienced this before around adults, and alone, too, walking out behind the barns, thinking of what I wanted to do with myself. There were times I couldn't come up with anything; right in the middle of a conversation—even at school—I'd go blank as if the language or the way of doing things or the world itself simply trailed off—simply quit—and I was left standing there, empty-minded. This was how it was now, a little, as the deputy, who'd held me first around the waist, then by the shoulders, then not held me at all, stepped back and looked at me. What was the man Jimmy doing right now? They had probably taken his photos away from him.

Years from then, in the women's prison in Kalima, out in the desert east of Jelidibad, I would remember that afternoon and think of how time on some days piled one thing upon another as if you couldn't get enough, as if time itself couldn't—as if there was all the time in the world and plenty to go around. I would think again about the deputy, who became embarrassed and shy like a boy and asked me to excuse him and walked quickly away around the side of the building. He was gone for a long time—he didn't come back. I climbed the fence, went into the graveyard, and lay down in the uncut grass on the grave of my sister Ronnie, who had died in pregnancy three days before Mama bore me. The baby, I knew, was still inside her body. They had buried them that way, in a grave belonging to her husband's family. I wondered if the baby was still waiting. Of course it wasn't—it had never lived, Mama told me—but still I wondered, and pictured it lying in the dark inside the dark—tiny, mute thing—waiting. When Papa came looking for me I was asleep in the grass and night had come.

Charlie Smith is the author of nine novels and novellas, including the forthcoming *Three Delays* and *You Are Welcome Here,* and seven poetry books, including the forthcoming *Word Comix.* He's won numerous awards, grants, and fellowships, including Guggenheim, NEA, and New York Foundation of the Arts grants and the Aga Khan Prize from the *Paris Review.* Five of his books were *New York Times* Notable Books. He has taught at Iowa and Princeton and was the Coal Royalty Fellow at the University of Alabama.

STAR BLACK

I've been pretty exclusively a writer of long fiction. Once in a while I'll rip a story out of the body of something much longer. That was the case with "Albermarle." It's from a biography of my mother (written by a character known to be a liar), called This Woman Here Skinned, *a book I've worked fitfully on for the last few years between or along with other projects. In the latest version the story does not appear so I thought I'd send it to my old barnstorming buddy Bret Lott at the* Southern Review. *I'm glad to know it had enough life for Bret and for Ms. Packer. My mother was born in eastern North Carolina, ten miles from Albemarle Sound. She said* oot *and* aboot *and* aroond the hoose—*very exotic for a boy born and hand-raised in south Georgia. She was a spooky smoky crazy woman hooked on hard drugs and still-run liquor who on her deathbed damned to hell whoever was closest. Just being in the same county with her was hair-raising. It was very moving to me to briefly inhabit her body and soul as an eleven-year-old.*

Jennifer Moses

CHILD OF GOD

(from *Glimmer Train*)

When Gordon first laid eyes on Lucy he didn't think anything of her, skinny little white girl with a limp and that
spaced-out, sideways-looking look of a newly clean junkie, which
is what she was, he was sure of it. Just one more white girl with a
bad habit trailing her around and maybe, too—who knew—she'd
done her time on the streets, going out to Airline Highway and
turning tricks for thirty, forty dollars, more if she blew them, less
if she was desperate; who cared just so long as she got her next hit?
Had the look: the shuffly walk, the squinty eyes, the raggedy hair,
not that he put much mind on her. Mainly she just stayed in her
room, anyway. Stayed in there, all curled up in a ball like a baby.
Didn't even watch TV. Didn't even turn the lights on. Just stayed
in there, in the dark, curled up into a ball like a baby.

Well, he'd seen them come and he'd seen them go, and this
one, he predicted, wouldn't last long: wouldn't last more than six
months, and then she'd disappear into herself, shrink and shrink
until she was no more than skin and bones, and then one day
there'd be a lit candle in her room, and Miss Dolly would call them
all together to tell them that there'd been a death in the family.
That's how she put it, Miss Dolly: "Bad news, there's been a death
in the family." And the others would all nod and shake their heads,
wondering if they'd be next, praying (if they had the sense to pray)

that they wouldn't, counting their lucky stars that they were still among the living, even if all they did at St. Jude's Home was sit around, smoking and watching TV.

Not that he was complaining: he liked the place just fine. He liked having his own room, all clean and private, all to himself, and no one could come in unless he said they could. He liked having hot running water, a toilet that always flushed, and three meals a day, thank you very much, though some of the other residents complained about the food all the time, saying it was bland. He had friends in the place, too. Louis, whose room was right across from his: before he'd taken sick, he'd been a welder. Martin, who'd done time in Angola, Gordon didn't know for what, but had served his time and come out clean, and then, *wham,* it turns out that he's got the virus. The social workers, the nurses, the cleaning ladies, even the volunteers. They were all just fine with him; better than fine. They were caring, decent people, didn't matter if you're black or white, a pimp or a whore or whatever you once were, or if you liked to do it with boys or girls, now you were at the place and they were going to take care of you and that was just fine by him; it was a blessing, yes indeed, it was a state of grace.

Praise Jesus.

They'd picked him up off the side of the road, is what had happened. Literally. That's how low-down he'd become. Picked him up off the side of the road like some dead animal, like roadkill, and hauled him off to Earl K. Long. Pumped out his stomach. Shaved his face. Pumped him up with medicine, with antibiotics, with Norvir and Fortovase and Viracept. Fed him on cherry Jell-O and Pedialite until his stomach was strong enough and they could switch him to real food.

His sister Ruthie came and said, You're nothing but a junkie, but the good Lord done saved you anyway, and now you gonna fall down on your knees and thank your Savior Jesus Christ for all he's done for you on this very day. His sister Martha said: I need to tell you now that if you're going to keep killing yourself, if you're going to keep living this way, then I have to say goodbye to you, because I can't just stand here anymore, watching you killing yourself. It isn't natural. I just thank the good Lord that Momma and Daddy have passed on so they don't have to see you like this. His sisters—both of them—were schoolteachers. They lived in fine brick houses up past the airport, and drove nice clean cars. And every day, it was the same thing: You gonna fall down on your knees and thank your Savior today for saving your sorry butt? Because if you don't, you are lost for good. And on and on they went, hectoring, haranguing, talking at him like he wasn't even there, and then one day, just like that, it happened. A nurse was telling him that he'd gained weight, and was even beginning to look human again, and just like that, *Boom,* Jesus came into his heart. Only it wasn't a *boom.* It was more like a flash. Yeah, that was it: a flash of brilliant, warm sunshine. Something he could feel in his entire body. *I'm here!*

And Jesus hadn't ever let go, no indeed, not one time since.

But Lucy: he was pretty sure that Lucy didn't know Jesus, and what's more, that she didn't *want* to know about Jesus. Some people were like that. They just couldn't take the Lord's blessings; they weren't ready for St. Jude's, and it was sad, but it was the way it was. They weren't ready for God's love, and no amount of talking to them helped, either. He knew that for a fact. After all, how many years had people been telling him about Jesus, and yet he'd stayed doing what he *had* been doing, which was sticking a needle in his veins, stealing money from his own kin, and for what? For drugs. For that next pure high. For a death in the gutter.

Skinny white girl who stayed in her room, curled up on her side, in the fetal position, no bigger than a kid. He figured her to be about thirty, thirty-one, the daughter of some kind of no-count rednecks, the kind that seemed to flourish like cotton in South Louisiana, white and black, it didn't make no difference if your father was a drunk and your mother was a slut, maybe hit the kids, or called them names; and then the father came home and whapped everyone around, or maybe even did it with his own daughter. Yup, he'd heard that that could happen too, more in white families than in black families, the father doing it to his own daughter. Made you sick just to think of it. Made you want to grab a gun and do some killing. Because there was evil in the world and then there was *evil,* and as down and out as Gordon had been, as much as he'd used people, and done dirty, and lived for the needle, he never did take a life away, or harm an innocent person. Because—and this is where his sisters had him—his parents had taught him right from wrong. From the very beginning, they'd told him never to take anything that you can't give back. His father had sat him down and drilled him, saying: What couldn't you ever give back? Until Gordon had finally figured it out and said: A person's life.

What else?

Their, I don't know, their arm or something like that? Like if you got into a fight or something. And you cut some guy's arm off.

What else?

I don't know. What else, Daddy?

A person's happiness. Don't never let me catch you being cruel, taking a person's happiness from them. Understand, son?

Yes sir.

No, he couldn't blame his parents for what he'd done all by himself. Drugging and drinking and whoring around, scaring his wife and kids off, losing his job, losing everything, his wife taking the kids all the way to Detroit to get away from him, telling him that she'd gone to the judge and he'd lost custody, that was that. Telling him to his face that he couldn't see his own kids, no sir, not now, not ever.

But Lucy, he thought, Lucy probably had been abused as a kid, and then went out and abused herself. She had the look, right down to the rabbity eyes. She had the look of a girl who was trained to be a whore by her own daddy, the look of a girl who couldn't die fast enough.

Which was why he was surprised when her folks finally came to visit, and it turned out that they were just as nice as nice could be. The mother brought cookies; the father looked nervous, pushing his hands deep into his trouser pockets, but saying hello and how-you-do like he was visiting a bank, and not just visiting his junkie-whore daughter and her junkie-whore friends at St. Jude's. Dressed all nice, the both of them; looking just like any ordinary couple, the kind you'd see at a shopping mall or the movies, the kind that go their own way, mind their own business. Drove in from Lafayette and when Lucy saw them she said, "Mom! Daddy!" and threw her arms around them. Happened right out front, in the common room, because that's where she'd been, watching TV. Watching *The Price Is Right,* because by then she didn't spend all day sleeping; she'd started coming out of her room. The mother passed around the cookies and the father looked at his feet, and finally all three of them went outside, out to the little closed-in patio area where there were chairs and a couple of potted plants— pretty plants, too, ferns and whatnot—and sat and talked. It was summer, hot as blazes. Gordon could see them from inside, could see the way their lips were moving, and how Lucy sat way up front on her chair, all squinched up to the edge like an excited child, waving her one good arm around.

St. Jude's wasn't all ex-whores and junkies; not really, though at first, when he'd first arrived there, that's what Gordon had thought: he'd thought it was a place for ex-whores and junkies to die in when they didn't have any other place to go. But it wasn't true. They didn't all die, even. Some of them even got better, and left. Louis was his best friend, and he was about as straight-up as you could be, doing welding at the big plants—Exxon, Geismar— that would have been until he got sick. Funny thing, too, that you could have a friend in a place like that, a real friend who you could shoot the breeze with, and tell stories; but there you had it, grace coming upon him like dew on the grass. When Lizzie, the volunteer, came, she'd drive them all over in her minivan, drive them up to the Kmart on Florida Boulevard for socks and under- shirts, things like that, or to the discount CD shop that Gordon knew about off Gus Young, he and Louis laughing like crazy when Lizzie fussed at them to put their seatbelts on, or bawled them out about minding their language. It was all in good fun, though: Lizzie didn't mean it, she was all right; rich white woman coming in once a week to drive a couple of niggers around, lecturing them to eat right and treat women good. Fellow across the hall, a fellow named Tommy who moved out a month or so after Gordon had moved him, he was a math teacher: went back to work, is what he did. Moved to New Orleans and got a job in the Orleans Parish school district, teaching seventh graders how to find the common denominator, and figure out the y factor when two plus y equals nine. And then there was that white boy, the one whose walls were covered with pictures of half-dressed men, and Miss Dolly fussing at him just about every day to take the pictures down, they were too provocative, they disturbed the other residents, there were *rules,* and if you can't abide by the rules, well, then, they'd just have to see you to the door. But everyone knew that Miss Dolly wasn't about to kick Alvin (that was the white boy's name) out; Alvin had been living at St. Jude's for years already; he'd lived there longer than any of the other residents, longer than a lot of the caregivers and nurses, too; he could practically run the place by himself if he had to, and what's more, he knew things before anyone else did, including who was bringing weed in and smoking it in the bathroom, and who was getting some of what they shouldn't be getting no more, fraternizing within the walls, and who had a wine bottle stashed in his coat pocket, and who was going to die before they even really understood that they were sick.

That was another thing: some of them were so young, so young and so lowdown, that they didn't even know what they had. That was what Gordon was telling Lucy the first time, ever, that the two of them ever really sat down and talked. By then she'd put on a couple of pounds and had lost some of her rabbity look, but she still walked with a bad limp, and was too skinny, leaning on her cane, her right arm hanging by her side, all bent up and use-less from the stroke she'd had—which was another thing the virus could do to you: give you a stroke, a storm in your brain, leave you all bent up, unable to walk, or worse, with half your face caved in like a fish, the other half alive and twitching.

It's sad, but it's true, he was saying, that some of them come in here—hell, I've seen 'em myself, and that was even before Jesus gave me the strength to walk again—and they're no more than babies. Kids. It's sad. They laying up there in the bed, don't know what's hit 'em. And when you talk to them about the virus, you know, use the word right out, they're in complete denial. Either that or they just too sick to know what's what. They look at you like you're from another planet. Or they start talking about faggots. You know: that only faggots get it, and they're all white. It's sad is what it is. A damn shame.

She'd looked at him then with shy eyes from behind her eyelashes, and he saw, for the first time, that her eyes were blue, and the lashes black and thick. And there was something else about her, too, that he hadn't noticed at first, not all those weeks when she was curled up on her side in her room, or even all the weeks since, when she first started coming out to the common room for her meals and to watch TV: there was a certain innocence about her, a certain way she had of holding her head cocked slightly to one side, which made her small chin look like it was pointing somewhere, or perhaps asking a question.

Gaud, she said. That's just gauddamn awful. He laughed then, hearing the Cajun inflection in her voice.

What's so funny? she said, and he could have sworn she was blushing, if only ever so slightly.

After that, he told her stories. Stories about growing up in Scotlandville, before drugs hit, and how it was back then; stories about the Gold Coast, which was what black folks called the neighborhood right around Southern, the area where the professors and the administrators lived in proud brick houses surrounded by myrtle trees. Stories about his crew; stories about his wife—or rather, his ex-wife, because he wasn't going to deny it, he had driven her off. Driven her off, her and his two kids, too, with his drugs. There wasn't anything he didn't do, either, back then, back before he'd been picked up from the gutter by the hand of the Lord, delivered back to the light of day. Heroin. Marijuana. Cocaine. Crack. Speed. Hell, he was a virtual laboratory of chemicals, a walking chemistry set.

Never did finish school, neither, he told her. My sisters, they both went on to college, earned their degrees. But me, I was too busy for that. Too busy getting high.

Ain't that the truth, she said.

She was easy to talk to, was what she was. Easy, and she didn't judge him. Unlike the black sisters, who looked at him like he was dog meat, like he was something they'd scrape up off their shoe. Or maybe that was just his wife, before she left him, before she finally got so disgusted that she took all her things and packed up the kids and got in the car and kept driving north until she couldn't drive any farther, driving all the way to Detroit before she finally stopped. Then had a lawyer write him a letter, demanding that he give up custody. Too high to even know what he was signing away. Didn't care. Didn't care about nothing, just so long as he could get his next fix. But Lucy wasn't like that: she'd sit beside him, nodding and laughing, and every now and then she'd give him this sideways kind of glance from underneath her eyelashes, making Gordon feel like he was special, like he was somebody, like maybe there was a reason he was still alive, when so many others were gone, track marks in their arms and the air around them stinking of death.

He told her this story: What finally made me scared? Well, you see, I had my friends—the fellows I called my friends, that is. You know how it is, when you're into drugs, you don't really know it, but your friends, the people you call your friends, are really your enemies, because they're the people you're doing drugs with. Let's see: there was Willy, I knew him from all the way back, from when we was kids, coming up. Me and Willy and his brother, Joe, we used to steal the girls' underpants and their brassieres from their mammas' clothing line, parade up and down the street with it on our heads, then we'd run like crazy, you know, when their mothers found out. Got a whipping anyway, but that was the way it was back then. Then there was a fellow named Craig, never did learn his last name. He held up a liquor store, ended up in Angola. Bunch of us, really, all of us in and around Scotlandville, just getting by, though honestly I don't remember it. I couldn't go to sleep in those days, thinking that if I had a single dollar on me, I'd get killed for it. But that's just the way it was, living the life. She nodded, and her hair—which was straight and brown and cut straight across, like a boy's—shimmered, catching the light.

Well, I'll tell you, because this is what happened. Willy? He was staying at his family home, you know, the same place where he came up. Ain't nobody else living there because the whole neighborhood, it went downhill. All the respectable people, the parents with kids to raise, moved out. Willy's brother, Joe, he moved out, too—moved all the way to Texas, if I remember correctly. The whole neighborhood ain't nothing but a place for junkies to shoot up and to get killed. But Willy stayed, because where else did he have to go? Stayed in the family house even after the plumbing and the electric had been turned off, and there wasn't nothing in it but maybe a mattress on the floor and a broken-down TV, because everything else had either been sold or stolen. So anyway, one day, we all kind of look around and realize that we haven't seen Willy for a while. For a week maybe. Go looking around. No one's seen him. No one's heard from him. Go knocking on his door, but the place is locked and ain't no one home. A few more days go by, and then I heard what's happened. All the dogs in the neighborhood? All the stray dogs, that the pound doesn't catch? They hanging out in Willy's yard, just standing around, barking, barking like they going crazy. Turns out that that's because Willy's in the kitchen— what *used* to be the kitchen before he sold all the appliances—dead on the floor, a needle in his hand, cockroaches the size of your fist crawling all over him—and the smell! And that's when I said:

I had enough. I don't want no one to find me lying dead with a needle in my arm.

I done some pretty bad stuff, too, Lucy said.

She was, he learned, thirty-five years old. Never been married. Had no kids. Spent time on the streets, just like he thought. Started using young—twelve, thirteen—because, she said, she wanted to feel good, wanted to be liked by the popular kids at her school. He had a hard time imagining that, what the popular kids at her school must have been like, because she had grown up in a new subdivision near Lafayette, in a three-bedroom house with air conditioning and a swing set in the backyard, and she was supposed to have gone to college, too. She was supposed to have followed her big sister to LSU, and gotten a degree, and made her folks proud. But instead she fell in love with the life and ended up on the street, spreading her legs or opening her mouth, she didn't care, just so she could get enough money for the next high, and before she knows it, no one's talking to her anymore: not her older sister (who became, of all things, a social worker); or her maw-maw, who had cancer, only Lucy was too strung out to go see her to say goodbye before she died; or any of her cousins; or her parents. She didn't blame her parents, though: they were Catholic. They went to church and prayed for her soul.

I just about did kill them, is what I did, she said.

They were sitting out back, because by now it was getting to be late fall, and the weather was cooling down some, especially at night, when the shadows fell, and everything got all soft and dreamy. That was the first time he noticed, *really* noticed, what she looked like. Not like before, when he'd seen her as a compilation of parts: round face, pointy chin, shiny hair, hips as narrow as a boy's, and not much in the way of female softness up top, either—all of that, no doubt, all hollowed out of her, all stripped away from her years on the street. But now, as she reached over to tap her cigarette ash into a glass dish, adding her ash to the heap of ash and butts already in it, he saw how long and delicate her hands were, even the hand that didn't work right anymore; he saw how graceful and lovely was her body. She was like some pretty little animal; like a pretty animal you'd see in a forest, the kind that would run away from you, scared. Not that Gordon knew a thing about pretty animals, or really any kind of animal, not to mention forests. Where he'd grown up, they'd had one park, that was it, and it only had a couple of trees; as for animals, the snakes and the lions and the tigers in the zoo were enough for him. He didn't much care for the animal kingdom, although once he'd had a dog, Barker, whom he'd loved like it was a child. Whatever had happened to Barker, he wondered, and then realized that he'd lost Barker around the same time that he'd lost Melinda and the kids, all of them gone, all of them as far away from him as was possible in this lifetime, making tracks, putting up a wall of miles.

Lucy was dressed as she always was, in loose cotton pants and a T-shirt, with flip-flops on her feet. No makeup, of course, because what was the point of putting makeup on when the highlight of your day was taking your morning meds and having the caregivers fuss at you because you weren't drinking your juice at breakfast? (Actually, he thought, that wasn't quite true either. Some of the women—particularly the sisters—put on makeup every day of the week, didn't matter how sick they were, laid up in the bed.)

I don't know, she said, exhaling a thin blue spool of smoke. I just don't know.

That's when he noticed that the insides of her wrists were threaded with spindly blue veins, a whole map of veins just there, just inside her pale white skin.

Did he love her? Sometimes he thought he did. Other times he just thought he was crazy. Crazy, or desperate, or both. He hadn't had a woman for a long time, and that was the plain truth, but now wasn't the time to be correcting that situation, not here, not at St. Jude's. Plus, right around the same time that he had that thought, a terrible thing happened. It was his friend, Louis. Louis, who he used to ride with, riding around in the car, every Tuesday morning when Lizzie, the volunteer, came. Riding in Lizzie's minivan, with Louis and sometimes another resident or two, going up to the video store to get Louis a whole bunch of horror videos, weird shit with titles like *Blood Friday* and *Evil Comes at Midnight* and *Satan's Crossing,* because Louis could sit in front of the TV, hour after hour, and watch that shit.

Louis, like Gordon, was a good-looking man, the flesh still on him, his face still shiny and bright. Had had him a life, Louis had, and from the looks of it, was on his way back to that life, back to life on his own, get himself his own apartment, get his job back. He was doing that well. But then—*wham*—Louis ends up in Earl K. Long, with a runaway fever, and the next thing you know, he's on a respirator.

That's when the volunteer drove Gordon over. Drove him over to see his buddy Louis at Earl K. Long. Drove him and drove one of the caregivers, too, a real nice woman, name of Judy. Because, the volunteer said, it would be awful not to say goodbye to him, it would be awful not to have a chance to say goodbye to your best friend. Talking the whole time, *blah blah blah,* about how he had to say goodbye to his friend.

When they got to his ward—ward 5C, intensive care—they were given masks to wear. But Gordon didn't want to go in; no, he truly did not. He didn't want to see Louis like that, all hooked up to machines.

The women went in first, while he waited in the hall.

I just can't, he said when they came back.

He needs you.

I just can't see him like that.

He's unconscious, but he'll know you're there.

By this time, both women were crying: the white volunteer, the one who came like clockwork every Tuesday morning, talked too much but otherwise was all right, and how many rich white ladies are willing to hang out with the brothers to begin with? She was crying. Judy was crying, too. Women and their tears. Made him uncomfortable, seeing them crying like that. Made him feel like scratching himself all over, like walking down the long windowless hall, walking and walking and never coming back; no, he did not want to see his buddy all laid out and breathing on a respirator, or watch women cry.

Just for a minute, he said.

He put the mask on and crept in, and at first it was hard to tell what was going on, whether his friend was alive or already dead, that's how weird it was—his friend's big strong body laid out, as if on a slab, and his rich brown skin, the color of dark caramel, covered with what looked like powder. His feet sticking out from under the sheet, and, up top, his big chest covered by no more than one of those throw-away bright blue coverings that they make out of synthetic materials. His eyes half-open but glazed over, and his chest heaving with the effort, straining against the machines. And his hands, upturned on the bed, the palms a whitish-pinkish color he had never noticed before, and the nails grown long from disuse. He was Louis, but not Louis. He was like a statue of Louis.

I've just got to take the bitter with the sweet, he told Lucy, afterwards, after he had returned from the hospital in the backseat of Lizzie's minivan, gone into his room, and had a few private words with Jesus. Just got to take the bitter with the sweet.

I'm sorry, Gordon, Lucy said. I really am. And she leaned forward, and with her one good hand she touched Gordon's knee.

I am too, baby, I am too, he said.

If he *was* in love, which he still wasn't sure of, it sure didn't feel like anything he'd felt before. Not like with his wife, Melinda. He'd been crazy for Melinda, and that had been the God's honest truth: that woman had made him crazy: crazy with desire, crazy with jealousy, and just plain crazy. First time he laid eyes on her, that was that: he had to have her. Big-boned woman with a generous behind and a quick, big smile, a smile that made her eyes dance, and her hair all teased up into one of those crazy dos like she was trying to be Angela Davis or something—women still wore their hair natural in those days. She'd only been twenty, maybe twenty-one when he met her, and he wasn't much older, but he'd gone after her like she was his own personal treasure; he was a treasure hunter and she was his gold, and by and by she agreed to marry him, laughing that she must be crazy to marry a crazy colored coon like him. But that had been way back, back when he still had his habit under control, back when he was still driving a truck, making a good living, too, driving those big babies, eighteen-wheelers hauling everything from factory parts to tulip bulbs, driving all over the continental United States, then coming home to Melinda. But no sooner had he walked in the door than it was: Honey, will you see if you can fix the sink? It's all backed up. Or: Praise Jesus, you're home, I got two sick babies and I feel like I'm coming down with something myself. She changed, too. What was once generous flesh became fat, and what was once a joyful laugh, a kind of crazy pride in how outrageous he could be, became a frown. So yes, he's not proud of it, but he did it: he had other women. It was easy, out on the road. He met them everywhere. At bars. At clubs. Bought them a few drinks, and if he got really lucky they'd invite him home with them, and sometimes, too, they came back to his truck, and they made love right there in the sleeping compartment of his cab.

There weren't that many of them, but each time he did it, he knew it was wrong. But he was young, young and stupid and horny and lonesome. Didn't know a good thing when he had it. Didn't know enough to leave things alone.

But with Lucy, things were different. He felt tender toward her, like he wanted to protect her. He wanted to put his big strong arms around her and breathe Jesus right into her mouth, so Jesus would flow down her throat and fill her heart and her lungs and her veins and her bones, so she wouldn't hurt anymore. So she'd never cry again. So she could go home to her mother and her daddy in Lafayette, and say: *Momma, Daddy, here I am, I've come home.*

When the word came down that Louis had died, dying there in his bed at Earl K. Long, surrounded by people who didn't know him, people who didn't know enough to hold his hand or touch his brow, Gordon felt a blow, as if he'd been hit in the guts, as if there weren't enough oxygen in the room. He went to Lucy, to tell her, and she looked at him with big eyes, eyes like a fawn, and stood there, nodding. But she didn't touch him, or do much of anything other than reach for the pack of cigarettes that she always kept in her right hip pocket, and offer him one. He prayed for guidance, but Jesus didn't answer him either, and then he had to pray for patience as well as guidance. And then, *boom boom boom,* things started happening at St. Jude's, like they sometimes did, real fast. A brother and a sister moved in together: Loretta and Laurence were their names, and when they weren't squawking at each other, they were squabbling with everyone else. Loretta was one of those big-boned women, tall and somehow raw looking, with lips that always looked shiny and puffed up, like the inside of a plum, and with hair sticking up all over the place, shuffling around in slippers; and what do you know, no sooner than she had moved herself in, gotten herself comfortable, she's coming on to him. Sliding her big-assed self right on up to Gordon and saying and doing all manner of things, all leading to the same one thing. Doing it right in front of Lucy, too, saying, You sure are one good-looking nigger, which was not only offensive, but embarrassing, too, talking that way in front of white people. Wiggling her big bottom in his face when he's having his breakfast, sliding her tongue around in her mouth. And the brother, if anything, was even worse, one of those poor souls who you don't even know how to start understanding, with a big head and enormous feet and hands—but what does the man do? He parades around in his sister's clothes, wearing her bright pink fuzzy slippers, her bra and skirt. Then another resident, a black boy who never did do nothing but listen to music on his headset and eat bowl after bowl of Lucky Charms, he wanders off one day and never comes back. It was downright confusing, and in the meantime, there was Lucy, always Lucy, hovering on the other side of the window, a hair's breadth away, a breath away. Lucy, who came to him now in his dreams, entering him in his sleep like a wind.

It was hot again outside, when he and Lucy smoked, summer

coming, and already all the scrub woods around St. Jude's looked like they were about to catch fire, everything on fire: the houses, the buildings, the billboards, even the pavement of the parking lot. Shimmering with heat, contagious, and day after day, no rain.

One day she told him a story. The two of them were sitting under the awning at the side door, looking out at the driveway, and there in front of them is the flower garden that some former resident had planted, planted and then died, because that's what happened here: they came here to die, everyone knew it, wasn't no secret. Came here to die because they either didn't have families or because their families didn't want them no more. His own sisters had given up on him which was why he was here, and as for Lucy, her parents had had to turn their backs on her, too, what with her whoring around, her drugs, the men she took in, her stealing, her cheating, her lying. Yup, she'd told him all about it, down to the last ugly little detail. Everything, or at least everything that she could remember, which left some stuff out because she was blacked out or nodding off or beat up and unconscious and in a hospital or beat-up and bleeding on some mattress somewhere; didn't much matter, she didn't care.

But this story wasn't about those days. This story was about a friend of hers that she'd had when she was young, when she was still just a little thing coming up in her parents' house, before she'd gone bad. This friend, she said—her name was Mary—was closer to her than her own sister was. She was her best friend, and that was a fact, the kind of friend that she did everything with, and told her dreams to. We were pretty much the same size, too, so we could borrow each other's clothes and everything, she said. When we grew up, we were going to go to college together, share an apartment, everything. We were going to be in each other's weddings, and name our children after each other, and live next door for the rest of our lives. That's what we planned. Plus, after college, we were going to join the Peace Corps. We used to talk about it, how we were going to go to Africa, see the lions and elephants.

Oh! I just loved those elephants. I probably spent the night at her house a thousand times. And you know what happened?

Gordon shook his head, no.

Ain't nothing happened except that Mary—l don't even know where Mary lives anymore because when she grew up, she left town, left Louisiana even, and every time for, I don't know, for ten years, every time I called her house, talked to her mother, her mother wouldn't tell me a damn thing, and then her mother, Mrs. Batiste, starts hanging up on me. Saying, I'm sorry, Lucy, but I can't talk to you, and then, click, she hangs up. Then the phone number gets changed so I can't call there no more anyhow. And Mary? She was *beautiful*. Just beautiful, I tell you, with these real big old brown eyes and crazy curly hair, and I just loved her. I did. I loved her so much.

You really loved that girl, Gordon said.

I did. I really did, Lucy said, sniffling a little, sniffling into her hands, because all this time, all this time that Lucy had been getting slowly better, slowly beginning to walk right, slowly beginning to put on weight, she had never cried or carried on in any way, leastways not in front of Gordon. But now a terrible thought came to him, and he didn't know why he hadn't thought of it before, that maybe Lucy preferred women, that maybe that's why she'd never opened up to him, not really, or at least not in any womanly way, not even when she'd seen Loretta go at it, switching her big behind back and forth. It was almost as if she were in love with this old girlfriend of hers, this friend from before all the bad things happened, like she could never want no Gordon, not all this time, not with her wanting Mary. Pain blossomed within him then, blossoming inside and spreading out through his veins and capillaries, his nerve fibers, his bones, until finally he was shimmering with it, aglow. He looked at her real long and slow then, looking at her in a way he'd never looked at her before, with wide-open eyes, with eyes that begged, taking all of her in, not caring if she was uncomfortable or self-conscious before his gaze. Taking in every little bit of her, from her small, sharp nose to her wispy straight brown hair, her narrow hips, her slightly pink, slightly freckled skin that stretched down from her neck and plunged under her blouse, encompassing her soft, wet, secret places, and when he saw the blush spreading across her neck and face, he kept looking at her, because he had to, because he had to know who she *was*.

Will you pray for me, Gordon? she said.

He took her by the hand then, her small pale hand in his, and right there, right on the patio outside the side door where the caregivers let themselves in, right there overlooking the parking lot and, beyond it, St. Stephen's Home, which was for oldsters, hundreds of them in there just drooling and nodding off in their wheelchairs in the sun, Gordon and Lucy got down on their knees, and began to pray. Jesus, Jesus, Jesus, Gordon prayed—aloud, because Lucy had asked him to—Lord God, come into this woman's heart, come and heal my sister Lucy, bring her closer to you, fill her with your love, heal her broken wounds. And on and on he went, praying to the Son, coming to the Father through the Son, praying for Lucy, but praying for himself, too, praying until he couldn't hear himself pray anymore, praying until the words were so deep inside of him that they leapt out of his throat before he knew what he was saying, praying without thought of time passing or awareness of his own body, his own breath, his own skin; and when he was done, his face was wet with tears and Lucy's eyes were closed and her lips were moving, her hand still in his, and he knew, right then, that Jesus was with him, that He was with the both of them, that Lucy, too, was a child of God, that she had been redeemed. And that's when he married her—because that's just what he was going to do, marry her and make her his wife—because he knew that Jesus was with both of them, working through them and in them, forever.

Praise God, he said.

Praise God, she whispered by his side.

Jennifer Anne Moses is a writer and painter
who lives in Baton Rouge, Louisiana, with her
husband, varying combinations of her three
children, and her beloved rescue dog, Marion.
She is the author of *Bagels and Grits: A Jew on the
Bayou* and *Food and Whine: Confessions of a New
Millenium Mom*. She can be found on her website
www.jenniferannemoses.com. This is her second
time in the pages of *New Stories from the South*.

LISI OLIVER

"Child of God" came out of my volunteer work at St. Anthony's Home,
a residence for AIDS patients in Baton Rouge, Louisiana. At St.
Anthony's, the residents come and go—some leaving for a better, healthier
life, some for the streets, and others to the grave—but the place itself exists as
a vessel of hope and holiness. The story came to me as if from a source outside
myself: it was my job to write down what I was being told. I hope I've done
justice to the real people at St. Anthony's whose dreams inform my work.

Stephanie Dickinson

LUCKY SEVEN & DALLOWAY

(from *Salamander*)

Lucky Seven squawks and wakes me. A wind tunnel of heat shakes the pickup. The windows are rolled down and Pepita's long hair, so thick and heavy it drapes her like a shawl, suddenly flies up and my head almost vanishes in it. Hector at the wheel keeps us on the highway, and the rooster goes quiet. They're salvage people. They also raise and show roosters. Pepita sits with the stick shift between her pretty terra-cotta-colored legs and burgundy sling-back shoes. She has the silkiest black hair I've ever seen. It probably weighs more than she does. In the bed of the truck are two hot water heaters. They're the rusted color of deep-fat-fried shrimp, and so is every tree and rock, every piece of scenery that passes by the window. I shift under the weight of the cage across my lap.

"Something bad must have happened for you to run, kid," Pepita says, patting my hand.

"Nothing really bad." I shrug. "I'm going to see my grand-mother in Corpus Christi. I was on the bus and then someone stole my bag and my ticket was in it." Suddenly, I worry that I already might have told them she has a condo in San Padre Island. I am a runaway, that part is simple. Hector and Pepita picked me up in Corsicana at the Dairy Queen when they stopped for chili dogs, and to get ice to cool down Lucky Seven's water. The rest gets complicated. My parents split up for a new set of partners. My father traded himself in and became a woman, my mother takes Botox injections. Her face looks frozen, and when she tries to smile her laugh lines land like knee drops on a trampoline. How can either of them believe they love anyone? They are terrified of quiet and talk and talk. I want to become silence.

"Dalloway, if Lucky Seven's too heavy for you, Pepita can hold him for a while," Hector says glancing over his wife at me. "She's used to it."

Pepita laughs. "But what you put in my belly isn't." She has on a red halter top and her stomach bump shows above the waist of her jeans. A cross hangs from the rearview mirror and a pickle jar sits on the dash.

"Are you bragging or complaining?" Hector asks her.

The wood crate on my lap is fitted with chicken wire for an entrance, and inside is a carpet sample for his talons to scratch. Also, a water dish attaches to the wire, and a newspaper is folded into a dainty triangle for his seaweed-like droppings. His feathers look like the duster Daddy used on his chandelier, a bouquet of dark brown and green, and hints of royal purple, but Lucky Seven's feathers explode with color, tropical fruit colors, mango and kiwi, passion fruit. I'm comfortable in the passenger's seat holding him even if I can feel his sharp eye piercing through the slats.

"If you like we'll train you to be a handler," Pepita says. "Maybe Hector will let me adopt you."

He laughs, "She can be the nanny for the bun in your oven.

The word *bun* doesn't sound graceless in his mouth. I do think of warm bread. I glance into the side mirror. I left Manhattan over seven days ago, and Hector says we're in Hill Country, stretches of dirt road and scorching sun. We're about thirty minutes from where the gamecock show takes place. In the distance, turkey buzzards circle, some so high they look like specks of pepper.

Pepita taps the crate with a perfect burgundy fingernail. "You'll be dancing soon, Lucky, honey."

Hector squeezes her thigh, which is not much bigger than my

forearm. "Poor Pepita, there weren't even toilets in her village. A stream ran under their house, and that is where they would go. Just a board with a hole in it."

Pepita elbows him "Stop it, Daddy."

"When we married I had to buy her father a pair of shoes."

Another jab into his ribs.

"Ouch, oh slugger," he groans. "Seventeen bridesmaids. I paid for everyone in the village to be in the wedding."

"When I first saw Hector I was on a pay phone and he was standing behind me. I thought he was Chinese."

He throws back his head. "I'm just good old Tex-Mex."

In an hour I've learned a lot, I've learned that Hector is a native of Tyler, Texas, and older than his wife by three decades. His eyebrows and hair are blacker than hers. In Bali, Pepita was the youngest of seven sisters. Hector tells me women rule the roost over there, women and roosters. "Instead of loving him, Pepita's mother gives her father black eyes and bloody noses."

This time Pepita pinches his arm, pulls one of the coarse salt-and-pepper hairs. He brought her to Texas as his wife. He was over there shopping for roosters, the most beautiful in the world.

"Pepita had a pair of flip-flops and one dress when she married me."

I think of my closet and all that my parents have given me. Expensive junk. Stuff probably sewn in countries where people receive a dollar a day, if even. Like in Macy's. Brown velvet jackets and tulle skirts, taffeta with spaghetti straps, front bows and back ties, party frocks for a lifetime, sugary outfits for a child, not a girl of fourteen.

"And how do you think I get treated over there when we go back to visit Pepita's parents. I'm an American and Jemaah Islaiyah terrorists will kill me if they get wind of any Great Satan citizen. Pepita's mother throws a rug over me in the truck and they go into the restaurant and leave me there for hours."

"Daddy, we're trying to protect you."

I laugh and feel almost warm inside. Like I could belong to

this family. I'm at that special twilight age when I'm leaving the dock of twelve and thirteen and heading into the turbulent waters of fourteen. I'm not one of those girls made of marzipan, or belly-pierced peach ass, who can sneak in wearing a baseball hat but with a jut of the chin turn the room moist as marmalade.

It's a mirage out the window. Instead of Broadway and Times Square I've gotten myself off the beaten track. I was frightened before Hector and Pepita picked me up. Cattle everywhere on their knees, tens of them in semicircles. They belong to no one, no order, answering to nothing but tangling strands of barbed wire. Then we crest a rise, and a cow climbs unsteadily from the ditch into the road. Cows wander in the ditch.

I look out at the fields of brush, and think of the city's dim crowded sidewalks hemmed in between cliff-like buildings, horns honking, and garbage blowing. Home of New York–style cheesecake, the island named after a cocktail, pasta primavera and egg creams, Eighth Avenue and Broadway. It's Shakespeare, the whole language of city. Puerto Ricans in gold high heels pushing a stroller with two babies. Homeless men in Hefty garbage bags and milk cartons on their feet.

"Hector, a cow!" Pepita cries out. "Daddy, watch out."

Hector hits the brake. The cow is so thin it must be sick. Its eyes are like mouths. It staggers across the road and into the opposite ditch. "Let me see Lucky Seven," he says, panic in his voice. "Open the crate so I can see if that thrust hurt him."

Pepita unlatches the crate and Hector peers across her lap. "Lucky Seven, did I jostle you? How are you doing, my little machismo man?"

"He's fine. See, Lucky Seven is smiling. Daddy, let's go," she says.

Each time she calls Hector *Daddy,* I think of my own. From thousands of miles away I can see clearly, my father and me in the old days walking for miles of blocks. "There is something I'm trying to tell you," he said three years ago. My heart skipped a beat. "I've decided to have my sex reassigned. I'm going to become a woman." We stopped in front of Paradise Bakery just as a girl roller-bladed down the sidewalk. She was a Latina beauty, dark ringleted hair, large breasts in an aqua tube top, and tight cheeks in watermelon-pink short shorts. My father seemed to lose himself in watching her. Like Hector is doing, looking at his rooster. He didn't want her, he wanted to become her.

I brush away my father, and try to see more of where I am. There seems to be a different hunger in this land than in the city. "What's wrong with that cow? It can hardly walk," I ask, feeling that choking sadness when animals are in trouble, and I'm not going to be able to help.

"It's probably loaded with ticks and running a fever," Pepita says, opening her lap notebook, a speckled black and white.

"Can we help? Please."

Hector reaches around his wife and pats my shoulder. "Say a prayer to the Maker. That's as best we can do."

I remember saying prayers to the Maker about my father who is now a good-looking middle-aged blonde named Kim, asking Him to change him back to Daddy. I thought of our last date at the Holiday Inn Crown, when Kim asked me to attend a seminar with her. I squinted but couldn't raise my father from the beige skirt and coral jacket. She whisked her and me up the escalator. INTERNATIONAL GENDER DYSPHORIA CONFERENCE was printed in block letters on a banner behind. I followed her into a frigid half-empty banquet hall that didn't have a drop of music in it, the tables under sheets of white paper.

Everything couldn't be more different here.

Pepita isn't interested in cows or sky; she's running a column of numbers on a sheet of paper with dollars signs, debits and liabilities. I feel huge and stupid next to her, although I'm supposed to be gifted. I like being with them because they chatter and I don't have to think about Daddy and Mommy and what they're doing in New York City, and if they're waiting by the phone or going about their business. Eventually, I'll drop them a postcard and tell them not to worry.

"We run a salvage store right out of the back of our truck," Pepita says. "We save rent that way." She takes out a notebook and shows me how much money they would have to pay for utilities if they had a shop. I like the nearness of the rooster, who smells like cinnamon. "We make our home in Ft. Worth. Hector can't provide better than a stockade of red dust."

Then we stop in the middle of the road; it's time to feed Lucky Seven. A mixture of maize, corn, sunflower seeds. Pepita sifts it through a strainer before she opens the cage. Hector's eyes shine at the sight of him; Lucky Seven struts out like a runway model, a preening weightlifter, his head up, his comb trimmed and flushed pink. "Look at him."

They take turns feeding him kernel by kernel. Hector picks up Lucky Seven and with his forefinger and thumb fluffs his feathers. Pepita massages his legs, and then bounces Lucky Seven up and down in her lap. She takes out a hand mirror and runs it between his tail-feathers, combing him for blemishes. Their eyes shine with true love. Lucky Seven is stretched and preened, then touches up his own feathers, pulling them through his beak, which glistens like a polished agate. He's the cock of the walk. Magical. Male.

I think of Kim nudging me at the seminar when Dr. Hickey from Manitou Springs, Colorado, a pioneering surgeon, stood up. "He's the doctor who operated on me." I tried to imagine Dr. Hickey, who resembled a Gold Rush prospector with his suspenders, grizzled sideburns and goatee, this man with a clicker in his hand that controlled the slide show carousel, bending over Daddy to cut off his male membership.

The overhead lights dimmed. A movie screen descended, and then a blurry image that might have been an alligator or a tree trunk appeared.

Hector waits for Lucky Seven to step back into his crate before shifting the pickup into drive and pumping the gas. "I wonder how high the center bets will be today," he says, nudging Pepita.

"They better be higher than in Laredo. Don't forget, Daddy, you owe me a twenty for the side bet you lost," she snaps.

It sounds like they're talking about boxing, and I let the hot breeze from the window and the sound of their voices, far away, wash over me. Three days I've had hardly any sleep, first the Greyhound from the Port Authority on 42nd Street to Pittsburgh, and then on to Dallas by way of Knoxville and Little Rock.

"Dalloway, today is my fifty-second birthday and my wife has no gift."

"Hector's gift was being born in America."

"I'm a Mexican American. Look how much better off Dalloway is. White bread."

"She was born with two presents every day," Pepita says. She keeps track of their mileage in a wide-ruled composition book. Funjino Stationery out of Mahwah, New Jersey. "And she has rich parents, I bet." She turns her pretty face with the black eyes to look at my mouth like she's waiting for an answer.

"Not really. My mother is a secretary. My father examines bank loans."

The truth is I'm forgetting them. I still have one hundred dollars. I cut my hair in the Trailways bathroom with a plastic razor. Now I'm a boy soldier with a buzz cut. When they look for me, they'll be trying to find a girl with long thin brown hair. I'm forgetting them, they're not the same people, and I'm different too. We were a family and now we're not.

Pepita coos through the chicken wire at Lucky Seven. The road is pristine. The sun reddens, a blood diamond, and the sky, boiling lobster. All the heat in the sky is nothing. She takes a perfume out of her woven purse, spraying her wrists and belly. The more she sprays, the more it is like humidity, the hottest summer day, the whitest petals. A Venus flytrap, the living flower that devours insects in its cloying aroma. Can you imagine a more beautiful death? Pepita spritzes her endless black hair with those petals, her twiglet wrists, under her chin. Then she aims the decanter and sprays Lucky Seven's hind side. "Lucky Seven was born with luck and he will bring us blessedness in the form of money. And seven is the beautiful number of transition. Seven," she repeats. "I expect him to win."

A classmate of mine raises golden-ruffed pigeons. Scott and his father are always going to pigeon shows.

Hector smiles and shows his fine white teeth; his incisors are pointed and sharp. I hadn't noticed that before. "Lucky Seven's bloodlines don't reach back generations. He's one of those exceptions, born with that special something. He has it."

Like Shakespeare had no before or after. Hector recognized Lucky Seven's qualities when other birds were being talked up.

I try not to, but my mind goes to Kim, who slapped me a month ago, the only time in my life anyone touched me in anger like that. Mom was on her honeymoon and when she got back I didn't tell her. Now I want to tell Pepita. How nothing makes sense. I'd tell her what a perfect father he'd been. And then how it felt to be sitting at that seminar next to Kim, while the surgeon—who made women from men, and less successfully, according to him, men from women—talked. The slide show seemed to go on forever. Like the stopped time in a classroom. "As we will see in these slides the most serious post-op problem is that the vagina will close." In the twilight, the surgeon looked gray like Dr. Kevorkian. He clicked and another grainy slide appeared. "In this case the vagina did close and had to be cut again." There on the screen was an unsuccessful outcome. The vagina crooked, the gash too pink, like defrosting meat. The patients wore black squares over their eyes to assure their anonymity but it would be obvious to anyone who knew them who they were. Their hands rested on the inside of their thighs to part themselves wider if required. The blindfolded bodies made me flinch, I wanted to cover them. Another click. Another execution about to take place.

We pass a shack, and an old woman sits on a kitchen chair beside the road. A sign nailed to her mailbox reads GLASS FOR SALE. Lined up for yards are green bottles, milk jugs, mayonnaise jars, and medicine bottles.

"Almost there," Hector announces, "once we see the bottle lady."

We turn at an intersection, one corner of which is occupied by one gas pump under an awning. The outside of the station is plastered with Salem and Pabst Blue Ribbon advertisements. Brands that I don't think they make anymore. But I could be wrong.

"We're almost there, Pepita. Better prime the boy."

We're in the middle of nowhere.

Hector takes a snap comb out of his pocket, the kind that guys used even before Daddy's time, and he licks the comb and then slicks it through his hair. When he catches me looking he winks and I laugh. Daddy used to be a winker, and make me laugh like that. Hector lifts a rabbit's foot necklace that dangles from the radio knob and puts it on. "We have to pile on the luck, right, Pepita? Both of us thought you would bring luck to us when we saw you. A shiny girl is always good luck. Right, Lucky Seven?"

Pepita chitnes in, "Lucky, my hero. Most beautiful and strongest. My gladiator."

"Like me, I'm her gladiator too," Hector winks, scrunching his eyes so you can see the laugh and tired lines scribble themselves over his face.

He hits the turn blinker although no one seems to be coming from any direction and pulls off the highway. We take another clay road toward a tin warehouse set down in the middle of a brush field. BMWs, Tercels, pickups, campers, motorcycles, and a boat rigged to the back of a Ford truck; almost every shape and size of vehicle has found its way here.

"You've probably never seen roosters compete, Dalloway," Hector says in a fatherly voice. "Stay close to us and you won't have to pay to get in. You're with us and Lucky Seven is competing."

"Lucky, honey, we're almost here. He's been a good boy, all cramped inside the box. Hasn't he been a sweet good boy?"

Lucky Seven shakes his feathers off. He's alert and aware, his head holding those fierce eyes jerking back and forth. How big is his brain? Any thoughts in there? Day hot. Stomach full. What to fear?

Will this be anything like the Westminster Dog Show? I wonder.

"You stay there, Dalloway, I'm coming around to get Lucky out," Hector yells.

When my toes hit the ground I feel the suck of raw earth. There's a car unloading its passengers, one of them a lady in her seventies trying to keep up in her blue spike heels pecking through the rivered dirt. A girl calls, "Grandma, where are we going?" Her grandma tells her they're going to visit the roosters. Then she smiles and I can see that her mouth is a red, brutal flower. She stops before we follow her inside to flour her face white and mark up her mouth until it bleeds fresh. I think of Daddy, in the beginning before he learned how to apply cosmetics. Daddy. Lipstick smeared on his lips, red but only in the center, the corners pale as cut bait. Daddy.

The tin shed looks like storage, nothing, not even a sandwich sign, advertising the rooster show.

Inside, a ticket man sits behind a rickety card table. Sawdust coughs itself across the floor. "Now there's a real Clint Eastwood," Pepita says, lowering her already low voice, squeezing my hand.

The grandma in the blue high heels stops the line from going anywhere. She must think the ticket-taker is Clint too.

"Ten dollars for adults. Your daughter's free," he says, his Adam's apple prominent.

"I'm a bit long in the tooth to be this one's mama," she says like a drag queen, squeezing the hand of the little girl.

Pepita giggles when the ticket taker lifts a long silver eyebrow and says to the woman, "I've seen stranger things."

"I'm still making gravy the old way with flour and blood," the granny says, laying the flat of her hand on one of her skinny hips.

"I can see you do, sweetheart," he says, shooing them along. "The little one gets in free." Next to one of his bony elbows is a pile of black T-shirts with flame-colored roosters printed on them.

His hand rests on burning feathers. His cold blue eyes check out Pepita and her stomach bump and the waist of her jeans and woven belt. "Twenty dollars for two adults. I believe you're both over ten although not by much."

Hector arrives, carrying the crated Lucky Seven. "Mister, my bird is competing this afternoon and these ladies are his handlers. No charge, am I right?"

"Whew," says the ticket seller, raising two lanky eyebrows. "Lucky Seven is one lucky bird. Ladies, nice to see you."

I follow Hector and Pepita inside the open room; you can see the rafters in the ceiling. I'm expecting long rows of tables with teams of judges roaming through, like the pigeon show. There's the English Trumpeter. There's the blue and there's the violet. But it's not like that. No rows of cages, no beautifully groomed rooster after rooster. In the middle is a dirt pit surrounded with chicken wire and tiers of aluminum bleachers. "Let me find out whose match is first," Hector says.

"Daddy, try to see that Lucky fights late," Pepita says, "that's when the bets get bigger."

Fights, I've never heard of roosters fighting, dog fights yes, pit bulls in Brooklyn and the Bronx. There are hundreds of people here: women in baggy T-shirts with writing on them and silver blond hair with one black strand to match the black circles around their eyes, bikers with strings of gray hair that haven't been cut since the summer of love; doctor men, oil-rigger men; boys pressed to the fence, fingers pushing through the chicken wire. Toward the dirt ring, a tall woman is dragging her shoe through lines of cornmeal. All the people who don't look like themselves or too much like themselves are everywhere.

"Daddy, I'm hungry. I want fruit, tangerine and pickles," says Pepita. "You know I always get famished before a match."

Hector shows us a table with fruits, bottled water and plates of shrink-wrapped cookies.

"Look, Pepita, it's Cort Kinker. He's going to be the pit master," Hector says, pointing to a short stubby man who looks like a

Grand Ole Opry banjo player in one of those shoestring ties and a fancy black shirt with blue stars printed on it. His whiskbroom ponytail sticks out in back but on top three strings of hair are swirled and take the shape of the letter K.

He waves at Hector. "You're up first. Lucky Seven versus Excalibur."

"Daddy, give me some money," Pepita says, and reaches out her hand. "I have to eat a tangerine for luck. Right away. You know I have to."

There are men carrying cages, big men with bigger fancier cages between them. They put their roosters down on the ground, their hands still caging their birds. Others hold the roosters stiffly, like they're carrying dynamite. Some aromas are the same as Manhattan, like somewhere in the Port Authority, past the Sea Delight, Pizza Cuba, Blimpie's, deeper into the atmosphere of despair and vomit. I don't know anything about this place.

"Dalloway, you sit with Lucky Seven in the handler's stall while I get my tangerine and Hector makes the bets. Guard him."

The handler's stall is just a dirt aisle with a folding chair. I sit on the ground next to the crate. Lucky Seven's bright eye presses between the slats, he's alert, wary, and watchful. I crouch down and peer into that intelligence. I wonder what he thinks. Maybe it's hot in his mind because the jungle country is where he's from.

When Pepita returns almost panting she smells of tangerine, a tiny golden dribble around her mouth. She has pinned her hair up and opens the cage door, coaxing the rooster out. "Now hold him, Dalloway."

"How do I do that?"

"Did you ever have a cat?"

"Yes."

"Hold him like you would your cat."

I place a hand on either side of this beautiful feather duster and feel a shudder go through both of us. There is so much pent-up tension. I'm surprised how soft his feathers are. Pepita kneels down with Lucky Seven and winds a string with a steel needle slowly around his leg. Like a medieval knight being mounted on his saddle with a lance. Her fingers are small and limber and I watch her make deft and deliberate movements.

"Stand back, Dalloway, this spur could put a hole in you."

I feel like I'm walking on a wire and there is nothing on either side. I'm stretched between the Empire State Building and MetLife. "What are you doing to him? You're not going to make him fight?"

"Make him? It's his destiny. His fate. What he was born and trained to do."

Hector comes back, his red face pale, his black eyebrows blazing. "Our Lucky Seven is up. He fights first. No changing it." He opens a ladies' makeup case, dresses his right hand in a rubber glove and then unpacks a spice jar of red pepper buds. "Okay, Lucky, my son. Open your beak." When the rooster's beak parts Hector feeds him red peppers. Then Hector has Pepita hold Lucky Seven as he lifts his tail feathers and slips a red pepper into his behind.

I take a deep breath but I can't find air. My heart races and I say nothing. What are you doing to him? I try to ask.

"Look at that Excalibur," Pepita hisses.

Across the dirt pit, the other rooster is being groomed. Excalibur has black wings with a tail of purple. Once, had I wanted a party dress, I would have asked Mommy to buy me those lilac wings and tails. Where would I go in such a dress of shivering feathers? Fly out of those lovely colors, fly, I want to warn Excalibur.

Pepita and Hector are huddled over Lucky Seven and I can't see what they are doing with their hands, but they're talking to him and now they're praying; Jesus and the saints. I know their hearts are racing. At the transgender seminar, there was a woman more beautiful than the others, willowy and white-skinned with luminous green eyes like a sea waif. Her wispy blond hair set off her fragile features and echoed the face of the young Marianne Faithful. Now Marianne was an old raspy-voiced songstress who

Mommy loved. Once she took me to hear her sing, and I fell in love too with the song performed in wisps and pieces.

"Sorry," the sea waif at the seminar whispered into my ear. "Dr. Hickey did me. Do you mind if I share your chair? There's nowhere else to sit." Her hand brushed mine. Cold as a wax lily. Dr. Hickey droned on. "The desire to be rid of one's genitals and live as the other sex is an issue of human suffering. We in the medical profession must ensure fruitful outcomes. Outcomes depend on how successful we are in fashioning a functioning vagina."

Bare bulbs pour glare down from the rafters. Cork Kinker promenades into the middle of the dirt ring. The pit master bellows like the first man to have walked on two legs out of the slime, pointing to the auburn rooster with the glistening feathers. "From Bali and Ft. Worth . . . Lucky Seven!"

Hector hoists the cock above his shoulders; the mouths in the crowd open all at once. The rooster for all to see is feathered like the duster for Kama Sutra body talc.

"That rooster is one beautiful bird. I've got three hundred bucks on him," one of the bikers shouts.

I understand how far Lucky Seven has traveled.

"They're wearing gaffs," a man behind me says, his Panama hat pitching low to his nose.

Then the pit master points to the lilac-tailed rooster. "Defan Excalibur!"

"Defan Excalibur's got red pepper up his ass," another man hisses.

It all swims together.

"Release your roosters. One! Two!" The handlers let them go and the roosters fly at each other, like rage that has come uncorked. Like genocide. Lucky Seven, the bright-eyed cinnamon-smelling bird from the truck, has erupted, wings flapping and legs kicking. Defan Excalibur's talon gouges like a chop-o-matic of hatred.

Why do they hate each other?

It is all the savage things, people loving a bowl of a beautiful girl's blood, homeless men having the floats in their head and space for bones in their shoes.

"Twenty on the red," the man with the Panama hat slurs.

"Fifty on the black." A man waves a greenback.

Pepita of the shining black eyes and hair like a sunrise, the body that moves like breeze through hot trees, leaps into the air.

Lucky Seven lands his spur in Defan Excalibur's breast but he can't pull it free, and the wounded bird hacks at Lucky with his beak.

I want my father of long ago. I want him to stop this, to make it all right. "He's going to be hurt. Oh, no." Then there is a lull in the fight. Hector goes in and pulls Lucky Seven's foot free from Defan. One of his wings is broken and flops at his side; the purple-tailed rooster kicks a gaff.

"ROUND," the pit master calls out.

Pepita and Hector scramble. Excalibur's handlers swab him with a cotton ball, squirt water with an eyedropper into his beak. Pepita is bright-eyed, she and Hector fluff Lucky's good feathers, salve the scratches with antibiotic ointment. Lucky Seven's shivering, beating the air with his good wing. I want to take him home, to the hospital; he must go to the veterinarian.

Hector lifts Lucky Seven, blowing air into his mouth. Then Pepita puts Lucky Seven's whole head into her mouth and sucks the blood from his neck and spits it out.

"Don't let him go back there. Please I'll give you a hundred dollars if you don't hurt him. Please don't hurt him."

"PIT!"

Eyes already stones, Lucky Seven and Defan shiver with rage. They bite each other's necks; peck the other's head, their beaks quiver when they draw breath.

A fat woman rises from the bleachers. "Three hundred on Excalibur!" She hikes up her blue terrycloth shift. Hector, on the other side of the pit, places his own bets. Pepita has a bill in her hand and waves it, shouting. "Three hundred and fifty on Lucky Seven. The gladiator!"

"Four hundred!"

"Sit your fat ass down. Hear me. You wouldn't know a fighter rooster if one flew in your face."

Blood spurts. The roosters are spurting because the crowd starts to moan. Lucky Seven gaffs Excalibur but this time he can't get free and his opponent pecks his eye. The crowd cheers. Blood is a hole you can fall into, taste and touch, stick your ear into, blood the shape of mouths and slippery fingers. In the bleachers the human faces turn to chins and teeth. The people are in pieces like the roosters they've come to watch who can't escape and run. Hector and Pepita spin. Defan collapses.

"AND THE WINNER FROM BALI AND FT. WORTH. LUCKY SEVEN."

Hector and Pepita are screaming about the won hundreds.

"Next is the long knife cockfight," the Panama hat behind me says.

The handler picks up Excalibur by his wilted feathers and pitches him into a giant wastebasket.

Now can we take Lucky Seven home? Pepita and Hector are jumping and hugging each other. I run to Lucky Seven who is falling and getting up, falling and dragging himself. I have him in my arms. I lean over him trying to stop the blood. No eye, his head is bleeding. Oh no.

I remember the first signs in my father. A cluster of red bumps on his neck above his collar. Tiny polka dots. "What are those?" I asked. The bumps went all the way around his neck. Like he had tried to hang himself. "Electrolysis, kiddo," he said. Electrolysis like a destination for the black ships from the *Iliad*.

I keep rocking Lucky Seven.

The pit master touches my shoulder. "Young lady, take your rooster and go." Then he snaps his fingers and says to Hector. "Come on, come on, get the kid out of there."

"Dalloway, let Daddy take Lucky. You come to the ladies' room with me. I don't like to go alone," Pepita says solemnly, but she's smiling.

"No, we have to take care of him."

"Hector will take care of the champion."

Then Hector's big hands ease the twitching rooster from me and he twists his rooster's neck, pitching Lucky Seven into the same basket with Excalibur.

I hear screams inside my mind but not in my mouth. I run to the barrel. Thousands of hearts beating in my body. "Why did you do that?" I shriek. "Why did you do that? HE WON! HE WON!"

Where the basket stands I lean against the chicken wire to see in. There is a pile of unmoving roosters, and one live strawberry rooster twitching, trying to breathe through a gash in its breast. I press my face against the wire, wanting to reach in and save it.

I don't even know why Kim wanted me there. I focused on a pitcher and poured melted ice into my glass. Dr. Hickey adjusted the focus on the projector lens. The tree shape sharpened. "Presently, we're experimenting with creating sensitive folds of skin with bowel lining," he said, reaching for his water glass. I stared at the screen. The crotches looked orange-red in white, or dark brown in black like cancers spreading between legs. "No ovaries, no uteruses, no menstruation," the doctor said. Mostly the vaginas were furred tongues. I tried to picture what my own looked like. Not a vagina or cunt. Not glossy or fluffy or slick, it was the rip between my legs that Granny Dunkin told me had to be washed and washed.

Pepita takes my hands, threads her fingers between mine. "You're a long way from home. That's why you're sad. I miss my mother and father too. Listen, for three years Lucky lived like a pasha. You'll get used to it, if you stick with us.

The clay road is still potted with ruts. The sky seems fiercer and bluer. Hector loves shortcuts and he's bragging to Pepita about how close he can get us to Austin without driving on asphalt. They both want to eat at Coco's, a family-style restaurant, although Hector warns Pepita that they have to live within their means no matter if they did win a little today. In the side mirror I can see into the pickup's bed where the empty rooster cage rattles between the hot water heaters, crusted with red rust, like every tree and rock, every piece of scenery that passes the window.

———————

Stephanie Dickinson has lived in Iowa, Texas, Louisiana, and now New York City, a state unto itself. Her fiction appears in *Salamander, Green Mountains Review, African-American Review, Storyglossia,* and *Gulf Coast,* among others. Her first novel, *Half Girl,* won the 2002 Hackney Award (Birmingham-Southern) for best unpublished novel of the year. Along with Rob Cook, she edits *Skidrow Penthouse* and is an assistant editor at *Mudfish.* Her story "A Lynching in Stereoscope" was reprinted in *Best American 2005 Nonrequired Reading.* Rain Mountain Press recently released her collection of stories, *Road of Five Churches.*

ROB COOK

I was/am working simultaneously on a linked story collection that features Dalloway—a savvy, sensitive Manhattan teenager whose father is a transsexual and whose mother is an animal rights activist—and a novel that takes place in pre-Katrina New Orleans. The cockfighting central to "Lucky Seven & Dalloway" began as a scene in the New Orleans novel. Although my writing group let me know that the scene didn't belong there, I hated to throw it out as I'd grown to love those fierce doomed roosters. I read a good deal about this "sport" both in the long ago and in the now, fictional and nonfictional, and began to wonder what would happen if my precocious yet naïve Northerner wandered into that Southern scene, how would she experience the pit world and those creatures bloodying themselves. It is a hybrid story, as if both parts of me are mind-melding, rural and urban, blue state meeting red state and mixing it up. I stopped thinking this is stupid and can't work. I stepped into Dalloway's shoes, stuck out my hitchhiking thumb, and took off. A peculiar way of making a story where the chicken came well before the egg.

Kevin Brockmeier

ANDREA IS CHANGING HER NAME

(from *Zoetrope*)

From the very beginning, Andrea saw the goodness of the world as something delicate and unpredictable, a slender green grasshopper that would tighten its legs and flick away from her the moment she brought herself to its attention. Her father spent his evenings carving blocks of wood into hunting decoys. Her mother lay in the bathtub listening to *American Top 40*. Andrea sat on the couch watching TV until the sun turned the screen into a square of blazing white foil, then went to her bedroom to play with her horses. Sometimes it rained while she was asleep; and in the morning, before anyone else woke, she would go outside to inspect the big puddle by the mailbox. She could see a picture of her face in the water, trembling and breaking apart at the edges, then disappearing as soon as she touched it with her fingers.

When she was ten years old, she returned home from school one day to find a moving van parked at a tilt on the street, its rotund rear tire flattening the grass above the curb. Her father was staggering across the yard with a Civil War chest in his arms, her mother waiting on the porch to take her inside. It came as no surprise to Andrea how brittle her family was, how tenuously made. For years it had seemed her parents were playing a game of make believe, a game that had only one rule: they would turn away from each other bit by bit while pretending everything was the same.

Andrea stayed with her mother, while her father moved to Colorado. In fifth grade she began to dream she was standing in a field of sunflowers that reached only as high as her knees, which meant she was in love with a boy she had not yet met. In sixth grade she won her school's spelling bee; her first period arrived while she was sounding out the word *quotidian*. It felt as if a tiny egg had cracked open between her legs. She knew what was going on.

She met her best friend, Rania, in junior high. They sat in the corner of Mr. Bailey's homeroom making friendship bracelets from embroidery thread, knotting them on diagonals so the colors would switch positions: green for the boys they liked, gold for the wishes they made, maroon for the secrets they kept. They spoke every night on the telephone, often for an hour or more. On weekends Rania would spend the night with Andrea, and they would stay up late eating pizza and watching MTV, or braiding each other's hair, or making a list of the ten people they would save in the event of a nuclear holocaust. Alone, Andrea liked to lie on the carpet and read: Sylvia Plath and Anne Sexton, Kurt Vonnegut and Henry David Thoreau. She began keeping a journal. She traced the lines on her palm with the tip of her finger. She bought a poster of the Beatles and tacked it to the wall above her bed. On days when she was feeling strong her favorite was John, and on days when she was feeling weak her favorite was George, perhaps because there was a vulnerability to John that she was afraid to indulge without an armor of her own vitality around her.

She turned fourteen the same year her mother remarried. Her new husband was a smooth-tempered, sardonic man named Jon, who brought to the house a strangely wily intimacy that slowly worked to soften Andrea's mother. One Saturday, she sat Andrea down at the vanity and showed her how to apply makeup like a grown woman—a little blush beneath the cheekbones, two contoured bows of lipstick. It was a lesson Andrea followed diligently until she decided that cosmetics were all so much folly and she no longer needed to wear them. In the summer of 1989, she learned she had been accepted into the arts magnet high school with a concentration in theater. On the first day of class, as she walked into the acting room, a feeling of nervous happiness overtook her; she had fallen upon a conclave of eccentrics. There was the boy with the Watchmen button on his beret, and the girl with the silent-film makeup, a flawless white geisha mask of it; and in the desk by the filing cabinets there was me, the skinny boy with the crowded smile and the flyaway hair.

At the back end of the high school, between the library and the cafeteria, lay a pair of carpeted open bunkers called the Pits. Each day at lunch a ring of students would gather in one of the Pits to pray while other students, jocks and cut-ups mostly, would make a running start and leap over them. Andrea sat in the other Pit with Rania and Carla and a boy known to everyone as Turtle because of the shape of his features and the slow glances he cocked. Sometimes Andrea would let her mind wander, holding little interior conversations with herself during which she pretended that someone had asked her opinion of the goings-on in the other Pit. Even in her own imagination she found herself fumbling desperately for an answer. There was a self-congratulatory exhibitionism to the leapers that exasperated her—but then, when she thought about it, couldn't she see the exact same quality in the prayers?

Finally someone did ask her. She was finishing off the corner bite of a tomato-and-Swiss sandwich when I sat down next to her and said, "So what do you think—would you rather be one of the people praying or one of the people jumping?" It was the first time she could remember me speaking to her outside of class. I was wearing the same thing I wore every day: blue jeans, high-top sneakers, and a button-up shirt with the sleeves rolled to the elbows, a uniform she supposed I had adopted so I could get away with thinking as little as possible about how my body was presenting itself to the world.

Andrea pointed instead to a boy with padded headphones over

his ears, running through a Lionel Richie song, singing it vigorously, majestically, as if no one were there to hear him. "I would
rather be him," she said.

She was not trying to be amusing, only honest, but her response
must have been a clever one, because I smiled and said, "Good
answer."

Then, just like that, I got up and walked away, rattling a ball-
point pen in my fingers. The intercom gave its five-minute warn-
ing. She did not think about me for long.

At the end of the day, Andrea always followed the crowd outside
to the parking lot, where her bus was waiting in a long file of other
buses, their outlines shuddering slightly as their engines turned
over. Sometimes, when the light was clear, she would gaze out at
the river as she rode across the bridge—at a bundle of sticks fanning open in the current, trailing streamers of brown foam behind
them, or at a motorboat carving a white line in the green water. It
was beautiful, but the beauty was always the same. She couldn't
wait to turn sixteen. One night she was at her desk finishing her
geometry homework when her eye was struck by the mound of
stuffed animals in the corner. Her bedroom had become a sort
of museum of her childhood: too much of her past there and not
enough of her present. She began to sift through her belongings,
boxing the old ones away. Her dollhouse, her Judy Blume books,
her porcupine pencil holder—one by one she said good-bye to
them. For a few days, looking at the sparseness of her bedroom,
she felt more capable than she had ever felt in her life, stronger and
closer to the center of her own experience. She gloried in the feeling, though she knew it would not last.

More and more she was immersing herself in the life of the
high school. She joined the French club and the drama club and
the environmental club—SAFE, Student Activists for Earth. She
started an Odyssey of the Mind team with Robin Crews and Cindy
Jenson, assembling a performance based on the seven wonders
of the ancient world. She played a street urchin in *Oliver!* and became a peer counselor. She was growing accustomed to being in

the school after hours. There was a sense of hibernation about the building once the other students had left, an atmosphere of still-ness and secrecy, as if she were watching it as it slept. She liked to think of herself as a hidden boarder there, creeping out into the hallways only after the sun had fallen.

For years she had spoken to her father solely on major holidays, but shortly after the new year, he began calling her every Sunday. He had turned a new page in his life, he said, and he wanted to make things right with her. He suggested that she spend the sum-mer with him in Colorado: "Just think it over. There's a mall less than a block from my house." The invitation concluded with an enticing little rise in his voice: "It has a Baskin-Robbins." To his mind she was still the five-year-old girl who liked nothing better than a scoop of bubble-gum ice cream, who would bruise her lips eating with the pink plastic spoon and smile like a ghoul whenever he let her steal the cherry from his sundae. He really didn't know her at all anymore.

That summer, in Colorado, she saw her father every morning before he left for work and every evening after he got home; but because he worked in an office building on the other side of the city, she was left to fill the long, sunlit middles of her days on her own. One afternoon she walked to the shopping mall to see *Pretty Woman.* The mall seemed bare and pitiless to her, with tinny synthesizer music coming from the speakers and pennies blacken-ing on the bottom of the fountain; the movie theater smelled like mothballs and stale tobacco. She did not go back. Walking to the grocery store later that week, she discovered a vacant elementary school that some local kids had refashioned into a skate park. That first day, she simply stood on the periphery of the lawn, watch-ing as they rode their skateboards down the staircase railings and hopped like performing fleas over the chains hanging across the end of the driveway. The next day, though, when she returned, one of the skaters asked her if she wanted to make a drink-run with them to the 7-Eleven.

"One condition—you stop staring at us, and you tell us your name."

"I'm Andrea," she said, and then somebody started singing "Candy Girl," and in less than a minute she had become Andi Girl.

The boy who had invited her to the 7-Eleven was named Justin. He was the quiet skater, just as George was the quiet Beatle; and only later did she realize how much courage it must have taken for him to speak to her. No one had ever thought of Andrea as funny before, but Justin did. She would drop a joke into the conversation, and he would screw his eyes shut and grin, producing a slow-growing laugh out of the privacy of his consciousness, the kind of laugh that seemed to have a bell ringing somewhere inside it. He began coming by the house to pick her up after her father had left for work. He gave her a copy of his favorite novel, Ray Bradbury's *The Illustrated Man*. He took her to the slope behind the Dairy Queen to teach her how to skate, but the best she could manage was to sit flat on the board as it rolled gently to the bottom of the hill.

She had known him almost a month before he kissed her. It was her first kiss, and she was prepared to shrug it off, but couldn't: she felt the entire gravity of her body changing as the two of them experimented with their lips, letting them go firm and then soft, moist and then dry, closed and then open. "Wow," she said, and he began to laugh.

She was having dinner with her father the night Justin attempted to skate the wall behind the shopping mall. He wasn't wearing a helmet—he never did—and no one could say why he fell backward onto the asphalt. He lay there in a loose pile of clothing as the other skaters tried to prod him awake using their shoes and the hard tips of their fingers. Someone flagged a motorist and convinced him to call for an ambulance. The technician who examined Justin found that he had fractured the back of his skull, chipping the point where its pieces joined together in an inverted Υ and sending a splinter of bone into his brain. And while all this was going on, Andrea was dining in a restaurant where the candles on the tables wore hoods of red glass and the waiters carried satin cloths over their arms.

For the rest of the summer she spent part of every day at the hospital. How simple it was to imagine that Justin had only fallen asleep on his back: His chest rose and fell with the compressions of the respirator. Every so often one of his eyelids would twitch. One day Andrea found a hair as long as a cherry stem growing from a pore on his neck. He was not yet shaving, which was why the hair had gone unnoticed for so long, she supposed, and she took it between her fingernails and tried to smooth the kink out of it. That night, she lay awake for hours, obscurely distressed by the thought that someone else might pluck it before she had the chance. Returning the next morning, she experienced an odd rush of relief when she saw it was still there.

Something was making Justin shrink further and further into the distance. First his friends quit visiting him, and then his aunts and uncles, teachers and cousins, coaches and grandparents. But not Andrea—she refused to allow him to sink into the bottomless world of her memories. Every afternoon she sat with his parents in the hospital room. "You've been such a good friend to Justin," they told her. "You truly have, dear. He's very, very lucky to have you."

At the end of August, a few days before her junior year began, Andrea flew back home. Despite all her efforts to wrest her bedroom into the present, the space seemed alien to her now, and it took the better part of a week for the sensation to pass.

When you have suffered enough damage, there are two roads you can follow: you can seal off all the cracks around yourself, putting up a thick casing of diffidence and reserve, or you can let all your protections fall and leave yourself open to every touch, every collision. Andrea—and she was Andrea again then, not Andi Girl—followed the second road. She began experiencing her life with a clarity and intensity she hadn't known before. It wasn't a matter of choice: the smallest nudge from any direction, it seemed, and she would find herself either laughing or crying. A song on the radio, a television commercial, a comment made by someone at school—that was all it took. Everything around her appeared to be shining from someplace just under the skin, as if no T-shirt or flagpole or blade of grass was anything more than a pair of hands cupped around a lightbulb, and at night, when she went to bed, she fell asleep right away, exhausted by the day's continuous play of shapes and colors.

Had anyone detected the change in her? she wondered. One day her chemistry teacher, Mr. Fuller, asked her to stay after class so he could find out why she kept excusing herself to go to the restroom. And there was the time in theater history when I passed her a note that read, "Are you all right? You've got this look on your face," and then a second note that read, "Not that you don't usually have a look on your face. It would be impossible to have a face without having some sort of look on it." But other than that, no one seemed to have noticed the difference. Sometimes she imagined it was only her spirit drifting past the rows of silver lockers, a tangled wind that no one was ever quite able to see. She looked forward to seventh period, her acting class, when she could take all the pain and delight and confusion she felt and put them openly on display, as if her whole life were just some sort of performance.

Her mother gave her a car for her birthday, an '87 Honda Civic, and she began driving herself home in the afternoon. She was asked to join the Key Club and the Honor Society, which she did, as well as the Y-Teens, which she didn't. She took a small role in Thornton Wilder's *The Matchmaker*. She signed up for a five-session PSAT prep course. In November, when Justin's parents took him off the ventilator, Andrea flew back to Colorado for the funeral. She missed two days of school, telling no one where she had gone except for Rania, her parents, and, months later, me. She was reluctant to need anything too much, or to express her need too publicly. Everything good in the world—everything she loved—seemed to be straining against the tightness of its own beauty. A single ounce of pressure, she thought, and it would burst open from the inside, vanishing forever.

Andrea had stopped writing poetry when she was fourteen, shortly after her Sylvia Plath phase, but she decided to start again and bought herself a journal bound in burnt-orange velvet. In class, whenever she was given a few minutes to let her mind wander, she ran her fingers over the nap, smoothing all the fibers carefully in one direction and then carefully back in the other. Sometimes, without thinking, she would begin drawing a word in the velvet—*fireplace* or *tangent, avenue* or *parsimonious,* any random word that happened to come drifting through the air. After a while she would notice the pattern she was making, brush the velvet clear, and slip the journal back into her shoulder bag. If it was January, the trees would be bare outside the window. If it was March, the first few oaks would be leafing out. She loved the feeling of peaceful melancholy that overtook her as she watched the blackbirds sailing over the branches and the gray clouds massing behind them. The air from the heater blew past her shoulders, and the sound of a distant car horn came over the hill, and I don't think she had any idea what people saw when they looked at her.

Andrea with her hair held back in a simple black band.

Andrea in her loose cotton shirt with the IMAGINE button over the chest.

Once in a while, she would perceive someone's stare, and her face would shift into a reflexive little expression of surprise. "I'm sorry, did you ask me a question?" she would say. "My mind was— you know—" and she would make a sound like a firework whistling into the sky. There is no form to this story because it is true, or at least as close to true as I am able to make it.

One Friday, the school turned everybody loose at noon so the teachers could attend a training session. Chris Bertram and I were lingering on the patio, trying to decide what to do with ourselves, when Andrea came out the front door with Deborah Holloway, shielding her eyes with a notebook. We convinced them to join us, and together we set off for the park at the foot of the mountain, where the gutters of the pavilion were stuffed with pine needles and the water from the drinking fountain tasted like iron pipe. Andrea had never spent any time with me away from school. She was wearing a silver ring with a band that was fashioned into a snake, and I kept taking it off her finger and singing a song: "I'm Sammy the Snake / And I have to confess / That I look and I sound / Like the letter *s*."

Over the next few months she saw more and more of me. We went to a Fishwagon concert by the river. We performed a scene from *The Crucible* at a drama tournament. For no reason at all, we bought an old surfboard at a garage sale, the wood beneath the wax already crumbling to punk, and propped it against the door of Rania's house. For a while it seemed to Andrea that I had lifted her free of something she had always believed implacable—of the endless search for company, those innumerable Fridays and Saturdays she spent driving from parking lot to parking lot hoping to recognize someone's car. One night we took a break from studying in her bedroom, and she twisted her desk lamp around to throw a hand shadow onto the wall. She linked her thumbs together and oscillated her palms. "Look at the beautiful butterfly," she said, and I transformed my hands into duck bills and started an evil marching chant: "We are *ducks*. We hate *butter*flies. We are *ducks*. We hate *butter*flies." There were moments when I could make her laugh so unselfconsciously that she felt like a child again, expanding into her past as she was moving into her future. Sometimes she thought of me as a John, other times as a Ringo.

She loaned me her journal so I could read her poetry, and I returned it to her with a note written on the velvet: "Hi, Andrea. It's me, your journal." My favorite poem, I said, was the one that ended, "I gave you my love in an acorn shell, but you left me anyway." It was a poem about Justin, though she had not yet told me about that part of her life; and when I read it out loud to her, the sound of her own sadness emanating from my mouth made her eyes well with tears. It was a Friday night in late March, and we had stopped to eat at a Wendy's, then gone to a showing of *L.A. Story,* where she gave me the toy car from her Kids' Meal: a "salad-mobile" with lettuce, tomatoes, and a radish on top, which would race forward whenever I wound the spring tight. She was amused by how much I seemed to enjoy it. During the coming attractions, when I tried to roll it across her temple, the wheels let go with a whir, snarling her hair up in the axle. I spent the whole two hours of the movie patiently untangling it, strand by strand. She could still feel the play of my fingers on her scalp, along with the soft tingle in her stomach, as I drove her home and she told me what had happened in Colorado.

She was trying to show me that things had changed between us, that I had occupied that small space she reserved for the people she genuinely trusted. The next week, she invited me to dinner with her mother and Jon. She introduced me to her father when he came to town for a business conference. She feigned an argument with me over whether the pencil holders that had been popular when we were kids had been hedgehogs or porcupines— I said hedgehogs, she said porcupines. We were standing in her driveway at the time.

We were rehearsing a duet scene from *The War of the Roses* the afternoon someone shattered the window of her car. "Do you think the Civic will be safe here?" she had asked as we pulled away from the high school in my Pontiac; and for the pleasure of sharing the drive home with her, I had said I was sure it would. When we returned a couple of hours later, we found a rock as heavy as a steam iron sitting on her front seat and jags of glass stuck in the upholstery and the carpet. Her stereo was missing, along with a box of her cassettes: the Lightning Seeds, the Sundays, Lenny Kravitz, the Jesus and Mary Chain. This was 1991, and the music she listened to—that we both listened to—announced that we were looking in on the world from its periphery, except for the Lenny Kravitz, which announced that we did not really believe in peripheries.

I drove Andrea to the gas station down the street so she could call her mother and Jon. Then I waited in my car with her for them to arrive. It was a spring evening, shortly past six o'clock, and the sun was setting over the tops of the repair bays, propelling the long shadows of the pumps onto the grass. The two of us sat there in the middle of my bench seat, Andrea wringing the tail of her shirt in her hands and gently repeating the words *motherfucker, motherfucker* as I held her from behind. After a while, I put my lips to the nape of her neck, touching them to that spot where the fine hairs began to taper away.

This is what I should have been thinking: *Andrea is in pain.*

This is what I was thinking instead: *I am kissing the back of Andrea's neck.*

Of all my memories of her, this is the one that troubles me most.

Andrea watched her senior year pass in a dizzying spin of standardized tests and college application essays: *Please tell us about your career goals and any plans you may have for graduate study. What quality do you like best in yourself and what do you like least? What event has most influenced your life? Explain.* I was a year older and had left for school at the end of August, enrolling at a university two states away, and she knew that she could not expect to see me until Thanksgiving or Christmas. Suddenly she had more time to spend with her other friends, particularly Rania. The two of them started talking on the phone again, going to movies, trading mix tapes. One night they even went to the craft store and bought a dozen spools of embroidery thread so they could fill a few hours making friendship bracelets, the way they used to when they were kids. Silver for the memories they shared. Blue for the years that had slipped away.

At school, Andrea was busier than ever. She was elected president of the drama club and secretary of the student council. She played the Wicked Witch of the West in a production of *The Wizard of Oz*. She wrote an essay on *The Metamorphosis* for Ms. Greenway's AP English class. Her mother said she was thinking about putting their house on the market, but promised to wait until Andrea had graduated and moved away. At college one day, in the yard beside the library, I came upon two acorn shells fused at the stem, and I cushioned them inside the smallest box I could find, one that had held a staple remover, then sent them off to Andrea in the mail. Three days later, the tiniest package she had ever received was waiting on the table by her front door. A mixture of joy and regret blew through her: she was aware of the feelings I had for her, aware of all the things she had neglected to say to me, aware even of the way I saw her features in the faces of women I didn't know as I walked through campus in my beaten old tennis shoes. And yet already she could sense me beginning to disappear from her life, another grasshopper preparing to tighten its legs and leap away.

During the last few months of high school, there was a feeling of such great ease in the air that it hardly seemed to her like school at all. She gave a reading of one of her poems at the launch party for the senior class literary magazine. She dedicated an evening a week to volunteering at a soup kitchen. The neighbor's cat died of old age, and a few days later there were two Labrador puppies chasing each other around the puddle by Andrea's mailbox, one called Jarvis and the other called Willie. It was a cold night in April when she dreamt she was a little girl again, watching her father haul all his possessions into the street. Her mother was leaving with him. And so was I. And so was Justin. And so was Rania. And when she woke up she couldn't shake the feeling that it all really had taken place that way: everyone she knew driving off in a big yellow moving van, and she the one—the only one—staying behind. She had hesitated far too long. She had missed her chance, and her childhood had reached out and snared her.

There were times she believed she would never get out of it.

But she did get out of it. She went away to college and then to graduate school, to London and Boston and Washington, D.C. She rented an apartment. She found work that was meaningful to her. She thought about me every so often, wondered where I was and

how I was doing, whether I still propped my glasses on my forehead when I spoke, whether I sang as much as I used to, whether
I could honestly say I was happy. I was living in our hometown
again and doing pretty well. I propped my glasses on my forehead
so reflexively that I frequently forgot they were there. I still sang,
though not as often as I once did, and I was still happy, though
not as often as I once was. Sometimes, driving past restaurants
that had once been other restaurants, big-box stores that had once
been woodlots and houses, I imagined that if I could just make
the right set of turns the place would unlock for me, and my car
would carry me into the roads of fifteen years before. From time
to time, in the narrow light of a late-autumn afternoon, Andrea
would find herself walking past the windows of a high school,
and she would remember how it felt to be sitting behind such a
window at her cramped wooden desk, looking out at the shadows
of the trees stretching over the lawn. She used to be there and now
she was here, and all of it, both the freedom and the constraint,
had happened in the same lifetime. How was that possible?

Not long ago, I was having lunch with a teacher of ours from
high school, Ms. Goss, who delivered the news that Andrea was
engaged to be married. I was startled to feel all the old adoration
come tumbling loose inside me, a great surge of it that made me
close my mouth and set my fork down on my plate. The look Ms.
Goss offered said she could see something like contrition on my
face.

"Is she taking his name?" I asked.

She thought about the question. "I don't know. I don't think so.
It doesn't sound like Andrea to change her name, does it? But then
it doesn't sound like Andrea to get married, either."

"I'm not sure why I should be upset by the idea," I said. "After
all, it's not as if I've been in love with Andrea all these years."

Which, of course, was just another way of saying *I've been in love
with Andrea all these years.*

But even that is not quite true. The truth is that I am slightly less
than half in love with all the other girls I knew back then—with

Jennifer and Erika, Vicki and Allison, Ara and Emily—but I am still, to this day, slightly more than half in love with Andrea.

The last time I saw her was several years ago. We met for coffee at a little restaurant on Kavanaugh, and she told me about her work, traveling to the Middle East as an advocate for democratic solutions to public policy issues. There was a confidence in her voice, a strength of purpose I had never before heard from her. She carried herself like a professional, with skillfully applied makeup and well-cut, sensible clothing. She was beautiful, and I couldn't help but admire her, but I was also saddened by how much she had changed, by the magnitude of the distance she had traveled, the terrible impenetrability of the past. In high school Andrea wore one long braided strand of hair that trailed past her ear like an ornament from a chandelier. Once, on a spring break trip to New York, she bundled everything she needed for five days into a small canvas backpack.

"Sometimes I remember the way I used to be," she said as we sat across the table from one another, "and I'm surprised nobody ever smacked me."

I took a long sip of my coffee so I wouldn't have to answer her. I wanted to tell her that she ought to be more generous to the girl she used to be, if not out of respect for herself then out of respect for me, or more specifically for the boy I used to be, who loved that girl, after all.

Kevin Brockmeier is the author of the novels
The Brief History of the Dead **and** *The Truth About*
Celia, **the story collections** *Things That Fall from*
the Sky **and** *The View from the Seventh Layer,* **and**
the children's novels *City of Names* **and** *Grooves: A*
Kind of Mystery. **His stories have appeared in such**
magazines as *The New Yorker, The Georgia Review,*
McSweeney's, Zoetrope, **and** *The Oxford American,*

BENJAMIN KRAIN

as well as in *The Best American Short Stories* and the *O. Henry Prize Stories* anthology. Recently he was awarded a Guggenheim Fellowship and named one of *Granta* magazine's Best Young American Novelists. He lives in Little Rock, Arkansas, where he was raised.

I had already made several attempts to write "Andrea Is Changing Her Name" before I stumbled upon its peculiar point-of-view strategy—a first-person narrative, but one that freely (and almost exclusively) adopts the perspective of a third-person character. This strategy gave me the license I needed to approach the story, which is, as you might have guessed, fairly intimate to me. In many ways, the piece is exactly what it pretends to be: a reconstruction of a certain period of my life, an effort to inhabit the mind of someone I loved, and a demonstration of the sentiment I express openly in the last few sentences. Certainly it is the closest I have come to writing a truly autobiographical story, which is to say that it is a four-part mixture of authentic fact, fact reshaped for the purposes of fiction, half-reliable speculation, and outright invention.

It could have been much longer than it is; I left out, for instance, the tale of how, the summer before I left for college, I drove three hours to Dogpatch USA (a Li'l Abner–related theme park that used to be located in the northwest corner of Arkansas), stayed just long enough to buy a large Shmoo doll for Andrea, and drove straight back home; I left out the story of the night the two of us found a downed street sign in the Denny's parking lot and began tiptoeing past the restaurant's window with it as if we were trying to steal it, over and over again past the same table of perplexed customers, until the manager came out and chased us away.

Because I was making use of the details not only of my own life but of someone else's, and because I was not sure how she would feel about this appropriation, I tried to treat the material with as much affection and understanding as I could. I haven't spoken to Andrea since I wrote it, and I still don't know how she will feel about what I've done, so in that sense, for me, the story is ongoing.

APPENDIX

A list of the magazines currently consulted for *New Stories from the South: The Year's Best, 2008,* with addresses, subscription rates, and editors.

Agni
236 Bay State Road
Boston, MA 02215
Semiannually, $20
Sven Birkerts

Alaska Quarterly Review
University of Alaska Anchorage
3211 Providence Drive
Anchorage, AK 99508
Semiannually, $18
Ronald Spatz

American Short Fiction
P.O. Box 301209
Austin, TX 78703
Quarterly, $30
Stacey Swann

The Antioch Review
P.O. Box 148
Yellow Springs, OH 45387-0148
Quarterly, $40
Robert S. Fogarty

Apalachee Review
P.O. Box 10469
Tallahassee, FL 32302
Semiannually, $15
Laura Newton

Appalachian Heritage
CPO 2166
Berea, KY 40404
Quarterly, $18
George Brosi

Arkansas Review
P.O. Box 1890
Arkansas State University
State University, AR 72467
Triannually, $20
Tom Williams

Arts & Letters
Campus Box 89
Georgia College & State University
Milledgeville, GA 31061-0490
Semiannually, $15
Martin Lammon

The Atlantic Monthly
600 New Hampshire Avenue NW
Washington, DC 20037
Monthly, $39.95
C. Michael Curtis

Backwards City Review
P.O. Box 41317
Greensboro, NC 27404-1317
Semiannually, $12
Gerry Canavan

The Baffler
P.O. Box 378293
Chicago, IL 60637
Quarterly, $24
Solveig Nelson

Bayou
Department of English
University of New Orleans
2000 Lakeshore Drive
New Orleans, LA 70148
Semiannually, $15
Joanna Leake

Bellevue Literary Review
Department of Medicine
New York University School of
    Medicine
550 1st Avenue, OBV-612
New York, NY 10016
Semiannually, $12
Ronna Weinberg

Black Warrior Review
University of Alabama
P.O. Box 862936
Tuscaloosa, AL 35486
Semiannually, $16
Lucas Southworth

Boulevard
6614 Clayton Road, PMB 325
Richmond Heights, MO 63117
Triannually, $15
Richard Burgin

Callaloo
Department of English
Texas A&M University
4121 TAMU
College Station, TX 77843-4212
Quarterly, $45
Charles H. Rowell

The Carolina Quarterly
Greenlaw Hall CB# 3520
University of North Carolina
Chapel Hill, NC 27599-3520
Triannually, $18

The Chariton Review
Brigham Young University
Semiannually, $9.00
Jim Barnes

The Chattahoochee Review
Georgia Perimeter College
2101 Womack Road
Dunwoody, GA 30338-4497
Quarterly, $20
Marc Fitten

Cimarron Review
205 Morrill Hall
Oklahoma State University
Stillwater, OK 74078-4069
Quarterly, $24
E. P. Walkiewicz

The Cincinnati Review
Department of English and
    Comparative Literature
McMicken Hall
Room 369
University of Cincinnati
P.O. Box 210069
Cincinnati, OH 45221-0069
Semiannually, $15
Brock Clarke

The Clinch Mountain Review
info at http://www.sw.edu.cmr
Warren M. Harris

\

Colorado Review
Department of English
Colorado State University
9105 Campus Delivery
Fort Collins, CO 80523
Triannually, $24
Stephanie G'Schwind

Conjunctions
21 East 10th Street
New York, NY 10003
Semiannually, $18
Bradford Morrow

Crazyhorse
Department of English
College of Charleston
66 George Street
Charleston, SC 29424
Semiannually, $16
Anthony Varallo

Crossing Borders
The University of Tulsa
Tulsa, OK
Semiannually
Geraldine McLoud

Crucible
Barton College
P.O. Box 5000
Wilson, NC 27893-7000
Annually, $7
Terence L. Grimes

Denver Quarterly
University of Denver
Denver, CO 80208
Quarterly, $20
Bin Ramke

Ecotone
Department of Creative Writing
UNC Wilmington
601 South College Road

Wilmington, NC 28403-3297
Semiannually, $15
Nina de Gramont

Epoch
251 Goldwin Smith Hall
Cornell University
Ithaca, NY 14853-3201
Triannually, $11
Michael Koch

Fiction
c/o Department of English
The City College of New York
Convent Avenue at 138th Street
New York, NY 10031
Semiannually
Mark Jay Mirsky

Five Points
Georgia State University
P.O. Box 3999
Atlanta, GA 30302-3999
Triannually, $21
Megan Sexton

The Georgia Review
Gilbert Hall
University of Georgia
Athens, GA 30602-9009
Quarterly, $30
Stephen Corey

The Gettysburg Review
Gettysburg College
Gettysburg, PA 17325-1491
Quarterly, $24
Peter Stitt

Glimmer Train Stories
1211 NW Glisan Street, Suite 207
Portland, OR 97209-3054
Quarterly, $36
Susan Burmeister-Brown
    and Linda B. Swanson-Davies

The Greensboro Review
MFA Writing Program
3302 Hall for Humanities and
    Research Administration
UNC Greensboro
Greensboro, NC 27402-6170
Semiannually, $10
Jim Clark

Gulf Coast
Department of English
University of Houston
Houston, TX 77204-3013
Semiannually, $14
Fiction Editor

Harper's Magazine
666 Broadway, 11th Floor
New York, NY 10012
Monthly, $21
Ben Metcalf

Harpur Palate
English Department
Binghamton University
P.O. Box 6000
Binghamton, NY 13902-6000
Semiannually, $16
Fiction Editor

Hobart
submit@hobartpulp.com
P.O. Box 1658
Ann Arbor, MI 48103
Biannually, $17
Aaron Burch

The Idaho Review
Boise State University
Department of English
1910 University Drive
Boise, ID 83725
Annually, $10
Mitch Wieland

Image
3307 Third Avenue, W.
Seattle, WA 98119
Quarterly, $39.95
Gregory Wolfe

Indiana Review
Ballantine Hall 465
Indiana University
1020 E. Kirkwood Drive
Bloomington, IN 47405-7103
Semiannually, $17
Cate Whetzel

The Iowa Review
308 EPB
University of Iowa
Iowa City, IA 52242-1408
Triannually, $25
David Hamilton

The Jabberwock Review
Department of English
Mississippi State University
Drawer E
Mississippi State, MS 39762
Semiannually, $12
Angela Fowler

The Journal
Ohio State University
Department of English
164 W. 17th Avenue
Columbus, OH 43210
Semiannually, $12
Kathy Fagan and Michelle Herman

The Kenyon Review
www.kenyonreview.org
Quarterly, $30
David H. Lynn

Land-Grant College Review
P.O. Box 1164
New York, NY 10159-1164
Annually, $14
Dave Koch, Josh Melrod

The Literary Review
Fairleigh Dickinson University
285 Madison Avenue
Madison, NJ 07940
Quarterly, $18
René Steinke

Long Story
18 Eaton Street
Lawrence, MA 01843
Annually, $7
R. P. Burnham

Louisiana Literature
SLU-10792
Southeastern Louisiana University
Hammond, LA 70402
Semiannually, $12
Jack Bedell

The Louisville Review
Spalding University
851 South 4th Street
Louisville, KY 40203
Semiannually, $14
Sena Jeter Naslund

McSweeney's
849 Valencia Street
San Francisco, CA 94110
Quarterly, $55
Dave Eggers

Meridian
University of Virginia
P.O. Box 400145
Charlottesville, VA 22904-4145
Semiannually, $12
Hannah Pittard

Mid-American Review
Department of English
Bowling Green State University
Bowling Green, OH 43403
Semiannually, $15
Karen Craigo and Michael
   Czyzniejewski

Mississippi Review
University of Southern Mississippi
Box 5144
Hattiesburg, MS 39406
Semiannually, $25
Frederick Barthelme

The Missouri Review
357 McReynolds Hall
University of Missouri
Columbia, MO 65211
Quarterly, $24
Speer Morgan

New England Review
Middlebury College
Middlebury, VT 05753
Quarterly, $25
Stephen Donadio

New Letters
University of Missouri at Kansas
   City
5101 Rockhill Road
Kansas City, MO 64110
Quarterly, $22
Robert Stewart

New Orleans Review
P.O. Box 195
Loyola University
New Orleans, LA 70118
Semiannually, $14
Christopher Chambers, Editor

The New Yorker
4 Times Square
New York, NY 10036
Weekly, $47
Deborah Treisman, Fiction
    Editor

Nimrod International Journal
University of Tulsa
600 South College
Tulsa, OK 74104
Semiannually, $17.50
Francine Ringold

Ninth Letter
Department of English
University of Illinois
608 South Wright Street
Urbana, IL 61801
Biannually, $21.95
Jodee Stanley

North Carolina Literary Review
English Department
2201 Bate Building
East Carolina University
Greenville, NC 27858-4353
Annually, $10
Margaret Bauer

Northwest Review
1286 University of Oregon
Eugene, OR 97403
Triannually, $22
John Witte

One Story
www.one-story.com
Monthly, $21
Hannah Tinti

Ontario Review
9 Honey Brook Drive
Princeton, NJ 08540
Semiannually, $16
Raymond J. Smith

Open City
270 Lafayette Street
Suite 1412
New York, NY 10012
Triannually, $30
Thomas Beller, Joanna Yas

Other Voices
University of Illinois at Chicago
Department of English (M/C 162)
601 S. Morgan Street
Chicago, IL 60607-7120
Gina Frangello

The Oxford American
201 Donaghey Avenue, Main 107
Conway, AR 72035
Quarterly, $24.95
Marc Smirnoff

The Paris Review
62 White Street
New York, NY 10013
Quarterly, $40

Parting Gifts
March Street Press
3413 Wilshire Drive
Greensboro, NC 27408
Semiannually, $12
Robert Bixby

Pembroke Magazine
UNC-P, Box 1510
Pembroke, NC 28372-1510
Annually, $10
Shelby Stephenson

The Pinch
Department of English
University of Memphis
Memphis, TN 38152-6176
Semiannually, $18
Lee Griffith

Pleiades
Department of English and
    Philosophy
Central Missouri State University
Warrensburg, MO 64093
Semiannually, $12
G. B. Crump and Matthew Eck

Ploughshares
Emerson College
120 Boylston St.
Boston, MA 02116-4624
Triannually, $24
Don Lee

PMS
University of Alabama at
    Birmingham
Department of English
HB 217
1530 3rd Ave., S.
Birmingham, AL 35294-1260
Annually, $7
Linda Frost

Post Road Magazine
www.postroadmag.com
Semiannually, $18
Rebecca Boyd

Potomac Review
Montgomery College
51 Mannakee Street
Rockville, MD 20850
Annually, $10
Julie Wakeman-Linn

Prairie Schooner
201 Andrews Hall
University of Nebraska
Lincoln, NE 68588-0334
Quarterly, $26
Hilda Raz

A Public Space
www.publicspace.org

Quarterly, $36
Brigid Hughes

Quarterly West
University of Utah
255 S. Central Campus Drive
Department of English
LNCO 3500
Salt Lake City, UT 84112-0494
Semiannually, $14
Pam J. Balluck and Halina Duraj

River Styx
3547 Olive Street, Suite 107
St. Louis, MO 63103
Triannually, $20
Richard Newman

Salamander
Suffolk University
English Department
41 Temple Street
Boston, MA 02114
2 years, 4 issues, $23
Jennifer Barber

Santa Monica Review
Santa Monica College
1900 Pico Boulevard
Santa Monica, CA 90405
Semiannually, $12
Andrew Tonkovich

The Sewanee Review
735 University Avenue
Sewanee, TN 37383-1000
Quarterly, $25
George Core

Shenandoah
Washington and Lee University
Mattingly House
Lexington, VA 24450
Triannually, $25
R. T. Smith

Short Story
P.O. Box 50567
Columbia, SC 29250
Biannually, $12
Caroline Lord

Small Spiral Notebook
172 5th Avenue, Suite 104
Brooklyn, NY 11217
Biannually, $18
Felicia C. Sullivan

Sonora Review
Department of English
University of Arizona
Tucson, AZ 85721
Semiannually
D. Seth Horton

The South Carolina Review
Center for Electronic and Digital
    Publishing
Clemson University
Strode Tower, Box 340522
Clemson, SC 29634
Semiannually, $28
Wayne Chapman

South Dakota Review
Department of English
414 Clark Street
University of South Dakota
Vermillion, SD 57069
Quarterly, $30
John R. Milton

Southern Humanities Review
9088 Haley Center
Auburn University
Auburn, AL 36849
Quarterly, $15
Dan R. Latimer and Virginia M.
    Kouidis

The Southern Review
Old President's House
Louisiana State University
Baton Rouge, LA 70803
Quarterly, $25
Bret Lott

Southwest Review
307 Fondren Library West
Box 750374
Southern Methodist University
Dallas, TX 75275
Quarterly, $24
Willard Spiegelman

Sou'wester
Department of English
Southern Illinois University at
    Edwardsville
Edwardsville, IL 62026-1438
Semiannually, $15
Allison Funk and Geoff Schmidt

Subtropics
Department of English
University of Florida
P.O. Box 112075
Gainesville, FL 32611
Triannually, $26
David Leavitt

Tampa Review
University of Tampa
401 W. Kennedy Boulevard
Tampa, FL 33606-1490
Biannually, $15
Richard Mathews

The Threepenny Review
P.O. Box 9131
Berkeley, CA 94709
Quarterly, $25
Wendy Lesser

Timber Creek Review
P.O. Box 16542
Greensboro, NC 27416
Quarterly, $17
John M. Freiermuth

Tin House
P.O. Box 10500
Portland, OR 97296-0500
Quarterly, $29.90
Rob Spillman

TriQuarterly
Northwestern University
629 Noyes Street
Evanston, IL 60208
Triannually, $24
Susan Firestone Hahn

The Virginia Quarterly Review
One West Range
P.O. Box 400223
Charlottesville, VA 22904-4223
Quarterly, $32
Ted Genoways

War, Literature & the Arts
editor@wlajournal.com
Donald Anderson

West Branch
Bucknell Hall
Bucknell University
Lewisburg, PA 17837
Semiannually, $10
Ron Mohring

Words of Wisdom
8969 UNCG Station
Greensboro, NC 27413
Quarterly, $18
Mikhammad bin Muhandis
   Abdel-Ishara

Yemassee
Department of English
University of South Carolina
Columbia, SC 29208
Semiannually, $15
Darien Cavanaugh

Zoetrope: All-Story
The Sentinel Building
916 Kearny Street
San Francisco, CA 94133
Quarterly, $24
Michael Ray

Zone 3
P.O. Box 4565
Austin Peay State University
Clarksville, TN 37044
Biannually, $10
Blas Falconer and Barry Kitterman

PREVIOUS VOLUMES

Copies of previous volumes of *New Stories from the South* can be ordered through your local bookstore or by calling the Sales Department at Algonquin Books of Chapel Hill. Multiple copies for classroom adoptions are available at a special discount. For information, please call 919-967-0108.

NEW STORIES FROM THE SOUTH: THE YEAR'S BEST, 1986

Max Apple, BRIDGING

Madison Smartt Bell, TRIPTYCH 2

Mary Ward Brown, TONGUES OF FLAME

Suzanne Brown, COMMUNION

James Lee Burke, THE CONVICT

Ron Carlson, AIR

Doug Crowell, SAYS VELMA

Leon V. Driskell, MARTHA JEAN

Elizabeth Harris, THE WORLD RECORD HOLDER

Mary Hood, SOMETHING GOOD FOR GINNIE

David Huddle, SUMMER OF THE MAGIC SHOW

Gloria Norris, HOLDING ON

Kurt Rheinheimer, UMPIRE

W. A. Smith, DELIVERY

Wallace Whatley, SOMETHING TO LOSE

Luke Whisnant, WALLWORK

Sylvia Wilkinson, CHICKEN SIMON

NEW STORIES FROM THE SOUTH: THE YEAR'S BEST, 1987

James Gordon Bennett, DEPENDENTS

Robert Boswell, EDWARD AND JILL

NEW STORIES FROM THE SOUTH: THE YEAR'S BEST, 1988

NEW STORIES FROM THE SOUTH: THE YEAR'S BEST, 1989

Rick Bass, WILD HORSES

Madison Smartt Bell, CUSTOMS OF THE COUNTRY

James Gordon Bennett, PACIFIC THEATER

Larry Brown, SAMARITANS

Mary Ward Brown, IT WASN'T ALL DANCING

Kelly Cherry, WHERE SHE WAS

David Huddle, PLAYING

Sandy Huss, COUPON FOR BLOOD

Frank Manley, THE RAIN OF TERROR

Bobbie Ann Mason, WISH

Lewis Nordan, A HANK OF HAIR, A PIECE OF BONE

Kurt Rheinheimer, HOMES

Mark Richard, STRAYS

Annette Sanford, SIX WHITE HORSES

Paula Sharp, HOT SPRINGS

NEW STORIES FROM THE SOUTH: THE YEAR'S BEST, 1990

Tom Bailey, CROW MAN

Rick Bass, THE HISTORY OF RODNEY

Richard Bausch, LETTER TO THE LADY OF THE HOUSE

Larry Brown, SLEEP

Moira Crone, JUST OUTSIDE THE B.T.

Clyde Edgerton, CHANGING NAMES

Greg Johnson, THE BOARDER

Nanci Kincaid, SPITTIN' IMAGE OF A BAPTIST BOY

Reginald McKnight, THE KIND OF LIGHT THAT SHINES ON TEXAS

Lewis Nordan, THE CELLAR OF RUNT CONROY

Lance Olsen, FAMILY

Mark Richard, FEAST OF THE EARTH, RANSOM OF THE CLAY

Ron Robinson, WHERE WE LAND

Bob Shacochis, LES FEMMES CREOLES

Molly Best Tinsley, ZOE

Donna Trussell, FISHBONE

New Stories from the South: The Year's Best, 1991

Rick Bass, IN THE LOYAL MOUNTAINS

Thomas Phillips Brewer, BLACK CAT BONE

Larry Brown, BIG BAD LOVE

Robert Olen Butler, RELIC

Barbara Hudson, THE ARABESQUE

Elizabeth Hunnewell, A LIFE OR DEATH MATTER

Hilding Johnson, SOUTH OF KITTATINNY

Nanci Kincaid, THIS IS NOT THE PICTURE SHOW

Bobbie Ann Mason, WITH JAZZ

Jill McCorkle, WAITING FOR HARD TIMES TO END

Robert Morgan, POINSETT'S BRIDGE

Reynolds Price, HIS FINAL MOTHER

Mark Richard, THE BIRDS FOR CHRISTMAS

Susan Starr Richards, THE SCREENED PORCH

Lee Smith, INTENSIVE CARE

Peter Taylor, COUSIN AUBREY

New Stories from the South: The Year's Best, 1992

Alison Baker, CLEARWATER AND LATISSIMUS

Larry Brown, A ROADSIDE RESURRECTION

Mary Ward Brown, A NEW LIFE

James Lee Burke, TEXAS CITY, 1947

Robert Olen Butler, A GOOD SCENT FROM A STRANGE MOUNTAIN

Nanci Kincaid, A STURDY PAIR OF SHOES THAT FIT GOOD

Patricia Lear, AFTER MEMPHIS

Dan Leone, YOU HAVE CHOSEN CAKE

Reginald McKnight, QUITTING SMOKING

Karen Minton, LIKE HANDS ON A CAVE WALL

Elizabeth Seydel Morgan, ECONOMICS

Pamela Erbe, SWEET TOOTH

Barry Hannah, NICODEMUS BLUFF

Nanci Kincaid, PRETENDING THE BED WAS A RAFT

Nancy Krusoe, LANDSCAPE AND DREAM

Robert Morgan, DARK CORNER

Reynolds Price, DEEDS OF LIGHT

Leon Rooke, THE HEART MUST FROM ITS BREAKING

John Sayles, PEELING

George Singleton, OUTLAW HEAD & TAIL

Melanie Sumner, MY OTHER LIFE

Robert Love Taylor, MY MOTHER'S SHOES

New Stories from the South: The Year's Best, 1995

R. Sebastian Bennett, RIDING WITH THE DOCTOR

Wendy Brenner, I AM THE BEAR

James Lee Burke, WATER PEOPLE

Robert Olen Butler, BOY BORN WITH TATTOO OF ELVIS

Ken Craven, PAYING ATTENTION

Tim Gautreaux, THE BUG MAN

Ellen Gilchrist, THE STUCCO HOUSE

Scott Gould, BASES

Barry Hannah, DRUMMER DOWN

MMM Hayes, FIXING LU

Hillary Hebert, LADIES OF THE MARBLE HEARTH

Jesse Lee Kercheval, GRAVITY

Caroline A. Langston, IN THE DISTANCE

Lynn Marie, TEAMS

Susan Perabo, GRAVITY

Dale Ray Phillips, EVERYTHING QUIET LIKE CHURCH

Elizabeth Spencer, THE RUNAWAYS

New Stories from the South: The Year's Best, 1996

New Stories from the South: The Year's Best, 1997

Dale Ray Phillips, CORPORAL LOVE
Patricia Elam Ruff, THE TAXI RIDE
Lee Smith, NATIVE DAUGHTER
Judy Troy, RAMONE
Marc Vassallo, AFTER THE OPERA
Brad Vice, MOJO FARMER

NEW STORIES FROM THE SOUTH: THE YEAR'S BEST, 1998

PREFACE *by Padgett Powell*
Frederick Barthelme, THE LESSON
Wendy Brenner, NIPPLE
Stephen Dixon, THE POET
Tony Earley, BRIDGE
Scott Ely, TALK RADIO
Tim Gautreaux, SORRY BLOOD
Michael Gills, WHERE WORDS GO
John Holman, RITA'S MYSTERY
Stephen Marion, NAKED AS TANYA
Jennifer Moses, GIRLS LIKE YOU
Padgett Powell, ALIENS OF AFFECTION
Sara Powers, THE BAKER'S WIFE
Mark Richard, MEMORIAL DAY
Nancy Richard, THE ORDER OF THINGS
Josh Russell, YELLOW JACK
Annette Sanford, IN THE LITTLE HUNKY RIVER
Enid Shomer, THE OTHER MOTHER
George Singleton, THESE PEOPLE ARE US
Molly Best Tinsley, THE ONLY WAY TO RIDE

NEW STORIES FROM THE SOUTH: THE YEAR'S BEST, 1999

PREFACE *by Tony Earley*
Andrew Alexander, LITTLE BITTY PRETTY ONE
Richard Bausch, MISSY

NEW STORIES FROM THE SOUTH: THE YEAR'S BEST, 2000

John Holman, WAVE

Romulus Linney, THE WIDOW

Thomas McNeely, SHEEP

Christopher Miner, RHONDA AND HER CHILDREN

Chris Offutt, THE BEST FRIEND

Margo Rabb, HOW TO TELL A STORY

Karen Sagstetter, THE THING WITH WILLIE

Mary Helen Stefaniak, A NOTE TO BIOGRAPHERS REGARDING FAMOUS
    AUTHOR FLANNERY O'CONNOR

Melanie Sumner, GOOD-HEARTED WOMAN

NEW STORIES FROM THE SOUTH: THE YEAR'S BEST, 2001

PREFACE *by Lee Smith*

John Barth, THE REST OF YOUR LIFE

Madison Smartt Bell, TWO LIVES

Marshall Boswell, IN BETWEEN THINGS

Carrie Brown, FATHER JUDGE RUN

Stephen Coyne, HUNTING COUNTRY

Moira Crone, WHERE WHAT GETS INTO PEOPLE COMES FROM

William Gay, THE PAPERHANGER

Jim Grimsley, JESUS IS SENDING YOU THIS MESSAGE

Ingrid Hill, JOLIE-GRAY

Christie Hodgen, THE HERO OF LONELINESS

Nicola Mason, THE WHIMSIED WORLD

Edith Pearlman, SKIN DEEP

Kurt Rheinheimer, SHOES

Jane R. Shippen, I AM NOT LIKE NUÑEZ

George Singleton, PUBLIC RELATIONS

Robert Love Taylor, PINK MIRACLE IN EAST TENNESSEE

James Ellis Thomas, THE SATURDAY MORNING CAR WASH CLUB

Elizabeth Tippens, MAKE A WISH

Linda Wendling, INAPPROPRIATE BABIES

New Stories from the South: The Year's Best, 2002

PREFACE *by Larry Brown*

Dwight Allen, END OF THE STEAM AGE

Russell Banks, THE OUTER BANKS

Brad Barkley, BENEATH THE DEEP, SLOW MOTION

Doris Betts, ABOVEGROUND

William Gay, CHARTING THE TERRITORIES OF THE RED

Aaron Gwyn, OF FALLING

Ingrid Hill, THE MORE THEY STAY THE SAME

David Koon, THE BONE DIVERS

Andrea Lee, ANTHROPOLOGY

Romulus Linney, TENNESSEE

Corey Mesler, THE GROWTH AND DEATH OF BUDDY GARDNER

Lucia Nevai, FAITH HEALER

Julie Orringer, PILGRIMS

Dulane Upshaw Ponder, THE RAT SPOON

Bill Roorbach, BIG BEND

George Singleton, SHOW-AND-TELL

Kate Small, MAXIMUM SUNLIGHT

R. T. Smith, I HAVE LOST MY RIGHT

Max Steele, THE UNRIPE HEART

New Stories from the South: The Year's Best, 2003

PREFACE *by Roy Blount Jr.*

Dorothy Allison, COMPASSION

Steve Almond, THE SOUL MOLECULE

Brock Clarke, FOR THOSE OF US WHO NEED SUCH THINGS

Lucy Corin, RICH PEOPLE

John Dufresne, JOHNNY TOO BAD

Donald Hays, DYING LIGHT

Ingrid Hill, THE BALLAD OF RAPPY VALCOUR

Bret Anthony Johnston, CORPUS

Michael Knight, ELLEN'S BOOK

NEW STORIES FROM THE SOUTH: THE YEAR'S BEST, 2004

NEW STORIES FROM THE SOUTH: THE YEAR'S BEST, 2007

Guest edited by Edward P. Jones